STONEWALL REVIVAL

STONEWALL REVIVAL
TALES OF 53 CHRISTOPHER STREET
& OTHER THEATRICAL ADVENTURES

Thomas Michael Garguilo

Christopher Street Books
Glen Allen, Virginia

Copyright © 2018 by Thomas Michael Garguilo.

All rights reserved. No part of this publication may be reproduced, distributed or transmitted in any form or by any means, including photocopying, recording, or other electronic or mechanical methods, without the prior written permission of the publisher, except in the case of brief quotations embodied in critical reviews and certain other noncommercial uses permitted by copyright law. For permission requests, write to the publisher, addressed "Attention: Permissions Coordinator," at the address below.

Christopher Street Books
4990 Sadler Place, #6680
Glen Allen, VA 23058
www.ChristopherStreetBooks.com

Stonewall Revival / Thomas Michael Garguilo -- 1st ed.
Library of Congress Control Number: 2018901358
ISBN 978-0-9998637-0-1

For Ron, my husband, my love.
You gave me the courage to try something new.

I'd like to thank the people who helped me on this adventure ...

Ron
Stuart
Angi and Rob
James and Greg
Suzanne and Annette
Joel and Laura
Diane and Bill
Rob
Jenni
Tim and Beverly
Anne
Alex
Kris
and dearest Lisa.

Author's Note:

This story is fictional.
It is inspired by the re-opening of a bar at 53 Christopher Street
in New York City in 1990.

Contents

Amuse Rouge 1
Baby, Dream Your Dream 3
Where the Underworld Can Meet the Elite 9
Welcome to the Theatre 20
Hey Big Spender 24
I Hope I Get It 35
I Am What I Am 41
There's No Business Like Show Business 51
Doin' What Comes Natur'lly 59
Beautiful Girls 75
Sunday 84
Love Changes Everything 100
Not a Day Goes By 109
Diamonds Are a Girl's Best Friend 116
Pretty Little Picture 130
What I Did for Love 151
Be on Your Own 163
We Need a Little Christmas 175
Everything's Coming Up Roses 192
Company 201
The Ladies Who Lunch 214
Every Day a Little Death 228
On the Steps of the Palace 236
Before the Parade Passes By 242
With So Little to Be Sure Of 251
The Apple Doesn't Fall (Very Far from the Tree) 259

Open a New Window 267
Put on Your Sunday Best 275
Giants in the Sky 282
Sweet Charity 293
Ever After 299

PROLOGUE

Amuse Rouge

I knew this would be the last time I'd be sitting in that fabled apartment talking with her. She was someone I had long admired, though before these encounters I'd only seen her perform, very briefly, late in life. Sitting here, in this time, she's still young. The press will come to refer to her as a muse. Her husband's muse. Tonight, I try to be her muse. To inspire her. To bring hope with a simple act of charity.

Some years earlier, another famous couple made this penthouse their own. William Randolph Hearst had owned several apartments in New York City. This one, atop 91 Central Park West, may not have been the most extravagant of the lot but, to someone like myself, it's jaw-dropping. The terraces alone, vast enough to accommodate hundreds of people for a cocktail party or other soirée, are film-worthy. Commanding one of the most enviable perches in all of Manhattan, it is superlative in a city that boasts excess. Hearst had ensconced his mistress, Marion Davies, here and in other urban palaces with all the trappings that unlimited money could buy. But that was many years ago, before the current lady of the house took up residence here.

Tonight, I have her all to myself one last time. Her living room, in contrast to our attire, is informal. Plants fill the vast space, creating a verdant indoor Eden. As I finish my beer, she hurries out of sight to refresh us. She'll never receive the credit that I think she deserves for all the things she's done. She taught Marilyn to bump and grind. Well before body doubles got credit for their contribution, she'd lent various parts of her anatomy — including her torso, her feet, and her behind — to some of the biggest film stars' most memorable moments on screen. But film would not be where she would make her mark. Broadway would make her famous and, if not Hearst-rich, at least very comfortable. Hearing the clinking of bottles caps as they dance across the kitchen counter, I wonder if she recalls anything from when she, at three years old, performed for Marion Davies at an MGM Christmas party. I won't ask about it. Just knowing it happened is satisfying enough.

My eyelids are growing heavier. As before, I'll fall asleep and this episode will be over. As I soak in those last few minutes with her, I can feel one cheek rise into a half-smile. She notices and asks, "What are you thinking about honey?" Staring at the photo she's returned to me, I conjure the man who brought us together. Once upon another time, he'd brought a legend back to life. Like her, he'd never received the credit due. In the foreground, I hear myself say, "Nothing really. Just, if my friends could see me now."

CHAPTER ONE

Baby, Dream Your Dream

I'm awoken by bright sunlight and a clattering of sound. Standing, I try to focus on something, anything, to get my bearings. But it is all enveloping, this place. Three hundred and sixty degrees of stimulus. I shudder in place, but the internal vibration soon gives way to a sense of calmness and familiarity. I've been here before, many times.

I know I'm standing at the crossroads. Times Square. My feet have touched this ground since the 1970s when my parents first started taking me to see Broadway shows. By the '80s and '90s, I knew this space so well that I could give guided tours.

Still, something is not the same. As people and cars all go rushing past me, the familiarity of this place shifts. I've seen all this, but not like this. I've only seen this Times Square in photos and film. Standing in place, my head stretches from side to side to give me the panorama that I need. The colors here are more vivid than my mind's recollection of this Times Square, as though the 8mm version of this place has been colorized to make it feel current.

Looking uptown, as the cascade of traffic flowing down Broadway and 7th Avenue starts to arrange itself for the upcoming funnel, I spot a landmark. A Coca-Cola sign that has called this place home for decades is not the behemoth that I know. This one occupies only a fraction of the advertising space running up the building at 47th Street. A red disk on a white background, it looks like something from a salvage shop. Below it, just above street level, sits an ad for Castro Convertibles. I haven't seen an ad for those couches-that-turn-into-beds for, maybe, 30 years.

Slowly, I start walking toward the Coca-Cola sign. Passing a newsstand, I see a stack of *The New York Times* and pick up the top one. It feels like I'm in a library, pulling an old edition from the stacks. It looks old, but feels new. Above the fold, on the right-hand side just below the masthead, the headline reads "Rockefeller Says He Can't Give City 600 Million More." To the left of that is a picture of John Lindsay, the mayor of New York City when I was child. Above that, in tiny print, I spot the date. It says Tuesday, January 18, 1966.

"What the fuck is this?"

What kind of dream or hallucination or joke is this, I think to myself, when I'm interrupted by the newspaper seller insisting, "Would ya like a cup of coffee with that?" Startled, I look up to see his displeasure and, reading his lips, I hear him bark, "Buy it or put it back. This isn't the public library." I toss the paper down and retreat toward a building behind me, wanting to have something solid against my back as I try to make sense of this. I was born in '62 and I'm 38 now. This can't be 1966, though everything begs to differ.

The billboards and signs that tattoo this intersection are not the electronic wonders that I've grown accustomed to, though they are still big and blanket most of the buildings around me.

With my back still pushed against the wall of a building, I feel my head moving rhythmically from side to side, as if watching a tennis match, and my eyes focusing on the people crossing in front of me. They're dressed in period costumes. At least to me they are. The men look like Dick Van Dyke clones in their tapered suits with thin lapels. The younger women have a vaguely Marlo Thomas *That Girl* look with more brightly colored coats than I'm used to seeing. In my New York, people mostly wrap themselves in blacks and greys. The thing I find most arresting about this place is the vividness of color. Films and TV shows that I've seen from the 1960s, even though shot in color, all had a more muted palette than what I see here. But this place is so extremely saturated with color. It makes it feel real, of today, not a distant point in time.

It's cold out and I have no gloves on. I reach into the pockets of my coat for warmth and that's when I find it. For a few seconds, my right hand runs along the edges of a piece of paper, or perhaps more accurately described as cardboard, in my pocket. I pull it out to see what it is.

It looks like a theatre ticket. I haven't seen something like it except for the torn stubs I used to find in my parents' collection of old *Playbills*. This one is intact. Unused. In small letters, it says "Palace Theatre B'Way at 47th St." and in bigger print it says "Gwen Verdon as Sweet Charity."

All of the swirling and confusion and trying to make sense of it all vanishes. I'm fixated on this ticket. It's my version of a Wonka Golden Ticket. Just to have it in my hands is an adrenaline rush. For someone who has collected theatre memorabilia for decades, having an untorn ticket from the original production of *Sweet Charity* is akin to finding a million dollars in a discarded duffle bag. It just doesn't happen. But if it did ...

I look up to see if anyone has spotted me holding this million-dollar prize and, thankfully, the world around me seems to have paid no notice. Now, I feel an intense need to go to the theatre, to go to the Palace, literally a stone's throw from where I'm standing. With determination, I dart into the human traffic in front of me and within less than a minute, I'm standing before it.

The six illuminated letters that sat above the marquee proper, the ones that spelled out P A L A C E, are still there. When lit, they would give off a reddish-pinkish tone. In present day parlance, we'd call it a girly color. It was like seeing an old friend. And even though they were only, perhaps, two feet tall and otherwise dwarfed by the marquee below and the surrounding shouts of other signage, they were always a beacon. From practically any spot in Times Square, you could see them. Maybe it was the color of the letters or maybe it was the insistence of the theatre itself that always drew your eye. I remember those illuminated letters so vividly, above the marquee for so many shows. I know I'd seen them there during *Woman of the Year* and *La Cage Aux Folles*. But at some point, they were taken down and replaced with an unnecessarily larger and less noticeable PALACE sign that ran vertically up the side of the building. When did that happen? More importantly, did anyone save those letters?

Standing in place on a New York sidewalk is never met with enthusiasm from the natives and even less so in this busy spot. I feel the annoyance of people walking around me, both from the front and from those behind, but I don't care. Not one bit. I'm now staring at a marquee I've only seen in photos. And sure enough it matches the ticket in my pocket.

I move toward the entrance, away from the crowds that stream by in all directions. The doors are closed and there doesn't seem to be any activity at all but, given that it's a Tuesday, at least that's what the paper indicated, surely there must be a performance today. I'd seen *Sweet Charity* performed by others over the years and even snagged tickets to a once-in-a-lifetime benefit performance back in '98 where the leading role rotated among the famous women who had performed as Charity, including one brief but exhilarating moment where Gwen performed the famous scene, inside a closet, where she tries to hide her exhaled cigarette smoke by blowing it into an oversized, clear garment bag. The entire audience at Lincoln Center went wild. I remember watching those five minutes or so and thinking, undoubtedly like the rest of the audience that night, how wonderful it would have been to have seen her do the original production. And now it was going to happen.

I pull out the ticket again and look for the date printed on it. It doesn't say January 18th as I expect. Shit. How could I be this close and not have this happen? It's not fair to be teased this way, especially in a dream. I start to rifle through all of my pockets, looking for my wallet. I'm going to pay for a ticket.

There is no wallet. There's nothing in my pockets. I start to become agitated and anxious and crazed when one of the doors of the theatre opens and out walks Gwen Verdon.

I abruptly spit out a "Hi" startling her a bit, I think. "I'm trying to get a ticket for today's show. I'm really looking forward to see *your* Charity," I say in a slightly more composed tone, though I realize that the *"your"* is wrong. At this moment, in this year, there is no other Charity to be wanting to see. They don't exist yet. I'm such an idiot.

She smiles gently and says, "Tonight's our first preview. We open on the 29th. There's still a few tickets available for tonight."

"I misplaced my wallet. But I do have a ticket, but it's for next month. I don't know if I can come back then. I don't know if I'll have another chance. I want to see you do this tonight," I start to babble.

My face must have fallen with disappointment because she then offers, "Are you visiting from out of town?"

I'm confused at the question. "No, I live downtown." I'd bought my dream apartment, a cozy pre-war one-bedroom at 59 West 12th Street a few years ago. I can't imagine why she would think I was from out of town.

I guess the frustrated look or the tone of my reply necessitated an explanation, and so she points to the top of my head. "The cap you're wearing. I just thought ...," she offers.

I pull the cap from my head and, turning it toward my face, realize where the question comes from. The front of the cap has the logo from *Chicago*. I start to laugh, just a small laugh, because I find the whole moment so ironic, so improbable, and perfectly theatrical.

Like a kid with a secret to tell, I say, "No, that's from a show that I really love. It's about these two women who murder people and end up being famous for it." Realizing that I'm telling her about a future she hasn't experienced yet, I cut myself off with, "But your show is the show I have to see."

Perhaps because she and her husband had, for years, been looking to acquire the rights to the play *Chicago* by Maurine Dallas Watkins to create a musical version of it but had still not been able to do so or, perhaps, because she was feeling sorry for me, or for whatever reason that entered her mind, she reaches for my hand and says, "Come with me."

She leads me into the theater and we walk just a few feet when she knocks on a door. An older man, maybe 60 or so, opens it and she starts to tell him, "Give this man ...," and then, looking at me, she asks, "What's your name?" After my speedy reply, she continues, "Give Tom a ticket to tonight's show."

As I turn toward him to consummate the deal, she quickly departs with, "Enjoy the show," as she pushes the door to the theater open and disappears into the street.

CHAPTER TWO

Where the Underworld Can Meet the Elite

It was a quarter past two o'clock when I exited the Palace lobby with my ticket in hand. Now I was faced with how to spend the intervening hours before the curtain rose. I was far less interested in finding out why I was in New York in 1966 or exploring the area or anything related to how I got where I was. I was solely and single-mindedly interested in seeing Gwen Verdon in *Sweet Charity*.

I felt naked without a wallet. I wanted to get some cash, if for nothing else than to get something to eat before the show. And as though I was being guided by some other force, I decided to make my way to the diamond district to sell my watch.

Exiting the theatre, I took two quick right-hand turns and headed east along 47th Street. In just a few minutes, I was surveying which store to enter. The block between 5th and 6th Avenues was littered with diamond, jewelry, and gold shops, remarkably the same as when I came here during the mid-1990s to sell some of Jimmy's old jewelry. Jimmy had been my first relationship and when he died I needed some money to keep his business afloat. I hadn't gotten anything near what I thought his belongings were worth, but beggars can't be choosers as they say.

At the first shop I entered, the man behind the counter indicated that he wasn't interested in buying my Cartier Tank watch but that a shop two doors down might be worth visiting. The second shop, a bit tinier and less organized than the first, proved to be the better choice, though I sweated a bit through the negotiation. As the man in this shop examined my watch, I saw a quizzical look come over his face. I had bought this watch while on a business trip to Zurich in the late 1980s as a treat to myself. I silently hoped that the fundamental design of such a classic watch was similar enough to what was being sold in 1966 as to pass muster with the man judging its worth.

He looked up to say, "It's not like any Cartier watch I've seen before."

Trying to find a plausible explanation, I offer, "It's a limited-edition model that I received as a gift. Go ahead and open it up, if you like. You'll see it's a real Cartier Tank."

With that he excused himself to the back, out of my sight. After maybe ten minutes, he returned and said, "I don't think I can sell this. I'm not interested."

I pleaded, "Surely, it's worth something. And I really need some cash."

With his head tilted to one side and his eyelids at half mast, he quietly said, "Maybe I could give you $20, but no more." I think he was expecting me to argue or negotiate the price, but I knew that if I pressed too hard I could walk out with nothing, so I quickly said, "Deal."

Exiting with my twenty dollars, I headed to the corner to grab a cab downtown. The decision to grab a cab down to the Village was almost a reflex, something akin to muscle memory for an athlete. Almost without thought, I said to the cab driver, "7th Avenue and Christopher Street." It was a phrase I had uttered countless times before, beginning in the '80s when I first started exploring downtown on my own and then, in the '90s, when I began living there, first in Jimmy's rented apartment on Horatio Street and ultimately in my own space later on at 59 West 12th Street.

With the same wonderment that I had gazed upon the PALACE letters above the theatre marquee, I wanted to see, in person, another sign that had long fascinated me. I had only seen it in old photos, mostly taken in 1969. Though it is a full three years before the riots will take place, Stonewall had become a brief but significant part of my otherwise ordinary life.

The Checker cab drove down 5th Avenue and then crossed over to 7th. With a bit of sentimentality and sadness, I thought how wonderful it was to be able to see my city in a different time, an earlier time. And while so much felt right, I also sensed a dirtiness that had not been part of my New York experience.

As we passed St. Vincent's Hospital at Greenwich Avenue, a series of still photos shuffled through my mind's eye. First, my mother's knee surgery, which had taken place sometime in 1972 or so at St. Vincent's, appeared. It was my first encounter with this neighborhood as a 10-year-old. I remember feeling scared of this place. To kill some time, my father had taken me to see a movie at a run-down theatre a block away. Everything from the film, *Fat City*, to the theatre to the neighborhood felt like it was dying a slow, painful death. Later, there would be so many people I would come to visit here. All of them dying from AIDS. St. Vincent's became a revolving door of misery and sadness. Ultimately, the most vivid memory would be Jimmy's death in a hospital bed there that filled up most of the slide carousel of memories. It was the first time I had seen anyone die.

With the cab slowing down on the east side of 7th, just before Christopher Street, I spot diagonally across the intersection the Village Cigars sign. Actually, it says United Cigars at the moment, but it's the same building, the same sign that I've known forever. It was a touchstone of sorts. While some things had changed at this crossroads, it seemed to remain a steadfast anchor of the Village's past. Exiting the cab, I looked up into the distance down 7th Avenue, expecting to see those beautiful towers that had always been there, at least in my lifetime. They are the architectural punctuation at the end of this small island, making New York the capital of the world and affirming that nothing more or greater will come after. And with characteristic brashness, we built two exclamation marks to end the conversation. But there was nothing to see. They've not risen yet. I momentarily think of a short scene in the film version of *Godspell*. It was an awful movie, save for a tiny segment during the "All for the Best" number. Stephen Schwartz cleverly twists the happy-go-lucky title into a scathing rebuke of how the rich always build on the backs of the disadvantaged, ending with "Someone's got to be oppressed. Yes, it's all for the best." The last seconds of the song, filmed atop the almost completed North Tower, are movie magic.

To my left, I notice that The Duplex, a piano bar and cabaret, isn't there yet either. Anchoring the north-east corner of the intersection is another building in its place. It's equally oddly shaped to fit into the irregular dimensions of this corner, as The Duplex is, but it is only two stories high. I hadn't known that *The Village Voice* once had an office on this corner, but there it is. I start to connect some dots. Fred McDarrah, who had been the photographic chronicler of the Village and its famous and not so famous inhabitants for decades had worked at *The Village Voice.* That's how he came to shoot those famous photos of the Stonewall Riots, the only visual testimony I had ever seen of it.

Above the second story of the building I can see an advertisement, painted on the wall of the three-story building next door. It's for Stonewall, but not my Stonewall. It's the legacy of a predecessor that reigned briefly in the same spot. This Stonewall Inn was a restaurant and nightclub that preceded my Stonewall with a straighter, more upscale clientele. This fading painted wall sign, touting its famous steaks and cocktail lounge, only reinforced what I had read about this incarnation. This Stonewall Inn was an outlier in the continuum of gay establishments that inhabited the space on Christopher Street for decades before and decades after.

This Stonewall Inn of the 1950s and early '60s had been preceded by Bonnie's Stonewall Inn, yet another restaurant and event space, that catered to a more bohemian crowd akin, I thought, to the late '60s Stonewall that the world had come to know and my Stonewall of the early '90s. For five years, I inhabited a premium seat with an unobstructed view of a 1990s revival of the Stonewall bar. And for one brief not-so-shining moment, roughly a year surrounding the 25th anniversary of the riots in 1994, I was the caretaker of this symbol.

Here I stood, wanting to round the corner to see that famous vertical sign that ran up the side of the building, straddling the spaces known as 51 and 53 Christopher Street. As I make my way past *The Village Voice*'s catty-corner entrance onto Christopher Street proper, I spot it. It's older and more distressed than I recall from the photos. Attached to the three-story building that is 51 Christopher, but next to the entrance of the two-story 53 Christopher that I called home, hangs a tired metal sign. Above those big vertical letters that spell STONEWALL sits a much smaller, horizontal RESTAURANT. And at the bottom, under the last L, again horizontally, sits the INN.

I'm still a good 50 feet away from it, a distance meant to allow me to soak it in. I realize that, when I'd seen this sign in black and white photos, the lack of environmental color allowed it to blend in. In person and in color, the blue of the sky and the familiar red brick of the buildings caused the sign to appear as a rotting appendage. Dark and rusting with a haphazard array of spots that marked the white lettering like lesions, it had been stuck onto the building a long time ago and hadn't been cared for since.

I crossed the street to look at it, this future symbol of gay rights, from a different angle. Standing with my back to Christopher Park, staring directly at the façade, it seems so remarkably the same to me. The only glaring difference is that there are two columns flanking the entrance to 53. They look odd to me and out of place, but they are sufficiently weathered as to suggest that they've been there for some time. Thirty years in the future, I'll walk past this place again and again, not realizing how remarkably untouched it was from the time it took its moment in the spotlight.

Though the space seems vacant, with the windows obscured and no signs of life, I'm startled to see the door of 53 Christopher open and two men emerge. They are well dressed in business attire, making them very out-of-place. I walk a bit further east toward 6th Avenue so that I am not so obviously staring at the building and them. Leaning against the iron fence of the park and casually looking back toward 7th Avenue, I allow my eyes to linger on them as they talk with animated gesturing.

Before 1994, I had only a superficial knowledge of Stonewall. Like many, I knew that a riot had occurred during 1969 at the bar when police came to conduct yet another raid of the space. Over time, that protest was christened the birth of the gay rights movement. Beyond that, I knew little else. It wasn't until Jimmy died and I became the guardian of Stonewall, and well after that when I relinquished my role to others, that I started to learn much more about the leading players in the history of that little bar on Christopher Street.

My initial research included Martin Duberman's book *Stonewall*, released in 1993. Duberman had done an extraordinary job of documenting something that had previously only received scant, incomplete coverage. His interviews with those people who had been a part of the rebellion, and the increasing social movement that came about after, in the 1970s and 1980s, were detailed and comprehensive. Duberman had described several Scorsese-like characters who purportedly ran the bar, including the vividly depicted "Fat Tony" Lauria who, according to Duberman, weighed-in at 420 pounds.

Starting in March of 1994, when Jimmy died and I became Stonewall's caretaker, I voluntarily assumed some duties which led me down paths that I hadn't thought of exploring before. My interest in real estate on this stretch of Christopher Street started when I began delivering the rent payments to the Duell property management office, Stonewall's landlord. Their office was at N° 5 East 57th Street, a prime location just above Chanel's flagship store. On several occasions, I'd scurry from work in midtown down to the bar to pick up the previous night's receipts before heading back uptown to pay the monthly rent. I'd stand in their office, sweating through my dress shirt — counting out tens, fives, and ones — praying that I'd have enough to keep us current. The people at the Duell office were immensely kind during that traumatic time, from when I first told them of Jimmy's death and each time I'd stand before them humiliated that I was paying them in beer soaked currency. They never made me feel that they would be the reason that Stonewall might have to close down. Other vendors weren't always as patient, leaving us in a constant state of fear that we'd close before the 25th anniversary in June. Those visits to the Duell office sparked an interest in learning who had owned the property back in the '60s.

As I gaze at these two out-of-place men, now walking slowly toward 7th Avenue, I wonder if they were the Mafia characters that Duberman and others had cited as running the bar in the late '60s or whether they were the real estate moguls I learned had actually owned the building. Hoping to catch a glimpse of their faces, I shadowed them until they separated in front of *The Village Voice*, not that that would have helped me identify them. Now standing directly in front of 53 Christopher, I flash-forward to the stall at the New York Public Library where I had learned far more about the ownership of that former horse stable than I'd ever imagined. Under the 52-foot-high beaux arts ceiling of the main reading room, I started to compile a list of the owners. And given that the bar itself mostly catered to those parts of society, shall we say, on the fringe, it was all the more ironic to find such notable men tied to the space.

Just a year earlier than my present situation, in 1965, the row of buildings from 51 to 61 Christopher Street had been sold for the first time in 150 years. This stretch of real estate had been in the hands of Henry S. Harper, the scion of the noted publishing family known later to many for Harper's Magazine, Harper and Row, and

HarperCollins. Harper had died in 1944 and the property had remained in his estate. But Henry S. Harper's claim to fame, other than being enormously rich and powerful, was that he survived the Titanic. I had found numerous articles about Harper from 1912 when he, his wife, his Pekinese dog, and his manservant were rescued from one of the lifeboats. It was one of those odd facts about the provenance of the Stonewall space that I'd never heard before and I found it fascinating. The sale of this stretch of Christopher Street went from Harper's estate to a company called Love Management.

Burton Handelsman, a real estate mogul, was the second name that caught my attention. His company, Love Management, was formed in the early 1960s and purchased the Christopher Street property from the Harper estate in 1965. Though not a household name in the late 1990s like a Trump or Lefrak, Handelsman's empire grew over the decades to include both New York and Palm Beach holdings. *The New York Times* archive contains a number of articles citing real estate transactions involving Mr. Handelsman, including some from 1976 when Citibank was trying to buy up property surrounding its new headquarters on Lexington Avenue. *The Times* reported "Citibank Buying Buildings to Keep Sex Shops Away From Its Offices." The buildings that Citibank was trying to buy were owned by Burton Handelsman. I did find it odd that I hadn't found any photos of him during my research. How is it that someone who owns this much of New York isn't photographed?

I had learned that from 1965 through the end of the decade, Love Securities Corp and Christopher Street Associates were two entities that traded ownership of the building where Stonewall stands, and the surrounding properties on Christopher Street, back and forth on a regular basis. Handelsman was a principal of both Love Securities Corp and Christopher Street Associates. Lucille Handelsman, Burton's wife, was listed as a vice president of Love Securities Corp. To me, the most indicative sign of Handelsman's immense power and wealth lies in the nickname that his wife goes by, Lovey. Lovey Handelsman.

Manny Duell, another real estate mogul, had an even more lasting role in the history of Stonewall. In a *New York Times* real estate piece in January of 1966 that linked Burton Handelsman to the property, Manny Duell is mentioned as having taken a 50-year lease, with an option to buy, on the Christopher Street properties that included the Stonewall bar, as well as property along Seventh Avenue. When I first found this tiny mention of the Duell name from 1966 I was surprised. I hadn't known that the people I was bringing beer soaked money to in 1994 were the descendants of the man who had leased the space in the late '60s.

Like with Handelsman, I could never find a photo of Manny Duell. Again, an odd thing for such a rich and powerful man. Literally at the same time as Duell has leased this space on Christopher Street, before he acquires it outright in 1970, he's building what is perhaps his greatest accomplishment. 1045 5th Avenue is a glass sheathed residential building near 86th Street that is completed in 1967. It is Manny Duell's masterpiece, and the duplex penthouse that he and his family will inhabit will be his castle in the sky for the following ten years until his death in 1977.

My hand reaches instinctively for the door handle at 53 Christopher, but there is no hardware to pull. The entrance is fortified, like a castle, to keep people out for the time being. For me, the space would become a living being, able to dictate how it was dressed and who it allowed inside. So many of the people that would be the regulars at my Stonewall, whether they worked there or were customers, seemed like actors playing a role, a revival cast of the 1960s Stonewallers. In addition to the drag queens and drug dealers, it wasn't uncommon for one of the less colorful inhabitants to describe themselves as a doctor or in other prestigious terms, even though they were working as a bartender or manager or sales clerk. Others freely offered fantastical stories of extraordinary accomplishments or experiences that went unchallenged by the rest of the denizens of my Stonewall. I had never before or since been with a group of people who projected such fanciful images. The odd thing, to me, was that no one ever called anyone else out on even the wildest stories. It was as though nothing was a lie, just a colorful story to consume. It was such a departure from the normal 9-to-5 job that I had in midtown. Every moment within those walls seemed like you were part of a theatre production. Years later, I even wondered whether the space itself was drawing the array of characters it did or whether it had the power to transform ordinary people into larger-than-life personas.

I take a few short steps and turn around to gaze up again at the not-yet-famous sign. Long after the riots are over in '69, it will remain anchored to the building as a tangible marker of what happened, happens, here. It gets some modest refurbishing and refinishing in the coming decades before it's ultimately removed, just before Jimmy signs the lease on the space. With its continued decay, it's certain that no one will bother to save that sign either. When I return to my time, I will hunt for where neon treasures go to die.

As I start my way back toward 7th Avenue, I glance through the obscured windows one last time, green-screening into place the array of characters who will come to this refuge. The original cast and the revival cast. Behind the scenes of this production, other Runyonesque figures join the real estate moguls.

Will B. Sandler appears as the attorney of choice for the transactions between the various parties selling, buying, and mortgaging the Stonewall property during the '60s. Later in life, he goes on to work for a very prestigious law firm. But the tiny reference of Sandler in *Broadway World*, suggesting that he once was part of the producing team for a show at the Astor Place Theatre called *Trumpets of the Lord* in 1963, adds just enough intrigue to an already theatrical story.

Joel Weiser also comes up as a name involved in the real estate dealings that surround this space. In at least one official "genealogy" of the property, Weiser is cited as the owner of the space. Oddly, that conflicts with the property records at that time, which show him as holder of a mortgage on the property, not the owner. There's not much else written about him, at least not much that I find, except for an interesting piece in *The Times* in 1967 that mentions him as the owner of buildings on the Upper West Side that were being studied by the city for potential abuses related to the eviction of tenants to make way for new construction. The tidbit that caught my eye in that article was a quote that *The Times* attributes to Weiser when asked about his ownership of those Upper West Side buildings. He had said something to the effect that he didn't really own the buildings, that they were owned by dummy corporations and that he didn't want to identify those entities. It reeked of fear. The more research I did on Stonewall the more I came to think, "you can't make this shit up."

Reaching the intersection, I glance at the clock above the entrance to *The Village Voice*. It's almost five o'clock. I had better get something to eat. I have a show to go to.

CHAPTER THREE

Welcome to the Theatre

I hadn't seen Lauren Bacall sing her warning to Eve Harrington in *Applause* in person at the Palace Theatre in the early '70s, but I had seen her do it on the Tony Awards telecast and in the television broadcast of the complete Broadway show from '73. Though it's something of a gift to be able to see a long-ago show captured on video, film adaptations of famous shows being another beast entirely, the lackluster *Applause* shown on TV made me realize a universal truth. The magic of the theatre is at least partly attributable to its ephemeral nature. You see a show and then, poof, it's gone forever. The moment can never be recaptured, except in memory. You can see a favorite show several times, something that I'm guilty of, and still no two performances are the same. Each one is a distinct gift. A decade or so later, I'd see Bacall return to this same theatre to do *Woman of the Year*. In person, it was thrilling. Had they tried to capture it on video, which thankfully no one dared do, I doubt it would have translated.

Tonight, I'm in Row C at the Palace Theatre, not far off center. I shake my head when I think that this prime spot commands a whopping $9.50, though I didn't have to pay for this privilege. In a few moments, I'll see Gwen Verdon create her Charity Hope Valentine for the first time on a Broadway stage. I'm grossly underdressed for 1960s theatre with khaki colored pants and a button-down shirt. I don't recall when people stopped dressing up and started to go to the theatre in jeans or other far too casual clothing. By 2000, theatre in New York had become irritating. People acted as though they were in their living rooms instead of being at a special event. For me, the collapse occurred when a family sitting in front of me during a matinee of *Chicago* started opening up bags of McDonald's burgers and fries and started eating in their seats before the curtain rose. At that point, I realized we were doomed.

The lights dim and I inhale deeply. The moment of truth has arrived, and I pray that this dream doesn't end for another two and a half hours.

Having listened to the cast album, I know how the score is supposed to sound but, hearing the first notes of the overture live, I realize that this will be a different experience from what I expect. I don't notice the amplification, or over-amplification to be more accurate, that has become a routine part of every Broadway show since sometime in the 1980s. The sound is full and rounded and, well, *live*. It's not amplified to the point of sounding artificial and recorded.

After the overture and before the "You Should See Yourself" number, Fosse introduces Charity to the audience with a Chaplin-style interlude called "Charity's Theme." It's an entrance only worthy of a star performer. From blackness, the scrims pull away in a trapezoidal shape to reveal Gwen, back to the audience and in silhouette, in that classic bent-knee pose. After a few of the trademark gestures and poses that define this Fosse/Verdon character, she turns and the spotlight illuminates her. The music has an almost silent-era comedy quality, or what I imagine to be an old-timey vaudeville tone to it, and she makes her way downstage with those exuberant, child-like arm swings that every other Charity in the coming years will try to copy. I had never paid much attention to this piece in audio recordings because the piece is instrumental and the lack of lyrics tends to make it less important in the overall soundtrack of the show. Watching her movements to the music, I think it's one of the most brilliant little gems I've ever seen. In this former home of vaudeville, now renovated into a red-velveted though still burlesquey legit theatre, the billboard-size show cards that lower down from the flies above the stage tell me what I already know. They say "The Story of a Girl Who Wanted to be Loved." And boy do I love this girl.

There is a moment in the first act that completely mesmerizes. It occurs during "If My Friends Could See Me Now." The whole song is a showcase for Gwen's unique talents, and the moment is crafted to allow an adoring audience to applaud wildly not only for the character she's playing, but for the star herself.

The collapsible top hat that pops open, as if by magic, to punctuate her innocently rendered bumps and grinds succeeds in revving up the crowd. The addition of the cane, toward the end of the song, allows for a sleight of hand, or feet in this case, that would make Houdini envious.

She's positioned herself down front on the right side of the stage, standing sideways to face the left side of the stage. She's planted the cane on her left side, toward the audience, and is standing perfectly straight. The top hat is in place over her fiery red tresses. As the sequence begins with a musical blare, she begins to step away from the cane, still being held perfectly vertical by her left hand. As her feet move further left, her back starts to arch into an impossible arc that allows her to keep the cane still planted in the same spot on the stage. The dainty march away from the cane continues until she's about three or four feet away, stretched into what looks like a backwards D-shape.

Just when you think that she's stretched herself beyond reason, she stops momentarily. Her right hand moves up to the top hat and draws a spitfire of imaginary circles on the lid. It's as though a spring is being wound very tightly. Or an archer's bow has been pulled to its extreme. Or a jet's engines have been gunned for take-off.

Still in that impossible back bending arch, she propels across the stage like an arrow streaking toward a target. Her feet have to have been moving, but the shuffling is near invisible to me. The cane remains steadfast at 90 degrees throughout. Forget Houdini, it's

Michael Jackson that should take note. I want to see the instant replay, to see how she did it.

During intermission, I mingle outside to overhear the crowd's reaction and to grab a smoke. Comments about the restoration of the Palace range from "it's a jewel box" to "it's a bordello." But the amateur reviewers have reached consensus on one thing. Gwen Verdon is a national treasure.

During the second act, I try to appreciate the talents of the rest of the cast, but Gwen is onstage for so much of the show that I have difficulty focusing on them. Sometime after "Where Am I Going" but before the "Finale," I must have dozed off because there's nothing more I can remember from that night's performance.

CHAPTER FOUR

Hey Big Spender

Sunlight is sneaking through the window blinds. My eyes open and I pull the comfy down comforter up to practically cover my head. I love this bed and this apartment. It's truly my perfect New York apartment. Sometime after I had resigned from my sentry duty at Stonewall, I decided that I needed to find a more adult space to live. The cute brownstone studio on West 90th Street that I had bought in the late '80s had served its purpose, but it was too small now and too far from where I had been spending most of my time for the better part of the '90s. Every time I took that cab ride from West 90th down to the Village, I thought of how ridiculous it was to be commuting so far to the center of my life.

When I first saw the condo at 59 West 12th Street, something inside told me that this was the place I had to live. It was rare to find a pre-war condo in the city. Most condos were uninteresting boxes. The vast majority of pre-war apartments, the ones with sought-after character, tended to be co-ops which, for those not well versed in the peculiar nature of New York real estate, are much more demanding in terms of who they let live in them and far more intrusive in screening potential residents. 59 West 12th Street, designed by Emery Roth, reminded me of all those magnificent, stately buildings that stretched up Central Park West. Positioned on, in my opinion, the most beautiful block in the Village, it exuded quietness and class.

The apartment itself, a 900-square-foot one-bedroom, was positioned on the second floor, just above the green canopy that greeted residents and visitors. Though I thought it was insane to spend $450,000 on a one-bedroom apartment, not counting the money I spent toward renovating the kitchen and bath, this apartment would turn out to be the best investment of my life. Jimmy had been a larger-than-life character, almost P.T. Barnum-like, and his influence on me, in living a bit more grandly than perhaps my upbringing would have cautioned, no doubt influenced me to take it up a notch. I furnished it with high-end pieces from Roche-Bobois and Maurice Villency. The pièce de résistance was a 42-inch flat screen television. I had seen it in one of those audiophile stores off of 5th Avenue on a lunch break and had to have it, even though the price tag was higher than some new cars. I had it mounted on the wall adjacent to the windows overlooking West 12th Street, and several of the doormen at the building would tell me that passersby would stop and stare up into my second-floor living room window in amazement. The rarity of being a pre-war condo combined with the numerous celebrities that lived in the building — which I hadn't known about when I bought my apartment — made this real estate investment a fortunate accident. Apartments like mine in this building would command more than double the price I paid in just a few short years. Perhaps I had learned something from Harper, Handelsman, and Duell. There are few things more valuable in the world than New York real estate.

Though I wanted to keep the afterglow of my wonderful dream alive a bit longer in that hazy fog of just waking up, I reluctantly slid out of bed and went to the kitchen to brew some coffee. It was a Saturday. No work today. My 9-to-5 job at a big multinational fulfilled the part of me that wanted to feel accomplished, but my life downtown, with all its highs and lows, was the thing that made me feel that I was living. I fired up the plasma equivalent of a Camry mounted to the wall while sipping the caffeine defibrillator. As I reached consciousness in the present, I felt increasingly uneasy about my consciousness in the past. You're not supposed to know that you're dreaming. It's an oblivious pastime. Somehow, I'd broken another rule.

I showered and dressed, ran a few Saturday errands, and generally lazed around for the rest of the afternoon. I was going to meet friends for dinner at Knickerbocker Bar & Grill, and I knew that we would gravitate to Stonewall after, as we had done on so many nights both during my Stonewall engagement and now in my retirement from the place where it all began. Sometimes we'd hit a few other gay bars in the neighborhood, just to feel as though we weren't being too predictable, but it was all a ruse.

While getting dressed for my daytime excursion, I had glanced in the small burl wood box where I kept the few pieces of jewelry that I owned, partly to satisfy a lingering curiosity left over from last night's dream, to see whether my '80s Cartier Tank looked too new to pass for something more vintage. I chuckled when I couldn't immediately find it. I put on the old Bulova instead, assuming that I had hidden the more valuable watch, as I would occasionally do, before having gone out on a previous evening with the anticipation of bringing a stranger home. After Jimmy died, and having seen so many other youngish men lying in caskets, the idea of having another real relationship wasn't something that I wanted to go anywhere near. I would look for the watch later. I had hidden it a bit too well before, sometimes as a last-minute impulse, when one of my "guests" was in the bathroom.

Saturday night dinner at Knickerbocker was always the same. It was the perfect embodiment of an old-time New York steak joint, complete with red leather banquettes, a lively but not boisterous crowd, big slabs of porterhouse steaks served sliced on oversized platters, the creamiest creamed spinach ever created, and the jazz combo that made everyone feel just a bit more glamorous than they really were. I was there with my usual partner in crime, Buddy, a friend who I had met at Stonewall and hung out with for much of the '90s, and his friend, Luke, someone who I had been attracted to but would never pursue. By 9:45, the usual ritual of "So what do you want to do?" would begin. Over a double espresso, intended to give us a boost after such a big meal, the banter would predictably wander over several not-serious choices of where to spend the rest of the evening. Buddy was my accomplice and would, according to our never-veered-from script, ultimately say, "So who are we kidding?" and that would be the cue to get up and head down 9th Street toward Stonewall.

After no longer being a caretaker of Stonewall, I didn't have the burden of keeping a place open that, by all rights, shouldn't have lasted in business. It made going back there more enjoyable, though perhaps the more accurate phrase would be that it was less of a hardship. For all that attracted me to Stonewall, I knew it was a place that was detrimental to many who inhabited it, including myself. For those that could enjoy its debauchery for a limited period of time, it was a fantasy playground. Lots of people, though, never escaped its gravity.

It had been such a circuitous path that brought about the re-opening of Stonewall and its persistence in remaining alive. Remarkably, this place found enough naïve or thickheaded custodians to keep it on life support. At some point in time, just before the turn of the century, the momentum of Stonewall having been open again for so long somehow guaranteed that it could no longer ever be not-Stonewall. Sure, a particular business owner leasing the space could go under or get tired of it and walk away. But, it would never be acceptable to the public for the space not to be called Stonewall and be a gay bar, *the* gay bar. It would be unthinkable for another bagel shop or Chinese restaurant, or any of the other squatters of the space during the '70s and '80s, to occupy the hallowed grounds again.

As we approach the bar, I always look for the plaque. It wasn't an official plaque. It was something that had been put up just outside the front door. It mentioned his name, Jimmy Pisano, and gave him credit for re-opening the bar. But, as I well knew, it wasn't there anymore. It had been callously removed from the exterior and in its place would follow other markers that designated the importance of the site. If not for Jimmy Pisano, none of what followed over the coming years would have happened. As proof, I offer the short-lived existence of another Stonewall incarnation, at 51 Christopher Street, at the end of the 1980s. Its tenure was nanosecond short and ended with no remorse, certainly not from the gay community it would seem. After it closed, an '80s-ish Stonewall sign that had replaced the original Stonewall Inn sign, the one that had lived there for decades, was taken down. The appendage had been amputated. Captured by Fred McDarrah in a sad photograph in 1989, it made the point to me that no one really cared that much about Stonewall.

Jimmy Pisano never set out to re-open Stonewall. When I met him at the end of the 1980s, he was working as a manager of the then popular Private Eyes nightclub on West 21st Street. I met him there on a New Year's Eve. Something about him drew me in. He was larger than life and a bit of a showman, totally the opposite of me. He had been in the bar business practically his whole life, from seedy bars to mega-hit nightclubs. Sometime after we started dating he told me he wanted to open a place of his own.

Fast forward to when he tells me he's found a great spot on Christopher Street and even then there is no interest or indication of re-opening the space as Stonewall even though we're all aware of the provenance of the site. To the contrary, this is his bar and he will name it New Jimmy's, not for himself but out of respect for another Jimmy who taught him about the bar business years earlier.

New Jimmy's was envisioned to be a stylish pub and eatery. Beautiful wood paneling was put up over some of the brick, artists came in and drew English-style caricatures on other faux painted walls, an appropriately old-time New York bar was put in place, elegant lighting was installed, and a host of other very expensive décor embellished the former horse stable. It was a work of art and far too upscale, including the finer dining choices on the menu, than anything that had ever been there. Within a year of opening,

Jimmy realized that it was too nice a space. The clientele he was seeking, the kind of gay crowd that frequented Private Eyes and much of Chelsea, weren't coming to Christopher Street to eat and drink and the clientele that did frequent the neighborhood establishments weren't looking for fancy food, fancy wine, and fancy drinks. Though it cost a fortune to create, a fortune Jimmy didn't have, within a year New Jimmy's slowly morphed into the place I was walking into tonight, a revived Stonewall bar, with a more appropriate level of grit and seediness that the original seemed to demand.

We enter and are greeted by staff and other customers as long lost friends, even though we've seen these folks regularly for years. There was a whole protocol to go through, partly derived from my former privileged status as, originally, the owner's lover and, later, my own stint as the person in charge. You made your way down the bar side of the room, ended up at the small service bar to say "hi" to whomever was working that night, took a quick look in the back room, a space that was originally the kitchen for New Jimmy's that was subsequently turned into a small, dark secondary bar with a few video games, and then headed upstairs to secure your belongings in the office, a holdover courtesy extended to me and a few others. The kitchen-turned-back-room space was something of an homage to real back rooms, painted black and very dark except for the lights of a pinball or other gaming machine. It was only missing casual sex, though after hours it did see some more lively moments.

Though lacking a formal reception line, the entrance was an important part of the show. I came to learn quickly that there was a pecking order in this society, the bar world, and that the closer one was to the seat of power, the more one would receive gifts, usually drugs, as a sign of respect and to court favor. I suppose it was no different than any other social order. It just seemed more illicit and, therefore, more exciting to someone like me.

Before we reached the staircase at the rear, we were gifted with some coke. This time it was from one of the resident dealers, though it could have just as easily been from a friend or customer of the bar. It was a regular practice that I first experienced when Jimmy was running the bar. Any number of people would offer him drugs and, by extension of my role, would offer them to me as well. Jimmy treated this all so nonchalantly that I came to think of it as just business as usual. It continued when I took over operations, though I had become more paranoid about accepting it because I constantly was in fear of having the bar closed down and didn't want to be the cause of that. Hanging our coats in the office, we paused to sample the second double espresso of the evening. I couldn't tell you if it was good coke or bad coke. I wasn't a connoisseur.

Leaving the office, I choose to go back downstairs instead of looking in on the new second-floor space that a subsequent Stonewall proprietor had put in place after my involvement with the bar ceased. I had known him from when New Jimmy's was originally built and again during my time as caretaker. Unlike me, he still believed in the potential of the place as a viable business and had arranged with the building owner to convert the second-floor apartment at 53 Christopher into an extension of the downstairs space. In addition to another sizeable bar, it featured a small stage area for performances. I liked this guy and hoped that he would succeed where I failed in building the business, but I wondered if he too had succumbed to the heady feeling of running a bar, and not just any bar. The most ironic thing about it all was that he was the straightest guy I'd ever met.

My friends and I settled into a space at the end of the bar, not far from the DJ booth. After the usual chit chat and gossiping with other patron-friends, I noticed a familiar face down the bar toward the front window. Peter was a very talented actor and singer. At the beginning of the '90s, not long after New Jimmy's opened, he was starring in what was then the biggest show on Broadway. Jimmy had known him, from where I never knew, and he came to the bar on a handful of occasions in those early years of the revival, when the place was still too upscale and serving food. The most memorable night, for certain, was when Peter brought about a dozen or so of his castmates to the bar after their performance. Jimmy had pulled together several of the dinner tables and chairs so they could all sit together to celebrate the birthday of one of the performers. When an impromptu cake was brought out, the ensemble burst into the single best rendition of "Happy Birthday" that I'd ever heard. It was like being at an audition for a ridiculously talented group of singers, all belting and harmonizing. They brought the entire bar to a standstill and then continued wowing the crowd by singing, with a few dancing, to the subsequent songs that were piped through the loudspeakers. The final showstopper number was this group of Broadway performers blowing the doors off the place with Frankie Valli and The Four Seasons' "You're Just Too Good To Be True." Broadway had come to Stonewall and I was loving it.

I walked over to say hello, and Peter introduced me to his female friend. It had been a number of years since I'd seen him at Stonewall, though I did know that he lived on the same block as I, having bumped into him on West 12th a year or so earlier.

"Do you miss running this place?" Peter asks.

"No, definitely not," I reply. "A lot of the people I was trying to keep this place open for screwed me over too many times. I much prefer being a customer. What are you up to?"

"I'm putting some concert and cabaret things in place," and, pointing to his friend, "Nancy is helping me with it."

"You owned the Stonewall?" Nancy asks with surprise, the same surprise that everyone seems to have, thinking that this place must be a goldmine.

"No, my partner opened the bar about 10 years ago and when he died I ran it for a while ... to try to keep it open ... for him and for all the people who wanted it to be here," I summarize. Then, looking at Peter, "But I'd much rather talk about theatre. I've got this amazing collection of theatre memorabilia that I'd love to show you someday."

"What kind of stuff?" Peter asks.

"Well, I've got lots of handwritten sheet music by Sondheim, Jerry Herman, Cy Coleman. Bebe Neuwirth's bowler hat from *Chicago*. Probably the best item is the original *Gypsy* script. Merman's *Gypsy* script," I say with enormous pride.

"Where the hell did you get that?" they both say, almost simultaneously, with laughter.

"Lots of it I picked up at benefits and auctions. During the height of the AIDS crisis, a lot of people in the theatre community were donating amazing items to raise money, as you well know. I got it at a Merman tribute benefiting GMHC," I explain.

"That's so cool. Merman's *Gypsy* script. That's like theatre gold," Peter gushes.

"Well, you know where I live. I can show it to you anytime," I offer, hoping that he'll take me up on it. Peter is not only talented, but boyishly handsome. I fantasize for just a moment about what it would be like to have him as my boyfriend. The three of us talk for another ten minutes or so and then I beg off, wanting to get back to my friends and realizing that tonight isn't going to be the night I get to show Peter my collection.

My friends are in the back room playing pinball, alternating with the occasional trip to the bathroom to take another hit. I join them and we blow the next few hours on nothing memorable. Being here is the point. What you do while you're here is secondary.

I won't end up staying very late tonight. We'll all depart around 3:15 and head home. A few years earlier, when I was part of it all, I could easily stay until six or seven, with the doors locked to the public and the shutters drawn. Fueled by the booze and the drugs, a dozen or more of us would keep the party going well after closing.

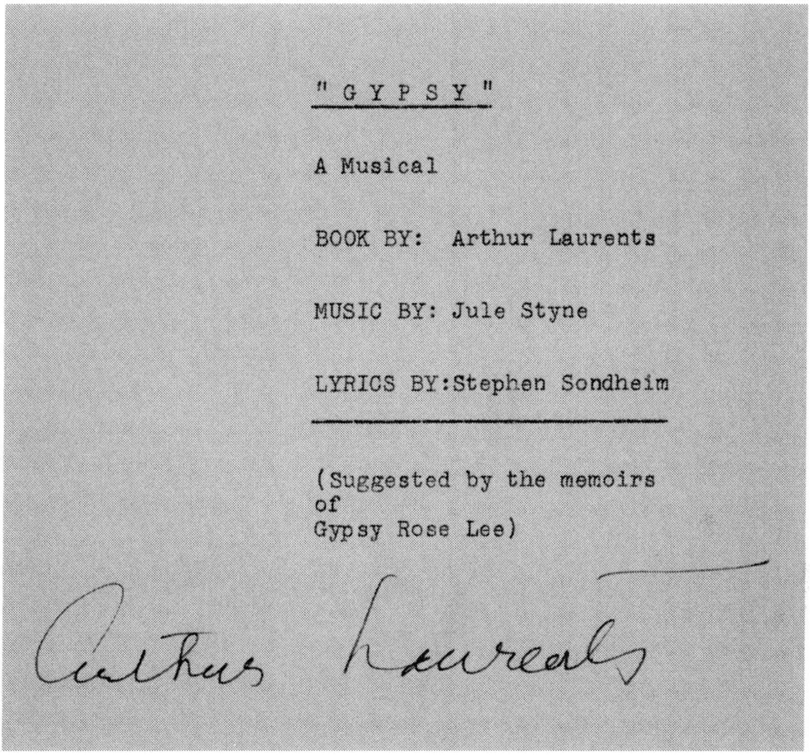

"G Y P S Y"

A Musical

BOOK BY: Arthur Laurents

MUSIC BY: Jule Styne

LYRICS BY: Stephen Sondheim

(Suggested by the memoirs of
Gypsy Rose Lee)

Arthur Laurents

CHAPTER FIVE

I Hope I Get It

When I open my eyes, I don't have the same jarring sense as I did the first time. I'm still a bit disoriented, but the whole "Where am I?" shudder is absent. I know I'm back in an older version of New York. The Checker cabs, green buses, mod clothing — all of it gives that away immediately. I know that this is Columbus Circle at the southwest corner of Central Park. It's still cold out, but whether it's the same day as before or another day is uncertain. I spot the newsstand and know that it holds the answer. Monday, February 14, 1966.

I'm tempted to walk down to the theatre district but, with no shows on Mondays, I start walking up Central Park West instead. The Upper West Side had been my first home in New York. In grad school, I ended up sharing an apartment with two other guys on West 76th Street. In 1987, a year after I landed my first job, I was able to buy the studio on West 90th. I knew this territory well.

The development and gentrification of this area is still a work in progress. Lincoln Center will help push out the seedier, crime-ridden parts of the area over time. But in 1966, you could still feel the upheaval taking place.

About ten blocks up Central Park West, at 67th Street, I bump into her again as she rounds the corner. She spots me at the same time I see her.

"Hey there. I guess you didn't like the show," she says with a laugh. "Otherwise I expect you would have been at the stage door after."

"Oh no, that's not it at all. I loved it. I loved you. It was brilliant," I say, and adding a small lie, "but I didn't want you to think I was weird or anything. I should have come back to say thank you for getting me the ticket. That was so kind and generous. I'll never be able to repay you."

"Well I was hoping you would have come back. I wanted to ask you about where you saw *Chicago* and who was involved," she says as we stand facing each other on the corner.

Realizing that I have to play this very carefully, I say, "It was sort of a college production. I saw it in Philadelphia at a small theatre." "It was well done, but I think it has the potential to be something more," I add, hoping that I've said enough that she'll want to continue talking about it, but also feeling miserable that I'm lying to someone I admire so.

"How far are you going?" she asks, indicating that she wants to know if I can walk further up Central Park West with her.

"Oh, up to 72nd Street," I lie again.

She starts moving, and I follow right next to her.

"So, what do you do? For a living, I mean," she asks.

"I'm in advertising. You know the Marlboro man. The cowboys in the commercials. That's what I work on." Technically, this isn't a lie. I have worked on Marlboro advertising at my 9-to-5 job at Philip Morris, but the fact that I won't be doing that for another twentyish years is something I choose to omit.

"That sounds important. Do you like it?" she asks with a sense of real interest.

"I enjoy what I do, but it isn't always as exciting as I'd like," I answer honestly.

"So whose job is?" she responds with another small laugh.

"I would imagine that what you do is very exciting. Creating new things. Bringing art to life," I say trying to sound thoughtful.

As we approach her building at 69th Street, she stops and we continue talking in front of the entrance to 91 Central Park West.

"It can be great, at times, but mostly it's pain getting something off the ground. Are you rushing to something or could you come up for a few minutes to tell me more about the *Chicago* production you saw?" she asks.

"Well, sure I could come up for a little bit," I answer, trying not to sound as thrilled as I am inside.

"Great," she says leading me into the building. "I have to get ready for tonight, so just for a little bit," she adds, making it clear that this will be just a short visit.

The tone of her remark makes me think that she's talking about the show. At the same time, I reach into my pocket and find that familiar cardboard feel. Pulling it out, I see that my original ticket, from my last visit to 1966 New York, is still there. This time, luckily, it's for tonight. Valentine's Day. I hadn't picked up on that the last time, just that fact that my ticket was for some time in February. How appropriate. I had assumed that there were no Monday performances because that's all I know from the world I came from. My mistake. My fortunate mistake.

In the elevator, I mention that the ticket I wasn't able to use last time was for tonight's show, hoping to make it sound like a coincidence versus an early instance of celebrity stalking.

"How lucky. The show's a little tighter now and the company has gotten over some of the harsher things that were said in the reviews," she mentions as we reach the top floor and exit the elevator, directly into her apartment. It was only the second time in my life that I had entered a New York City apartment where the elevator opened directly into the apartment rather than a hallway. It was a rich thing.

"Everyone loved your performance," I say, though that's not entirely true. Overall, the reviews had been lukewarm at best, though Gwen had been spared the harshest criticisms.

"Yeah, but they sort of have to say that about me. I hate that they criticized so much of the show. It's a good show and everyone's working really hard. Bob got some positive comments, but he internalizes every negative thing that was said about the score and John and the rest," she says referring to Cy Coleman and John McMartin, her co-star.

Standing in her apartment, once home to Marion Davies, a Hearst apartment, is surreal but disappointing. Perhaps I was expecting something Xanadu from *Citizen Kane*. It is, for certain, enormous and worthy of a titan. But the imperial touches are largely absent. There are no giant European statues or suits of armor or ancient tapestries in sight. Then again, that was another resident's style. There are lots of potted plants, some rather large, all around. It's a mixture of styles, in my uniformed opinion. There's a chest or armoire against a wall. It's a bit ornate for my taste, about six feet tall, and has a slightly Asian feel in its extensive detailing. Walking further, I see a long, sleek console against the windows. It is white, understated, with a few pieces of small sculpture on top. It's more to my taste, but not Hearst-worthy. Though I don't get, nor ask for, a tour, I can spot some elaborate gold wallpaper and ornate woodwork that may be a holdover from the previous power couple. I do insist on a quick look out on the stunning terrace overlooking the Park, but the cold weather brings us quickly back inside. Imagining the grand parties that had been held here and could be held here, I sit on a couch and she sits somewhat cross-legged on a nearby chair. A housekeeper brings me a hot chocolate but mostly disappears during my visit.

"You must have really liked *Chicago*," she says glancing toward my hat. I don't bother to look at it, knowing it's the souvenir I bought during the 1996 revival. "Were you involved with it?"

"I don't remember what drew me to it. Maybe it was the darkness of the premise. Two women become famous for murder. Celebrities, in fact," I mention, adding, "The whole jazz-age timeframe begs for it to be made into a musical." I'm feeding an interest that I already know she has for the story.

"Was Watkins involved in this production?" she asks referring to Maurine Dallas Watkins, author of the original play, whose later embrace of a more Christian lifestyle caused her to refuse Fosse and Verdon's attempts to buy the rights.

"I don't think so, but I don't really know. Why?" I ask, knowing the answer.

"I've thought it would be a good musical, but she's refused to consider it. She's found God or something," she summarizes quite succinctly.

"Well, she is rather old by now, considering how long ago she wrote the play. Maybe you just need to bide your time. An estate might be more apt to consider an offer, even if the deceased had no inclination," I say, trying to offer what I think sounds like practical advice.

"True, but I'm not getting any younger. I can't wait ten years," she responds, though in fact she will.

I blurt out, "I understand. But when my boyfriend died and I inherited his bar, everything changed for me. It's not the same, I know. I'm just saying that the world can change very quickly." I regret bringing that passage of my life up with her. I want this to be a conversation about her and theatre and making *Chicago*.

"I'm sorry. You own a bar? I thought you said you worked in advertising. Marlboro," she responds with a mixture of empathy and confusion.

"That's my day job. I had to run his bar. I needed to keep it open. It was, is, an important gay bar," I try to explain.

"An important gay bar?" she asks, as if that was an impossible idea, which at the time it was.

My mind starts to scramble to find something to say that makes what I'm referring to plausible. As I do, she reaches for a cigarette for herself and then offers me one, saying "I assume you smoke."

"Yes, thanks," I say, lighting the cigarette. The exchange allows me to construct an explanation.

"Well, it's important to me because it was important to him. It was the first and last bar he would ever own. He died just a few years after opening it and it's a legacy of sorts."

"What did he die from? Was he much older than you?"

Unable to explain the truth about him dying from complications brought about by the AIDS virus, I focus on the proximate cause of death. "He had a very aggressive cancer. It overwhelmed his body. By the end, one leg was so blackened from cancer lesions that it would have had to have been amputated had he lived any longer. Everything just started shutting down. He was only in his forties," I describe in as dispassionate way as I can.

"I'm so sorry honey," she says with the most genuine sympathy.

"I didn't mean to bring it up. I just wanted to give you hope that things could be different. That you might be able to get *Chicago* after all. Things sometimes can change very quickly. I didn't mean to bring up all this sad stuff. I don't know why I did that," I say regretting how I've altered the conversation from theatre to my personal life.

"Don't worry about it. And I do hope you're right. It's the kind of story that doesn't come along very often. Bob would love to turn it into something remarkable. Something that would last," she says.

Taking the empty cup of hot chocolate, she heads to the kitchen. I'm so comfortable on the sofa. The conversation has drained me. I almost never talk about Jimmy's death, keeping it a very personal moment. Even mentioning it briefly to this stranger, albeit a known stranger, makes me feel exhausted. Before she returns from the kitchen, my eyes close. I never did get to see Charity Hope Valentine on Valentine's Day.

CHAPTER SIX

I Am What I Am

I didn't remember the trip home from Stonewall, but the dream of talking to Gwen Verdon in her apartment was still vivid when I awoke in my apartment around noon on Sunday. Getting fucked up at Stonewall was nothing new, though I was much better now at restricting it to nights where I had the following day to recover. During the early '90s, there was many a morning that I'd call in sick to work. Initially, after Jimmy died, I had fooled myself into believing that I could run the bar and still do a good job at my 9-to-5 place. Over time, I compounded this foolishness with hiring and overpaying several staff members who I thought I could trust to do the right thing when I couldn't be there every night and weekend.

The conversation with Gwen was fresh, and I started to think about how parts of our lives were similar. She would become the keeper of Fosse's legacy after he died, fighting to keep his name and work alive and relevant. I, too, felt a need to preserve the good things that Jimmy had done in re-opening the bar at 53 Christopher. Despite the mismanagement of the place, something that I did not fully appreciate until after he died and I surveyed the financial ruins, I was determined to make it all work — to ensure that the bar would remain open, that people would remain employed, and that everyone would have a chance to step into a living icon of gay rights.

I called Joe Jr.'s, a coffee shop at the corner, for my bacon, egg, and cheese on a roll hangover remedy. It was one of those quintessential New York spots, worthy of a *Seinfeld* visit. When you called Joe Jr.'s to order something for delivery, it was mandated by the gruff counterperson who answered with a shouting "YES" that you speak very quickly with your address and order. There could be no hesitation whatsoever or he would start barking your order to you because, apparently, he recognized every caller and knew what they wanted. I don't remember ever being on the phone with him for more than five or six seconds. He practically slammed the phone down before you even finished ordering, but your meal would arrive within 10 or 12 minutes. It was a New York miracle.

After pulling out some old photos of the construction of New Jimmy's, when everything was hopeful, and lingering over them and a third cup of coffee, I got showered and dressed. I needed to pick up some groceries for the week, but I decided last minute to head over to a day spa on Christopher to see if I could get a massage. It would help with the hangover, I thought. It had been opened by a longtime friend of Jimmy, someone he had known from the bar world, and, like New Jimmy's, it was a bit fancier than the neighborhood was used to seeing. The people who worked there now were a bit less colorful than the original crew, especially the massage therapists who, at the start of the business, could generally be counted on for providing the happiest of endings. The original owner had died a year after Jimmy, also from AIDS. One of his boyfriends, someone I knew briefly, would eventually get into all kinds of legal trouble at a different day spa. Apparently, he thought he had learned enough at this place to literally play doctor and set up a practice. There was no shortage of characters on Christopher Street.

Heading back up Christopher Street after my massage, I see that there's a drag show of some kind going on at Stonewall. I step inside, intending to only spend a few minutes to see who's performing, but I end up at the bar with a Bloody Mary. The allure of drag at Stonewall is almost a religious calling, both for the performers as well as the audience. To the performers, especially the ones that impersonate Judy Garland or other stars of an earlier era, Stonewall is akin to "playing the Palace." But there aren't many of them anymore because there isn't much of an audience who knows or cares about those half-forgotten stars. To the audience, it's like seeing a reenactment of history. It feels passé, given the abundance of far more provocative entertainment nowadays and the preoccupation with self-indulgent talent shows on television.

As I watch the lip-syncing from my chair, thinking that some of these girls have a hardened look that would have appealed to Fosse when casting *Sweet Charity*, I start to chat with the new bartender. He isn't really new to Stonewall, but I refer to the bartenders and managers that came after Jimmy ran the place, and during my short tenure running it, as *new* to distinguish them from the revival crew of the early '90s. A sort of BC / AD demarcation. Carlos is straight out of central casting — young, charming, and cheerful.

"What are we raising money for today?" I ask Carlos, noticing the queens soliciting the crowd for cash.

"I don't know. Probably some AIDS thing," he responds without much thought or interest in the proceedings. "Did you have all this drag when you were here?" he asks referring to mine and Jimmy's tenure.

"It was more about entertainment, less about fundraising for charity," I reply.

"That must have been better. My tips take a hit when there's some charity thing going on," he complains, though I doubt it's true given his obvious charms and the tendency, at least for the older patrons, to want to curry favor with the handsome bartender.

"Have you mentioned it to your manager?" I ask.

"No, he wouldn't care. This place really isn't managed well. Nobody gives a shit about the staff," he confides.

"I think you have it pretty good, actually. In my day, we had the craziest managers. Really. Some of them were really out of their minds. At the time, I couldn't believe it. Now, I look back and laugh."

He goes off to sell some drinks, but returns asking, "So like what did they do? What was crazy?"

"Well, for instance, I remember being woken up one night at Jimmy's apartment. Around three in the morning. Jimmy answered the phone and one of the bartenders was calling to say that the manager had stripped completely naked and was sitting on a bar stool in the middle of the floor," I say, pointing to where it happened. "He was twisted out of his mind and just decided to take his clothes off and rant from the barstool about nonsense."

"You're fucking kidding me," Carlos says, his interest having been piqued.

"I wish I was," I say, laughing with him. "There were others too, most of them dead now. Another guy who worked here thought it would be funny one night to spray the customers with a fire extinguisher. And when he was fired, he couldn't understand why such a big deal was being made out of it. There were so many outrageous moments sometimes I have a hard time remembering them all. But you're right about the drag. Today, it's different. Most of the drag queens create their own character. Back then, it was more about capturing a famous performer."

"Who was the best one?" he asks showing far more interest in the topic than I expected.

"Well, there was one performer, Electra, who was the best that I ever saw. And he had so many famous characters that he could do perfectly. It was amazing. He impersonated Lucy and Judy and Marilyn and Bette Midler. Lots of icons. I could try to describe it, but it was one of those things that you had to see," I say.

There was also a slew of not-ready-for-primetime drag queens who graced the stage at Stonewall. Vinny, who went by the stage name of Vee Martense, made regular appearances, mostly performing as Shirley Bassey. He had been one of the characters at Stonewall that most made me think of the late '60s crowd that had been here. He was old-school. He had become a customer of the bar from the re-opening, and Jimmy and I hung out with him often. He could be wildly generous and kind, though he often didn't have a pot to piss in, as they say. But he, like many others, always took the fun too far. He'd get blind drunk, snort a boatload of cocaine, and become this very loud, very grand persona. He had a really good job as a court stenographer, but he basically screwed that up. I remember being told that while at work one day, at the courthouse, he dropped a bottle of coke in the men's room and ended up snorting the whole thing up from the floor so as not to waste it — from the filthy floor, amongst the shards of glass of the vial that broke. And yet, I liked the guy. As fucked up as he could be, there was something genuinely likable about this man. He died alone in his apartment, having ground up and snorted too many painkillers. It was a sad, but not entirely unexpected, ending.

One of the current queens comes over to my spot at the bar and makes some small talk, presumably to solicit a donation. She knew Jimmy, so there's a respectfulness to her speech that I appreciate.

"Is he taking good care of you?" she asks me, nodding her head toward Carlos. Then, speaking to him, "You know his lover opened this place. You wouldn't have this job if it wasn't for Jimmy Pisano." She actually pronounces his name as Paesano, the Italian word for friend or countryman. It's a common mistake that a lot of the acquaintances make. It used to bother me, but given that the translation of their mispronunciation is a kind, fitting description of Jimmy, I have stopped correcting people.

"It's very kind of you to remember that. Most people don't know that this place exists because of him," I say.

"Honey, as long as my big mouth is workin' everyone will know that Jimmy brought this place back to life," she announces loudly, as if to an audience, while her right and heavily bejeweled hand gestures in an arc across the room. Nothing is done without a sense of theatricality in Stonewall.

We chat a bit more and I put a twenty-dollar bill in her container. Finishing up my drink, I say goodbye to Carlos and head home.

With the TV on in the background, I look through some more of those old photos of the opening of New Jimmy's as well as some priceless pictures from Gay Pride, the best being a series with an attractive black drag queen strutting in front of New York's Finest. Twenty-some odd years after the riots, the police and a drag queen are hilariously posing in front of 53 Christopher. The pictures are all stuffed in a photo album that had been made for the first anniversary. It had been a well-organized collection, documenting the first year of the re-opening, but, over time, I had haphazardly added other photos to the point where I wasn't always sure what year a given picture was from.

The first year was a happy year because everyone believed that the place would be successful. The construction and decoration of the place were masterfully done and terribly expensive. Even at full capacity, I doubt Jimmy could have made a go of it. I came to know, later on, that the borrowing that would sink this place financially started from day one. Jimmy had gotten his best friend Bobby to put money in New Jimmy's, as well as his cousin Robert. Neither would see a return on their investment. The contractor also put some big bucks into the place and, although he wasn't an owner in the legal sense, he became a de facto silent partner given his stake in New Jimmy's success. Even after a year of running what was then Stonewall by myself, I couldn't figure out just how much was owed to everyone. Investors, the tax authorities, suppliers — it was an enormous sum. The hole was too deep to climb out of, but I ignored that reality just as Jimmy had done.

Vinny, who became a fixture in the bar, appeared in several photos, both in and out of drag. As crazy as his behavior could be, on the night Jimmy died he was there with me in the hospital and a profoundly sober presence. Even years later, every moment of that day is as clear as if it happened yesterday. It started with Jimmy feeling very sick and unable to breathe. I insisted that we go to the emergency room, but Jimmy was having nothing of the kind. He had been hospitalized several times before and each time was worse and more foreboding than the previous stay. Finally, I convinced him to let me take him to his doctor, thinking that he'd have to listen to his doctor about going into the hospital.

The cab ride downtown from Jimmy's apartment on 73rd Street to his doctor's office in the Village was difficult because his breathing became more and more labored. I told him that we should head for St. Vincent's instead of the doctor's office, but he refused. By the time we entered the doctor's waiting room he could hardly breathe and was about to collapse. The nurses and doctor were stunned at his condition and scrambled to bring him into a room and started administering oxygen. His doctor was angry that we had come to the office instead of going to a hospital until I quietly explained that the only way to get Jimmy to a hospital was to bring him here first. An ambulance was called and Jimmy was stretchered for the short ride to St. Vincent's.

Unlike previous visits, Jimmy got a room rather quickly, a semi-private space that fortunately didn't have another person in the next bed. I was calmer now knowing that we were at a place where something could be done to help him.

After calling his cousin Robert, who lived with us in the 73rd Street apartment, to let him know what was going on, I waited for the usual array of nurses, doctors, and technicians to come to administer all the testing and ask all the questions that they invariably would at this stage of an admission. Jimmy was anxious. While we were at a place where something could be done to help him, the truth was that there was nothing that really could be done to alter the trajectory. You never knew whether a particular hospital stay would be the last one. During a prior visit to the emergency room at St. Vincent's, I had let the nurses and doctors know that Jimmy had a do not resuscitate order in place. At that time, though, he clearly wasn't in the mindset of letting go, insisting that he wanted every available means of technology to keep him alive. It had become a big scene in the emergency room because Jimmy's longtime friend, Michael, arrived and, in my mind, convinced him to rescind the DNR, causing a great deal of arguing and confusion.

Within a short time, Jimmy's doctor appeared. He spoke of Jimmy's current condition and what treatments he was going to pursue to help Jimmy recover. He examined Jimmy's lower leg, the one that bore the lesions from Kaposi's Sarcoma. Prior to AIDS, it was a very rare cancer that no one had heard of. When people started referring to it as, simply, KS you knew it had crossed into the vernacular. The black lesions that had spotted portions of Jimmy's lower leg when I first met him were now completely covering his lower extremity, turning it black and hard. The doctor said nothing about the leg. Jimmy told his doctor that he was in extreme pain.

After the doctor left the room, I tried to reassure Jimmy but he was anxious and agitated and started to pick at me. I continued to try to calm him down, but it was not happening. At one point, he turned onto his side, almost fetal and practically crying, but angry, and whispered, "You said you would help me."

Jimmy was hooked up to various machines and drips when Vinny came to the door of the room. I was surprised to see him, until he explained that he had called the apartment and Robert had informed him that Jimmy had been admitted to the hospital. I brought him up to speed. The next few hours were quiet, primarily because Jimmy had fallen asleep. Vinny and I split our time sitting in the room with him and, when we wanted to talk, moving to the nearby visitor lounge. I remember little of my conversation with Vinny that night. I think he asked if I wanted something to eat. But whatever we talked about was a separate autopilot dialogue that part of my mind took care of as I dwelled on what was happening in that hospital room. I was anxious and uncertain. Though I'd been in this situation before with him, this admission felt more foreboding, more surreal.

After several hours, Vinny had fallen asleep in a chair in the lounge. I returned to Jimmy's room and sat in a chair at the foot of the bed. There was only the dim fluorescent overhead fixture behind the hospital bed illuminating the room. At times, I wanted to move up the side of the bed and hold his hand or touch his face but I was too scared to do that. Shouldn't I be more comforting if, in fact, this was going to be the end? He was not awake, but I didn't know if it was sleep or something else. The back of the bed had been raised to a 45-degree angle, so I could look directly at Jimmy's face as I sat there. A few times I whispered, "It's OK. It's going to be OK," because it seemed like that was what one was supposed to say. For the remainder of the next hour or so, I silently thought, as though trying to communicate telepathically, "You can go if you need to go." It felt better to talk to him that way.

The first thing I noticed was that the peaceful sleep was interrupted with a heaving sound and motion. Jimmy's upper body, from his chest up toward his head, lifted slightly off the bed forming an arch between his back and the bed. It happened just once, but it looked like a gasp for breath. I wasn't sure if it was an inhale or an exhale. His mouth had opened halfway, eyes still shut. For a moment, I thought about getting a nurse before I decided to just sit and be with him. He was still again.

Within a short time, it happened again. His body arched, almost reaching up to something, with his mouth opened and the sound of air. I realized I was witnessing it, the final moments of the life of someone I loved. I was relieved that I was alone, that Vinny was still sleeping in the lounge, and that no nurse had come into the room. I wanted this to be a quiet, private moment. With the subsequent movements of his upper body arching upward to the ceiling, I had a feeling that I was witnessing his soul's departure from the body. The feeling comforted me. The dreaminess of the moment, though, is shattered as I start to see foam pouring out from Jimmy's mouth. It's white and bubbly. The more his body is arching upward, the more the soapy mix comes streaming out and down his chin. His body continues to heave upward and his throat and mouth become more extended as though he's trying to vomit something from his body. And then it stops.

The moment you see a human being go from breathing to not breathing is a demarcation. To see the exact second of death is the most sobering moment of life. There will be nothing, ever again, that will truly scare me. Everything else is made small and irrelevant. The next day, when I phone my 9-to-5 boss to explain why I won't be at work for the next week, I describe the moment as being "like a miracle." During the call, I feel like I'm listening in on someone else's conversation. I can sense that my boss thinks I've lost my mind. The words coming out of my mouth are not mine. Someone else is describing it and they cast it, inexplicably, as a miracle.

After some indeterminate silence, I get out of the chair at the foot of Jimmy's bed. I'm still too scared to go up the side of the bed to look at him closer or to touch him. The absolute stillness, of the room and his body, is noticeable. I go to the nurse's station and say, "Could you please come. I think he's dead."

CHAPTER SEVEN

There's No Business Like Show Business

I didn't remember going to bed that night in my apartment. I must have fallen asleep in the living room while looking at the old photos. But my eyes open up in the old New York that I've become recently acquainted with in dreams. I'm on the Upper West Side again, at Lincoln Center. I'm sitting at the famous fountain that will be captured in so many films, especially during the late '60s when the complex is new. All three of the main buildings that surround the fountain are there, but the space seems somewhat bare or incomplete. As I look toward the Metropolitan Opera House, it looks like there is still some work being done to the façade and the familiar Marc Chagall murals are not yet there. Sometime around 1967, Zero Mostel and Gene Wilder will parade around this fountain, with the Chagall murals in view, when Wilder's Leo Bloom character agrees to become Max Bialystock's partner-in-crime in *The Producers*.

Reaching into my pocket, I find no theatre ticket, only the remaining money from the sale of my watch. I head toward Columbus Avenue to find a newspaper and to get some breakfast. Though I don't know what day it is, I can tell that it's about midday. *The New York Times* tells me that it's Monday, May 30, 1966. I take the paper and head into a coffee shop.

Sitting at a small table next to the window overlooking the street, I peruse the menu and order coffee and an omelet. It's Memorial Day and I catch a small article in the paper that says that certain Broadway shows are running a special matinee performance for the holiday. There's no *Sweet Charity* mentioned, but I notice that there is a preview performance of *Annie Get Your Gun*, a limited-engagement revival taking place at Lincoln Center. Merman had done the show some 20 years earlier and, now in her late 50's and at the end of her career, was reprising one of her signature roles. I wonder whether I have enough money left to get a cheap seat or if they offer standing room tickets.

I flip to page 23 and scan the theatre listings to see what else is running. I practically break out into laughter when I see what's playing in New York. In addition to Merman in *Annie Get Your Gun* and Verdon in *Sweet Charity*, there's a banquet of riches for anyone with even a modest interest in live theatre. There are five more weeks to see Henry Fonda in a comedy called *Generation*. Angela Lansbury has opened to rave reviews in *Mame*. Lee Remick is starring in *Wait Until Dark*. Vivien Leigh and John Gielgud are winding down the final two weeks of *Ivanov*. Ginger Rogers is playing Dolly Levi. Lauren Bacall is in *Cactus Flower*. There are productions of *Show Boat*, *The Odd Couple*, *Barefoot in the Park*, *Fiddler on the Roof*, *Funny Girl*, *Man of La Mancha,* and *On a Clear Day You Can See Forever*, plus productions of less universally known shows. The fabulous invalid is being attended to by the likes of Julie Harris, Hal Holbrook, Bea Arthur, Ray Milland, Barbara Bel Geddes, Larry Bliden, Barbara Harris, John Cullum, Barbara Cook, Constance Towers, Mimi Hines, Joan Van Ark, Alan King, George Rose, and Tony Roberts. Had I lived in this time, I'd have starved to death, choosing to spend any money I had on theatre over something trivial like food.

As I'm digging into my omelet and reading the paper, suddenly there's rapid knocking on the window on my left. It's her. Gwen. She smiling and waving at me. I try to stand up, knocking the table and spilling some coffee when she mouths something and makes her way to the door of the coffee shop. Entering and making her way to my table, she's carrying a small shopping bag that looks like it has produce in it.

"Oh my God, I wasn't expecting to see you again," she says. "Did I say something to offend you?"

We're both standing at my table and I motion for her to sit down. "No. Why would you think that?"

"Well, you just left so abruptly. I went to the kitchen and when I got back, you weren't there. You must have raced out of the apartment," she explains.

"No, no, I wasn't offended. I was just upset. I never talk about the things that I was mentioning to you with anyone," I offer, trying to simultaneously think of a plausible reason why I disappeared and trying to understand the peculiar nature of these dreams where another character, in this case Gwen Verdon, is trying to makes sense of things that don't need to make sense in dreams.

"I thought that, maybe, I had gotten too personal. Asking too many questions. About your life and your involvement with *Chicago*," she says.

"No, really, it was just that I got too emotional and I had to leave. I'm so sorry that I was rude. I didn't want to do that. But I didn't want to break down in front of you," I say, adding, "I'm just so happy to see you again so that I could explain. You startled me just now. I wasn't expecting to see you."

"I saw that hat of yours as I was walking by and doubled back."

"Yes, the famous hat. I guess it's my trademark by now," I say and we both laugh.

I ask her if she wants anything to eat and she declines, saying, "No, I'm running over to Lincoln Center to drop this stuff off. It's all organic ... so much better for you than the stuff that they sell in the supermarket. That stuff is just poison for your body."

Knowing that she becomes a big and early adopter of organic fruits and vegetables, actually to the point of growing her own tomatoes and greens on those incredible terraces of hers, I remark, "I think more and more people should eat that way. The stuff that's in food nowadays isn't real food."

"It's for Ethel Merman. She's opening tomorrow night and I can't go because of my show and she came to my opening. I wanted to bring her something that would be good for her. She thinks she's indestructible, but none of us are. Though, she's probably a bit sturdier than most," she says, smiling at the slight dig that she's made.

"That's very thoughtful of you. And certainly original. You're giving her the gift of health," I add.

"Exactly. Do you want to come with me?"

"To see *Annie Get Your Gun* and meet Merman? I'd kill to ...," I say before she cuts me off.

"No, not to see the show. I'm just dropping by to say hi and give her this. Before the matinee," she explains.

"Still. I'd kill to go with you."

I pay the check, leave a tip, and we head out of the restaurant toward Lincoln Center. It's a beautiful spring day in New York and I'm heading to meet a Broadway legend with another Broadway legend. These dreams are insanely good.

We enter through a stage door. Though there are people just inside who would otherwise intercept us and ask our intentions, that's not the case when you're walking in with Gwen Verdon. There are simply a lot of greetings and smiles and complements offered to her as we make our way to a dressing room. She knocks, but starts opening the door before receiving a response.

"I've come to return the favor," she says walking toward Merman who is seated in front of a mirror, partly dressed in the garb that makes her Annie Oakley.

"Thanks a lot, kid. But don't you know you're supposed to wait before entering a lady's dressing room? What if I was naked or something?" Merman bellows.

"I would have if I was entering a lady's dressing room or something," Verdon swipes back playfully. They both laugh, Merman's sounding like a truck driver and Verdon's sounding like a little girl.

Verdon gives Ethel Merman a kiss on the cheek and says, "I wanted to bring you these. It's what I was telling you about. These aren't grown with pesticides and chemicals. They're much better for you. You need to start taking better care of yourself."

"You bring me vegetables for my opening? What am I a rabbit?" Merman says in a way that sounds like a caricature of herself.

"I'm bringing you the gift of health," Verdon says, smiling toward me.

"And who is this?" Merman asks looking annoyed

"That's my friend, Tom," Verdon replies. I'm dumbfounded that she's used the word *friend*, given that we've met a total of three short times and I'm still an absolute stranger to her, but I'm absolutely thrilled inside.

"Hello Ms. Merman. It's wonderful to meet you," I say.

"What's so wonderful about it?" she says, speaking at a volume two levels above that which is called for in normal conversation.

"Cut it out, Ethel. I bumped into him on my way here and I asked him to come along. Do you think you're going to extend the show?" Verdon asks, changing the subject.

"We'll come back to New York in the fall, after we do the tour," Merman replies.

"Well, then it's even more important that you eat better. I don't know why you'd want to put yourself through all that. I would hate being on the road," Verdon adds.

"I have to work. I can't stand the routine when I'm doin' it, but I hate it even more when I'm not. Haven't done anything since *Gypsy*. I thought those fuckers were going to give me the movie, but they screwed me. Going back to this," Merman says, pointing to her Annie Oakley outfit, "seemed to be the best thing."

"I'll try to see the show before you leave town," Verdon says.

"Great. Now let me finish gettin' ready," Merman says, indicating that our visit is over.

We walk toward the door of the dressing room, exchange good-byes, and head out into the hallway.

"Thanks for coming with me," Verdon says smiling, putting her hand on my shoulder.

"I loved it. She's just like you imagine her to be."

"And then some."

She starts walking back toward where we came in and I stop her with, "Do you think ... I mean I really hate to ask ... but do you know Jerry Orbach?"

"Yeah, sure. Why? You want to meet him?" she asks.

"Well, yes, if it's not too much to ask. I think he's amazing."

"OK. Let's go find him," she says leading me down the hall.

Not sure where to look, we hunt for another room where Jerry Orbach might be getting ready for the matinee. Turning around to explore some other doors, I spot him.

"There he is."

She walks in front of me toward him, pulling me by the hand, and says, "Hey Jerry, I want to introduce you to my friend, Tom, he's a big fan."

Flustered, Jerry Orbach extends his hand and as we shake, says, "Well, any friend of Miss Verdon is a friend of mine."

"I think you're a remarkable actor and performer. I've always admired your work and career," I praise, though he's still not halfway through his theatre career and even further from becoming *Law and Order's* Lennie Briscoe.

"Thanks," he replies with a smile, though he seems uncomfortable that a fan has caught him backstage.

"We don't want to take up any more of your time," I offer. "Just wanted to say hello," and with that I grab Gwen's hand and lead her toward the exit.

As we step into the sunshine, she asks, "You got some sort of crush on him? He's straight. Married."

"No, nothing like that. I just think it's really cool when someone devotes themselves to their craft so much. Doing it so well and for so long," I say, then realizing that he hasn't done it yet, "He's got a long career ahead of him."

"Men do have it easier in this business. They grow into their looks and nobody minds if they don't perform at the same level as they did when they were younger," she says.

I lead her toward the fountain and we sit at its edge.

"When you get the rights to *Chicago*, you might want to consider him for the role of Billy Flynn," I suggest. "He's just perfect for the part."

"So, now you're casting a show, my show, that I don't even have yet," she jokes.

"You'll get it. I'm confident of that," I say, momentarily wondering if my being here can change anything that's to come, but then realizing how silly the thought is of changing a future that has already happened.

"Your boyfriend ... what did you say his name was?"

"Jimmy."

"What was it that attracted you?"

"He was just larger than life. He came from a world that I found exciting and slightly dangerous. I've always lived on the straight and narrow. He exposed me to things that I wouldn't have seen or done on my own," I tell her, adding, "He did a lot of drugs too. It became very self-destructive. That made me crazy. I thought I could fix him. I went to therapy. We went to therapy. Even broke up with him for months. But, we got back together. The attraction was that strong."

"I get that. It's a choice you make. To be around someone who can make you crazy but the alternative makes you crazier," she confides and I wonder how much of what she's saying about my relationship parallels her life. Fosse would go on to be with many other women, yet she was alongside him even after they ceased being a couple and, perhaps most fittingly, when he succumbed to a heart attack in Washington, D.C., on the opening night of a revival of *Sweet Charity*.

"I'm going back to the apartment. You wanna come?" she asks.

"No, I think I'll just sit here for a bit longer," I say. "But, hey, why don't you take my hat. You seem to like it and it'll be a reminder of what I've told you. You're gonna get this show made into a musical."

"Ok. You're sure? You seem to be always wearing it. It must be your favorite."

"Yes, I'm sure. Maybe next time, I can take you to see the bar. Stonewall. So you can see the place that was so important to him," I offer, unsure as to when our next encounter might be or if there will be one at all.

I watch as she walks away, still marveling at the fact that I've been able to get to know her. I've never had such vivid dreams. My mind has never been so creative before as to construct these episodes, with all their detail and depth, into what feels like real conversations in real places. And, for whatever reason, I don't seem to mind that I know I'm dreaming. The sun is warm and I close my eyes to relish the moments I've just had.

CHAPTER EIGHT

Doin' What Comes Natur'lly

Another workweek had gone by. When I had awoken on Monday morning, in the living room chair with photos spilled out onto the glass coffee table, I realized that I had sunk into one of those wormholes. Even a decade after meeting Jimmy, and a good half-dozen years after my place at Stonewall ended, I could still easily fall into watching those film loops in my head. Every memorable moment, and there were so many, would fill the widescreen in my mind. It was like being trapped in multiplex theatre that only ran films from your memories, where you'd teleport between the different showings, sitting in the dark for a few minutes in each theatre to watch something you'd seen repeatedly, unable to not watch your life flash before your eyes.

It was Saturday again. Joe Jr.'s delivered the ritual breakfast. As I dive into the perfect bacon, egg, and cheese sandwich, a thought comes out of nowhere. I start to imagine whether I could direct these dreams of 1966 to be more intentioned, rather than the roulette wheel random path that they had been taking. Could I pick the time and place to be? The places and times that my dreams had taken me to, on their own accord, were insanely good. After all, I did get to meet Gwen Verdon, see *Sweet Charity*, visit the fabled Hearst apartment on 69th Street, and meet Ethel Merman and Jerry Orbach. It wasn't as though there was anything lacking in how things had transpired so far. Greedily, I wondered if I could pick a situation, just by thinking about it.

My mind filled with possibilities. Angela Lansbury was making theatre history in *Mame* at the very same time that *Sweet Charity* was running. That would be amazing to see. And even if I was just limited to 1966, there were so many remarkable shows to see that year that these dreams could go on for quite a while. For a moment, I even wondered if I could see myself, a four-year-old living in Queens, or Jimmy or my parents or other relatives and friends, some of whom were dead by 2000. But the thought of observing myself or other real people started to feel creepy. Going to the theatre or meeting the people that ruled that world was fun, a fantasy. Observing myself or my parents, in their 30's, felt too much like science fiction. Maybe I could hang out at the pre-riot Stonewall. As if I hadn't spent enough time in that bar, now I was thinking about visiting it in another era.

I throw on some clothes and run out to pick up the paper to see what's going on in the world according to *The New York Times*. Fittingly, the *Chicago* baseball cap is nowhere to be found. Anything that makes these dreams feel even more real than they already do, I embrace wholeheartedly. I don't even bother to search for the hat because, upon finding it, I'd be disappointed that the illusion had been broken. I browse through all the sections of the paper, save for Sports. Though I've already seen it, I stop at the ad for *Annie Get Your Gun* starring Bernadette Peters. I decide to see it again. It seems like I'm fulfilling some cosmic prophecy or theatre equilibrium, given the last '60s visit.

At seven o'clock, I dress appropriately enough for the theatre, with black jeans and a white button-down shirt, but not so properly that I can't go out after to a bar and fit in. The cab ride up from West 12th and 6th Avenue is short, even with theatre traffic.

The show is playing at the Marquis Theatre, the least Broadway style theatre in New York in my opinion. Swallowed and surrounded by the Marriott Marquis Hotel, the theatre opened in 1986, bearing none of the charm of the old theatre houses. I crawl over too many other patrons to get to my seat, as does everyone else, because the design of the space is more commercially-driven than artistically-minded.

Bernadette Peters is always a joy to watch. I was a latecomer in joining her fan club, having first seen her in *Into The Woods* in 1987, but have seen everything else she's done since. As the overture begins, I try to remember what shows she was in during the late 1960s and whether it would be possible to see her back then, but her eternal youthfulness seems to make that redundant.

Like the last time I saw it, I thoroughly enjoy the show and Peters' command of the role, though having stood face to face, as it were, with Ethel Merman, at least in my head, I have more fun this time, imagining Ethel onstage behind Bernadette chastising her for not being as big or as loud as Merman.

As we leave the theatre, I glance toward the Palace where *Aida* is playing. Though I had enjoyed seeing it, it left me feeling "entertained." Perhaps I was too old or old-school, thinking that all the best musicals were already written, except of course until Sondheim decides to write something new.

I walk to 9th Avenue to find a cab to avoid the jousting that occurs when too many theatre-goers vie for too few cabs. "7th Avenue and Christopher Street" flows out of my mouth like a recording. While I'm in the cab, I roll up the sleeves of my shirt to look more casual and push the shirttail down as far as possible into my jeans to minimize the gut that has come with age.

Fifteen minutes later, I'm walking in the door. Since it's a Saturday, not a school night, I can be naughty.

I find an empty bar stool, right at the end of the bar, near the entrance. At various points in time over the last decade, bar stools would come and go at Stonewall depending on who was running the establishment at the time and whether the place was trying to be a lounge where people would come to enjoy a few cocktails over several hours or whether it was a beer joint trying to serve as many bottles as possible to a more transient crowd. I preferred the happy medium that seemed to be in vogue now, where bar stools were in place from the afternoon until nine o'clock or so. As the happy hour customers departed, their seats were summarily evicted to make way for the anticipated rush of standing room patrons. The fact that a stool was still at the end of the bar at this late hour meant that a valued, probably older, customer had been holding court here for an extended period of time. Whatever the cause, I was happy to have one of only three stools still in place at this late hour. Being at the far end of the bar, so close to the entrance, enabled me to avoid passing through the receiving line just yet. I waved and nodded to a few faces toward the back, but was happily situated in an outer orbit that did not necessitate engagement.

I ordered a Budweiser to fit in and spotted a familiar face roaming around the room picking up discarded beer bottles and empty drink glasses. It was Ben, formerly one of the most attractive customers of Stonewall when it was first re-opened by Jimmy. I was surprised to see him bussing drinks, but not surprised to surmise that he had fallen on hard, or should I say harder, times.

As he made his way around the far side of the room picking up the empties, he spotted me and circled around the bar rail that divided the bar area from what used to be the dining side of the room toward my bar stool.

"Hey, how are you doin'? I haven't seen you in a while," Ben greets me.

"I'm great. Just got out of a show," I say, showing him the folded *Playbill*.

"Was it any good?"

"Really good. Second time I've seen it," I reply.

"You're such a theatre queen," Ben jokes.

"Yeah, guilty. So, you're working here?"

"Yeah, just trying to pick up a few bucks. For spending money. The assistance I get doesn't go very far. And now that Jimmy and you aren't here anymore, I have to pay for my drinks. Can you believe it?" Ben explains.

Ben was introduced to us by another patron a decade earlier. Back then, Ben was extremely desirable, though he could probably still have his pick of any man in the bar tonight. In the early '90s, he was in his prime. The product of perfect Italian and Spanish genes, Ben had the face of a young Anthony Perkins or Warren Beatty. His body wasn't the product of a gym, but it was flawless nonetheless, with broad shoulders and a defined chest that tapered down to a slim waist and runner's legs. His chest was covered with a perfect mat of black hair that ran down his stomach and into his pants.

"Sorry about that. If you weren't working, I'd buy you a drink," I offer.

"I get off between one and two, whenever it slows down. You can buy me a drink then if you want," he flirts.

Ben had been given a nickname by some of the patrons of Stonewall. I remember the first time someone referred to him as "Mullet." I asked why they were calling Ben by that name, especially since his hair was short and parted on the side and he wasn't a Southern boy or redneck type. The explanation was obvious, after the fact, and hilarious. Borrowing the silly expression that had described that unfortunate hairstyle, they explained that Ben was "business in the front and party in the back."

"Sure thing. Happy to spend some time with an old friend," I respond as he walks away to continue his business picking up the empty bottles and glasses.

Ben did have one of the most impressive cocks I'd ever seen and, apparently, it had been viewed by lots of folks. Another friend delighted in telling me that it was "the size of a baby's arm," laughing hysterically as he motioned with his hands to draw an air painting of the size of Ben's endowment. Years earlier, I first got a sense of the scale of it when Ben would stand behind me while I played pinball. He'd stand so close that I could feel the bulge through whatever pants he was wearing. When another player's turn came up and I was standing further back from the pinball machine, Ben would still be right behind me, allowing me to run my hand over his mound and, if he happened to be wearing shorts, reaching under the leg of his shorts to stroke it. All of this done as people roamed about the back room of the bar.

Ben loved coke and alcohol, and I was happy to offer both. He rarely paid for a drink during the early years of the Stonewall revival. His physical appearance and effortless charm paid the tab. When I had coke in my pocket, it was always available to share with him. If I had bought it myself, versus the gifts I'd receive, it was often in anticipation of sharing it with him in private. Usually, we'd slip into a bathroom or to the office upstairs. He was easily the sexiest man I had ever seen, someone I would never have presumed to get the time of day from otherwise. But booze and drugs were the currency that put us on equal footing.

I ordered another beer, my third, and roamed toward the back of the bar, the belly of the beast as it were. I mingled with another friend, a hairdresser, who had also known Ben's reputation and was eager to gossip about what had brought Ben to Stonewall as a busboy. I feigned ignorance, but I knew that Ben escapades were legendary. Though he was known as an aggressive top, he'd apparently bottomed enough times without protection that he became infected. I remembered when he told me, sometime after I left my duties at Stonewall, that he was HIV-positive. He had laughed as he told me something to the effect of "that's what I get for takin' it up the ass." I couldn't help but feel the same profound sadness that I felt whenever I had heard someone tell me that they were infected. At that point in time we all knew how it was transmitted. People like Jimmy had had no idea that what they were doing was going to kill them. But, those that followed, the no longer naïve victims, they knew and yet they still succumbed.

Sometime just after one, Ben had finished his duties and came up to me. I bought him the promised drink and we stood for a while without saying much. He knew what Jimmy had gone through and it painted an unpleasant roadmap that we silently shared as we sipped our beers. Though we had never had sex, just several near misses, there was an intimacy between us that ran deep. He had taken me home to his apartment one night as dawn was breaking after one of the frequent after-parties had finally concluded. Pushing the couches and ottomans together to form an impromptu living room bed and relocating a six-foot mirror to be able to capture the anticipated fucking from multiple angles, he stripped quickly and presented his enormous but still not fully erect penis. It wasn't that I hadn't seen it before, having snorted numerous lines off of it in the bathroom and office at Stonewall. Yet, at that moment, it seemed threatening. I panicked and said I couldn't go through with what I had clearly wanted to do just prior to that. A second near miss occurred in similar fashion, after another very late night at Stonewall. That time, we headed up to my studio on West 90th. Still fearing intercourse with him, I asked if we could just jerk off together. The amount of alcohol and coke consumed was so much that Ben had to unstring the laces of his sneaker to fashion a cockring of sorts to be able to sustain an erection.

"You mind if we go somewhere else after this one?" Ben asks, gesturing with his beer bottle. "These queens are like a bunch of old fucking biddies." He follows with a mocking imitation of the kind of clucking he's heard, "Hey baby, there's some other empties you can take care of now that you're done bussing tables."

"Sure," I say, "we can go back to my place and continue the party without all the interruptions from your fans."

"Great. Where's your apartment?"

"Over on 12th," I reply and after another two or three minutes we head out.

As we walk toward my apartment, I wonder whether he's looking to hook up with me or whether he just wants to be with someone he trusts. Amid the casual conversation between the bar and my apartment I conclude that his intentions are more the latter.

Entering my apartment, he surveys the living room and remarks "You've got a really sweet apartment. When did you move here?"

"Oh, about two years ago. I wanted to have a real apartment, with more than one room. And to be down here."

"You can't get away from that place, can you?" he asks, stating the obvious.

I put the TV on for background noise and open the liquor cabinet. "I don't have beer, but I do have vodka and gin. What would you like?"

"Bring the Absolut. How much blow do you have?" he asks.

"Hopefully enough," I tease, as I bring two glasses with ice to the coffee table and set them down with the bottle of Absolut.

"You mind if I get comfortable?" he asks as he removes his sneakers and socks. "I know you don't want to get fucked and I wouldn't want my poisoned load either," he continues as he takes off his shirt. "I just feel better with no clothes on."

As I sit down on the leather love seat next to him, I kiss him gently on the lips and say "Come inside. We don't have to do anything. Bring your drink."

We move into the bedroom and I pull back the comforter and top sheet. I put on the bedroom TV, setting down my drink and the coke on the night table as I take my clothes off. He follows suit, taking off his jeans and we crawl into bed. Even though almost ten years has gone by, with some flecks of grey now in his hair and laugh lines that are etched deeply into his gaunt face, he is still remarkably handsome. I hand him the coke and he does two very big hits into each nostril.

"Did you know Jimmy was positive when you met?" he asks, handing back the coke.

"I did, but I didn't. I knew he was positive, but I really didn't understand what that meant. I mean ... I *knew* what it meant, but I just sort of ignored it," I say, and continuing for clarification, "I had had a crush on this guy who used to work at Limelight in the 1980s. His name was Joey. He was the first person I saw develop full-blown AIDS. I used to visit him at St. Vincent's during my lunch hour, at the end when he was dying. So I knew what happens, what it looked like. But I guess I just didn't want to think about that with Jimmy."

I snuggle up close to him, on my side, realizing that we're sharing one of those rare, profoundly honest conversations that people only have when they're talking about mortality.

"But you left him, at least for a while," he says. "Was that because he was getting sicker?"

"No, it wasn't about that. I just couldn't stand all the drugs," I say as I take my own hit from the vial. "He loved coke and Special K. I couldn't understand it. I even tried Special K once to see what was so great about snorting an animal tranquilizer. It was horrible, like being in a hole with dirt being thrown on you. It felt like I was drowning or something."

"And I was angry that he wasn't trying to take better care of himself. I thought if he took better care of himself he'd live longer. I thought the drugs would cause the disease to progress. I was certain of it and couldn't understand why he'd want to accelerate it. It caused all sorts of fights. Eventually, I had to leave him or it would have made me insane."

"What made you come back?" he asks.

"I guess it was the same stuff that attracted me to him in the first place. He was a thrilling person to be around. It was a whirlwind in the beginning. Meeting people. Going places. Being the lover of the guy who owned his own bar. It was like always being on stage in this hyper-theatrical existence."

He starts to stroke his cock, almost absent-mindedly, and I stare at it as he says, "I don't want to die alone, but I don't want to be with anyone either."

"Don't think about that. That's not going to happen," I say dismissing the notion that his fate is sealed. "You're doing fine and lots of people are doing fine." I rattle off a list of people we both know that have been positive for a long time and are still healthy.

I start to mirror his stroking to avoid talking about this particular topic further, knowing that my diversion will cause him to shift fully into his sexual persona. In a few moments, we're grinding our bodies against each other and, within a minute or two, I ejaculate all over his hairy chest.

"Sorry, I just can't help it. You've always been the most beautiful man I've known," I say as he resumes masturbating his engorged penis to completion. The release allows me to redirect the conversation.

"Why are you assuming the worst? I think that having a more positive attitude helps ... but what do I know?" I try to reassure but falter.

"It's not that. It's just that you see all this shit every week. Somebody getting sick. Going into the hospital. Another wake. Another funeral. It's just fucking depressing, even if you're healthy. And if you're lucky enough to be infected, it's like standing in a line where you don't know how far you are from the front," Ben says staring at the ceiling.

I nestle my head in the crook of his neck and let his words linger in the air. I notice a picture of Mariah Carey on the quietly playing TV.

Motioning my head toward the background chatter on the TV, I shift the conversation with "She's such a diva."

"Did I ever tell you about the time at Rao's when she had to move tables because she didn't like us smoking near her?"

"No, what was *that* about?" he replies with a bit of a chuckle.

"Oh, back when the bar first opened, Jimmy's friend used to take us up to Rao's on a semi-regular basis. He had one of those standing reservations on Tuesday nights," I start to explain.

"You mean Jerry?" he asks, referring to the man who everyone knew as the guy who supplied all the vending machines at New Jimmy's.

"Yeah, Jerry," I confirm, adding, "It was a heady trip, going there. I mean it was *the* impossible reservation in New York. You either had a standing weekly reservation for a table *forever* or you didn't. And the place was always this cinematic mix of celebrities,

New York power brokers, and wiseguys. Jerry would drive us up there to East Harlem. Nobody ever worried about their car on that block. It was as though everything was protected by some unknown, unseen, unnamed crew. We'd go in, sit at the bar and Nicky the Vest — I kid you not that that was what he was called — would make you a drink while you waited a few minutes for Frankie to sit you at your table. There were only about eight tables, I think."

"You're fucking kidding, Nicky the Vest?" he laughs.

"Yeah, I'm not shitting you," I say emphatically and continue painting a picture of the scene. "It was like out of a movie. A Scorsese movie. We always got seated in one of the booths. Frankie would come over, pull a chair to the table to chat with you, well mostly Jerry, about nothing in particular and then he'd ask you what you wanted to eat, offering some suggestions. It felt like Frank Sinatra was greeting you at his personal restaurant."

Ben laughs at the description, and I'm happy that this little sidetrack has shifted the mood to something more lighthearted.

I continue, "Well, this one particular night we were seated in the booth at the far end of the restaurant, next to an empty round table big enough for four people. The whole place looked like it was frozen in the '50s or '60s, and the jukebox only played those standards, you know Sinatra, Dean Martin, people like that. The fact that you could smoke anywhere, at any table – no smoking and non-smoking sections – only added to the feeling that you were in another era."

I take the glass of vodka from the nightstand and swallow more than a sip, in some sort of Rat Pack tribute. Ben follows suit as I continue, "So, we're all smoking at this small table in this small restaurant. The first couple of times we went there, I was self-conscious about it, but Frankie insisted that everyone have a good time, always bringing over one of those big old amber colored ashtrays to the table after we ordered. So, on this particular occasion, we're all smoking and laughing and enjoying ourselves when this couple walks in and gets seated at the round table next to us."

"Mariah Carey?" Ben asks.

"Yep, but at first I didn't notice it was her. She was with Tommy Mottola," I say, with a short singing segue into the lyrics from the Dr. Buzzard's Original Savannah Band song, which Ben joins in for. "Jerry points out who they are. I try not to be obvious about looking over, but I'm starstruck. Not Jimmy, though. He just took all that sort of stuff in stride. As if, why wouldn't Mariah Carey be sitting next to him. Anyway, I notice them talking very quietly, sometimes whispering into each other's ears, as they look over in our direction. Mottola comes over to our table after a few minutes and asks if we'd mind not smoking, looking toward Mariah as he explains 'cause it's not good for her voice.'"

"You guys get into an argument or something?" Ben asks.

"No, nothing like that," I say. "Out of nowhere, Frankie comes over and says that we should continue to smoke and that they should move to the table at the front of the restaurant. I didn't know the politics of the place, but it seemed to me that they were banished to the least desirable spot, especially for a celebrity, because the table was right next to the front door and looking into the kitchen."

"Go Jerry," Ben cheers.

"Yep, Jerry apparently had a lot more clout there than I imagined. It was one of those 'you don't fuck with my people' moments and my head swelled with the thought that we were being treated like kings in this place that most people could never go to," I recall with almost the same ego-inflating thrill as when it had happened.

"I never could figure out what his shtick was," Ben adds, referring to Jerry. "He's like the most unassuming guy but you know there's something serious going on there."

"Yeah, I've had some hunches over the years about him, but he was always so kind to Jimmy, and then to me after Jimmy died, that it was a place I didn't want to go," I reveal. "I never wanted to know anything about him that might alter my feelings for him. He was the person I called the morning after Jimmy died to ask about where to make funeral arrangements 'cause I knew he had buried his younger partner not long before Jimmy died. He helped me so much in those months right after."

"Was he an investor in Stonewall?" Ben asks.

"No, but Jimmy had borrowed money from him, so he had an interest of sorts in the place," I reply. "Jerry even went down with me to the IRS after I started opening up all these threatening letters that were sent to the bar about back taxes and things."

"What the fuck was that about?" Ben asks as he slips out of bed and goes into the bathroom to pee.

"I didn't know it, but Jimmy had fallen behind on paying pretty much every tax and fee and charge that you're supposed to pay when you're running a business," I answer joining him at the toilet for a side-by-side-by-side (just me, him, and his still enormous penis) recess. "I freaked when I started opening all the Stonewall mail and saw how bad things were. I don't think he paid anything near what he was supposed to for like three years. Jerry went down to the IRS with me, so I could explain that Jimmy had died and that I was going to try to pay everything that was owed."

"What happened?" Ben asks, finishing up in the bathroom and heading to the kitchen to replace the ice in our glasses.

"This horrible woman at the IRS just started threatening me," I start, feeling the same tension from years before. "After I explained that I wasn't the owner, that he had died, that I had no formal relationship with the bar, but that I would try to keep it open and get everything paid, she just rails into me about how they're gonna seize all my assets to pay for what's owed."

"Fucking bitch," Ben shouts.

"I was just ... just flabbergasted," I say. "I mean I've come down here to try to make things right. I'm not responsible for what had happened before, and here I am getting attacked as though I'm the one responsible for not paying what was due. Jerry calmed me down afterward, explaining that they threaten all kinds of stuff that isn't true to scare you. But I was fucking scared. I'd been such a fucking goody-two-shoes my whole life and here I am taking the rap for something I didn't do ... while I'm trying to do the right thing. I was such a naïve idiot."

"No, you were just being yourself," Ben says trying to calm me down, asking, "How much was owed?"

"I couldn't even tell you," I answer in a calmer tone, as we move back into the living room. "It was in the tens of thousands of dollars. A couple of times I would pay these bills with my own money, just to keep the wolves at bay, until Jerry told me not to do that. I must have sunk twenty or thirty thousand bucks into Stonewall, hoping for things to get better so that the place could operate on its own."

"You ever get any of that back?" Ben asks after retrieving the remaining coke from the bedroom.

"No, of course not. I never expected to and when I left I didn't care about that. I was just so disgusted."

We're sitting luge-style on the loveseat, Ben at the rear, watching but not watching the drivel that's playing on TV at four in the morning. A little more coke and a little more vodka take center stage before I resume my tirade on how everything was working against me in trying to keep Stonewall open.

With a second wind, I start my Peter Finch in *Network* "I'm mad as hell" speech. "I was just so fixated on the 25th anniversary of Stonewall. I was so sure that having the bar open for that would fix everything. There'd be so much publicity. So many visitors between that and the Gay Games. People would rally around Stonewall. The gay community would come out in droves to support it. Jimmy would get the credit for re-opening the space as a gay bar when it hadn't been one for like 20 years since the riots. It was a fucking bagel shop. A Chinese restaurant. Nobody gave a shit about it before. But now they would."

Ben lets me continue venting, as I move into overdrive. "I was so fucking stupid. Nobody gave a shit about it for 20 years as they ordered their schmears and General Tso's and nobody really does now in 2000, not really. Oh, yeah, there's all that gay landmark talk, but that's bullshit too. I fucking realized that no one, least of all the gay community, whatever that is, cared about keeping the place open when I got approached by the people who were in charge of the Stonewall 25 March. They were supposed to be responsible for pulling off a series of big events to commemorate the 25th anniversary. So, when they came down to the bar, did they come to talk about how the place would be featured during the festivities? No, of course not."

Ben wraps his arms around me in a bear hug, trying to contain me as I rant. "What did they want to talk about? They fucking tell me that the homemade Stonewall t-shirts that are being sold in the bar — the black ones and the white ones that are taped up on the big mirror over the bar for visitors to buy, a souvenir of this special place — that I can't sell these t-shirts. That they violate their trademark of 'Stonewall 25' and that they'll sue me and boycott the bar if I continue to sell them."

"It's OK, it's over," Ben whispers trying to bring me back.

But, as though it was 1994 all over again, I continue the tirade. "I couldn't fucking believe my ears. I'm fucking killing myself to keep this place open, working my day job and spending almost every other waking moment there, so that there *is* a Stonewall to go to and all they're concerned about is that I'm selling t-shirts commemorating the 25th anniversary. That was the first betrayal."

"But there was more than one Judas. There were several. A year later, when I was faced with proof that people on the staff were stealing, and not just the expected over-pouring or giving away the odd free drink to boost their tips, that was the end. I was surrounded by traitors. By people only worried about their own self-interest. One of managers I fired on the very last day I ran the bar asked me whether I really believed if he was stealing from me, trying to raise doubt as to whether he was complicit in what I had learned about some bartenders. I told him that it didn't matter, either he was colluding with them or he was incompetent to spot the thefts. Either way it didn't matter. He was gone. And so was I."

I had run out of steam. These monologues would do that to me, bringing out all the pain, anger, anxiety, and resentment that had been compartmentalized inside. Once the speech started, I had to deliver it fully. It was like running an emotional marathon. Now that I'd crossed the finish line, I could drift off to sleep. Sometime between drowsiness and REM, Ben must have led me back to the bed.

CHAPTER NINE

Beautiful Girls

This transition back in time was softer. Despite the absence of dream sequence music, my awakening on West 44th Street, in front of Sardi's, is smooth and fluid, lacking any jarring or turbulence that accompanied the previous landings. My arrival on a block full of theatres makes me think that I may get to see another long-ago show, and I'm full of anticipation.

Looking across the street, I see the Shubert Theatre, the Broadhurst, and the Majestic. Lee Remick in *Wait Until Dark*, Barbara Bel Geddes and Gene Wilder in *LUV*, and Mimi Hines, having replaced Streisand, in *Funny Girl* fill my theatrical menu. While the chance to see a young Streisand do *Funny Girl* would have been my first choice, there's still a veritable feast to consume. On my side of the street, the Little Theatre, which eventually becomes the Helen Hayes, and the St. James require perusal. The Little Theatre isn't running a show, at least not a Broadway show, because it's currently being used as a television studio. But the St. James beckons a few steps down, showcasing Ginger Rogers in *Hello Dolly*.

I'm not exactly sure what date it is, but from memory I know that it's still the late '60s because Merman will close *Hello Dolly* in 1970 and Streisand has already left *Funny Girl*. The street is oddly empty at what I think is late afternoon. It would be criminal to have this selection of shows to see and arrive on a day where the theatres are dark. Maybe it's a Sunday, I guess, but to be certain I head toward 8th Avenue to find a newspaper.

As I pass the St. James, I reach into my pocket to find, hopefully, the remainder of the change from that original twenty-dollar bill. I'll need that to get the paper and, if things pan out, to buy a ticket for whatever shows might be playing today. Reaching inside the pocket of the black topcoat that I'm wearing, something decidedly more formal than the apparel I'd be given on my earlier dream-visits, I notice some remaining bills and something else. The familiar shape and cardboard feel cause a flood of endorphins. Pulling it out, I see it's a ticket of sorts, but not for a Broadway show.

This ticket is for something entirely unexpected and somewhat confusing. It seems to be for a fashion show. Or a ballet. Or some strange mix of both. I'm disappointed that I haven't been gifted another Broadway show and am half tempted to push the ticket back into my pocket and find a *New York Times* theatre timetable to change whatever plans this episode seems to have made for me. The oddest thing of all is the name of the theatre on this ticket, the St. James.

I know, with absolute certainty, that the St. James Theatre hosts *Hello Dolly* for a large swath of the 1960's, from its opening in '64 through Merman's closing of the show in 1970. Even if I had had a lapse of theatre memory, though unlikely, my presence now in front of the theatre with Ginger Rogers' name above the title reaffirms my conviction. What kind of obscure, failed show is this ticket for and how can the date of the performance selected for me to see be September 25, 1966? It makes no sense, so I head to find a newspaper to hopefully bring some clarity.

I stop in a bodega, at least that's what I would call it in my time, on 8th Avenue. *The New York Times* confirms that today's date matches the ticket I have in my pocket. Still confused, I walk back around the corner, eastward on 44th Street, toward the theatre. In front of the entrance, under the *Hello Dolly* marquee, I spot someone inside. I try to open the door and, finding it closed, motion to the woman arranging a sign inside the lobby.

She comes to the outer lobby door and says loud enough to be heard through the locked door, "We're closed."

Pulling out the ticket, I motion to her and through the still closed door mouth, "I've got a ticket but I don't know what it's for."

She looks at the piece of cardboard that I've pushed up toward the glass and with palpable aggravation says, "That's for tonight. We're still rehearsing now. You can't come in."

Pleading, and somewhat lying, I say, "Someone gave me this ticket and I'm not sure what it's for."

She motions for me to wait and disappears for a moment back into the lobby and, upon her swift return, I see she's carrying a book.

Opening the door just enough to push the book toward me she says, "Here, look at the program. Tonight, they're doing a benefit for American Ballet Theatre. Come back at eight o'clock."

She recedes back into the lobby and pulls the door closed behind her effectively ending our prison-like, between a pane of glass, conversation. The cover of this book, or program as she called it, bears only a blue and white sketch of a very well-dressed woman, sitting in a balcony seat with opera glasses raised to her unseen face. She's gazing toward a barely sketched stage where a coterie of dancers from *Swan Lake* are in performance.

Leafing through the first few pages, I come to understand what this ticket is for. Yes, it's a benefit as I've been told. But, not like any benefit that I've been to or read about. It's a mash-up, though that word doesn't exist yet, of ballet dancers, couture clothing from the leading fashion designers of the day, and, as printed in the program, "Stars of Stage and Screen." That's why I've been gifted with this ticket. My unknown benefactor does indeed understand my preferences.

A Fashion Show in Dance will play this night, one night only. Mixed in with the fashion names that I recognize and the ballet names, which I don't, are Lauren Bacall, Gwen Verdon, and Angela Lansbury. It's not clear what they'll be doing, but it doesn't matter.

When else and where else will I get to see these three leading ladies on stage at the same time.

On page seven of the program, I notice another name. She's listed as the Chairman of this event, a pre-feminism title, and I'm suddenly appreciative of the attire I'm wearing, a conservative dark blue suit. Above the names of the Honorary Committee members, which include Rockefeller, Mellon, Blass, Hammerstein, Rodgers, and Bernstein, sits the name of the most famous woman in the world, at least in the late 1960s, Mrs. John F. Kennedy.

Still standing outside the entrance to the St. James, I close the program and close my eyes. I'm shaking my head in disbelief at the good fortune I've received. I ask a passerby what time it is and realize that I've got several hours to kill before tonight's event. I've clearly dismissed the notion of buying a ticket to another show and hope that my ingratitude in not trusting the theatre gods, or whomever is responsible for this, for their choice of show does not court their disfavor. The possibility of seeing Jackie Kennedy in person, the after-the-assassination-but-before-Onassis Jackie, in addition to the "Stars of Stage and Screen," is a once-in-a-lifetime event. Not my lifetime, per se, but this alternate universe lifetime that I've been relocated to temporarily.

Heading back toward 7th Avenue to catch a downtown cab, intending to see if Stonewall has opened yet, this time as a gay bar on its way to infamy, I see a few fashion-types and dancer-types entering the St. James via the stage door. I half expect to see Gwen Verdon, given my past dream encounters with her. But she's not there. Maybe she's already inside for the rehearsal. I recognize no one else on the street but, then again, the fashion and ballet worlds are not in my repertoire. I continue my march toward Times Square, hoping to make some good use of my spare time here.

The cab ride down is a straight shot and I'm down at Christopher and 7th by four o'clock, at least that's what the clock over *The Village Voice* says. It's fairly warm out so I remove the topcoat and carry it over my forearm as I walk toward 53 Christopher. I feel significantly overdressed for the neighborhood, where I only see people in more beatnik-inspired clothing, and for the time of day.

There's no sign of life yet for this Stonewall or, better said, about-to-be Stonewall. I knew that the bar did not become operational until 1967 as the gay dance club that would attract a cross-section of highlifes and lowlifes that would mingle together because there were few choices for my people back then, but I thought there might be some activity that hadn't been documented in the books and newspaper articles that I'd read. I try to stare into the obscured front window of 53 Christopher to see if there's been any progress on renovation, recalling that the Stonewall Inn Restaurant predecessor had succumbed to a fire that permanently shuttered it. As I try to peer inside, my hands framing my eyes against the glass to eliminate the interfering daylight, a man steps outside from 53 Christopher and he is agitated.

"What do you think you're doing?" this gruff, 30-ish, would-be hoodlum barks.

Slightly stunned, I reply, "I was just trying to look inside. To see how things are going."

"What the fuck is it to you? Get the hell out of here," this combination construction worker and bouncer fires back.

While in my normal world I would have quickly retreated and apologized for my nosiness, I instead elected to call his bluff. It was something I learned during my tenure at the '90s Stonewall, especially with drunk or unruly customers, that a louder and more forceful counter-punch could quickly bring down the nastiest of opponents.

"I was told I could look at this place anytime I wanted to. Who the fuck are you?" I shout back.

"None of your goddamn business. Who the fuck told you you could look inside?" he shouts back, but with enough uncertainty in the latter portion of his attack that I realize that he's not entirely certain if I belong or not.

In a split-second I have to decide which of the two names that I know that have a relationship to this place, at this time, to use to call his bluff.

"Manny Duell told me to take a look anytime I wanted," I lie to him, hoping that I've picked the right name.

He's taken aback, I know, because he doesn't come back at me with a quick response. I look at him, trying to figure out what he's thinking when he more softly states, "Nobody told me that anyone would be coming."

Apparently, I'd guessed correctly, or correctly enough, to put him on the defensive. Now I just had to carefully manage the lie so as not to expose myself.

"He told me *anytime*," I say matter-of-factly. "He didn't say I had to make an appointment."

I'm still not sure whether I've surprised him with a name that he knows and fears reprisal from, should word get back that he's denied me entrance, or whether he's just uncertain of who I might know that could cause him some grief. The fact that I'm too well dressed, I'm certain, has helped me throw him off balance in either case.

"Look, can I go inside or not?" I throw in for good measure.

"Yeah, fine, come in and look around. What are you lookin' for?" he asks in the more moderated tone that we've shifted to.

As we enter into the darkness, I reply, "I didn't realize I had to explain my business here," joking, but with an edge, in the style of Joe Pesci in *Goodfellas* when he asks "So you think I'm funny, funny how?" I'm enjoying this turn of the table.

"I didn't mean nothin' by it," he replies respectfully. "I just want to make sure you get what you need."

"What's your name?" I ask, keeping him against the ropes.

"Angelo."

"Well, Angelo, I'm just looking to see how much progress has been made," I respond, trying to be sufficiently vague but specific to help carry on this charade.

My eyes have adjusted a bit to the darkness and I see that not a whole lot has been done to fix the place up or, more aptly, clean out the debris and junk in anticipation of next year's opening. Perhaps they haven't decided yet, that peculiar mixture of characters that are purported to open this place as a gay bar, what they're going to do with the space.

Stepping toward the space where there will be the long bar that I will occupy a seat at on too many nights some 20-odd years hence, I feel nauseated. The place is a mess and I know, from what I've read, that very little will be done to make this place ready for its most famous role. The toilets in this late '60s Stonewall won't work. There won't be sinks to wash the drink glasses, just tubs of dirty water. It's the polar opposite of what Jimmy Pisano will do to this place. I don't want to look at it, any of it, anymore.

"When is all this shit getting cleared out?" I ask Angelo.

"I don't know. Nobody tells me anything," he replies with certain truthfulness.

"I don't need to see any more," I reply looking at him. "I'll let Manny know you took care of me."

"Thanks," he replies as we both head back toward the door to exit.

Shaking his hand, I say, "I'll let you get back to your business," and I walk toward 7th Avenue, relieved that I was able to pull it off but depressed that that the bar looked no better than the horse stable that sat here in the early part of the 20th century. Jumping in a cab, I head back to the St. James, wanting to shake the detritus off my good suit.

In a blur, the hours have passed such that I'm standing now in front of a theatre that looks like it's preparing for an opening night. Cars and limos pull up. Well-dressed and well-heeled patrons assemble outside to gaze and be gazed at. Some of them know each other. Actually, a lot of them seem to know each other, judging by the greetings and kisses and handshakes that are exchanged. I don't know a soul. I try to wait nonchalantly outside, even after many of the attendees have entered, in hopes of seeing Jackie Kennedy. But, unsure as to whether she might already be inside or whether she's entered through a different door, I give up and enter to find my seat.

While the seat itself, B114, sounds promising, I find that I'm in the second balcony, above the mezzanine. It's Siberia and I'm pissed off. I won't be sitting anywhere near the President's widow nor will I have a close view of Lauren, Gwen, or Angela. Why the fuck would my dream-maker go to all this trouble of getting me here, only to ruin the experience with a seat this far away from the stage?

I'm paging through the program, looking at the advertisements that have undoubtedly helped to defray the cost of this event, when the gentleman in the next seat, B115 on the aisle, asks me, "Are you by yourself?"

"Yes," I respond.

He has the appearance of a middle-age suburban businessman, a little thick around the middle, with black horned rimmed glasses like my father wore at the time. He offers, "My wife and I got these tickets at the last minute and they only had two single seats left. She's down there," he says pointing to the front of the mezzanine. "Would you mind switching with her so that we can sit together?"

"What?" I say, more inquisitively versus as a direct question.

He adds, "We asked the person sitting next to her if they would switch, but he's sitting with a group of other people and wouldn't move."

"Sure, no problem," I say, delighted at this turn of events.

"She's the fifth person in, off the aisle, first row, wearing a sapphire jacket with a mandarin collar," he says, offering enough detail about his wife's attire to suggest that he was in the fashion business.

I quickly get up, offer a "Thanks so much," and make a beeline for the lady who's occupying the much better seat that I will be inhabiting.

Standing at the front of the mezzanine, which hangs over Row G of the orchestra, I catch her eye and mouth, "Would you like to sit next to your husband?"

She smiles and eagerly relinquishes her seat, something which I find unfathomable but am grateful for nonetheless. Near the center of Row A of the mezzanine, I've now got a perfect vantage point for finding the former First Lady and watching my beautiful girls unobstructed.

I notice my new neighbor's watch says it's 8:45 and wonder why the show hasn't begun yet. I go back to flipping through the program and find an insert buried midway through. In addition to the triumvirate that was listed in the bigger program, this insert, obviously printed closer to show time, also includes the names of Elizabeth Ashley, Phyllis Newman, Arlene Francis, Bobby Short, Barbara Walters, Lee Remick, Betty Comden, and Jane Morgan as performing tonight. It also indicates which designers each of the ladies will be wearing, that the performance is broken into two acts, that the strawberries are being provided by the Four Seasons restaurant, and other gay tidbits. As I read, the house lights dim.

CHAPTER TEN

Sunday

I awaken to the sound of the shower. Feeling well hung over, I stumble out of bed and make my way to the bathroom to pee or throw up, I'm not entirely sure yet. As I stand at the toilet, Ben pulls back the shower curtain. He's smiling and happy and entirely too awake.

"Sorry, did I wake you up?"

"No, well maybe. It's OK," I reply.

"I'm gonna make you a nice breakfast. Why don't you come in?" he asks motioning for me to join him in the shower. "You'll feel better."

"Sure," I reply, entirely unconvinced that I will ever feel better.

As I step into the shower, he, thankfully, steps out and dries himself off. The last thing I want to deal with right now is his dick. I hear him walk toward the kitchen and wonder what I even have in this house that would make a suitable breakfast. But if that's what he wants to do, I'm not going to stop him.

The warm water has washed off some of the haze, but I'm still not feeling sober or clear headed. Slipping on the oversized white terry robe that I love, I walk into the kitchen to find Ben, still completely naked, trying to make coffee. He hadn't found the paper filter that holds the grinds for brewing, so the muddy mess that's pouring into the carafe will need to be thrown out.

"You only have two eggs and the expiration date is last month," Ben says, indicating that he's surveyed the tiny kitchen thoroughly as well as the refrigerator that sits in a closet near the front door of the apartment. The man who did the renovations to this apartment thought I was crazy to put a full-size refrigerator in what was supposed to be a spare closet. Yes, it was a bit off-center to do that, but by taking the big machine out of that tiny kitchen I was able to create a beautifully streamlined space that seemed much bigger than its actual 6-by-8-foot dimensions. And the small, under-counter unit that was placed in the kitchen was sufficient to hold the few things that I did need to keep handy.

"Let's call Joe Jr.'s," I say as I pour out the swamp coffee that Ben has made.

"But I wanted to make you breakfast," he says endearingly.

"Thanks, babe," I reply kissing him on the cheek, "but I really need some sustenance and there's nothing in this apartment. Besides, I want your full attention for something else."

He wraps his arms around me, pulling the fabric at the back of my robe so that the front opens enough for him to rub against my body.

"Not until after I get something to eat and some coffee," I say, pulling the robe closed.

"What else could you want my full attention for?" he teases.

"No, seriously, I've been having these wildly vivid dreams. And the one last night was the strangest of all. The other ones I could have made up in my head, I suppose, but this one ... I don't know how I made this one up," I explain.

With breakfast ordered and delivered, with no qualms from my friend at Joe Jr.'s that it was after two o'clock, we eat our food in bed as I relate my remarkable night at the St. James Theatre to Ben, after first giving him a synopsis of the previous visits to 1966.

"So, you've never heard of this show before?" Ben starts.

"Benefit, actually," I interrupt.

"Well, it's not like it's out of the realm of possibility to get a bunch of Broadway and movie stars to do a benefit for the ballet. It happens all the time, doesn't it?" Ben asks, not understanding my amazement.

"Yeah, but how does your mind make up such detail for something like that, especially the ballet parts that I have no idea about, never been to, have no interest in, with such excruciating detail that I really feel like I was there," I attempt to explain.

I continue, as though trying to convince a jury, "OK, I suppose I could have imagined that Lauren Bacall would be wearing a dress by Norman Norell. I know he was like the pre-eminent American fashion designer of the time. I've heard the name before. But the fact that Angela Lansbury is wearing a dress by John Moore, who I've never fucking heard of, and Gwen is wearing something that is listed in the program as a mink burnoose, which it turns out is kinda like a cape, when I've never heard of the word burnoose before — you tell me how someone imagines things that they've never heard of before."

"Maybe you read it somewhere and just forgot or something," he answers, trying to bring rationality to my confusion.

"Maybe, I guess, but I don't know ... I can tell you about the whole night like I was there, really there," I insist, "even to the point of telling you that Jane Morgan ..."

"Who is Jane Morgan?" Ben interrupts.

"She was a nightclub singer who did a bunch of Broadway but never became super famous," I explain, continuing, "So this Jane Morgan, who's listed in the program as having a big number in the second act, well there's no Jane Morgan performance. Nothing. Why would anyone have a dream where they imagine each and every musical number, dance, and speech in a program and include someone they've never had any interest or fascination in, only to have them not perform. It's just weird."

"How much *do* you remember about this show?" he asks, coming around to the fact that my recollection is bizarrely detailed.

Like a radio sports announcer broadcasting a big game, I recount, "My God, it's like a film in my head. I can remember it all so vividly. When the house lights dimmed, the overture started — Leonard Bernstein's *Candide*. The program listed him as being on the Board, so that choice wasn't unexpected. *Candide* was a flop when it opened in the late '50s, but it was supposed to be one of Bernstein's great opuses, so it was recorded and persisted as a 'notable work' largely on the reputation of Bernstein as this genius composer."

"The opening of the show is this big ballet number, supposedly by George Balanchine according to the program. I wouldn't know. There are these two principal dancers, a prima ballerina and her male counterpart, and then the company of ABT. Lots of leaps and twirling. Very 'classical.' It kind of made me think of *Swan Lake*, the way they were dressed and the way they moved. This segues into dancers modeling high fashion clothes from all the big designers of the time, you know ... Norell, Bill Blass, Geoffrey Beene, and a bunch of other presumably big names that I'd never heard of. It's all very hoity-toity. It felt a little disjointed, I mean jamming together a fashion show and a ballet, but the clothes were super theatrical, not the kind of things any normal woman would wear, so, in that sense, I guess it worked as an art piece."

"Then Lauren Bacall comes out. She looks stunning in this white number with a mandarin neckline. They must have been popular at the time. It looked like it was crepe. It was sooo white. It could have been sheer, but you really didn't see anything. She looks like a goddess or a princess. When I saw her in *Woman of the Year* and later in other things, she was much older. Still attractive, but more regal than stunning. In 1966, she's still got that movie star thing. But it's the voice that really makes it incredible. She delivers this speech about fashion and the arts. The program said it was written by John Fairchild, who ran Women's Wear Daily and was the Anna Wintour of the time. It was a perfectly fine speech, extolling the value of fashion and art in society. Just what you'd expect. Culture, culture, culture, blah, blah. But when Bacall says this shit, it raises it to another level. She just makes everything she says sounds so much more sophisticated and important than if any other human would say it," I drone on, intending to give Ben the CliffNotes version of the night but unable to stop myself with the color commentary that I deem necessary to fully explain what I saw.

"Then there's *another* ballet routine and, like the first one, there's this chorus of ballet dancers, not the ones doing the number but other ones, modeling all this expensive fashion," I continue. "Then Arlene Francis comes out and Elizabeth Ashley after her," I speed up. "It just kept alternating between these ballet numbers and all of this clothing being modeled and the celebrities. There had to be hundreds of dresses."

"Did you meet Gwen Verdon in this one too?" he asks, apparently having been more engaged than I imagined.

"No, I just saw the show. She was wearing this Geoffrey Beene outfit, white crepe with big ruffles around the neck, after having shed the mink cape," I detail. "There wasn't a performance really. She didn't do anything from *Sweet Charity*. And I didn't meet or speak with her or anyone else."

"It is a little strange," Ben concurs, moving closer in bed to me. "I get why a theatre queen would imagine all that stuff about *Sweet Charity* and Ethel Merman, but I don't get why'd you have a dream about all this other stuff."

"Exactly," I say, "and stop calling me a theatre queen." I push Ben back to his side of the bed.

"But ya are Blanche," he imitates and falls into laughter.

"Stop fucking around. I'm serious. This is all just totally amazing. These crazy fantasies, dreams, I don't know what to call them," I say, returning to the subject at hand. "The second act was equally over the top and it culminated in this big number called The Diamond Ball. It was really Angela's showcase — she sort of paraded around in this silver-sequined white silk dress with all these other women, ballet dancers in white gowns, until all the other stars come out for the finale."

"Did you end up seeing Jackie Kennedy?" Ben asks.

"No, I don't know if she was there or not. Certainly, you'd have expected a stir or something from the crowd or some sort of acknowledgement from the stage if she was. I just assumed she wasn't, though I could have easily dreamt her there if I had wanted to. I know what she looked like then, unlike Jane Morgan who I wouldn't know from a hole in the wall. See that's what's so strange. To put Jackie Kennedy in your dream, but then have her be a no-show."

"So instead of obsessing on how you dreamed this, why don't you just enjoy it and leave it at that," Ben says with abundant practicality.

Calmer for having shared as much detail of the night as I thought Ben could stand, I exhale and agree. "You're probably right. I shouldn't be so fixated on the how and why. But I do want to do some research ..."

"You mean like all that crazy Stonewall research you did?" Ben asks.

"It's not crazy. Someone should know that stuff. Maybe I know a little too much, but people should know more about that place than they do. It's shameful, really, how little people care about it, except until it's something they can take advantage of ... for political purposes or money," I say, getting animated about it.

"Whoa, whoa, let's not go there again," Ben whispers, grabbing me and turning me around so that we're spooning.

"OK. No more pontifications. Not today. I'm still feeling like shit," I admit.

As if on cue, he wraps his left hand around my dick and proceeds to jerk me off. I'm still tired from the excesses of the night before, so I let him service me and offer no reciprocation. Licking the cum off my belly and chest, he softly says, "I can still do that. You can't."

"I'd like to," I reply truthfully, "but you're right."

"You had Jimmy cremated, right?" Ben asks. "What did you do with the ashes?"

"Eventually, I went out to East Hampton and spread them on the beach and in the water. That's what he wanted," I answer. "Part of me had this evil thought that I should just take all his ashes and put them in lots of coke bottles and give them to all his friends, his customers, his dealers. Not tell them, at first, but not let them snort him either."

"You are one sick, twisted fuck," Ben laughs.

"I *didn't* actually do it, I just thought about it. And that was enough," I laugh also.

As we're snuggling in bed, I continue, "I did have this one strange thing happen, though. With his ashes. After I brought them back up to his apartment, where his cousin was still living, for safekeeping. I went into our bedroom, or what was our bedroom, wanting to open the cardboard box to see what ashes looked like. I had never seen cremated remains before. The box was yea big," I draw the size in the air for Ben to imagine.

"It was sealed with tape," I continue, "so I had to use a knife to open it. I'm kneeling on the floor, next to the bed, opening the box, lifting out the top of the clear plastic bag that holds the ashes, which is knotted on itself to keep the remains inside. I'm struggling to unknot the plastic bag cause it's really thick and has been knotted tightly. Finally, I wriggle the knot at the top open and start to unwind the twisted plastic to look inside. I could see through the plastic that it was kind of white and grey, like sand almost. But I wanted to look at, to touch, Jimmy's remains. As I complete the untwisting of the plastic bag, ready to look inside, I feel this big rush of cold air on my neck from the ceiling fan. Except when I look up, the ceiling fan is not on. It was the creepiest feeling. I'm not making it up and I wasn't hallucinating or having some breakdown or anything. It was several weeks after Jimmy had died that I had finally picked up his ashes from the funeral home, so it was well after the shock of seeing him die. And this big arctic blast of air hits the back of my neck. I think I even felt my hair move from the breeze."

"Wow. That's really strange or wonderful, depending on what you want to believe," Ben notes.

"Yeah. I looked at it only for a very short time. The breeze on my neck really scared the shit out of me. It was finely ground, mostly. Some things were bigger, but not like identifiable or anything. I tied the bag up and closed the box, not to re-open it until his ashes were spread."

"Do you believe in that sort of stuff — that the dead can communicate with you?" Ben asks.

"I didn't before that, though I had gone to some psychics with friends and heard stuff that they couldn't have known. And not so much anymore. Even after the ashes and the pen incident."

"Pen incident?" Ben asks, as if on cue.

"I sort of forget the details, but I was trying to decide who to be with after Jimmy died. There were these two guys vying for my attention or affection or whatever. One of them was older, more secure. The other was younger and more flakey, you know, the attractive kind that you want to fix. One day, as I was leaving my apartment to go to work, I put both names on a piece of paper on the small kitchen counter. This was in the 90th Street studio apartment that you came to. And I put the pen that I had written the names with right down the middle of the page, between the two names. Like I was asking for supernatural guidance or something on who to choose. Remember, this is in the middle of working my day job and trying to keep Stonewall open, so I'm pretty fucked up or overwhelmed at the time trying to balance these two things. Anyway, I come home from work and the pen has moved. It's now pointing to one of the names. The older guy. I never tried that again. It kinda spooked me. But, if you're asking if I believe you can talk with the dead, that's my best example that it might be possible."

Ben switches subject, "You said you also visited Stonewall during these dreams. What was it like back then?" I'm not sure whether he's really interested in this part of my dreams or whether he just wants to end the talk about death and the supernatural.

"Well, up to this point, it hasn't opened yet. That doesn't happen until 1967 according to what I read, but you know a lot of those accounts aren't the most accurate. That's why I keep going down to see what's going on in the space," I reply.

"And ..." Ben prods.

"Well, it's really a shithole at this point. Not that they fix it up or anything to open it. There was a fire. That's why it's closed. There's all this debris and crap everywhere from the previous business, the restaurant. I did notice some crappy wood paneling on the walls. It looks like it could be the same that you see in photos from just after the riots. But who knows." I explain.

"And those guys you saw, the ones in the suits the first time," Ben probes, seemingly as fascinated with identifying the characters that I claim to have witnessed.

"I really didn't see their faces well, not that it would have mattered. I haven't seen a picture of Duell or Handelsman from that time, or anytime really, to know if the guys in my dream are supposed to be them or not. It's like a big mystery. This whole thing. Why am I pursuing Gwen Verdon in these dreams? Aside from the obvious. What's the connection? But I do sort of feel like I want to take her there for some reason," I admit.

"Why would you want to take Gwen Verdon to Stonewall?"

"I don't know exactly. I'm almost embarrassed to say this out loud, but I kinda want her help. I know it sounds crazy, but I think I'm supposed to have her help me stop AIDS or something. At least to minimize its impact," I confess.

"That's fucking crazy," Ben answers with a tinge of anger in his voice. He's gotten up from the bed that we've been lazing around in for the past hour or so and puts on his jeans.

Seeing that I've broached into dangerous waters, suggesting that AIDS could be prevented or that certain people could be spared or warned about it, I join him in getting dressed and plead, "Hey, I'm sorry. I didn't mean to make light of it, if that's what I did. I'm so sorry. Please forgive me. I was just telling you what I really felt.

I've never been so honest with anyone. Telling them what I'm truly thinking."

"I'm not mad at you," Ben responds. "I'm mad at myself. I didn't need anyone to go back in time to prevent this or warn me about what not to do. I fucking knew it and I did it anyway."

"Shit, I get it," I whisper. "I never want you to be angry with me. There's a part of me that loves you. I can't explain it. I know we're not supposed to be a couple or anything. I just feel attached to you in some strange way that I don't understand."

"It's fine, really," Ben assures me. "Let's get out of here for a while. It looks nice out. Let's go hang out in the park."

With that, we finish dressing and head out. A subway ride later, we're in Central Park. There are people playing softball on the fields near the 65th Street Westside entrance to the park. We sit down in the grass and casually watch the game.

Pointing up toward the roof at 91 Central Park West, I say, "That's where she lived. In the penthouse. But she moved out around '93 or '94. Gwen, I mean."

"How do you know this shit?" Ben asks with amazement.

"I don't remember exactly. I think I read it in an old newspaper clipping," I respond. "She started renting there in the late '50s, before it went co-op in the early '60s. It's a huge apartment, but the terraces are almost bigger than the apartment itself. Something like 3,000 square feet or more of terraces. She starts growing her own fruits and vegetables up there. A veritable farm in the sky. She got on the organic train very early. Fosse dies in 1987. And around the early '90s there's this big news story about how lots of people, including celebrities, are living in these magnificent rent-stabilized apartments in New York. The big story is about Mia Farrow. She's in this 11 or 12-room huge apartment on Central Park West. Woody films parts of *Hannah and Her Sisters* there. And she's paying something ridiculously low in terms of rent for that apartment. There's all this outrage over how people are taking advantage of the rent-stabilization laws. So they started changing the laws. Carly

Simon moves out of her huge place in that same building when they start to raise the rent," I say pointing toward the Langham at 73rd Street.

"She didn't own her apartment?" Ben asks, referring to Gwen Verdon.

"I don't know. In a bio about Fosse, it said that part of the reason he did *Chicago* was to make Gwen financially secure. So I don't know if she bought the apartment then, in the mid-70s, or before, or ever," I reply. "By the early '90s, she was doing a little TV work, guest shots, and other things around dance and preserving Fosse's legacy. She moved up to Bronxville. And the apartment was sold to some young investment banker type. I looked at the real estate records, but I never saw her name on any transfers. But, back in those days, co-op sales weren't required to be recorded by the City, especially if it was a cash transaction. Now, it's owned by Giorgio Armani and he's redone the whole thing. So, even if you could get into the apartment now, it wouldn't look like it did when she was there."

"And Hearst owned the apartment originally?" Ben asks, indicating an interest in this piece of real estate.

"Actually, he owned the whole building at one point. Marion Davies, his mistress, lived there. The penthouse itself was much larger when Davies lived there. At some point, it was divided into two penthouses. The one Gwen lived in, at the rear, and the one in the front, which is a duplex with this wild tower space on the upper level," I say, pointing to the phallic appendage at the top of the building. "The same family has been living there for like 20 years. When it was one whole floor, one apartment, it must have been something like 7,000 square feet of living space, not counting the terraces."

"Fucking amazing," Ben remarks.

"I wish I had met her at some point. In real life. I really like her. She seems so genuine, so vulnerable and kind," I say. "I've met so many other Broadway people over the years. From charity work or just by accidentally meeting them. She's the one that got away. Maybe that's why I'm fixated on her."

"Maybe you'll meet her again in your dreams," Ben offers.

"Maybe. That would be cool. Last time we spoke, I told her I wanted to take her to Stonewall, to see what Jimmy had built. Not really built. But re-opened so that it could become the symbol that it is. A living symbol. It's so funny how in these dreams, I'm so reluctant to tell her about the time travel. That I don't live in her time. You wouldn't think it would make a difference in a dream. But for some reason, I feel the need to protect her. Or maybe it's protecting myself ... from not seeming like a kook who says he's from a future time."

"I think you're overthinking this whole thing," Ben says. "I think this is some huge gay theatre fantasy that your mind has created from all the stuff you've seen and read about. And you can't just enjoy it. You're overanalyzing it. You need a boyfriend. Why aren't you with anyone? You're a great catch. Living alone with all that theatre memorabilia in your apartment isn't doing you any favors."

"I don't need a boyfriend," I state emphatically.

"Haven't you been attracted to anyone since Jimmy?" Ben asks. "It's been, what, like five years."

"More like six," I confirm, "and yes I have been attracted to a couple of guys, but I doubt that I'll ever have a normal relationship again."

"You don't have to be with someone positive," Ben replies, helping me dance around what he thinks is my presumed criteria for a next lover.

"Yeah, I know," I reply, "but that's not all of it. That alone wouldn't make it OK to open myself up again. It was such a shit show, being with him during that time. Stuff that had nothing to do with AIDS. I thought he was cheating on me. Not like on purpose, but he'd get so fucked up and everyone throws themselves at people like him, guys who own bars."

"Was he?" Ben asks. "Did you ever catch him?"

"No, I never did," I respond, "but the possibility made me crazy. Even though he had this decent apartment over on 73rd, he had to go and rent a big apartment down on Horatio Street. It was hugely expensive and unnecessary. The 73rd Street apartment remained vacant, so he was paying for two places in Manhattan. The new apartment was a two-bedroom duplex, with the master bedroom on the lower level. His cousin moved downtown with him, but the separation of the spaces meant you could do anything downstairs and no one would know. He insisted that he needed it to be nearer the bar. That it was too far to cab back and forth from 73rd Street down to Stonewall every day, multiple times."

"Were you living together down there?" Ben asks.

"Not really," I respond. "I'd stay with him on weekends and the occasional weeknight. I didn't want to move in permanently and give up my apartment on 90th or pay for something I wasn't using. And we were just working such different hours. It made it impossible to have a normal life like before he opened the bar. I'm working 9-to-5 in midtown, and he's at the bar during the afternoons, to do business, and in the evening to play host."

"Well, I can understand why he'd want to live closer. You always need to be there. Daytime and nighttime. Otherwise, they steal you blind," Ben remarks.

"Yes, I suppose," I reply, "but I'd get so worked up wondering what he was doing at 2 a.m. that I couldn't sleep. A couple of times I even got dressed in the middle of the night and cabbed down from 90th to Horatio to check on him. To see if he brought someone home to party with. I was paranoid about how the drugs would cause him to cheat. And everyone was throwing drugs at him. He bought his own, of course. But every lowlife in the Village seemed to want to court favor. I'd run into the apartment and find him in bed, alone, twisted out of his mind."

"Hey, it's not like you didn't know what you were getting into," Ben assesses. "He always was a big cokehead from what I heard."

"You have no idea," I reply. "There was one time, when he was hospitalized, that he started to call people to bring him coke in the hospital. I know because one of the guys he bought from, Eddie, who also happened to work at Stonewall at one point, told me about it. He said that he kept getting calls from Jimmy begging him to bring it. Eddie told me because he figured, when he refused Jimmy, that Jimmy would just end up calling someone else to get drugs delivered to St. Vincent's."

"That's pretty fucked up."

"Yeah," I concur. "Shortly after that we broke up for a couple of months. I couldn't take it. I was afraid of losing my job. I wasn't getting any sleep. He was always high. We even had gone to a shrink for couple's therapy. Get this ... this crazy motherfucker tells me, somewhere during our second or third session, that I should not go to work every time that Jimmy gets high. The first time he does it, I should not go to work for a day. The second time, not for two days. The third time ... you get the idea. He said that it would help Jimmy stay sober."

Laughing, Ben replies, "You're fucking kidding me."

"Nope," I say, "not one bit. I told this therapist that I thought it was the craziest thing I'd ever heard of. To risk my job, hoping that it would stop Jimmy from doing drugs. But he said he'd seen it work in similar situations. I told Jimmy there was no way that I was going to put my career in his hands. That pretty much meant there was no solution for us. Right after that, we separated."

"You didn't speak or see him at all?"

"Not at all," I answer, "though I did hear through other people that he just kept spiraling downward. That he'd be in some public place or a store and he'd reach into his pocket to pay for something and bottles of coke or Special K would come falling out of his pocket. He'd scramble to pick them up, but he was so twisted that even that embarrassment didn't faze him."

"When was that?"

"Oh, sometime in late '92," I confirm, "shortly after *Guys and Dolls* had opened. I remember because I ended up briefly going out with this guy in the cast. But only very briefly because he was a dick."

"Leave it to you to relate every conversation to a Broadway show," Ben jokes.

"What can I say?" I joke back. "I am what I am."

"When did you get back together?"

"I don't remember."

"What, no theatre reference point?" Ben interrupts.

"At some point, he begged me to go out to dinner with him. He kept just calling and calling and leaving these messages, begging me *just* to go to dinner. Nothing more, he promised. But we both know how that turned out. As soon as I saw him, I wanted to be with him again. The dinner started out as though we were just trying to be friends. Both of us playing a part that neither of us believed. But we ended up back at my place, of course. And while I was fucking him, he looked up at me with this expression. Like he'd never been in love before and was experiencing it for the first time. I'll never forget the look. Like he was seeing God or something. And then, as I'm climaxing, he says 'I'm cumming and I'm not even touching myself.' And sure enough, he did."

"Cue the music," Ben teases.

"Oh, fuck you," I laugh. "It was really very sweet. Tender. Real. As immensely fucked up as the relationship was ... it just had to continue. By that time things had gotten so bad financially that he had given up the Horatio Street apartment. Moved back into 73rd Street. I ended up spending almost every night there from then on. And he didn't stay late at the bar or go there every night, which was something that helped make it work, but only made the dysfunction at Stonewall worse."

"Nobody minding the store," Ben says. "That's when it really became a free-for-all."

"Exactly," I say, "in every sense of the word. Receipts went down, even though liquor purchases went up. He never really said it, but I think he knew that it was all over then. That the place was never going to make a go of it. Even through the haze and self-denial of all the drugs, which he still did of course. He didn't *do* anything about it really. Just kept juggling things, as he did, to keep the doors open. He had that gambling machine installed in the back room to make a few extra bucks. Like that was going to make up for all the debt, all the lost money."

"When did he die?" Ben asks. "I'm sorry I don't remember."

"March 4, 1994," I respond, "just three months before the 25th anniversary. I remember walking back into the bar after he died. Asking the DJ to play *Get Here* by Oleta Adams. I told the manager and a few of the staff that Jimmy had just died and the news then spread organically through the crowd. I just stood at the DJ booth and realized that it was going to be my job to keep Stonewall open. I guess I was in shock, but it was all so calm. Or, at least, I was calm. Trying to reassure people, the staff, that Stonewall would remain open. Some of them cried. Some of them just went on with their jobs. It was such a strange feeling. What's that expression? When the world ends, it doesn't go out with a bang but with a whimper. That's what it felt like."

After we grab a couple of burgers at Big Nick's, a frequent spot Jimmy and I had ordered in from, Ben and I catch a cab downtown. We both exit at 7th and Christopher. Ben heads down 7th Avenue and I choose to walk home via West 10th to avoid Stonewall. Walking past Julius', I knew, wasn't going to be as tempting. Finally home again, I jumped right into bed, determined to be rested for my 9-to-5 workweek. As I lay in bed with the TV on — a habit that I acquired after Jimmy died which some psychologist would surely find meaning in — I hear the opening credits of *The Cotton Club*. Gwen's part is small, playing the mother of Richard Gere. So, instead of falling asleep to some background noise, I prop myself up to watch my friend.

CHAPTER ELEVEN

Love Changes Everything

I've become an experienced flyer, in real life thanks to a corporate job that necessitates twice monthly visits to our ad agency in Chicago and in my time traveler existence thanks to my desire to revisit old New York. This landing is smooth and, again, in Times Square. The scene is essentially the same as my first trip, people-wise, dress-wise, and Palace Theatre marquee-wise. *Sweet Charity* is still running, so it's still 1966 or 1967. I do notice that the movies being advertised are different from the first visit, so I know this isn't some *Groundhog Day* repeat. Then, I remember seeing a billboard shilling *Our Man Flint*. Now, I see Raquel Welch, in the famous fur bikini, luring us to *One Million Years BC*. I'll see her at the Palace much, much later replacing Bacall in *Woman of the Year*. It was an odd casting choice that I've always attributed to Bacall's desire not to have anyone too talented replace her.

There's no theatre nor ballet nor fashion show ticket in my pocket. Just a few singles from the first $20. I make a mental note to try to bring something else of value with me next time, God willing, to hock for cash. I don't like being without money in these dreams, but it hasn't seemed to be a problem thus far. I find the nearest *Times* to situate myself and discover it's almost exactly one year since my first visit and more than three months since the last. It's January 13, 1967, which happens to be a Friday and Gwen Verdon's birthday, which I of course know.

I honestly don't know whether I'm supposed to buy a ticket to see the show again or, perhaps, another show like *Mame*. That's a very tempting idea, so I take a tally of my worth. I'm not flush, counting only three dollars and change from my pocket, so I won't be buying a theatre ticket. Yes, I probably could get something in the second balcony for some show, maybe even *Mame*, but why would I want to do that. It would be torture being that far back.

I take it as a sign, given the significance of the day, that I should set out to find my new friend. As it's after five, I decline the notion to head uptown to the apartment. Instead, I decide to find some flowers and wait outside the stage door for her to arrive for tonight's performance. She's notorious for arriving early to prepare, so I make haste to find a real florist, given that the profusion of flowers being sold in every bodega and grocery store has not become a thing yet. Between 5th and 6th Avenues I find a small flower shop and I'm pleased to see that my meager funds are sufficient to purchase a small but tasteful arrangement.

It's not long before I'm back on 47th Street, just off of 7th Avenue, judiciously standing some 25 feet or so from the stage door of the Palace. I don't want to attract too much attention standing outside, especially with the bouquet in my hand. That would just invite interception by some stage manager or similar well-intended person trying to relieve me of my gift and send me on my way, hoping to spare Gwen Verdon from my approach. Not knowing which direction she'll be coming from, my head pivots back and forth to keep surveillance. Recalling some mention by Fred Ebb in later years that she would often take the bus home after a performance, one of those factoids that I found so endearing about her, I try to remember which public transportation routes she might likely take from Central Park West. Fortunately, before my brain hemorrhages from trying to recall all the different bus and subway lines on the west side of Manhattan, I spot her walking toward the door. And, equally fortunately, she sees me as I walk toward her and lights up with a smile.

"Well, hello stranger," she greets me.

"Hello to you to," I say, "and happy birthday. These are for you."

"Oh, you really shouldn't have," she responds. "I don't want people making a fuss on me today. But thank you. They're beautiful."

"I found myself in the neighborhood," I say truthfully, but with a deeper meaning than the words literally mean, "and I thought I'd just pop by on the off chance I could wish you a happy birthday."

"I'd like to stop counting," she jokes, "if you don't mind. What have you been up to?"

Before I can answer, the stage door opens and a gentleman is standing in the doorway looking at me talk with Gwen. Clearly, he's been expecting her and has taken keen interest in who this person is that is holding her up.

"Hey Gwen," he says at sufficient volume to put me on notice. "How is everything?"

I start to tell her, "Well, I saw you at the fashion and ballet benefit," when she interrupts to answer him.

"Oh, this is my friend Tom," she says to him and, leading me toward the door, "Tom, this is Paul. He takes care of me. He takes care of everybody."

We're standing literally a step outside the stage door as I shake hands and exchange a smile with Paul when Gwen says to me, "Hey, why don't you come in. We can talk a little while I'm getting ready. Paul, can you help me find a vase for these?"

I've been backstage before, many times at the 46th Street Theatre during the run of *Nine* when my college roommate and I became fan-friends with some of the ladies in the cast. Though it's been renamed the Richard Rogers Theatre, I can't seem to make the switch in my head. Later, when I started heavily collecting theatre memorabilia, I even found myself onstage at the Shubert in *Chicago* as a result of one of those Broadway Cares auctions when I was the highest bidder for a second act walk-on as one of the background news reporters. The best part of that experience had been the pre-performance rehearsals and mingling with the male dancers in their communal dressing room. I had even gone backstage to meet Harvey Fierstein on two occasions when my friend Stuart, who had known Harvey from his salad days, invited me to join him for a visit after the performances. I distinctly remember Harvey kvelling, on one occasion, about how he was using the same dressing room as Ethel Merman. But this time it would be a different experience because I was personally being invited by the star of the show to spend some unknown amount of time with her backstage before her performance.

Though the back of the house of most Broadway theatres is, generally, a stark environment, I was particularly taken aback by what I saw as I followed Gwen and Paul into the bowels of the Palace. Paul is leading us toward a metal staircase, with the flowers in his right hand and his left hand holding Gwen's to presumably ensure that she doesn't trip or lose her footing. We're walking downstairs to my surprise, having assumed that the star's dressing room would have been at stage level or conveniently located to the stage. Not so here. The staircase is a bit rusty with whatever paint that had been applied in ancient times flaking off the industrial handrail. The staircase wraps around a central open column where enormous pipes, no doubt part of the theatre's mechanical systems, run from way above us to someplace subterranean. Clearly, whatever monies had been spent by the Nederlanders to restore the theatre for its return as a legitimate venue didn't make their way here. It's rather a mess, not as bad as the Stonewall debris I had seen on the last trip, in significant need of cleaning and restoration.

I've known Paul for all of five minutes and I already love him. Watching how he holds Gwen's hand as he leads her to her dressing room speaks volumes. He is clearly not just an employee, but someone who truly cares about her. As we enter her dressing room, I take notice of her name, painted in gold, on the door and this makes everything real. I am in Gwen Verdon's dressing room at the Palace. If I pulled out a pocket camera to take a picture, which I can't because the higher authority has not sent me back here with one, I'm sure they'd have paid no mind to my indiscretion at not being cool. But, it's just as well that I don't behave like the fawning fan that I am inside. Paul excuses himself to find a vase as Gwen offers me a seat.

The dressing room isn't big, certainly smaller than Harvey's and Ethel Merman's, but comfortable and organized. Toward the left, after you walk through the door, sits a wall of mirrors above a make-up table. It's about seven feet long, I estimate, with a sink on the right-hand side of the counter. Straight ahead, I spot a wardrobe of clothing, not theatre costumes but her regular clothing. Toward the right are a few places to sit, so I take an out-of-the-way place to park myself as I try to continue surveying the inner sanctum, facing her make-up counter. I don't know how long I'll be permitted to stay and I want to remember everything. I think it may be around 6:30 or so, but I won't ask anyone for the time because I don't want to hasten my departure if it's getting close to when she starts preparing.

Gwen reaches for the opened pack of Marlboros on the dressing counter and a pack of matches. As I look at what she's doing I must have that "I'd like one too" look on my face. Without asking, she offers me one and says, appropriately, "So how come you never seem to have any cigarettes on you? I mean for someone who smokes *and* works for Marlboro," she continues, gesturing with the familiar red roof pack.

"I didn't get a chance to go to the bank today," I say, trying to offer a reasonable explanation, "and I thought I still had some in my pocket, but I ended up spending all my cash on the flowers."

"Well, it was really sweet of you," she says kindly, "but you can't be spending ..."

Paul interrupts her thought as he returns with the flowers in a vase, placing them on a small table just behind the door and out of the way. He's asking her about someone I've never heard of, whether she plans to see them or not, and I take this pause as another opportunity to scan the room. This space, which she has inhabited for about a year, is painted with a greenish-khaki color that is soothing, but somewhat unexpected. I would have expected something more feminine, though I don't know why I've made this presumption. There are some fleurs-de-lis on the wall above the mirror that catch my eye, as well as a handmade, pinwheel-shaped collage of pictures.

With Paul taking his leave, Gwen returns to me with, "You were saying something outside about the ballet benefit ..."

"Yes," I reply eagerly. "I was able to snag a ticket, principally because of you and the other stars, and really enjoyed it, though I'm not really a ballet fan."

"I'm sure most of the people there that night weren't real ballet fans," she confides, "but it helped raise money for a good cause and all dance, even the kinds we don't like or understand, is related. It's all important to know."

We've finished our cigarettes and she starts to move items on the counter, as if to start the process of transforming herself into Charity Hope Valentine.

"Do you need me to leave?" I ask, hoping that I'm not intruding on her routine.

"No, you can stay," she says, "if you don't mind me getting ready while we talk."

"Of course not."

We chat a bit more about the benefit, she trying to help me understand the ballets and I commenting mostly about the fashion and the stars. I know that she, like many of the Broadway stars of the time and even into my time, donate their time and talent for various worthy causes. Part of it is business, keeping your name and face in front of the ticket-buying public. But I can't help but believe that her instinct is purer, that she does this because she sincerely cares. Certainly, the childhood illnesses that forced her to wear knee-high boots to correct her legs has made her sympathetic to those who are sick. Remembering my conversation with Ben about how I wanted to ask her help with AIDS, I segue our discussion about the Fashion Council benefit to something more general.

"Have you ever thought of starting your own charity," I start, "not all by yourself, but something that you lead to help people with a particular disease?"

"No, not really," she replies. "There are so many worthy causes and I really don't have the time, especially now, to take on something like that."

I encourage her to think more broadly, beyond the here and now, to a later time when she might use her celebrity more deliberately, but she can't possibly imagine the world that I'm thinking of and she, naturally, gravitates to supporting the things, the diseases, she knows. As we're talking, she's begun to apply her make-up and I'm fascinated with some of the little details that I notice, not the least of which is how she applies her eye make-up. I hadn't noticed it from my seat when I watched her play Charity a year ago, but now I clearly see that she's drawing the slightest of vertical lines from the center of her lower eyelids downward from her eye. It's only a few millimeters long so it's certainly not going to be visible, certainly not past the first few rows. But, I surmise that this is one of those tricks of the trade to draw attention to the eyes. Up close, it has a faint clown-like or, more appropriately, harlequin quality that I find endearing. I also notice the freckle or mole under her right eye. It's not something I've really noticed before in pictures, perhaps because it was concealed or airbrushed away. Now, the transformation that she's going through before my eyes makes it into a beauty mark.

"Was he sick for long?" she asks, segueing my segue back to something more personal.

I know she's referring to Jimmy and I reply, "Well, it was there when I met him, but kind of dormant. Containable. It wasn't 'til the last year or so that it ravaged him."

"So you knew he had cancer when you fell in love?"

"Well, yes, I guess," I answer, "but it's not like the mind can control the heart now, is it?"

"No, it really can't."

She asks me more about Jimmy and our relationship while finishing up her preparation. I answer truthfully and, fortunately, don't have to lie or modify things too much to explain what the last year was like. Paul returns as I tell her about a song that Jimmy used to sing at the top of his lungs, and totally off-key, from a show that we saw together early in our relationship. They both listen attentively as I describe Jimmy singing "Love Changes Everything" from *Aspects of Love* around the 73rd Street apartment.

"It was so bad," I say, "so loud and so bad that it was funny." I do my best version of how it sounded, though not as loudly lest I draw too much attention from the people who I hear walking in the hallway outside. Switching back to my normal voice, I continue, "The neighbors must have hated it. But it was just so loving and done without any fear of how embarrassing it sounded."

They both laugh at my impersonation as Paul pulls out a colored pencil and Gwen gives him her left shoulder. He's going to paint on the heart, the one that surrounds the name Charlie, that is a trademark of her character.

As I watch this almost tender moment between them, Paul asks, "What show was that from?"

"Oh, something called *Aspects of Love*," I say, but add, "It closed before it opened, so no one's ever heard of it." I hope this sufficiently explains why it's a song that these theatre professionals wouldn't have heard of, at least not yet.

As he finishes and she's standing there in that iconic black dress, I'm grateful that I've had this hour or so, mostly alone with her. I surmise that my time here has ended and stand.

"You don't have to go if you don't want to," she says. "You could stay and talk with Paul or just hang out here."

I surmise that she's possibly doing some match-making, noticing the ease with which Paul and I have connected. Paul is indeed handsome, but starting a relationship of any kind with someone from a different point in time is not something I want to comprehend. It reeks of complexity. I politely split the baby with, "Well, I may stay for a little bit, but I wouldn't want to get in Paul's way or take up too much of his time. I'm sure he has stuff to do."

As she leaves her dressing room, she smiles and says, "Well, if I don't see you, take care. And help yourself to a cigarette if you want."

They've both departed and I'm alone. I move closer to her make-up table to look at all that's arrayed on it. I feel like a spy, but it's harmless I rationalize. There's a small saucer with crackers stacked on it. The kind that are wrapped in pairs and sealed in cellophane. And a coffee cup and some bouillon. Amidst the make-up brushes, the box of Kleenex, a small magnifying mirror on a stand, various kinds of make-up, and a hair dryer sits a small round clock. It's just after 8:30. Curtain time. Not knowing how long it will be before Paul comes back downstairs and potentially catches me snooping, I return to my seat on the other side of the room. It is a moment of bliss. I expect to hear the first notes of the overture from the Palace stage upstairs. But before Paul returns or the music starts, I drift to sleep in the chair and another magnificent episode rings down the curtain.

CHAPTER TWELVE

Not a Day Goes By

Friday night after a long work week is earmarked for dinner with my friend, Stuart. We had been introduced by Vinny, the court reporter by day and drag queen by night bar-friend. Stuart had had an extraordinary, better-spent youth. As a very young man in the '50s and into the '60s, he'd often skip school to take the train into Manhattan to see Broadway shows. As he once told me, "I think going to see Ethel Merman in *Gypsy* was a better use of my time than learning about geometry." He ended up seeing so many of the great shows and stars of that era and even turned a fan letter to Vivien Leigh into an unlikely friendship that spanned her later Broadway runs. I could listen to his stories of sitting in her dressing room or her limousine, before, during, and after a performance, ad infinitum.

Stuart's collection of stories and memorabilia no doubt inspired my years of collecting and should have been committed to paper. But he never seemed interested in memorializing it, preferring on occasion to pull an item or photograph from his satchel to show to me or other people he felt close to. As remarkable as the artifacts were, including several very personal items from really big stars, the stories he told were even more remarkable. Sometimes, when we were out with someone he didn't really know well or had just met, I'd ask him to tell them about the Christmas story. He'd very matter-of-factly tell them that, at 20 years old, he went with a well-connected friend to see Judy Garland open the Felt Forum at Madison Square Garden on Christmas Day in 1967. He'd explain that the show itself was a bit disappointing, as Judy wasn't in her best form that night. But after the show, this friend took him along to Tony Bennett's home —Bennett had joined Judy on stage that night to sing a Christmas song — and that Judy ended up singing all night at this after-party of sorts. While sitting on the floor eating pizza with Lorna and Joey, Stuart enjoyed Judy rattling through a private mini-concert, suddenly now in top form, with Cy Coleman accompanying her on the piano. It was the kind of story that left people's jaws on the table and fairly succinctly explained the term better-spent youth to these newcomers.

Our Friday night ritual was fairly consistent. Stuart would show up at my apartment around 6:30 or so. We'd chat a bit and then head around the corner to a hole-in-the-wall Italian restaurant called La Dolce Vita. It was a throwback to an earlier era and rarely crowded. We affectionately referred to it as "the dump" because it was the least pretentious joint in Manhattan and the staff was colorful to say the least.

Dropping his bag as he enters my apartment, Stuart heads toward the far end of the living room where I display the finer pieces of my theatre collection and asks, "Anything new that I should see?"

"No, not really, but I have rotated some pieces. I took the handwritten Cy Coleman *Big Spender* score and found a place on top of the piano for it."

"I'm sure Cy would appreciate that ... not being hidden in a cabinet," Stuart responds.

"I don't have enough room to put everything out. Maybe I need a bigger apartment?"

"Your apartment is perfect," he replies and then teasingly, "You've got all this wall space that you could use, but I know that you prefer the minimalist look."

"Yeah, I hate putting nails in the walls," I tell him what he already knows. "And this way I get to keep changing it up, leaning things on top of the piano."

"I did get that Bob Fosse note framed, finally," I say while walking toward the cabinet where the excess memorabilia not on display is stored.

As I pull it out to show him, Stuart remarks, "This was a really good find. It's such a personal piece."

Stuart is referring to a note card that I found when we both were hunting through the bins at a small autograph dealer, a rare exception to my usual collecting modus operandi. It's about five-inches square, with Fosse's name and address printed across the top of the heavy card stock. The majority of the note, a thank you to Ruth Gordon for a note she sent to him praising *Chicago*, is typewritten. But below his signature is a handwritten afterthought expressing more personal appreciation because, as he writes, "Your note arrived at just the right time too! I was a little down just before receiving it. B.F." For a man that had won an Academy Award, a Tony, and an Emmy all in the same year, just a few years before, the sentiment captured in that little fragment seemed to illustrate how he always seemed to be fearful or worried about failure. With *A Chorus Line* having eclipsed *Chicago* in terms of reviews and awards, his tendency to anticipate a fall had been adequately fed.

"Have any more of those dreams?" Stuart asks, having been fully apprised of my adventures in theatreland because of our shared interests.

"Yes, and they've gotten even stranger. Now, I'm dreaming of things that I don't know anything about. I'll tell you over a cocktail," I reply as I grab my things and we head out.

Over a recession martini, a proper martini served in a near munchkin-size glass and so named because La Dolce Vita wanted to keep prices down, I explained the last trip back and the ballet-fashion fundraiser. I could give Stuart a more detailed screening of the evening because, unlike Ben, he loved theatre, ballet, fashion, and hearing about celebrities. It took until we were halfway through our appetizers, baked clams for me and eggplant parmigiana for him, before I finished.

"I wish I had your dreams," Stuart confides.

"You've had real life experiences better than that," I insist. "You don't need to dream about meeting these people or seeing these shows because you did."

Stuart starts to analyze why I'm linking the theatre world and Stonewall and AIDS. "We've both lost a lot people. Seen a lot of them die. Maybe your subconscious is trying to cope with it by finding a way to prevent all that loss and agony. I know it's been a long time, but I don't think you're over losing Jimmy and dealing with that Stonewall mess."

The entrees have arrived and we continue analyzing, as one of the waiters with no customers currently sits down to play at the ancient upright piano near the entrance to the dining room. Even on a Friday night, the place is never occupied by more than three or four parties in a space that could easily seat 50 or 60 people. It's one of things we like about the place, the fact that it's almost a private dining experience each week and the surreal *Sunset Boulevard* aura of having the staff routinely sit down to play bad piano music in the middle of the dinner hour due to the lack of customers.

"If anything, I'd agree that I'm still angry at a lot of it," I muse. "I don't miss Jimmy. His death was a relief. Not at the time. But now. We'd have never been able to escape the insanity of that relationship if he didn't die. Maybe I'm feeling guilty about being relieved that it freed me to move on."

"So, what are you still angry about?"

"I'm still angry that, despite his many flaws, despite the fact that he was no hero figure, despite his mismanagement of everything about the re-opening, that it was still his doing that makes that place exist," I explain.

"I know how you feel," Stuart commiserates, "but that was a long time ago and there have been many people who have kept that place open, yourself included. So, I don't know that I'd agree that Jimmy is solely responsible for there being a Stonewall again."

"I disagree," I respond firmly. "Yes, he didn't intentionally go down the path of wanting to re-open Stonewall. But his actions singularly brought it about. There was no one, not in the decade after the riots, that thought that the space should be restored to a gay bar. Aside from the annual marches in the '70s and '80s, it was as though the riots were a non-event."

"I'm older than you and I wouldn't say that what happened after the riots made it a non-event," he says. "It took many years for it to take hold. The change has come slowly. People point to the riots as the birth of gay liberation, but no social change happens like that. It's the product of hindsight."

"I suppose," I say, accepting that my friend has a different perspective on it.

"Listen, the fact that it wasn't a gay bar for a very long time doesn't mean that no one wanted it be one or that there was some rejection of Stonewall being a physical place to come to, a marker," Stuart concludes.

"Yes, I understand," I reply, "but even in the '80s, at the height of the AIDS crisis when the community was looking for support, it could have been a powerful symbol. Even then, it existed as a bagel joint and a Chinese restaurant."

"I think that's just business. The landlord had a space and that's who rented it" Stuart argues.

"Ok. Then explain why," I reply, "when it did re-open briefly at the end of the '80s as Stonewall, by whoever did that, that it failed miserably, went out of business right away and that the sign got ripped down. That, to me, proves my point. When there was a chance to reclaim the myth, it just evaporated. And the single marker of its existence, that sign outside the building, was stricken from the world."

With some exasperation, Stuart replies, "I have no idea why that happened. No one does. It could have been for a thousand reasons that have no bearing on Stonewall being a landmark, being revered as the birthplace of all the progress that's taken place. It could have been mismanagement of that bar too. People weren't going out to bars like they used to during the '80s. I remember. People were scared. You didn't know, in the beginning, how it was contracted. A lot of places went under."

"Again, I think you're proving my point," I say. "It was only about a year after that failed attempt to bring Stonewall back that Jimmy took over 53 Christopher. And, yes, he didn't call it Stonewall in the beginning. But he also faced that same, how do I put this, lack of traffic. Lack of people coming in. But he was stubborn. Thickheaded. For his own personal reasons, his ego, to make his bar a success. So, even in the abysmal mess of losing money every month, he persisted. He kept it open. He eventually relented and made it more of a bar and less of a restaurant and put the name in the window. I can't imagine anyone keeping something alive like that, something that didn't want to seem to live, for as long as he did. We're talking about three or four years of losses before he died. I'm not saying he did it for noble reasons. But the lack of credit he's received for making it happen, it pisses me off."

"OK, I understand your point," Stuart concedes. "If not for his persistence, it would have closed again and probably become another Chinese restaurant or something. I get it. He gave it enough longevity as a bar again to make it unacceptable to be something else."

Feeling a sense of victory, I ask, "Shall we see what they've got for dessert?"

"But of course," Stuart answers with a laugh.

As my double espresso arrives, Stuart returns us to a favorite topic of conversation, "So, what are you going to ask Gwen Verdon to do when you meet her again?"

"Oh, I don't know. Maybe this will all end abruptly and I'll start dreaming about something else," I start.

"Oh, I don't think so. This is too good to stop. You want it to keep going, don't you?"

"Of course, forever. Or until it's run its course. I think I want to take her to Stonewall in 1967 before she heads out to California to start preparing Shirley McLaine for the movie. But, I'm a little scared of showing her it as dumpy as it is then. How will I explain what Jimmy did, or what I told her he did, to make it this famous gay bar? When all you can see at that time is this crappy gay bar. I don't get how that's going to unfold."

"Maybe you'll tell her the truth," Stuart ponders.

"Yeah, that's one of the many strange things about this. Why am I reluctant to really dive right into this ... to make her a co-conspirator to what's going on? Maybe that's how the dream ends. I tell her I'm from the future and she blows me off."

Laughing, Stuart says, "Maybe she has you committed to a mental hospital and you remain there in every subsequent dream. No more original Broadway shows for Tom."

We both laugh at the scenario, but I return to being a little more serious, "I do want to see how I get her to help me with AIDS, whether it's to eliminate it or just warn everybody so fewer people die."

"And you're going to make her think you've helped her get the rights to *Chicago* so that she's obliged to do you a favor," Stuart says continuing our impromptu scripting of my future dreams, adding, "Did you ever find your hat?"

"No, that's the crazy thing. It's nowhere to be found. I looked everywhere. Can't find it or my Cartier watch."

"Your last trick probably stole both of them," he jokes.

"It's a possibility," I reply. "Shall we head back to catch *SVU?*"

With that, Stuart pays the check and we walk back to my apartment for the final part of our near weekly ritual. Chris Meloni is on the TV as I pour an after-dinner drink for both of us. More often than not, I'll fall asleep sometime before the end of the episode, and Stuart will quietly let himself out of the apartment. Tonight is no exception and, despite the double espresso, I miss the summation.

CHAPTER THIRTEEN

Diamonds Are a Girl's Best Friend

I'm beginning to think that I do have some influence on how these episodes are scripted. Upon awakening on 47th Street, between 6th and 5th Avenues, I feel a small protrusion in my right jeans' pocket. Reaching inside, I discover two rings. They are the wedding or, given the lack of marriage rights at the time, commitment rings that Jimmy had made for us. He had taken the diamond studs that had belonged to his mother and had them inserted into two gold bands at a small jewelry store in the Village. There was no ceremony, nor party, nor dinner to mark this exchange. It was, simply, his way to mark our union and I was touched that he had used his mother's earrings to do so, especially since he could have used that money for so many other things.

Though I had sold much of his jewelry on this block, including several gold chains and some gemstone rings, in order to pay some of the unending bills I'd receive at Stonewall in 1994, I couldn't part with these rings at first. It wasn't until sometime later, faced with mounting financial pressure, that I somewhat reluctantly sold them for cash. Seeing them again felt good, but as I had given them up once before, it stung less to sell them again. This time I'd use the money to fund whatever adventure this sequence would bring.

I returned to the shop that had helped me during the pilot episode of this series and was able to secure a rather tidy sum for the pair. At one point, I hesitated selling both rings and thought that I'd try to ration them for a subsequent visit to the 1960s, but concluded that I shouldn't try to outsmart the theatre gods that brought me here. If they've given me two rings to sell, then that's what I'd do.

With $200 cash in hand, a tidy sum at that time, I walk westward on 47th Street to head to the Palace. Along the way, I spot a newsstand and give a cursory look to note the date. It's June 23, 1967. A Friday. President Johnson will be meeting with Premier Kosygin of the Soviet Union in New Jersey of all places. I also notice that some organization called the Board of Estimate has voted to approve the building of the World Trade Center after seven years of disputes and delays. This small article at the bottom of the front page indicates that the towers will probably be finished in 1970. Considering it took only one year and 45 days to build the Empire State Building, I conclude that the decline of America into a tangled mess of bureaucracy must have begun in the early 1960s.

As I approach 7th Avenue, I spot Paul, the ever-present, ever-kind Verdon guardian I met during the backstage visit. We shake hands and he places one arm around my back, in a half-hug, to indicate his affection or approval of me, I'm not certain which.

"Nice to see you again," Paul says with a smile.

"It's great to see you too."

"Do you work around here?"

"No and I'm not working today," I indicate. "Just thought I'd catch a show. Hey, maybe I'll pick up a ticket for your show. I'd love to see it again. Maybe stop by after to say hi to Gwen too."

"Oh, that's not going to be possible," he says with a look of concern. "Gwen had some minor surgery yesterday and she'll be out for a little while."

As Paul tells me this, I remember that sometime during the second year of the run Gwen has surgery, reportedly for the removal of a cyst, and that she never returns to the cast. Helen Gallagher, a fine performer in the show in her own right and Gwen's understudy, takes over the title role and the show closes not long after that. Prior to this, it's been announced that Shirley McLaine will be doing the film role and, as a testament to her love of the work and her devotion to Fosse, Gwen will spend time during the latter part of 1967 in Los Angeles prepping McLaine to be Charity Hope Valentine.

"Oh, I'm so sorry to hear that," I say. "I hope it's nothing serious. Is she home recuperating now?"

"I don't think so. She had it yesterday," Paul states, "but everything seems to be OK."

"Thanks for telling me," I reply. "I think I'll leave a card and some flowers with her doorman. When you speak with her, please send my best wishes."

"Of course," Paul indicates, "not a problem."

With that I give Paul a full hug and say goodbye. I walk up to 7th Avenue and see her name still above the title on the marquee. That sign will be changing soon. I walk aimlessly up 7th, trying to figure out what get-well gift I should bring to her. I debate whether leaving some food or some chocolates at her apartment would be appropriate but dismiss the idea given that I don't know when she'll be released from the hospital and given that I don't know what foods she might like to indulge in. I conclude that the best course of action is to do exactly what I had said to Paul by simply leaving a note and, instead of flowers, a small plant. Given the abundance of plants at her apartment, it's something that seems to be a better bet and will last longer than a bouquet.

There's a nice stationery store further up 7th that I stop at to buy some note paper. I find a nice 5x7 card stock that will let me write a few thoughts, something that will feel more personal than a mundane greeting card. The clerk indulges me by allowing me to borrow a pen and lets me commandeer a small space at the counter to write my note. It takes me a good five minutes thinking about what to write before the pen ever touches the card stock. The clerk seems a little miffed that I'm spending so much time composing my thoughts, but I give her a nice smile and she demurs. Eventually, I simply state the truth — that I heard from Paul that she was recuperating and that I just wanted to wish her a speedy recovery. I end the note with a suggestion that we might get together again before she heads to California. Though I worry that she'll may think Paul was too loose-lipped with me, otherwise how would I know such a non-public thing, I decide that showing her I know things that I shouldn't know yet as a comparable stranger to her is a small step toward, perhaps, telling her the truth about how I'm here. With the note finished, I make my way toward Columbus Circle to find a lovely plant in an exquisite pot. The thought that I'm going to give her something that will remain in her apartment makes me smile.

Though I find two florist shops on my trek northward, neither of them have the kind of exquisite pot that I want. Though in my time there will be plenty of high-end stores of all kinds in this neighborhood, in the late 1960s the area was still, decidedly, the poorer part of town. I conclude that I'll use the abundance of cash in my pocket to go someplace I know will have something worthy, Madison Avenue. Grabbing a cab, I instruct the driver to head over to the eastside and drive up Madison slowly. He balks at not having an address, but I hand him a twenty-dollar bill, the equivalent of maybe a Benjamin in my time, and tell him that this is a special trip and that I will take care of him. That seems to make us best friends. I explain that I want to find a really good flower shop, the kind that also sells very premium plants, and he joins me surveying the shops as we meander up the avenue, him taking the left side and me taking the right. Somewhere in the upper 60's, he spots a shop and asks me if it looks impressive enough. I tell him that it seems to and he pulls into a spot at the curb. I indicate that I want him to wait and that I might be awhile. My new friend tells me to take all the time I need.

Inside, I find the proprietor of this boutique or emporium, the fanciness of the place being so high that the words "shop" or "store" would not suffice. I tell him that I'm looking for something special, for a great lady. He leads me toward the back when I spot an amazing orchid plant, standing almost three feet tall, in an antique-looking Chinese pot.

"I'll take this one," I say, without inquiring about the price.

Looking at my casual clothing, jeans and flannel shirt, he seems to doubt my ability to afford my selection and says, "Well, this is very special indeed. But it's quite expensive. It may be a bit more than you're looking to spend."

"How much is it?"

"I'm afraid that's $60," he says with an assurance that I'll flinch.

"That's all?" I say, trumping his snobbery, and reaching into my stash to pull out the required amount.

With the exchange having been completed, I carefully wrestle the too-large-to-be-put-in-the-back-seat orchid plant into the cab and instruct the driver to head to 69th and Central Park West. When we arrive at the building, a doorman greets the cab and opens my door, stunned at the size of the orchid plant I hand to him as I exit the cab. Though the meter still hasn't used up the first $20, I hand the driver another $20 and tell him to wait. Inside the vestibule, I tell the pleasant doorman that this is a special gift for Ms. Verdon. He looks at me strangely.

"For who? Mizverdun? We have no one by that name," he responds.

I realize that "Ms." has somehow thrown him and, assuming that the title has not become widely used yet or at least not with this gentleman, I restate, "This is for Gwen Verdon. Please make sure you take good care of it until you can give it to her. And please don't lose the note." Still feeling rich as Rockefeller, I give him ten-dollar bill from my pocket and he beams with appreciation.

"Why, yes, certainly sir," he assures.

Jumping back into my personal yellow limousine, I utter the familiar "7th Avenue and Christopher Street" and we zoom downtown. I'm fairly confident that Stonewall has finally opened for business and that I'll be able to see it as a patron for the first time since my roundtrips to the '60s began. Given that it's only late afternoon, I'm not sure if I'll find Stonewall open or not. The things I had read suggested that it was a more night and late night venue, especially the references to being a private club, but the lack of commentary on being open earlier will not deter me. I figure that the proprietors, whoever they really are from that mix of characters I'd researched, wouldn't leave money on the table by not being open for happy hour on a Friday evening.

My instincts are right, and as I approach 53 Christopher, I see that there is activity. The original production of Stonewall has opened and I approach the door to see if there will be any screening of patrons trying to enter as was reported. The window is still obscured, but one of the double doors is open and a tall, lanky man stands guard. He's perhaps late 30's or early 40's, with a short-cropped haircut. I pretend to know what I'm doing, trying to look as though I've been inside before, to minimize any potential interaction.

"What are you looking for?" he asks, blocking my way inside.

"Same thing I looked for last time, an overpriced drink and some scintillating conversation," I reply, trying to gay it up enough to assure him that I belong.

I keep stepping forward, hoping my forward momentum will cause him to stop blocking the door, and, luckily, the sassy response and lack of hesitation in my gait cause him to move aside.

As I enter, I prepare to turn right because the main bar in the original Stonewall, which comprised both the 51 and 53 Christopher parcels, is in the 51 Christopher side of the combination. From behind I hear the doorman/bouncer aggressively say, "Aren't you forgetting something?"

As I turn, I see his outstretched hand, palm up, pointing toward me. Trying not to appear flustered, I say, "Oh, did I forget the cover charge?"

"You know the drill," he says. "Three bucks and sign in."

I recall reading that patrons would be asked to pay to enter this "private club" but I hadn't heard about a sign-in sheet. Not wanting to piss him off, I pull out a five-dollar bill, the lowest denomination I had, and give it to him saying, "This is the smallest I've got, so I guess you're going to have to keep the change."

He seems a bit thrown off by my giving him more than necessary but, not surprisingly, doesn't argue the point. Instead, he hands me a notebook, similar to the composition notebooks I recall from grade school, the kind with the black and white speckled covers, and a pen. I flip through the pages, filled with lists of names after names catalogued by date, until I get to a page where it seems that I can add my name. Above the blank space that I will write in, I notice several previous entrants have elected to sign in with the names of celebrities, authors, and other pseudonyms. Though I doubt my opponent would mind if I spent a moment trying to think of another clever non-name to add to his list, I instinctively write down the only appropriate name I can think of, Jimmy Pisano.

He looks at my entry, perhaps somewhat perplexed that I've entered a name that appears to be my real name, and in a nod to my overpayment tries to make a joke, chuckling, "Diamond Jim Pisano. Welcome back."

"It's Jimmy Pisano, and thanks," I reply. As I say the words, his name, out loud in this place, I feel a cold shudder rush through my body. Though Jimmy is still alive in this time, a teenager in fact, it's as though his future self, no longer living, has joined me here to see the origins of his unintended achievement.

I make my way to the 51 Christopher portion of the building as originally intended. There has been very little in the way of preparation for this opening since my brief tour with Angelo. Much of the debris that littered the floor back then has been removed, but the overall feeling is still dismal. Everything paintable is black. The lighting is dim. There's a musty smell of something rotting. With a quick look at the bar and the back of the room, I estimate that there are between a dozen to two dozen patrons, mostly white and under thirty. I make my way to the long plywood island trying to impersonate a bar near the far wall.

Thankfully, I don't have to immediately decide what I'm going to have to drink because the sole bartender on duty is engaged with another customer to my left, about four feet down from me. I take note of a sign behind the bar, affixed to the wall with what looks like an old bicycle chain, listing the drinks available. I can have scotch, rye, or bourbon for one dollar, a soft drink for 35 cents or, inexplicably, champagne for $1.25. I shake my head in total disbelief that, in this dump, someone could or would order champagne. Still feeling, or hoping, that Jimmy is standing beside me, I offer a silent, "Can you fucking believe it?" to my imaginary companion.

The bartender breaks his conversation and makes his way to me, asking, "What'll you have?"

Though I want to ask for a beer, I don't see it on the list, which makes perfect sense if you're in the business of watering down the drinks. Not wanting to break the illusion that I've been here before, I elect to order something off the short bill of fare I've seen on the wall.

"I'll have a scotch."

The bartender reaches for a glass and gives it a perfunctory rinse in a basin of cloudy water. I'm disgusted by seeing how unclean everything is, especially the glass I'm about to drink from. I momentarily run a scenario in my head, trying to guess whether contracting some disease or infection in this time would transfer back to my real life, as he places the glass before me.

"Thanks," I say and handing him a five, "Could I get some change for the cigarette machine please?"

He nods and faces away from me to make the change, not out of a register but out of a metal box behind him that looks like the cash tray from a proper cash register. As he makes his way back to me, I take further notice of his appearance. He's wearing a leather vest without a shirt, which in my day would have been a bad choice, given that he's somewhat paunchy with no definition of anything that should be defined. With a little work, he could be attractive. But it's a seller's market, and if one didn't like the atmosphere or the lack of hygiene or the bartender's appearance, there isn't exactly an abundance of other choices.

I pick up my drink, walk to the back, pick up a pack from the cigarette machine, and head back to my original spot, only a little bit closer to the patron that the bartender was talking to when I ordered. He's very tall, very thin and, though I'm no longer able to accurately judge the age of anyone under 25, I think that he might be 15 or 16 years old. It doesn't surprise me, though, since complying with the law isn't part of their business plan.

With the bartender taking care of other patrons further down the plywood faux-bar, I decide to chat up the young man-boy. I figure that if he is as young as I suspect, I stand a better chance of soliciting information from him about this place.

"Do you have a match?" I ask, pulling out the first tube from the pack.

"No, I don't smoke, sorry," he responds. The timber of his voice is thin, attributable to his age and, I suspect, nervousness.

"You're better off. These things are no good for you," I reply, hoping to find some common ground to start a conversation.

"Then why do you do it?" he answers, with childlike naiveté.

"Well, cause it feels good," I say with a smile and a bit of a laugh.

He nods up and down, answering, "Yeah, I guess that makes sense."

He looks as though he's about six foot and a half, but it's his extreme slenderness that makes him seem even taller. With the standard issue short blond hair, parted on the side, cut that he's sporting, I figure he's a suburban kid.

"Do you come here a lot?" I ask.

"Nah, it's my first time, but don't say anything please. I just wanted to see what this place was like," he responds with surprising truthfulness.

"You come here a lot?" he asks of me.

"Well, truthfully, it's my first time too. But, I'd appreciate it if you could keep that to yourself," I admit, hoping to gain his trust.

"Sure," he answers, "I heard about this place from a friend and kind of skipped out of ..." he cuts himself off.

"School," I say, finishing the sentence he didn't intend to complete.

"Ah, yeah," he confirms, continuing with noticeable anxiety, "You aren't police are you?"

"No man, don't worry," I assure. "I'm not the police. I don't care that you're here. They're known for liking underage guys here."

By most accounts, the original Stonewall had more than just the occasional minor. Ed Murphy, one of early staffers at the door, had been characterized as, among other things, a wrestler, blackmailer, and a pimp of young boys. I wonder, briefly, whether my encounter at the door was with Murphy or another standup guy employed here. Murphy polishes his reputation over the years by devoting time to AIDS and runaway/homeless teens, the latter being one of the most reviling ironies I'd encountered. His riding in subsequent Gay Pride parades as an honored Stonewall veteran and assuming the unofficial title of "Mayor of Christopher Street" was shocking to me when I first learned of it. By the time Jimmy died, it was further down the list of things I despised about the gay community. By that point, thanks to Jimmy's networking, I had met a couple of elder statesman, some claiming to have been at the riots, who seemed to relish their unconfirmed reputation as chicken hawks.

"The bartender's been teasing me about my age," he says, "telling me I'm not old enough to be here, but kinda hitting on me at the same time."

"That's not surprising. By the way, my name is Tom, what's yours?"

"Dick," he says, and I suppress a laugh. He's a little confused, asking, "What's funny?"

"Nothing. Really," I answer, trying to hide my amusement at his name. "I just think that this whole set-up, this place, is a bit of a joke. Entry fee. High-priced watered-down drinks. Plywood bar.

No sinks. I haven't even been to the toilet yet, but I'll bet that's pretty fabulous too," I say, concluding my review.

"I haven't been to many places. I live on Long Island," he says, confirming my suspicion, "but this seems pretty standard. And they have dancing, which is what everyone's talking about."

Indeed, there are a handful of guys toward the back, past the end of bar, dancing together but apart, as if not standing directly face to face would somehow protect them during a raid. The bartender makes his way back to us, asking if we'd like another round. We nod yes and he fetches them quickly. Dick pulls out a ticket and hands it to the bartender.

"What's that?" I ask.

"Didn't you get one at the door. I got two tickets when I paid," Dick informs me.

I sneer at the bartender, but pull out money to pay for my next drink anyway. I don't want to make a fuss, in an illegal bar run by the mafia with a doorman/bouncer that's probably a thug and done time. It's not worth wasting what precious time I have here.

The bartender looks at me and comments about Dick, saying, "Doesn't he have such small hands? Those look like a kid's hands, not a man's hands."

Not wanting to tug at the bait, I reply, "His hands look fine to me. Now, you, you could stand a few days in the gym. It would bring you bigger tips." I half-smile, half-smirk to indicate that I'm not going to gang up on the man-boy.

"My tips are fine," he answers back as he tugs at his crotch. "Especially this one."

Seeing that this threesome conversation will go nowhere, and still wanting to pry Dick for what he knows about going to gay bars in this era, I pull him by the arm and lead him toward the 53 Christopher side of Stonewall.

"Let me take you on a little tour," I say to Dick.

"Sure, but there's not much to see," he says and he's right. We walk through the opening in the wall that previously separated these two buildings, into another dance floor area. This side, as black as the other, only has a small makeshift bar toward the rear, where my Stonewall's back room would inevitably take shape.

"You're right. But I didn't want to engage him," I say, referring to the bartender, adding, "besides, this place could be really cool if someone just put in a little effort. I can picture it."

"What would you do?" Dick asks.

"Well, for one, I'd get a really great antique bar, one of those really long ones that curves around the end," I say pointing to where the '90s Stonewall bar would sit. "I'd have a beautiful antique mirror above the bar and stair-stepped shelves to show off the liquor."

"You want to own a bar?"

"At one point I did," I answer, "but I've come to realize that it's a miserable business. I'm not cut out for it. It takes a special person to handle it and to do it well. The people you employ are largely looking to steal as much as they can. And many of the customers are messes, either alcoholics or drug addicts or mentally unbalanced. For a *fun* environment, it sure can be depressing."

"So why are you decorating a bar that you don't want to have?" Dick asks astutely.

"It's just a fantasy," I say, wanting to give a reason as to why I'm describing the Stonewall that Jimmy built. "I'd put a long bar rail here, to divide the room and give people a place to put a drink and have a conversation. At either end, there'd be tall columns with lights on top ... kind of like antique streetlamps. On this side of the room, I'd have comfortable banquettes against the walls to create more places for people to congregate. The fabric would look like the kind you see on expensive furniture. And this paneling they've got up, it's cheap shit. I'd get the kind of beautiful old paneling you see in an English library, with old wall sconces casting a nice glow over the room."

"It sounds expensive, but really nice," Dick says, joining my architectural fantasy.

"Yes, it would be expensive. And it would make people feel good about being here. This place, the way it looks now, makes you feel as though you should be hiding in a closet, instead of being proud. It's a swamp," I add for good measure.

"Do you live near here?" Dick asks suggestively, profoundly changing the direction of the conversation.

I'm flattered that a much younger man would be attracted to me until I remember that he's only 15 or 16. I panic. "I'm afraid I don't," I snap. "Listen, Dick, I'm going to have to go now, but I'm going to tell you something. And it's going to sound strange. But, believe me, it's important. When you're older, sometime in your 30's, you're going to hear that you're supposed to have sex with a condom …"

"I'm not going to sleep with women," he interrupts.

"No," I say emphatically, "when you're sleeping with men. When you're fucking. They'll say you should wear a condom. I know it doesn't make sense. But please believe me and promise me that you'll do it. Every time. No exceptions."

"What are you talking about?" he asks with a tone of disbelief and anger because I've replied to his overture with an insane rant that will make no sense to him for some time.

Knowing that my warning can easily be forgotten in the coming 12 or so years, I aim to be even more outlandish so that he won't forget this otherwise unmemorable day in his life. I stare him directly in the eyes, like a lunatic that I hope he'll remember, insisting, "Starting in 1980, you need to have sex with a condom or you will die."

"Oh, Jesus, you're fucking crazy," he shouts, throwing his hands up in the air and storming off to the 51 Christopher Street side.

Good, I think to myself. That was potentially crazy enough to be remembered. Maybe I've just saved one life. The scene I've caused has brought the attention of the few other patrons on the 53 side and the larger number on the 51 side. I need to depart before I'm asked to or, worse yet, draw the attention of doorman/bouncer. I want to return here, if I'm able in some next episode, and I don't want to be perceived as a troublemaker that gets stopped at the door. I walk to the front door, exit, and cross the street. Sitting down on a park bench, I stare at the building. More people are heading in, getting intercepted by the possible Ed Murphy and parting with their Mafia tithe. I don't know how I feel about what's just happened. I've been wanting to see this original Stonewall since I first landed back here. Reading about it was one thing. Seeing how shabby it is, how unlikely it feels for anything of historical note to take place here, I feel nauseous. I can't imagine bringing Gwen here now. I put my head down toward my lap to gain my composure and the moment passes.

CHAPTER FOURTEEN

Pretty Little Picture

Sometime during the *Tonight Show* I had woken up on the loveseat, and seeing that Stuart had already let himself out, I had hazily made my way to the bedroom. The sound of the TV, which I hadn't bothered to turn off, awoke me mid-morning. I turn it off so that I can make some coffee in quiet, only to turn it back on when the brew is ready.

After the Joe Jr.'s requisite breakfast, I call Buddy to see what he's up to today. Saturday is usually his pampering day at the Christopher Street day spa. He tells me when his appointments are scheduled for and I call them to try to align at least our manicures and pedicures so that we can chat for a bit.

At just after two o'clock, we sit side-by-side for dueling manicures at this gay version of Sydney's from *The Women*, though arguably that's redundant. Most of the manicurists and other female staff are Russian transplants living in Brighton Beach which gives the place an exotic feel. The hairstylists are a mix of younger, gay pretty-boys and old-school queens with loyal followings. The massage therapists include a handful of vegan waifs and 30-something bodybuilders. During the early years of this establishment, I'd book my appointment with the same therapist, a short, beefy lost soul who would usually, but not always, reward me by completely disrobing during the first half of the massage while I was face down. His ability to silently shed his clothes, while performing the massage, was worthy of Lili St. Cyr or Gypsy Rose Lee. Nowadays, I just take whichever massage therapist is available. Like Giuliani's scrubbing of 42nd Street, this spa had become Disneyfied.

"I made a reservation at Knickerbocker for 8:30," my friend announces. "It was either that or 6 o'clock. I should have called earlier in the week."

"That's fine. Maybe you can come to my place first for a drink. I have some old photos of Stonewall I want to show you."

"Old photos of Stonewall?" Buddy laughs. "I hope it's not some embarrassing picture of me doing who knows what or who knows who."

"No," I join in the laughter that now includes both manicurists, "they're just some pictures from the beginning. I'm thinking of donating some of them."

"To who," he asks, "like a library or The Center?" referring to the Gay, Lesbian, Bisexual and Transgender Community Center on West 13th Street, though no one ever referred to it as such.

"I don't know to who, actually," I admit. "It's not like there's some central repository for gay history, at least none that I know of."

"Sure, I'd love to look through them and help you get it in order," he replies, "but I wouldn't know who to give them to either. Maybe somebody over at amfAR or Broadway Cares would know where to donate them. I can ask."

"Ok," I say not convinced, "but I don't think they're the kinds of places that deal with archives. But it's worth a shot."

We go on to discuss, though gossip is a more accurate word, the comings and goings of shared acquaintances, bar friends, as the manicures segue to pedicures in an adjoining room. As we finish up, he lets me know that he's got some shopping to do and that he'll by at my apartment around seven. I still have a massage to enjoy and fate has paired me up with Anton, the least attractive massage therapist here. Anton's been working at the salon for a couple of years, far longer than anyone else. I originally didn't understand why a place that seemed to only hire hyper-attractive people would continue to employ someone with no body to speak of and a bad case of facial acne scarring. After I received his first meticulous hand job several years ago, I realized why.

Back at the apartment, in preparation for Buddy's arrival, I put out some cheese and pulled the old photo album out of safekeeping. I hastily tried to arrange the pictures into a better chronology, but some didn't neatly fit into my four impromptu categories: Building New Jimmy's, The First Anniversary, The Second Anniversary, and The Conversion Back to Stonewall. The last category was the most difficult to define because the transformation from New Jimmy's to Stonewall proper did not happen overnight. It was an on-going neutering that started sometime before the first anniversary of New Jimmy's and culminated with the removal of the New Jimmy's name from the front window and its replacement with a red neon Stonewall. New Jimmy's was decidedly masculine, a gay gentlemen's pub. Stonewall was neither masculine nor feminine. It just was.

At 7:10 the doorman buzzes that my friend has arrived. He enters the apartment and beelines to the impromptu bar set up in the kitchen. Pouring himself a vodka on the rocks, he joins me in the living room and scans the photos laid out on the glass coffee table.

"So, what is it exactly that you're trying to do?" he asks.

"I want to document the re-opening of Stonewall. To memorialize the rebirth. And to give credit to the people that made it happen ... especially Jimmy," I reply with a greater sense of clarity and focus. "Now that the place has been open as a bar for a decade, there's no chance that it will ever be put back to sleep. It's a living monument now and forever."

"OK," he says with some uncertainty, "but what are you going to do ... ask them to put these pictures up in the bar or give them to some organization?"

"I won't ask them to be placed in the bar," I say. "There's no guarantee that they would stay there or that they wouldn't be vandalized or stolen or just removed."

"But that *is* where it took place." "Wouldn't the most people get to know about Jimmy and the re-opening there?"

"Yes, but this is meant for history," I say pointing to all the photos. "If they ended up at the bar too, I guess I wouldn't object, but I want them to be archived — to be the permanent, indelible record of the beginning of the re-beginning. Like at the Smithsonian or..."

"What? You want these pictures to go to the Smithsonian?"

"I'm just using that as an example," I say, interrupting his interruption. "I don't know where they should go. Someplace that documents gay history and the people that made things happen. Maybe I'll give copies to several places."

"OK, OK," he says calmly. "Let's not worry where they're going, let's go through them and see what tells the story."

"OK, that sounds good," I agree and start pulling a few of the photos together into a pile in front of him. "I think that part of the story is how Jimmy converted the space back into a bar for the first time since the riots. How he went all-out to honor the space with something really special."

"But it was called New Jimmy's then. Don't you want to start when it became Stonewall again?"

"No, no," I insist. "The changing of the name back to Stonewall isn't the beginning, that's too obvious. It starts when he signed the lease, I think it was for seven years, and made the commitment. Here, look at these ..."

"Oh my God, that kitchen," he sighs. "It must have cost a fortune and then to rip it all out ... what a shame."

"Yeah, the kitchen, all of that expensive wood paneling that was installed, the charcoal sketches on the walls," I reply. "It was a shame that he spent all that money to make it a really nice place and nobody cared. What really killed me was when people would come in and vandalize stuff ... usually in the bathroom so that no one would see them doing it ... stealing or breaking fixtures, cracking a vanity ... just fucking lowlifes ... wanting to destroy something beautiful."

"Oh, Jimmy looks so good in that picture," he says pointing to a shot where Jimmy is beaming as he holds a vinyl sign that was made for the first Gay Pride March that would go by the newly re-opened bar.

"And I want to make sure everyone knows that Jimmy didn't name the place for himself and that he wasn't hiding the fact that New Jimmy's was the original Stonewall bar, or at least half of it," I insist.

"And this one with Joe, he was always loyal to Jimmy," I say pointing to another shot from the first year.

"What a hunk," Buddy remarks looking at Joe, and I concur.

"Jimmy had even borrowed money from *him*. And after he died, I made sure that I paid Joe back first. I couldn't stand that Jimmy was borrowing from friends."

"But that's what was so special," Buddy smiles. "Everyone felt that they wanted to help Jimmy make it work."

"Not everyone, but a few people really made a difference."

"Look at Sal," Buddy continues, pulling up a few photos from the coffee table.

Sal DeFalco, who had been an early part of the Stonewall revival, was a legendary New York bartender having started at a very young age serving drinks to the rich and famous at Studio 54.

"He once told me that he 'dated'," I say, gesturing the air quotes, "Peter Allen and that he was waiting for him to land at LaGuardia when Peter wrote 'When You Get Caught Between the Moon and New York City' while the plane was in a holding pattern."

"I didn't hear that story," Buddy laughs, "but Sal did have quite the life. I wonder how he and Claude are doing in Florida. I haven't heard from them in a while."

"And here's Pool," I say, showing a picture of one of the most famous figures of Fire Island, Johnny Pool, who started bartending there in the 1960s. Johnny Pool and Sal DeFalco were exceptionally well-known and well-respected bartenders, and yet even with their followings the crowds didn't come to Stonewall.

"I only wish I could find a picture of Marsha," I say. "I know she came in a few times."

Along with Sylvia Rivera, Marsha P. Johnson had been at the original riots in 1969. Though dozens of people would claim to have been there, many falsely seeking some status in the gay community for having been an eyewitness, they are among the few whose presence hasn't been disputed.

"These pictures from the Pride Parade have to be part of it too," Buddy says, pointing to a handful of the snapshots.

"Yeah, definitely," I say. "I love this one. A guy in drag flirting with a NYC police officer while his fellow cops look on laughing. That's the money shot. They're there to protect the place and do crowd control and she's bumping and grinding in front of him. The entire change captured in one picture. It kills me that I can't remember his name. He was working there as a waiter, I think, and he dressed up in that outfit for Pride and I just can't remember his name. I better finish all this before I totally forget everything."

"Oh, look at that handsome bunch," Buddy cuts in. "Ah, to be remembered for posterity."

Laughing, I say, "Oh you'll be remembered too, but for what I'm not sure. Look, those two pictures are from May, a Carnival Night party, two months after Jimmy died. It was the fourth anniversary of the re-opening, in 1994. We were getting all ready for the 25th anniversary in June. Throwing all those parties to drum up business and keep the place going. Nobody but you and a few other people realize how close we were to closing down right before the 25th. I was so thin and exhausted."

"Listen, honey," he says, "I'm getting thin and exhausted. We better head over to Knickerbocker. I need me some meat."

"I have a feeling I'll hear that again after Knickerbocker."

Leaving all the photos strewn across the coffee table in makeshift piles, we head out for another Saturday night. Maybe someone will come in and package all this undocumented history for me while we're out carousing. The conversation during the 10-minute walk migrates to family drama.

"So my dad and stepmonster will be coming to New York for two weeks."

"It's only two weeks. You can live through that, you've done it before."

"I can deal with my dad wanting to check in on the business, even though it's painful," he says, "but after eight hours of him questioning everything, then we have to go out to dinner with her and that just kills me. I can kill time with her shopping, but across the table at dinner there are no distractions. Every day and every night, it'll be the same thing."

"Will I meet them this time?"

"I wouldn't put you through that," he affirms. "I wish you could have met my mother. When she was alive, that was the best of times."

Buddy had often told me of his youth and before, when his parents were first married, and how they all lived the most charmed of existences. His parents would fly down to Cuba, pre-Castro, to gamble, with Desi and Lucy of course. And in the 1960s, Sinatra and the like would drop by their fabulous Long Island home for cocktails, which he, as a child, would prepare. It was a Patrick Dennis story that he'd share freely with anyone in earshot. Even his closer friends would comment, out of earshot, as to why he insisted on telling them over and over again, given that nobody believed they were true or, at best, that they were one-tenth truth juiced up on gay steroids. I chose to never question the tales. He had been a loyal friend to Jimmy and myself and there was no reason to unravel that.

We're seated, by Ron, at the first booth, just behind the reservations desk. Liza and all the other Hirschfeld characters hover on the walls above us. Diane or Patricia would typically take care of us. Both had been there a long time and treated us like family. Diane, a pretty blond with a quieter demeanor but razor-sharp sense of humor, was engaged with other tables as Patricia made her way to our banquette.

She greets us with, "How are my favorite guys tonight?" Patricia brandishes her fiery red hair and oversized personality better than any comedienne on Broadway or TV. Her entire persona wraps you in a warm hug.

"Great. And you?" we reply almost simultaneously.

After some chit-chat about a workshop she's gone to, Patricia returns to the business at hand with, "Are you boys hungry?"

"Starving," my friend says, as though he hasn't eaten in days.

"The usual, please, Absolut martinis, a dozen oysters each, steak for two, rare, fries and creamed spinach," I recite almost nearly as well as "7th Avenue and Christopher Street."

Over this blissfully the same Saturday night ritual, we talk more about his upcoming visit from dad and stepmonster and my obsession with righting the Stonewall story.

"Well if anybody should put it all down on paper, it's you," he says. "No one else has that perspective, behind the scenes and front of the house."

"It's daunting," I say, "trying to correct a story, or tell a story that hasn't been heard. I'm not even sure why I feel the need to do it. Maybe I'm just trying to hold onto something. Something that's not there anymore or maybe never was there."

"Whatever the reason you're feeling this need to do this," he says, "just go with it. Don't second guess yourself. Jimmy's opening of the bar is as much a part of the story of gay liberation as anything else. There wouldn't have been the push to make the site a national historic landmark if it was still a Chinese restaurant."

"But maybe it's all in vain," I say. "Maybe I'll put all this together and nobody will care or notice. You know my feelings about how people have used Stonewall for their own agendas."

"It doesn't matter," he pronounces. "Just put the story together, use the pictures to document it and let it go. Stonewall's become a myth. Myths aren't truthful. They're stories. Just tell your truth."

"If I had a dollar for every joker who came up to me when I was running the bar who told me that they had been there on the night of the riots, I'd be a multi-millionaire," I say and we both laugh.

The jazz combo is in full swing and our practically ringside seats give us prime viewing of the bass player's riff. Dinner always starts out fast but downshifts to a more languid pace once the oversized steak platter arrives and live music fills the room.

"I had another one of those dreams," I tell my friend, though I haven't revealed half as much to him of my past episodes as I had to Stuart. Something inside made me skittish about telling him too much. Maybe it was because I feared he'd commandeer my story with his own tales of how he'd poured Frank a martini.

"What show did you see this time?"

"No show this time," I reply, "but I went to Stonewall and ended up talking to some kid."

"You dreamt that you went to the bar?" he asks, unaware of my previous forays to the not-yet-open Stonewall in 1966.

"Yes, I walked in, looked around and ended up speaking with this young guy. The place was a dump," I start explaining.

"Some things haven't changed," he interrupts.

"No, really a dump," I continue. "It's dirty and the bar is made out of plywood. There's some crappy paneling near the entrance where they've set up an office of sorts and a coat check. The bartender kind of looks like Joe, he had that manly face with a big bushy mustache, but he's paunchy and not very nice to the customers."

"And the kid ... was he one of those homeless kids?"

"No, suburban kid in the bar for the first time," I say. "He seemed very innocent. I ended up telling him about AIDS."

"You told him what about AIDS?"

"I just kind of went off on him. Telling him that he'd die if he didn't use a condom after 1980," I answer a bit sheepishly.

"Oh, honey," he says, "there is all kinds of deep shit going in your dream. You've been looking at all these pictures of dead people and now you're dreaming about stopping people from getting AIDS. Have you had any other dreams like that?"

"No," I lie.

"Well, maybe you should hurry up and donate those pictures," he offers, "so that you're not looking at them all the time. None of us need to remember all those funerals. At least not all the time."

We finish up with double espressos, pay the check, and kiss Patricia goodbye. As morning must always follow night, we make the necessary pilgrimage.

It's after eleven when we enter Stonewall. The downstairs is full but not packed. I scan the room to see if Ben is working again and am relieved to see that he is not. I don't need that kind of bender tonight. The receiving line protocol having been completed, we settle in to enjoy ourselves with some pinball in the back room. Assorted guest stars rotate in to play with us, making each round take far longer than I prefer. Adam, a formerly handsome and thin junkie, though because he was white and well-educated the term junkie was never used to refer to his indulgences, has joined the gathering in the back. He doesn't have a drink in his hand and shows no interest in joining our pinball play, which tells me he has no money in his pocket.

"Hey, Tommy," he smiles broadly. "How are you doing?" Adam has gained about 50 pounds since quitting whatever drugs he was previously taking, on what seemed to be a 24/7 basis. His overly solicitous greeting, using "Tommy," which no one ever called me, makes me feel like I'm about to be bombarded by a doesn't-take-no-for-an-answer telemarketer. When he was thin and continuously high, he'd never bother engaging with me. Now that he was sober, except for alcohol, and fat, he acted as though we were best buddies.

"I'm good," I reply, and not really looking for an answer ask, "How are you?"

"I'm doing great since I quit," he says trying to muster an altar boy's halo over his head. "But I really haven't been able to find a job. I was working at Boots and Saddles, but they let me go."

As I call up the lyrics from *A Chorus Line* about strays and losers, I go against my better judgment and say, "Would you like a drink?"

"Oh, yeah, that would be so nice," he smiles. "Thank you."

As I head to the front bar to get him a drink, I think that I must be an idiot to show kindness to someone who, on so many occasions, would ignore me talking to him or, in those rare instances where he'd grant a momentary audience, flit away while I was in mid-sentence if he saw someone better looking — or a dealer.

"Here ya go," I say, conjuring the best fake smile I can.

"You're really too nice," he says, and while I silently agree with him, I'm waiting for the other shoe to drop. "I wasn't very nice to you while I was fucked up."

"That's true, but it doesn't matter," I lie. While I'd always thought he was stunningly attractive, I internally professed never wanting anything more from him than friendship. That too was a lie. In his worst state, he was even more desirable because he needed to be fixed.

"Well, I just want to say I'm sorry for being a dick," he begins his contrition. "I should never have been so fucking rude to you."

"Oh, so you were aware of what you were doing?" I seize the moment. "I thought, or wanted to think, that you were just too fucked up to know any better. But you've clarified that."

Realizing that he's undone all of his penance, he tries to apologize again with, "I wasn't doing it on purpose. I'm sorry. I was treating a lot of people like that. But I'm really sorry that I treated you that way. You were always nice to me … you were always trying to be nice to me."

"Look it's fine," I say. "It's in the past. I accept your apology. Where are you living now?" As the words come out of my mouth, I realize I've made a tactical error. Never ask someone who's noted for being a user and is currently down on his luck any question that might open a door.

"I've been renting a room in a boarding house in Chelsea," he says. "It's pretty much a tenement, but at least it was a place to sleep."

"Was?" I ask, bracing myself.

"When I lost my job at Boots and Saddles, they kicked me out. I've been sleeping in the park until I can get some sort of emergency housing or another job."

Over the next forty minutes, while still playing pinball and intermittently chatting with Adam, I recognize that I'll be taking him home with me. Just for one night. To sleep on the loveseat. I'm decidedly the most gullible person I know.

On the short walk to my apartment on 12th Street, I let him know what the rules of the road will be tonight. I inform him that he'll be sleeping in the living room and that, in the morning, we'll go to the boarding house where he'd been staying. I will pay his back rent and pre-pay for two weeks so that he has time to get another job, any job, to get back on his feet.

"I'll make up the couch," I announce as we enter the apartment.

"Can I take a shower before bed?"

Though at first I'm annoyed that he seems to be making himself too comfortable, I realize that he probably hasn't showered for days and, disgusted at the thought of him sleeping on my furniture like that, I consent with, "Sure. Here's a towel."

He's still showering when I've finished setting up his bed, and I'm reluctant to start undressing to go to sleep lest he think that there's the possibility of anything happening tonight. But it will look strange if I'm still standing in the bedroom fully attired when he exits the shower, so I strip down to my underwear and turn on the TV. Lying in bed, I have a direct line of sight into the bathroom. When the sound of the water ceases, he pulls back the shower curtain, reaches for the towel, and steps out onto the bathroom floor to dry off. In that single moment, I realize that whatever charming qualities he did ... does ... did have that we would never be compatible. He is dripping puddles onto the bathroom floor as he runs the towel over his Rubenesque figure. I'm also aggravated that, despite the 50 pounds, he still looks too good for someone who's put all that toxic shit into his body.

Now thankfully dry, he walks into the living room and calls out, "Why do you have all these pictures out?"

Getting up from bed, I come in to make sure he's not handling them too much. "I'm putting all the pictures I have from Stonewall together to document all that happened to re-open the bar. Please be careful with them. I don't have negatives for a lot of them."

Adam gravitates to a pile and pulls up several 5x7s, asking, "What is this from?"

"That's from the Bartender's Ball," I explain. "Every year there's this black-tie event for bar owners and their staff to get together. When we went, it was at the Copa. It's kind of like the Academy Awards for the New York bar community. These are from before the event, when we all got together at Stonewall."

"And this one is at the Copa."

"Jimmy looks wrecked or pissed off or both," Adam says pointing to one photo.

"Yeah, he was. And you can see from that little portion of my face that we were having a fight," I say. "It was supposed to be a great night. He could finally stand among all the bar owners that he had known for years and be proud of what he'd accomplished. Achieving his dream. Joining their ranks. But, he got wrecked on coke or K and I got pissed off that he was ruining it."

"That's too bad."

"Yes, it was," I explain. "Jimmy was far from perfect. Maybe the least perfect person I've known. But for all the flaws, he managed to do something that we all benefit from. And his name has been wiped away. Ripped off the wall. I prefer to remember him during the happy times. Especially in the beginning."

"Who's the strange looking guy with the bandana?" Adam asks.

"He used to come to the bar in the very beginning, before you started coming," I say. "I'm not sure who he really was. He had some affliction, some impediment. He spoke very slowly. Anyway, he was this harmless guy. Always polite. But didn't fit in. He'd just sit there drinking bad red wine and talking about 'Mother' in a way that made us think that he came from some wealthy family. Jimmy was always very compassionate with him. Always brought him a stool to sit on, even if the bar was full, because the guy also had some difficulty walking. When this guy was ready to go home, Jimmy always took him outside and made sure he got him safely into a cab. Jimmy even ran out and got a birthday cake for him one night when he found out it was his birthday."

"That's really sweet."

"Yeah, that's what I choose to remember," I nod, "the kind person always wanting to make people feel comfortable, always wanting people to have a good time."

"It's getting late," I say rising from Adam's makeshift bed. "Time for both of us to go to sleep."

"Thanks for letting me stay here," he replies as I turn off the light and head into my bedroom.

CHAPTER FIFTEEN

What I Did for Love

"Are you feeling OK?" she asks, and I'm temporarily confused. I see that I'm in Gwen Verdon's apartment, on the same couch that I sat on before, but I seem to have entered this episode mid-conversation, rather than on some New York sidewalk.

"Yes, I think I'm fine," I answer. "I just lost my place for a moment."

"Have another sip," she says, pointing to a glass of what looks like lemonade. "You might be dehydrated."

Based on the beverage, our mutually light attire, and the view outside, I can only assume it's summer, but I don't know the year. She starts to resume whatever conversation that we must have been having and I try to listen for clues in what she's saying to orient myself. There are mentions of getting ready to go to California for the movie and I surmise that it's July or August of 1967, just after she's left *Sweet Charity* and just before she goes to train Shirley MacLaine to do her role on-screen. She'll spend several months on the other coast, dutifully working alongside her husband and making the occasional guest appearance on variety shows before returning to New York. I don't know what I've said before in this conversation with her, prior to my landing mid-sentence, so I cautiously let her do most of the talking and inject a few positive affirmations to keep things moving along until I can say something that hopefully isn't redundant or contradictory to what I might have said to her a few minutes earlier in this alternate universe.

Ready to jump back into the pool, I say, "It's a noble thing you're doing."

"I'm doing it because I want to do it," Gwen replies. "What you did for Jimmy, for that bar, keeping it open after he died, that's noble. This is what *I* do."

Apparently, the conversation that I'd missed was more extensive than I'd imagined. I correct her, saying, "No, it wasn't noble. I did it because I wanted to do it. And it wasn't some selfless act. It was a heady experience to run the bar. It fed my ego. I even deluded myself, for a short time, that I'd quit my job and do it full time. And I've never told this to anyone before, but I sort of imagined that people would think of me as this hero figure, stepping up after my partner died to keep his dream alive and to preserve this icon. But I hadn't put in any effort to open it up or keep it afloat for the first couple of years. I was an unworthy successor. I was just a sentinel."

"That's what I still don't get," she says. "This whole thing about it being a gay icon. I've never heard of it."

I've slipped up and I know it. Talking about keeping your lover's bar open is plausible. Referring to it as a gay icon is premature. I try to think of a way to fix my mistake, saying, "Well, it's not an icon really. At least not yet. But there's something special about it that will last and will be remembered. You'll see. Anyway, let's get back to your trip."

"I've already told you," she says with some irritation. "We'll be there for a couple of months. We're going to stay in Westwood. I'm helping Bob get it ready for shooting. It's his film and it's really important to him. Universal has backed it with a big budget and given him free reign, except for that one thing."

"Maybe it's better that you're not in the film," I say, trying to find a way to make lemonade from something that was certainly hurtful to her. "Your Broadway performance is legendary. It will be remembered for years. If you did the film version, that would be the definitive recollection of it, not the Broadway run. And who's to say whether it will translate as well to film and how the critics will receive it. I mean look at *Birdie* or *Forum* or *Gypsy* or *Camelot* ... none of them was as good as the stage version."

She was nodding her head in agreement as I rattle through the shows until she pauses with, "Camelot hasn't come out yet." She's right. In my rush to provide evidence, I've neglected to stick to films that I'm certain came out before our present date.

"Well, yes," I say, "but Vanessa Redgrave singing. That has disaster written all over it."

Gwen laughs, but then returns with, "I have only one thing to say ... *The Sound of Music*," effectively trumping my red-suited heart play.

"Ok. You win that hand," I concede.

"It's not like I'm getting any younger," she turns serious. "Even if I do another big show that gets made into a movie ..."

"Like *Chicago* ..." I interrupt.

"Even if that does happen," she continues, "by then I'll be close to 50 and no one in Hollywood is going to back a picture with a 50-year-old dancer."

"OK. I get it," I reply. "But nothing will ever change the fact that this role is yours. You are Charity and Charity is you. Anyone who does this role in a revival will try to recreate your Charity. Not hers."

That seems to have satisfied her, at least partially, such that she changes the subject, asking, "So, when did you want to take me down and show me your bar? That icon in the making."

Though I'm happy to have gotten out of the no-win conversation about losing the starring role in a motion picture taken from a show that was tailored specifically to her talents, I've now got to explain why I no longer want to take her to Stonewall. "I'm not sure that I want to take you there, at least not in the short term," I reply. "The people who run it now have turned it into a real dump.

You wouldn't see what I see. You wouldn't be able to appreciate what Jimmy did."

"Well, OK," she replies, "I thought you wanted me to see what he had built."

"I did," I explain, "but it isn't that place anymore or yet again. Maybe next year when you get back and I'm feeling less embarrassed about how it looks."

"Sure thing," she stands. "I don't want to be rude, but ..."

"Oh, I'm sorry. I've taken up a lot of your time."

"No, it's fine ..."

"Can I just take a look out on the terrace before I go?"

With that, she opens the living room door to the narrow terrace outside. This portion of the vast terracing, though not park frontage, hangs over 69th Street facing south with an unobstructed view over Central Park and diagonally toward midtown, thanks to the lack of a tall building on the opposite side of the 69th Street. Looking to my left, eastward toward the Park, I see where the other penthouse apartment on this floor starts, just past Gwen's dining room. A heavily scrolled iron gate, housed in a brick-arched surround, separates the spaces. To the right, looking westward, I see a high brick wall that nearly cuts off this roughly 8-foot-wide patch of terrace from the vaster, Olympic-size terrace that wraps around the back of the apartment.

"I probably won't see you for a while," I say. "Can you show me the rest of the terraces before I go? I've never been in an apartment in the city with this much outdoor space. It's unbelievable."

She leads me to the biggest terrace, roughly 2,000 square feet, give or take. It forms an L-shape around the parts of the apartment I have yet to see. I remember an article in which Gwen told famed columnist Earl Wilson, shortly after moving in, that she was going to put an enormous Italian tent back here. That, plus an awning and trees and other greenery would fill the space, and I see that she's kept her word. In the foreground, I marvel at the countryside garden in the sky and in the background, I try to mentally photograph the vistas. With mostly brownstones and low rise apartment buildings filling the streets below, the panoramic view of the Upper West Side is celestial. The skyscrapers that will dot Columbus Avenue and Broadway and beyond have yet to rise. Only God has a better view of New York than I do right now.

"I don't know what to say," I mumble. "It's extraordinary."

"This isn't all of it," she says, indicating that I should follow her to see more. She leads me back into the apartment, through the rotunda. In other apartments, the space would certainly be called a foyer or entry or landing because it is the space one enters the apartment directly from, upon exiting the keyed elevator. But not in a Hearst apartment. In a Hearst apartment, it's a rotunda.

I ask my famous tour guide, "So how big is this place?"

"Three bedrooms, around 3,700 square feet they say."

I see one small bedroom to my left, just off the rotunda and opposite the living room we exited when the tour began. We're heading down a hallway, past the elevator and a maid's room. There's another slightly larger bedroom to the left, and at the end of the hallway we take a quick right and left to enter her master bedroom where I spot a fireplace against one wall and two doors leading out to another huge terrace on the opposite wall. The Hearst touches are still evident. There's a chandelier in the bathroom and what I can only describe as "décor and finishings" from a French chateau in the bedroom. It reminds me of the old oak paneling that Jimmy had installed over the brick walls at Stonewall to give it a gentlemen's pub feel, except that this stuff is authentically antique. For a moment, I picture the scene from *Citizen Kane* where boxes and crates of European art, furnishings, statues, and the like fill the halls of Xanadu and wonder whether that scene was replayed in this room 30-some years ago. As she opens one of the terrace doors to show me the final spot on the tour, I'm amused to see that the furniture that she's brought to this former palace is nothing like what I imagine Marion Davies enjoyed. Her contributions to the space are decidedly normal, not baronial, and suited to any eclectically designed New York apartment.

"This one isn't as big," she says, referring to the roughly 1,000 square feet of outdoor space that I'm now admiring.

I laugh and say, "This is three times the size of my first apartment."

"Mine too," she says with a "If My Friends Could See Me Now" wonder in her voice.

"It must have cost him a fortune to outfit this place the way he did, Hearst I mean," I say as we walk back into her bedroom and then back down the hallway to the elevator.

"It was even more ornate than what you see now," she says. "Charles Van Doren, the quiz guy, had it before me and it was a bit of a mess when I got it. There were exposed electrical wires all over the place. The wallpaper had been solid gold leaf ..."

She continues to describe aspects of the Hearst transformation of the apartment that are still visible as well as those that had been removed, not unlike the way I had painted the picture of Jimmy's renovation of Stonewall to the man-boy. An invisible tear runs down my cheek as I think of how that Italian fashion designer will strip this place of all traces of its former grandeur.

Standing in front of the elevator, I say, "Well, I guess I won't see you for a while." She allows me to give her the slightest of hugs and a kiss on the cheek.

"If you give me your number, I'll call you when I get back," she offers.

Since I can't give her a phone number to reach me, I counter with, "Oh, I'm almost never home anyway. I'll just check in with your doorman from time to time."

"Oh, and thank you again for the beautiful orchid plant," she smiles as I enter the elevator.

Riding down, I feel aglow from the visit. As I walk out into the street, I pause to think of what other places or people I might try to see in whatever remaining time this dream offers. But my destiny pulls me to that place again. I hop in a cab and utter the Pavlovian phrase. On the way to the bar, I daydream within the dream about how both she and I need to serve the ambitions of two imperfect men. She will do it without falter. I, one the other hand, have not completed my duty.

Inside now, on the 51 Christopher half of Stonewall, I scan the room from my vantage point at the bar. Having spotted another customer with a beer bottle, I've ordered the same from a different bartender than the one that previously served me and the man-boy, hoping to fend off as many germs as possible. The room is full of patrons, though that word doesn't suit the crowd. They are, mostly, too poor and bohemian. It's early evening and the mixture of people is far more diverse than last time. There are street kids, drag queens, the occasional professional, and the precursor to what we'll eventually refer to as transgender men and women. Johns Hopkins was ground zero for the first sex reassignment surgeries in 1966, from male to female, but the people here now are unlikely to be able to take that step in their transitioning. The music from the jukebox, as eclectic as the crowd, vacillates from Petula Clark's "Don't Sleep in The Subway" to The Doors' "Light My Fire."

One of the more feminized black men reminds me of a young Marsha. She's hanging out with a Hispanic friend who could easily be Sylvia. An overweight drag queen is using a cane to walk. Though she's barely 35, I assume, she looks like she's had a harder life than people twice her age. Her wig is enormous, almost two feet around her head and kaleidoscopic, as if it was tripping. She catches me staring and makes her way toward me.

"How are ya doin', sweetie?" she asks, taking the empty space next to me. She slurps the last of whatever she's been drinking through a straw and places the empty glass on the bar in front of me. "Care to buy a lady a drink?" she asks in a husky voice that is meant to sound sexy, but isn't.

"I'm doing just fine," I reply and pause just long enough to leave doubt as to whether I'm going to play along. "And, yeah, I can buy you a drink ... that is, if you'll talk with me for a little while."

"Talking is *one* of the things I do best," she responds, again adding an overly theatrical flirtation. "Can I get a bourbon and coke?" she directs to the bartender. "My new friend is buying." The bartender, a twenty-something brunette with short hair parted on the side and requisite porn mustache, hears her and starts to refresh her beverage. I order another beer and pay for both.

"Do you come here a lot?" I ask.

"About as much as I can," she answers, adding, "I don't recall seeing you here before."

"I've only been here once before, but I have a fondness for the place," I reply.

"You live around here?"

"Sort of," I answer, trying to be noncommittal. "Do you mind if I ask you a few questions?"

"Shoot away, sweetie," she replies. "I love to talk about myself."

"Your outfit, the wig and all ... are you trying to impersonate someone or are you creating your own character?"

"Well, *that's* kind of specific," she replies, taken aback by the unusual nature of the question. "What are you getting at, exactly?"

"Oh, just that a lot of drag queens that I know like to create their own characters. I was wondering if you were doing the same thing," I explain, staring at the garish wig.

"You mean this?" she asks pointing to it.

"Well, yeah, it's quite ... well, distinctive," I fumble for a polite way of expressing what I'm thinking.

"Sweetie, I wear this to distract from my face," she says, bursting into laughter, and I join her.

"Do you leave the house dressed up like this or do you change here or somewhere nearby?" I ask, certain that this attire would attract too much attention even for her and even in seen-it-all-before, liberal Greenwich Village.

"I'm mostly dressed when I leave the house," she explains, "but I do add some of the finishing touches in the bathroom."

"And nobody bothers you, walking on the street?"

"Sometimes, but usually not," she becomes serious. "At night, I have to watch out, leaving here late. I can't walk fast, but if some punks try to fuck with me I just start swinging my cane like a crazy woman. That usually scares them off."

I'm treating the discussion as though it was an anthropological discovery, wanting to understand how the less "passable" parts of gay society managed to live in the late '60s in New York. "I'm just curious," I continue my dig, and pointing to the Marsha and Sylvia doppelgängers, "Those people over there, what do you call them?"

"Mercedes and Porsche."

I laugh at the literalness of her answer.

"What's so funny?" she wants to know. "Do you want me to introduce you?"

"Sorry," I apologize, "I didn't mean 'what are their names?' I meant 'what does someone call someone, a man, who presents themselves as a woman?'"

"Sweetie, you sure do ask a lot of strange questions," my subject correctly observes, "and I don't even know your name yet."

"It's Tom ... uh, I mean Jimmy," I blurt out.

"Pretty funny," she rightly notes, "someone who can't even answer what their name is wants to diagnose other people. Well, Tom-Jimmy, if you're trying to classify them, like they're in a zoo or something, then you'd call them transvestites. Me, I just call 'em the girls."

Realizing how smug I must seem, I try to apologize, "I'm so sorry. Really. I just was trying to understand how they think of themselves. Where I come from, people have created all these different words or terms. To distinguish different, ah, sexuality or gender. I was just wondering ..."

"Where are you from, baby?" she interrupts.

Searching for the plausible, I answer, "Well, I was born here in New York, but I've lived in Europe for about five years."

"*So* international," she gushes. "I knew there was something I liked about you. So, what do they call the girls in Europe?"

Finding no harm in making up a story that she'll likely never question or remember, I explain, "Well, men who change into women, physically that is, they're called transgender. They used to be called transsexual, but that term has fallen out of favor. Actually, there's a lot of terms to categorize the spectrum of sexuality and gender. I can't even keep up with all the names to distinguish the different groups."

Finishing her drink, she raises an eyebrow indicating that I'll have to refresh her again if this conversation is to continue. "Hi," I call out to the bartender. "Can my friend and I get another round?"

Having paid the piper, she engages, "Seems like somebody had a lot of time on their hands. I mean why do they need to do that? We're all just people. Who we love or how we want to live ... does everything need a name? Me, I'm just a simple girl. You can call me Marlo, that's my girl name. Or you can call me Tad. Thaddeus is what's written on the birth certificate."

"That's an unusual name," I remark.

"Not really. Marlo's become quite common," she jests. "Yes, Thaddeus gave me all sorts of problems in school, that's why I go by Tad, but I'm actually getting to like it better as I get older. It's was my grandfather's name, but my parents divorced when I was young so I really didn't know him."

"How did you hurt your leg?"

"I fell in the subway ... actually, I was pushed. That's why I lost my job at Bloomingdales. Can't exactly have a gimp selling all that high-priced shit. Anyway, I didn't like that job anyway. Too structured. I'm more of a free spirit."

"What do you do for money?"

"I find nice men like yourself to help me out," she starts her pitch. "I mean I know I'm no beauty, but I do OK. Some men like a big personality."

"Yes, some men do," I say to be agreeable without opening a door. "Do you really know Mercedes and Porsche?"

Without response, Marlo grabs my hand and pulls me toward the dance floor where the subjects of my fascination are half-dancing and half-talking.

"Hey girls," she announces. "This is my friend." Looking at me she asks, "Which of those two names do you want to go by?"

"Jimmy's just fine, thanks," I reply.

"Here's my new friend, Jimmy," she continues. "He's been asking me about you two. But don't get any ideas 'cause he's mine."

The Marsha analogue looks at me with some disdain and dismissively declares, "Well, he's too white for me anyway."

The Sylvia analogue, more inquisitive, asks, "What are you asking someone else about me? Why not come to the source?"

"Hi," I try to recover from this less than desirable introduction. "I was just talking with Marlo and wanted to know more about you two. You're easily the most fascinating people here."

"Oh, is that so?" Marlo feigns being offended.

"I mean you remind me of some of the customers at this bar my boyfriend owned," I say.

"In Europe?" Marlo asks me, and then looking at them says, "Jimmy used to live in Europe."

I wasn't planning to take the ruse in this direction, but it seems easier to go with the flow of what has started rather than to make up something new. I embellish, "Yes, he owned a bar in Europe. In Switzerland. We had a lot of trans-women customers."

"Trans?" Marsha analogue questions.

"Yeah, it was the word that they used to describe themselves," I deflect.

"Is that so?" Marsha analogue remarks. "Seems like you've got some opinions about me and you don't even know me."

"Leave him alone," Sylvia analogue says, coming to my rescue. "He looks nice. I don't think he meant you no harm."

They seem to have assumed good cop / bad cop roles and I take a few more jabs from Marsha analogue while Sylvia analogue defends me, as though I was on trial. I'm not sure where this is leading and I'm just about to bail when the jukebox switches to a new song, just released and climbing the charts as I would come to learn later. Aretha is singing. And spelling. And they both start to lip sync along, putting on an impromptu performance in the middle of the dance floor. It's not as professional as Peter and his Broadway chorus, or Electra, or any of the other performers that would grace the stage at Stonewall for me, but the moment is infinitely more profound.

Before they reach the "sock it to me" finale, I catch, out of the corner of my eye, the man-boy Dick. He's saying something to the bartender and pointing at me. As much as I want to stay, I know this is my eleven o'clock number. I swiftly move toward the 53 Christopher exit, but before I reach the door I spot another familiar face. It's Barry, a friend of Stuart that I meet in the late '90s on Fire Island. As a young man, in this time, he helps Judy Garland with some free legal work during some of her more destitute moments. I'm flustered to see, in real life, the young man that he showed me in photographs of himself and Garland. "Barry, you look amazing," I blurt out, "just like in the pictures."

He is, of course, stunned to have a stranger call him out by name, with such a nonsensical remark. But, before I can explain, I hear a small commotion behind me which I assume is the man-boy and others looking to confront me. I rush through the archway out to Christopher Street and into darkness.

CHAPTER SIXTEEN

Be on Your Own

Adam is decidedly more adept at coffee-making than Ben. I awaken to the wonderful smell of a fresh brew and, throwing on the oversized white robe, head into the living room. There, I see Adam has obviously spent some time rearranging the photos. They are not clustered into the categories that I was trying to create. Instead, they are laid out in a line like the headshots from the opening number of *A Chorus Line*, stretching across the love seat and across the coffee table.

"What are you doing?" I say with mild annoyance at his presumption, but also with fascination.

"You were still sleeping, so I didn't want to wake you up with the TV," he says. "I just started looking through the pictures and tried to put them in a timeline."

"These here," he says pointing to the lineup, "they're interesting. They tell a story about the beginning and the people."

"These here," he says pointing to a pile on the small dining room table just off the front door, "they don't really do anything for me."

I'm impressed with his focus and his selection. "It's interesting," I say sincerely, "but even I don't know exactly what dates all these pictures were taken on. I mean a timeline is supposed to be in chronological order and I can't do that."

Heading into the kitchen to pour a cup of coffee, I hear Adam explaining his choices. "I guess I wasn't so hung up on being exact. Some of them are obviously earlier and some are obviously later. I don't think it matters if they're in the exact chronological order."

Rejoining him in the living room, I challenge his thinking, not because I don't agree with it but in order to see how committed he is to this direction and how he can defend it. It was something that I had learned and gotten used to at my day job. "Some of these photos ... I don't even know who these people are. How can I call them a chronicle of the re-opening of Stonewall if I can't name all the players and can't give an exact date and context?"

"I don't see that as being a big deal," he says with assuredness. "It's not like people look at those photos from the riots in '69 and discount them because all the people aren't named and the exact sequence of events isn't documented."

I'm astounded that someone who has poured so many drugs into their system for so many years is as articulate and thoughtful about this as he is. "Maybe you're right. Maybe I'm trying to make this too perfect. It's probably from the way I've been trained at work. Everything has to be so precise and so perfect. I tend to discard anything that I can't defend six ways to Sunday."

"I was just trying to take it all in and *feel* it," he says. "Once you put it out into the world, other people can add to it, raise their hand to identify the names you don't know, help you correct the timeline. But, if you just keep them locked up here, well, it's not like you're gonna suddenly remember things that you can't remember."

I walk over and hug him, planting a tender kiss on his cheek. There is a second where this embrace could become intimate. He's been talking to me all this time without any clothes on and, despite the girth or perhaps because of it, he looks angelic. But, grabbing his dick would only demean the moment. He's given me clarity and I'm grateful.

"What's going on in these pictures?" he asks, thankfully helping me to return to the task.

"Oh, God," I sigh, "that was during the first year. You can see that it's still a restaurant with all the tables and banquettes. Anyway, this guy had come into the bar and told Jimmy that he was the world's first man to become pregnant. He was dressed as a woman. Maybe I can find a picture of him somewhere." I start to shuffle through the stack of discarded photos, hoping to find a picture of him and his accomplice.

"Here we are. That's the guy — huckster actually — that claimed to be the first pregnant man. And the little blond thing in this picture kissing Mike the bartender ... well, Mike's expression says all you need to know."

What did Jimmy do?" Adam asks.

"Well, that's the funny part," I answer. "Jimmy just went along with it, especially after Miss Thing said that she had numerous TV and news interviews coming up. She wanted a place to hold a baby shower and hold the interviews. She thought Stonewall would be the perfect spot. I thought it was a fraud from the moment I heard about it, but Jimmy didn't seem to care. He was from the 'there's no such thing as bad publicity' school. So, he figured it could only help to build business."

"What happened?" Adam asks.

"Well, nothing really," I continue. "She had promised all this media, she announced that it was a boy before the actual shower, she just kept fanning the flames of this ridiculous story, but everyone went along with it because Jimmy went along with it. We had the shower. There was a decent size crowd, but no media. I guess that Jimmy thought that any excuse for a party was a good excuse. It was like so many of the things that happened there. Way too over the top and nobody called bullshit."

"Are these pictures from the baby shower?" Adam says handing me a small stack.

"No, the balloons here are pink," I explain. "For the baby shower, we used blue balloons because it was a boy. Whoa! Wait a second! Oh my God! I never noticed that."

"What? What are you looking at?" Adam says excitedly.

"On the balloons ... here," I point. "You can just make out that it says 'Gay Liberation 1990' on one side. That's from the night before, actually early morning, of the 1990 Pride Parade. Everyone, all of Jimmy's friends and a lot of the faithful customers, stayed after closing to help blow up all of those balloons. To line Christopher Street with all these pink bouquets. I had totally forgotten. There I am at the bar with Jimmy's friend Cathy and what was his name — oh, yeah Gary. He was a friend of the bar and actually worked there for a bit. All of these people coming out to help Jimmy on that very first Gay Pride Parade after we opened. It was so wonderful!"

"Well, now we know where to place it in the timeline," Adam smiles.

"Yes, yes we do," I beam. "I can't thank you enough. For your help. Say, why don't we get dressed, grab a bite, and go pay your rent at that place you were staying at."

Behind a big smile, there's a sad reflection that I catch in Adam's eyes, as though he was thinking that I'd ask him to stay with me for some period of time. And in that same flash of almost-hidden sadness I do pause for a second to consider it. To help the man who has just unlocked a puzzle for me. But, rationality or selfishness prevails. Having Adam stay with me for some indefinite time would only lead to chaos. He'd quickly end up moving from the love seat to the bed and never find the need to get a real job. And for a time, I'd be happy with that. The leap from the rooming house to a luxury apartment on 12th Street was not in anyone's best interest, I reassured myself.

Dressed, we head out to Joe Jr.'s. The small space is packed on this early Sunday afternoon, so we sit side-by-side at the counter. I enjoy witnessing first-hand the brusque man who normally answers my phone call putting all of the other denizens of the neighborhood through the same paces. With a small crowd waiting at the door and just outside the restaurant for seats, we follow proper protocol and consume our late breakfasts without delay. It's a happy assembly line of dining.

I stop at an ATM and withdraw far more money than I think Adam will need. Heading up 6th Avenue toward Chelsea, I'm dreading seeing the tenement that I will abandon him to. I know that seeing it and merely knowing about it are vastly different. I hope that I can withstand the shock of how bad it will be and remain resolute about not inviting Adam to stay with me.

Somewhere around 18th Street, we head west, eventually crossing 7th Avenue and almost reaching 8th when he leads me up the steps of a row house. Just a half a block away, a similar building is the magnificent home of some lucky family. This building, though, has been carved up into so many units that it feels like we've entered some third world country. The air is stale and the sound of multiple TVs and boom boxes mixes into an unintelligible din.

Because of my discomfort with the surroundings and the fate that I'm bestowing upon Adam, I don't say anything. I merely follow him as his ascends the long staircase that is in serious disrepair. How could such a place exist in New York now? It's an artifact of a squalor that persists despite the multi-million dollar neighboring properties. Rounding the landing, we walk past several rooms with doors ajar. The glimpses that I gather are depressingly the same. Like some gypsy internment camp. I try not to look anyone in the eyes as we ascend the next flight of stairs, but three junkies are stumbling down the staircase, speaking incoherently to each other, and I can't avoid looking into a 20-something's empty eyes.

"Where are we going?" I whisper to Adam as we get to the third floor.

"I want to see if my room is occupied or not," he explains. "I had one of the better rooms with a window out on the street. I'd like to get it back."

"OK," I respond, feeling like shit for the way he's been living and will be living again.

As we get to the last door on the third level, just opposite the staircase going up to another layer of cells above us, Adam stops. "This is it," he says looking at me. He knocks loudly, too loudly for civilized society, but I attribute the aggressive posturing to a societal norm that I don't understand in this place. He raps again loudly and it seems that the flimsy door might just come off its hinges. Instead, we hear the sound of a lock clicking and find a rail-thin boy staring at us. He's naked, with half of a hard-on. We've seem to have interrupted him while he was conducting business, which I conclude because I hear the faint voice of another male asking him to come back to bed.

"When did you move into my room?" Adam interrogates the drugged-out call boy.

"When you didn't pay your fucking rent asshole," the call boy slurs.

"I left stuff in there. I want to get it," Adam insists, pushing his way in.

"What the fuck?" the call boy protests, but he is so strung out that he is unable to put up any resistance.

Adam flicks on a light switch and I take in the space, all 30 square feet of it. There is a window straight ahead of me, just above a filthy mattress upon which an obese middle-aged troll lies face down. But the window is useless because it's covered in a century's worth of grime. To the left, there are some cabinets or built-in closets, which Adam is riffling through. The call boy seems to have accepted that he isn't going to stop Adam from conducting his investigation and resorts to, "Just fuckin' hurry up, will you."

The entire space is packed with junk and filth. I want to flee the room, but I can't abandon Adam, at least not yet. The beast on the bed begins to stir, rotating so that I can see his face and enormous belly. He's trying to see what has interrupted his 30 minutes of freak show pleasure. I want to vomit thinking about him and the call boy grinding away on that mattress. As Adam continues to toss garbage from the closet onto the tiny patch of open floor space in search of his missing belongings, another figure enters the cramped room. Tall and unshaven, this man looks like an angry prison warden.

"What the fuck are you doing back here?" he bellows to Adam.

"I'm getting my stuff. You locked me out before I could get my stuff," Adam says defensively.

"It's not here. When you pay me what you owe me, you can get that shit back," the authority figure commands.

"Where is it?" Adam insists, standing inches away from the man who controls this prison.

"Pay me my 200 bucks," he replies.

Sensing that an escalation of this impasse may impede Adam's return to the hostile hostel, I interject with, "Hey, let me pay what he owes."

Reaching into my pocket, I try not to pull the entire wad of cash out in front of these lowlifes. "Here, 200 bucks, just like you asked," I say, pushing the money in the direction of the nameless warden.

He counts the money and, seemingly satisfied, says, "Come with me you fuckin' loser and get your shit." Adam and I follow him as he heads down the hallway, leaving the room to the call boy and his beastly client. The warden stops short of the stairway down and opens a door to what appears to be a broom closet. I'm amazed that the proprietor hasn't tried to rent the closet to some wretched refuse. As he pulls a cord above our heads, a faint light from a single bulb illuminates the dank closet. Adam spies something familiar and pushes his way past the warden.

"If anything's missing," Adam starts to threaten when I interrupt him to engage the man who runs this horror show.

"Do you have any rooms available to rent?" I ask.

He gives me a what-the-fuck look and I realize that I haven't been explicit enough. "I want to pay for Adam to stay here. Do you have any rooms available?"

He seems inclined to say no, but then, looking at my clothes and general appearance, apparently decides to see what price the market will bear. "I have something on the second floor in the back. It's 250," he says.

Adam, hearing the bartering beginning, stops pulling clothes from the pile of debris and says, "That's 50 more than I was paying. No fucking way."

"Shut up," I say, shutting him down.

"You want a room for your friend, it's 250," the warden says, looking at me with an unsaid, "This is my final offer."

"Let's see it," I reply and he leads me down the staircase.

"C'mon," I say to Adam, "you can get the rest of your stuff in a minute."

On the second floor, the warden opens the door to a room and flicks on a light switch. A boy and a girl flopped on the bed are thrust into view. She is startled by the light but the boy, hypodermic needle still in his arm, is unfazed.

Enraged, the warden grabs the boy by his hair and yanks him off the bed, throwing him into the hallway. The girl screams and struggles off the mattress to help rescue her companion. The warden, grabbing her by the back of her t-shirt, pushes her into the hallway and onto the floor where the boy has landed. "Get the fuck out. Both of you," he erupts.

Adam and I are standing on either side of the door with the pile of bodies between us. My knees start to buckle at the sight of all this and I become sickened with the thought that Adam had sunk so low as to have made this hellhole home. Any thought of rescuing him evaporates as I imagine what things he must have done to land here. There can be no redemption for one who has fallen so far.

Dispassionately, I look to Adam and say, "Take a look," nodding to the interior of his new abode.

Adam sees the absence of feeling in my eyes and steps over the pile of junkies, now whimpering and moaning on the floor, into the room. "There's no window. It shouldn't be 250," he says, trying to restart the negotiation.

"Well, you're not paying for it," I say with loathing, "so the only question is whether this will do or not."

"Yeah, it's fine," Adam replies without looking at me.

I pull the full wad of remaining cash from my pocket and count out $750. "Here it is," I say handing it to the warden. "Three weeks rent in advance."

Looking at Adam, I shake my head in disgust and say, "This is the end of my help. You need to make this work. I won't allow myself to be pulled down by you or anyone else."

With that, I stretched a leg over the junkie pile to make my way down the staircase and out of this place. I don't remember the walk back to my apartment. Twenty minutes later, having banished Adam and his misery from my consciousness, I look at the timeline and make some adjustments.

CHAPTER SEVENTEEN

We Need a Little Christmas

The bed is large and comfortable, but it isn't mine. As the room comes into focus, I'm strangely calm considering that I don't recognize anything and I'm naked under these freshly pressed sheets. There's an old crystal chandelier above me, in the center of the room. The ceilings are very tall, maybe 15 or 20 feet high. The vibe is definitely old-world European, with ornate molding and heavy brocade drapery. Leaning up in the bed, I look around for evidence of another person and, seeing none, quietly slide off the bed to inspect the surroundings for clues.

There's a phone on the end table and, conveniently, it tells me everything. I'm in Room 719. At the Plaza Hotel. Technically, it's Suite 719, but I haven't ventured out of the bedroom yet to verify the size of my quarters. There's something grand and faded about the space, but I'm not sure if the shabbiness is intended or an artifact of some 1960s neglect. In either case, it's certainly not to my taste. I make my way to the bathroom and put on a robe that bears the famous double-P logo, a secondary clue in the triangulation of my location. I know where I am, but not yet *when* I am.

I've decided to make myself at home and head into the living room to survey the remainder of this famous room, immortalized in Neil Simon's comedy. It doesn't look exactly like the room depicted in the late '60s film but, then again, that room was probably created on a soundstage. Still, it has the same feeling, with the tufted sofas and French armchairs. I pull back the heavy curtains to look outside. The General Motors Building is facing me, directly across 5th Avenue. It's winter, judging by the attire of the passersby below. And it's around Christmas, given the small smattering of lights and wreaths that I can spot from this post.

I head over to a table and pick up the phone. I've decided to dial the operator to ask about getting a *New York Times*, my preferred method of orienting myself. She's apologizes for there not being a copy of the paper outside my room and I ask her to hold as I run to the door to find what was always there, a massively thick Sunday *Times*. Excusing my mistake, I thank her and she wishes me a Merry Christmas at the same time that I scan the front page of the paper. It's December 24, Christmas Eve 1967.

The thought of spending Christmas Eve in New York is both exciting and depressing. I won't be with family or friends, and based on what I've learned previously about theatre schedules in the 1960s, the likelihood of there being a Broadway show playing tonight is slim. Feeling far too comfortable considering I have no idea how I'm going to pay for this room when checkout comes, I pick up the phone and order some coffee and some eggs from room service. I then call the front desk to try to tease out what my checkout date is at the Plaza Hotel.

"Good day, sir," the gentleman answers. "How may I help you?"

"I'd like to ask if it might be possible to extend my stay by another day?" I ask, not wanting to sound like an idiot by asking for the information directly.

"So, you would like to check out on the 27th?" the man asks after flipping through some pages. I smile at hearing *that* sound rather than the clicking of a keyboard.

"Not necessarily," I backpedal. "I just wanted to ask if it were possible to extend my stay if that should become necessary. I didn't know how booked the hotel was."

"It wouldn't be a problem sir," he confirms. "Just let us know as soon as you can if your plans change.

Relieved that I don't have to check out today, or tomorrow for that matter, and have to find far more cash to pay the bill than I surmise will be in my pocket, I start pulling apart the sections of *The Times* to see how I might spend the holiday. I could try going to midnight mass at St. Patrick's, something that I had never done, or perhaps, I'll take the path of my Jewish friends and go see a movie and eat Chinese food. The paper is enormous. Far more substantial than the Sunday *Times* that I am acquainted with. The Arts & Leisure section isn't called that yet. I find the movie and theatre listings in a combined Sections 2 and 10, which seem to have been merged in light of the holiday. The cover of this merger carries a headline — "At Christmas Remember the Neediest." Below, I see several short stories of needy families, a subsection of 100 cases that *The Times* has published for the holidays. Each story has a case number and there are instructions on how to help these people and others through the Catholic, Jewish, and non-denominational organizations listed at the bottom of the page. I glance at a few of the cases and feel guilty about excommunicating Adam.

Though it takes entirely too long for room service to deliver such a simple breakfast, the coffee and eggs are tasty. While eating, I scan the theatre listings to see what new shows have opened since my last episode and which have closed. Again, there is an embarrassment of riches on page D7 that I barely comprehend.

Most appropriate is the listing for the opening of *Plaza Suite*, scheduled for February 14 and starring George C. Scott and Maureen Stapleton. There are other pre-announcements for shows set to open in the new year, including *The Prime of Miss Jean Brodie* with Zoe Caldwell, Arthur Miller's *The Price* with Jack Warden and Arthur Kennedy, and *I Never Sang For My Father* with Hal Holbrook.

Among the shows that have opened since my last visit is a limited run of Lillian Hellman's *The Little Foxes*. Bizarrely, there are no actors named in the listing, and since I've seen the show, or will see the show to be accurate, with Elizabeth Taylor in the '80s, I have no interest in this production. Of great interest is a show called *More Stately Mansions* with Ingrid Bergman, Arthur Hill, and Colleen

Dewhurst. That would certainly be an acting tour de force, even if the show itself was shit. But, as expected, Ingrid Bergman will not be giving up her Christmas for my benefit. Melina Mercouri is in *Illya Darling*, but not today. Never on Sunday.

Pearl Bailey is the new Dolly, Lloyd Bridges and Betsy Palmer have moved into *Cactus Flower*, *Cabaret* is still running with its original cast and, thankfully, Angela is still Mame. That would be the show I would kill to see, but it won't be running again until Tuesday, after my presumed checkout at the Plaza Hotel and, certainly, this episode. But, as if by divine intervention, there is something playing tonight at the Palace. It's a musical I've never heard of called *Henry, Sweet Henry* with Don Ameche. It must be awful if they've resorted to playing on Christmas Eve which none of big hits has had the need to do. Michael Bennett, long before becoming Fosse's only real competition — but not really — in the 1970s, is listed as the choreographer. That alone makes it interesting. Well, that and the fact that it is at the Palace and I have no other options, save for films.

I check the pockets of my clothes and find a still sizeable sum of cash, just over $40. I'll be able to get a ticket, maybe some dinner, and still have some money left for drinks afterward. There's nowhere near enough to pay the bill that I expect upon leaving the Plaza, but I choose not to worry about that. If the theatre gods have placed me here, they must have figured that out for me. It's at this point, while still casually leafing through the paper, that I spot it. I'm embarrassed that I haven't remembered it on my own. On page D4, near the bottom, a small ad calls out Judy Garland's opening of the Felt Forum at Madison Square Garden tomorrow night. The top ticket price is $12, something that would be affordable even with seeing Don Ameche tonight. But I quickly grow fearful that all of the Judy fans will have gobbled up the best seats long ago and that I'll need to pay a scalper, if they exist in this time, something far more.

I call the phone number, PLaza7-8870, at the bottom of the ad to ask about ticket availability. A polite but unhelpful lady tells me that there are no $12 tickets available, but still a few $10 tickets for tomorrow's opening and a good amount of $8 tickets. The absence of mental floor plan of the Felt Forum makes any further discussion with her about the available seats pointless. I don't even know if I'll still be here tomorrow, given that all previous episodes have concluded within a single day. Trying to remain hopeful that I'll have my first overnighter, I decide to spend the afternoon in my lush environs. I catch a couple of movies on Channel 5. *David Copperfield* with Lionel Barrymore and W.C. Fields is a classic. *The Silver Chalice*, a pseudo-religious film with Paul Newman, is a mistake. Both for Paul and myself.

Around five o'clock I order some room service dinner instead of going out, to preserve as much cash as I can. By seven o'clock, I'm itching to head down to the Palace even though show time isn't until 8:30. I walk down 5th Avenue to see the store decorations, the Rockefeller Christmas Tree, and St. Patrick's Cathedral. At this late hour on Christmas Eve, there aren't the crowds and jostling that I know. It's serene. At Rockefeller Center, there are no white wire angels blowing brass horns lining the promenade as I expect. Instead, in their place are oversized characters dressed in Dickensian period attire. They look like they're made of white plaster or fiberglass, but I can't be sure. The female figures are dressed in ball gowns, welcoming the tourists and locals to an imaginary Christmas gala. Male figures play musical instruments. And above the heads of each of these lavish characters is a white tiered chandelier with long tapered electric candles. The overall effect is quite impressive. For a moment, I feel as though I've just been welcomed into a magnificent Christmas Ball in Victorian England. Just beyond, the tree is even more magical than I imagined and somehow more authentic than what I remember from my time. It's as tall and full as any I have ever seen in this spot, but the lights aren't so "electronic." They burn steadily in primary colors with an analogue, retro comfort. I want to spend more time, but the theatre calls and I know, or hope, that I can come back to see it again tomorrow. Lord & Taylor, just down the road, doesn't disappoint either. This year, the theme for their legendary windows is old Vienna. There's a miniature recreation of the Vienna State Opera replete with a choir of altar boys singing carols. In another window, I watch the rhythmic movement of the lord and lady dolls dancing through the Schonbrunn Palace. *Do I Hear a Waltz* accompanies in my mind. As per my Sondheim-y tendencies, everything's suddenly Viennese.

My lingering causes a delayed arrival at the Palace. Just after eight o'clock, I stand at the box office window and purchase a front mezzanine ticket for just under $9. Inside, I find the theatre only half full, that's if I'm being generous. The usual audiences for a Broadway show have abandoned *Henry, Sweet Henry* tonight. The Gays apparently don't idolize Don Ameche and are resting up for Judy tomorrow night. The Jews are either at the movies or in a Chinese restaurant, or so I've been told. The Suburbanites are nestled in their own faux Rockwell Christmas illustrations. And the Tourists are in Chicago or Cincinnati or wherever.

Some 30 minutes after the overture, I make my exit. It's just too painful. The show is bad and I have no patience for seeing this cast desecrate Gwen's stage. Times Square is eerily quiet as I hail a cab. I've wasted almost $9, money that I may need tomorrow to scalp a ticket to Judy. But I'll waste a bit more and go down to Stonewall. I've never spent a Christmas Eve at Stonewall. The thought is depressing. A bar will draw lonely souls on any given night. On a night where everyone is supposed to be in the company of loved ones, the crowd is bound to be pitiful. But I have no place else that I want to be.

I'm surprised to see Angelo at the front door and greet him by name. He recognizes me from my surveying visit a year ago, before the bar opened, and allows me to enter without signing the guest book or paying the cover. Apparently, my name dropping had a lasting impression and I'm grateful to have saved a few dollars for tomorrow night's scalping. I had half expected the man who I assumed was Ed Murphy to be lording over the front door tonight given the likelihood of street kids spending their Christmas Eve here and his corrupt Father Flanagan reputation. But as I make my way into the 51 Christopher side, my instincts are proven right as I see him holding court with three down on their luck young men in a bizarro-world *Boys Town*. He's seated and they're all standing around him at the far end of the bar, toward the back of the room in front of the roughly 20-by-40-foot dance floor.

Opting to steer clear of that unspeakable union, I find a stool at the mid-point of the lengthy bar. There are no other patrons to my immediate left or right, which suits my preference for not engaging with the lonely boys tonight. The nearest bartender is a black-haired beefy type who reminds me of Gary, the quiet and shy bartender that worked for Jimmy and me during the revival. He's wearing a black guinea tee to show off his uncommon-for-1967, gym-swollen upper body. He makes his way toward me and our eyes connect in a don't-I-know-you-from-somewhere uncertainty.

"What'll you have?" he asks hesitantly, as though there's another question that he's really wanting to ask.

"I'd like a gin and tonic. But if you don't have any clean glasses handy, I'll take a beer," I reply honestly.

He smiles knowingly and reassures, "I'll make sure your glass is clean. Promise."

After pouring the drink and delicately placing it in front of me on a cocktail napkin, as though we weren't actually in the filthiest bar I'd ever been in, he asks, "Can I have your ticket?"

"Angelo didn't give me any," I reply. "I know him from when I was doing an inspection of the bar last year for Mr. Duell. So he didn't charge me or give me any tickets. I'll just pay cash, if that's OK."

"Uh, wait a second. I'll be back in a minute," the beefy Gary analogue responds as he heads down to the far end of the bar. To my horror, I see him saying something to the Flanagan figure, who leans forward to look down the bar at me. He says something to the bartender, looking none too pleased at the interruption.

"It's OK. There's no charge," Gary analogue announces upon coming back to me.

I lift the glass and, looking back toward Flanagan, give a non-smiling nod to acknowledge the largess. Then, looking at Gary analogue, I put a $5 bill on the bar, saying, "Thanks, I appreciate it. This is for you. What's your name?"

"Kurt," he responds.

"Well, hey Kurt. I'm Jimmy. Merry Christmas," I offer.

"Merry Christmas to you too."

"It's a bit busier here, and happier, than I expected," I note.

He gives me a slightly perplexed look, but acknowledges part of my statement with, "Well, yeah, it is a pretty good crowd."

"Sorry," I explain, "I had just assumed that there wouldn't be many people here tonight and those that were here would be a little on the depressing side, you know, considering it's a holiday."

"Oh. Well, everyone seems to be having a good time," Kurt observes.

"I just kind of figured that people would want to be home with family tonight. You know, like in the movies," I add.

"I think we're all here because we want to be," Kurt explains. "I don't want to be with my family. Tonight or otherwise. That's why I moved to New York." With that, Kurt moves down the bar to take an order from a 20-something couple, best described as a 1960s Will and Grace.

The dance floor behind the *Boys Town* crowd is rather full, as is the 53 Christopher side of Stonewall that I can see through the opening in the wall. Most everyone I see seems like they're celebrating, not despondent or lonely, and I'm filled with a Christmas glow that I hadn't expected. I'm somewhat sad that I don't see Marlo or Mercedes or Porsche, but relieved that I don't have to explain my previous quick exit under pursuit. Kurt makes his way back to me and I think he genuinely likes me. Either that or he thinks he should court favor with someone who has been deemed a non-paying friend of the bar.

"So, where did you come from, originally?" I ask.

"A small town in Pennsylvania," he responds without further specificity. "You from around here?"

"I grew up in Queens. We moved to Jersey when I was a teenager," I explain, trying to be as brief as possible. "After school, I moved into Manhattan and that's where I've been ever since."

"I don't remember seeing you here before," Kurt mentions with a bit of a question mark.

"I haven't been here lately. But, I'm well acquainted with the place."

"Can I ask you something?" Kurt starts and I nod in the affirmative. "If you thought that we were going to be empty tonight and it was going to be depressing, why did you come?"

"Oh, I don't know. This place is important to me. It's got a lot of ghosts from my past hanging around. Besides, I didn't have anywhere else to spend Christmas," I admit.

"Not speaking with your family either?" Kurt asks, thinking that we are kindred spirits.

Though it isn't true, I won't refute his assumption. "Something like that. I'm just glad I did come here tonight," I smile.

"Me too," Kurt responds in kind. "Where's your place?"

"I'm over on 12th Street."

"Cool. I'd really like to spend the night with you," Kurt begins his come-on. "I'm supposed to work until closing, but maybe you have enough influence to get me off early." We both chuckle at the lascivious way he says "get me off." Kurt sees that my glass is almost empty and, without request, takes it for a refill.

"I don't think I have that much clout," I say, "and I don't mind waiting for you to get off."

Kurt places the refreshed drink down in front of me. "Sure," he says unconvincingly. "But, I'd really like to have some better hours here. The manager doesn't know what he's doing. Maybe you could put in a good word. I could run circles around him."

Without changing expressions, I say, "I'd be happy to see what I can do."

I realize that, for whatever modicum of sincerity there may be in Kurt's flirtation, all of this is just a lie. A means for Kurt to improve his standing here because he thinks I have some influence with the guys that run Stonewall. I can't say I blame him, given that he's a good 15 years younger than me and in great physical shape. But the bluntness of the transaction, the lack of any finesse, is what galls. As Kurt goes to refill another patron's glass, I mull the possibilities. I can continue the transaction and seek my satisfaction in bed knowing that he won't be getting any advantage here for his efforts. That could be a just retribution for the affront. Or I could shut him down totally and make him think that his offending me will result in some unintended consequences from the powers that be.

In the midst of the internal debate, one of the street kids that had been with Flanagan makes his way toward me. He stops short, maybe four feet away from me, and just stands there alongside the bar. He's wearing an old flannel shirt over another shirt and worn, dirty jeans. He's carrying a tattered backpack that surely contains all his worldly possessions. His sandy brown hair is disheveled and there's some stubble and a few bruises on his pudgy, Iowa-handsome face. He is neither talking to or looking at anyone, just standing silently and bearing the international sign of someone looking for a place to crash — an open fly.

Out of a sense of pity or in a desire to rescue him from Flanagan, I decide that I will take him, not Kurt, back to the Plaza. I chug the remainder of my gin and tonic, stand up, and call out to Kurt who is still tending to another customer, "Hey man, sorry but I just gotta go now."

Kurt flees the other customer mid-sentence, anticipating that something has gone awry. Coming up to the space where I had been sitting, he says, "Is something wrong?"

Standing in front of the street kid, I look back toward Kurt and just shake my head from side to side without saying anything, but saying everything. Then, facing the lost soul, I say, "You're coming with me. To someplace nice. And warm."

I grab his hand and lead him out of Stonewall without pause, bidding Angelo a Merry Christmas as we exit and walk to 6th Avenue. In the cab ride uptown, my street urchin says nothing. Somewhere north of 24th Street he takes my right hand and starts to put it into his open fly. I pull my hand away and, not wanting him to feel rejected, plant a gentle kiss on his cheek and say, "Don't worry. We're good."

Thankfully, there's virtually no one, except a single doorman, standing outside The Plaza or along the path we need to take to get to the elevator up to Suite 719. He's still uncannily silent, given that I've just taken him through a fancy hotel lobby and into an equally overdone suite. With the door to the suite closed and locked, I take a breath of relief that we've gotten here without incident.

"You can put your backpack down anywhere you like," I tell him.

He removes it and puts it down beside him on the floor in the vast living room. Without even scanning the room to take in the environment, he continues to stand there not looking left, not looking right. Just staring straight ahead.

I start to grow a little anxious that he may have some mental issue and that my decision to bring him here could have been very flawed. I walk over to him, standing right in front to break the blank gaze he has looking toward the window. "What's your name?" I ask gently.

He pauses and then very quietly says, "Michael. My name is Michael."

"Hi Michael," I reply with equal quietness. "My name is Tom."

I take him by the hand again and lead him to the bathroom. Turning on the shower, I look back at Michael and say, "Maybe you'd like to take a nice hot shower?"

Without response, he starts to take off the two shirts and the worn, dirty jeans. At about five foot eight and 180 pounds, he's pudgy for a kid that presumably has nothing. His body is completely covered with hair. Front and back. Thick golden hair. He resembles a woodland creature of sorts.

"Are you hungry?" I ask, but he doesn't answer. Instead, he steps into the shower and begins to wet himself down.

"When you're done, you can put on this robe," I say as I leave the bathroom.

I debate ordering up some room service, but decide against it given his lack of enthusiasm to my question. I pull back the sheets in the bedroom and put on the TV. It's almost eleven, and I catch the very end of *Mission Impossible*, waiting for Michael to finish getting showered. After 10 minutes or so, he appears at the bedroom door wearing the Plaza robe. I get up from the bed and walk over to him.

"Did that feel good?"

He nods his head up and down and reaches to start unbuttoning my shirt. I'd rather that he not undress me because I don't want this to be a transaction. That was Kurt's intention, not mine. But, seeing as how I will need to get undressed anyway and not wanting to create more awkwardness than there already is, I stand there completely still as he removes my clothes.

Fully undressed, I look at him and say, "Thank you, Michael."

He reaches, as if to grab my penis, but I step backward. "Let me get my robe," I say.

Coming back into the bedroom from the bathroom, I see that he's still standing in the same spot. I grab him by the hand and lead him to the bed where we both lay down as the Channel 2 newscaster talks about Christmas services in New York and around the world. Sometime before the end of the news, he rolls over toward me and tries to kiss me. I push him away.

"It's late," I say to him. "Let's just go to sleep," and with that we drift off watching Roberta Peters, the Metropolitan Opera soprano, sing holiday music on a Christmas Eve special.

I awaken before Michael on Christmas Day and slip into the living room to call room service. By the time I return, he is awake and smiling.

"Merry Christmas," Michael says.

"Merry Christmas to you too," I say. "I've ordered us some breakfast. You must be hungry. I know I am."

"Yes, please," he replies and then heads to the bathroom. He's still in the bathroom when breakfast is delivered.

As I'm signing the check for our Christmas morning feast, Michael steps into the living room stark naked and sporting a full hard-on. I glance toward the Plaza employee, who's had the unfortunate luck of working on Christmas and now is greeted by a furry beast fully aroused, expecting the worst.

"Enjoy your breakfast gentlemen," he says without missing a beat and exits the room.

I run into the bedroom to retrieve Michael's robe and, bringing it back, say, "There's no time for that now. Breakfast is getting cold."

We eat in silence. Michael polishes off everything on his plate and consumes the bread basket bounty as well. He also enthusiastically consumes a large lunch that I order a few hours later. I tell him that I'll be needing to go out later, to see a show, and that I can't take him with me. But, I explain that he's welcome to come back to sleep here again tonight after the show and I tell him to wait for me in front of the General Motors Building around midnight. He nods to indicate that he's understood what I've said, but when I come out of the bathroom after taking a shower later that afternoon, he's gone.

Around six o'clock, I head down to Madison Square Garden in search of a scalped ticket to tonight's show. For a good 45 minutes, I patrol the 8th Avenue side of the building, occasionally going down 31st and 33rd Streets, to find someone who looks like they may be selling a ticket. The box office still did have seats available and that will be my last recourse if nothing better is available outside. Out of frustration, I decide to park myself at the corner of 8th and 31st Street under the supposition that someone exiting a cab from downtown will land there.

I do see a number of gay men exiting cabs every few minutes from my vantage point, but they all walk with determination toward the Felt Forum entrance indicating that they're not parting with any tickets tonight. The last cab I spot, though, deposits some familiar faces. The 20-something couple at Stonewall are making their way toward the theatre when I intercept them. He is wearing a black turtleneck and black pants. She has a mod dress on that's a little too short for her.

"Hi," I interrupt them. "You guys were at Stonewall last night, weren't you?"

They're both a little startled, but she looks at me with some recognition. "You were they guy who took that dirty kid out. Boy, were they mad at you when they realized what you did."

"Huh, what do you mean 'mad at me'?" I ask.

"The bouncer guy at the bar," she explains, "he wasn't happy that you took that kid out of there."

"He's a fucking pig," her young male companion interjects.

"Yes, he is," I agree. "I couldn't let that kid go home with him. I just felt so bad that that was going to be his only option if I didn't do something."

"Are you going to see Judy?" the waifish boy in black asks.

"I want to but I'm having a hard time getting a good ticket," I say with self-pity. "I just have to see Judy up close."

The girl, who I now confirm is the straight girlfriend of Mr. All-in-Black, looks at her companion and says, "Why don't you take him to see Judy tonight?"

"What do you mean, you don't want to go with me?" he answers.

"No, but I've seen her before with you and this guy did something really nice last night and you hate that jerk who keeps trying to get you to go home with him and ...," she rambles, adding more and more reasons as to why he should take me inside to see Judy Garland.

"You're sure?" he asks her.

"I'm sure," she says. "I can meet you later at your place."

With that, the switch is agreed to by all parties and I walk to the Felt Forum entrance with my new best friend, Jeremy. I don't want to be ungrateful, but I am concerned about where we're going to sit and I'm about ask him when I see him pull out the tickets and hand one to me. It's a $12 ticket. Row C. Hallelujah. Get happy.

The stage includes a section that juts out into the audience, not unlike the staging that was used for the Judy Garland Show on TV, and some runway lights that illuminate the edges. The crowd couldn't be more adoring. Several have brought Christmas-wrapped gifts and flowers for their queen.

Jeremy and I talk, exchanging some getting-to-know-you niceties, but I'm really focused on scanning the crowd to find the young version of my friend Stuart. He's told me about this night a dozen or so times and the possibility of seeing him here is almost too good to be true. I'm not sure what I'll do if I see him here, at 20 years of age. The 8:30 start time has come and gone by more than a half hour. Not unexpected for a Judy show. It's frustrating because I've run out of polite conversation with my benefactor Jeremy and the surveillance has yielded nothing positive.

Some 45 minutes late, the star finally makes her appearance. She's wearing a reddish cocktail dress, not unlike the color of the PALACE letters above the marquee, that lands just above her knee.

It's trimmed at the bottom and on the sleeves with matching color feathers. It's flouncy and bouncy, like much of the crowd that hands her Christmas presents during the first songs. She opens with a Happy Holiday medley, the only non-repertoire piece during the evening. The sound is too low and muddled and Judy's voice is not quite there yet. But her fans don't care. They are ravenous.

As the first act proceeds, the voice gets stronger and the audio becomes better, but it's still not top form. I've only seen two other mega-singers perform live, Sinatra, past his prime but still a commanding force with Liza and Sammy by his side, and Streisand in June of 1994 from the 10th row of the Garden. She, at full command of her powers, was something to behold. This Judy is a shadow of her once staggering self. The only thing I can think of is why I can't go with Stuart to Tony Bennett's house later to hear her in full voice. Jeremy comments that she's getting better as the evening unfolds, and I want to tell him, "you have no idea how much better she'll get as the evening unfolds."

The second act carries a lot of favorites: *Zing Went the Strings of My Heart, Ol' Man River, Rockabye Your Baby, Battle Hymn of the Republic,* and *Over the Rainbow.* The white-beaded pants suit that she wears for this set is more typical Judy. The cheers and screaming of her most ardent admirers make the whole scene feel more like a revival meeting than a concert. Still, I'm happy for having had the privilege of seeing it.

I tell Jeremy that I'm profoundly grateful for his generosity, but I excuse myself abruptly as the show concludes so that I can run outside to find Stuart before he heads off to the private performance at Tony Bennett's house. On the street, I spot a limousine idling. Something in my gut tells me to stay there and wait, rather than running about to search for him in the still exiting crowd. Maybe 20 minutes go by before I see a group of four leave the theatre and walk toward the waiting limo. They stand out because two of them are children, Lorna and Joey. The other two include a young woman that I don't recognize and a young man that I do. He's wearing a white turtleneck and dark coat. I want to run over to him, to get a closer look and maybe to say something. But, I stand frozen, like Michael in the Plaza suite. Before getting into the passenger side door, Stuart's head turns and faces me. We're a good 50 feet apart, but I get the feeling that he has seen me, just for an instant, staring at him. He won't remember the stranger staring at him on this night 30 years later when he tells me the story. But I won't forget it.

Back at the Plaza, I stare out the window to see if Michael is in front of the General Motors Building. I wait until two o'clock before turning out the lights and going to bed, even though I knew all along that he wouldn't be coming back.

CHAPTER EIGHTEEN

Everything's Coming Up Roses

Meetings at work have gone very late for a Friday, so I get to my apartment at the same time Stuart arrives for our weekly get-together. We walk into my apartment, and I go to the bedroom to remove my suit and change into normal clothing.

"What happened that you're so late tonight?" Stuart asks as he turns on the TV.

"Somebody got a bug up his ass about something and thought that keeping us at work past six o'clock, reaming us out, would send the right message."

"Oh, the big corporate world. There's more guys waving their imagined big dicks there than there was at The Anvil," Stuart notes correctly.

Laughing, I agree, "Yep. All we're missing is leather and the smell of musk."

"Any new things I should see?" Stuart inquires in our established routine of sharing new theatre finds.

"No, nothing new but I did want to get your opinion on something," I mention as I pull a rolled-up t-shirt out of a cabinet. "I picked this up at the 10th anniversary concert of *Into The Woods*. There wasn't really any great memorabilia being auctioned that night, but it was one of the most incredible nights I've had."

As I unroll the commemorative t-shirt to show Stuart, he starts to suggest an answer to the question I've yet to ask. "Well, you could display the front face in a shadow box. I've seen that done quite nicely. But it really isn't up to the quality of the rest of your collection."

"Yeah, I know," I say. "But the performance and the after-party were just so amazing. I got to spend a few minutes talking alone with Sondheim. I'll never forget telling him what his work meant to me. I must have sounded like a blithering idiot, but he just was so nice and personable. He made it seem like he really cared about what I was telling him."

"Well, unfortunately, you don't have a picture of that and you can't shadow box a memory," he notes. "Besides, you have other Sondheim pieces that are really remarkable. Personally, I wouldn't try to display the t-shirt. Just keep it tucked away for yourself."

"You're right," I say. "It was such a special show. The songs about people leaving you. People dying. Not being alone. A story about AIDS wrapped up in familiar fairy tales. Just brilliant."

"Yes, that's why he's Stephen Sondheim and we're not," Stuart says as he stands and puts on his coat.

We walk around the corner to La Dolce Vita for that deliciously unremarkable dinner. A little cocktail conversation about some galleries that Stuart has been to during the week is intermingled with plans for going to an autograph show next month. During appetizers, I decide to tell Stuart about my latest adventure.

"So, I didn't want to mention this on the phone when we spoke because I wanted to see the expression on your face when I told you," I begin.

"Oh, this sounds portentous."

"It's nothing bad," I reassure. "I had another dream. At least I think it's a dream. But we can debate that."

"What are you talking about?" he says, perhaps for the first time not being able to predict what I'm going to say.

"I was in New York at Christmas," I begin, "in 1967. I was staying at The Plaza, though I didn't actually have to check out and pay the bill."

"Did you see Gwen again?"

"No, no Gwen," I answer. "I ended up going to see a show with Don Ameche at the Palace but it was so bad that I left before intermission. I went down to Stonewall. But that's not the important part."

"Go on."

"The next day, Christmas Day," I explain, "I went to the Felt Forum to see the Judy Garland concert."

Stuart's eyes light up. "Oh, this is going to be good. Now, you're meeting Judy Garland."

"No, no," I stop him. "I saw the show. It was just as you described. Judy wasn't in top form, but it was good. But the remarkable thing was that I saw you. Going into the limo with Joey and Lorna."

"Why is that so remarkable?" he says looking confused.

"Well, because I really saw you," I insist. "You even glanced at me as you were entering the limo."

"Tom, I've told you that story a thousand times," he cuts me off. "Of course you think you saw me because I told you all about that night."

"Yeah, yeah, I know," I say. "But you never described it with the level of detail I saw."

"I think you may be losing it," he says affectionately. "Now you're making it sound as though you think these things have really happened. I really love that you're having these theatre fantasies, but let's not get carried away. They're dreams."

As dinner arrives, I prepare to unleash the proof that he's yet to find in my explanation. "I understand what you're saying. But you were wearing a white turtleneck. How could I have known that?"

Stuart pauses, as if to mentally scour the pictures of that night in his mind. "Yes, I was wearing a white turtleneck." Another pause follows before he says, "I must have told you that at some point."

"Stuart," I say confidently, "just now you yourself had to think back to what you were wearing that night. It wasn't top of mind or an integral part of the story you've told me about that night. It's not a detail that you would have thought to share because the important details — what the concert was like, what Tony Bennett's house was like, who was at the after-party, what Judy sang, the fact that they ordered in pizza — all of those things are details that you've told me because those are the important things about that experience. Just like you've never told me that you got into the front passenger seat, next to the driver."

Stuart's face turns to shock. I've just hit him with another detail of that remarkable evening that even he knows he's not told me before. "Holy shit," he mutters. "That's right. Nancy got into the back with the kids and some packages. I jumped in the front. I'd almost forgotten that."

There's a profound silence for the next few minutes as we look at each other and half-heartedly finish our entrees. Though I knew what I was intending to tell him tonight, I honestly hadn't fully realized the implication of it until the words came out of my mouth and I saw his reaction. We skip dessert, but order espresso to provide more time to digest both the meal as well as what's been discussed.

"I don't know what to say," Stuart remarks. "I'm literally speechless."

"Yeah, me too," I manage to utter. "This …. well, this changes everything. If it happens again, going back, I'll know that it's real. I don't know what I'll do. I'm a little scared."

"What are you scared of?"

"When I thought it was a dream," I start to find the words, "it was safe, fun, harmless. Now what am I supposed to do?"

"About what?"

"Am I supposed to *do* something?" I ask out loud though to no one in particular. "When I used to say that I wanted to do something about AIDS, to warn people or to stop it, that was when I assumed this was all a fantasy. Now, I'm confused as to why this is happening to me."

"I need another drink," Stuart announces.

"Me too," I agree. "Can we go to Stonewall instead of going back to watch *SVU*?"

"I don't know," he answers. "You usually hook up with Buddy or your other friends and disappear. That's why I don't go with you there anymore. I'm long past my partying days."

"I'm sorry. I promise I won't do that tonight. I just think we need to think about this more and get a drink. And that place is what's driving this. It's calling."

Stuart agrees and the check is paid. As we walk toward the bar, some backpedaling ensues. "I'm still not sure that you should be treating this as ... supernatural or whatever," Stuart begins. "It's entirely possible that I did mention these things to you and that we both forgot that I did. Or that I've forgotten the details and your description of what I was wearing and where I sat in the limo just happened to seem correct. I don't know."

"That's a lot more comfortable to think about than the alternative."

We enter Stonewall and head directly to the nearest open space at the bar, avoiding the contingent of bar friends and others that might interrupt. Carlos brings two glasses of Amaretto on the rocks.

"Let's not debate the reality of this," I say, "or deal with it right now. Help me think of what I should do in the next dream or episode or whatever we should call this."

"Ok," he concurs, "but that would depend upon what day it is when you go back and who you meet, wouldn't it?"

"Yes. I guess so. But, so far, the timeline's been advancing a few months at a time. So, I'd assume that next time would be in 1968."

"The riots don't happen until '69," he continues the thought, "so, something else must be happening in 1968 that you're meant to see. Can you think of what it might be?"

"I don't know," I continue, "maybe I go to other shows, meet other people."

"What is Gwen doing in '68?" Stuart asks.

"The only thing I can think of is that she's back in New York helping out with the filming of the sequences of the movie that are shot on location. You know ... down on Wall Street, at Yankee Stadium, at Lincoln Center, in the Park," I say, listing as many scenes as I can remember from the film.

"So, maybe that's where you meet again," Stuart suggests.

"But what am I supposed to do if that happens?"

"Tom," Stuart answers with some frustration, "I don't know what to tell you. I don't think you can plan this. And, so far, you haven't had to. So, just see what happens and go with it. You'll know what to do."

Buddy and a few of the other bar friends make their way over to us. Stuart and I can't continue the conversation and, just as well, are exhausted from what we've already discussed. He says goodnight to everyone and leaves me with the gang.

I have another Amaretto, hoping that staying with an after-dinner drink, instead of switching to a cocktail, will remind me to go home sooner rather than later. Buddy is excited to tell me that he's spoken with some of his friends at Broadway Cares and amfAR and that they suggest donating whatever I have to The Center.

"They started a gay archive in 1990," he says, "and it sounds like just the kind of place to house your collection of photos."

"Thanks," I reply, "that really helps. Maybe I'll go over tomorrow to check it out."

"Have you seen Ben yet?" Buddy asks.

"No, why?"

"He's in the back room sniffing around for someone to hook up with," Buddy informs me. "Or, should I say, he's looking for a sugar daddy."

"Well, you are the right age," I tease, "and I've always said you're sweet."

Laughing, Buddy pretends to be disinterested, "Oh, I'm not taking anyone home ... or at least not taking them home to support."

Despite his protest, Buddy suggests we head to the back room, "Just to play a little pinball," though I know he'd be quite happy to land Ben in bed.

As we walk down the bar toward the back, I notice Adam sitting next to a 40-ish guy who's been an infrequent customer of the bar going back to the beginning. The guy isn't particularly attractive or well built, maybe five eleven and 150 pounds with a face like Jerry Seinfeld. But he does own his own printing business, which Adam is keenly aware of given the overdose of flirting and touching and laughing way too loud that I witness while passing them.

The pinball machine is occupied by a threesome that seems entrenched. We wait for about 15 minutes for an indication that they'll be vacating, or at least sharing the machine, before I call it quits, down the remainder of my Amaretto, and leave.

Saturday afternoon, I head over to West 13th Street to survey the archives of The Center and, hopefully, speak to someone in authority about what's in my possession. I toy with the idea of bringing over a sampling of photographs to substantiate that I have something of value for a place concerned about gay history. But I elect to leave it all home, thinking that it's their responsibility to prove to me that they would be a suitable repository for the Stonewall Revival Collection as I've now decided to call it.

Despite their longstanding presence in the Village and my former role as Stonewall caretaker, I'd never had the occasion to visit The Center before. A volunteer near the entrance kindly explains that the archives are upstairs but doesn't seem to have any other information to share. When I reach the entrance of the room that houses their collections, I don't see anyone around. I stand quietly at the reception desk near the doorway, hoping that someone will appear so that I can ask some questions. I see a notice on the edge of the reception desk that states that visits are by appointment, but without any indication of how to make an appointment.

In the silence of the room, I scan the shelves that run up and down the walls of this fairly small space. They are full of folders and other containers that seem to house the photos and letters and books and other ephemera that constitute "the archive." I wonder if this is the entirety of their collections. The roughly 600-square-foot room is packed with memorabilia of all kinds, but very little is on display. I'm tempted to start looking through some items on the lower shelves, if nothing else than to see when and if someone comes to tell me that I can't freely browse the contents of the room. But no one comes. Twenty minutes go by. Then and there I decide that, regardless of how appropriate this place may be to house the photos I have of the re-opening of Stonewall, that they haven't proven themselves worthy. However well-intentioned they may be, a real archive shouldn't be a converted office space that is left open and unmanned.

Back at the apartment, Stuart calls to tell me that he hasn't slept well after my revelation from the night before. "I just couldn't make sense of it," he says. "And it bugged me that I couldn't figure out how you knew what you knew. So, I've figured out how to test what you think is happening."

"OK," I say, "I'm all ears."

"What you need to do, the next time you're back there, is to hide something in a place that no one but you could find. And then, after you've done that, you go to that place to see if it's there now."

"Whoa," I interrupt, "you're telling me to try to hide something in New York City in 1968 and then try to find it 30+ years later?"

"Yes," Stuart says, "but it obviously has to be a place that no one else will find it or move it in the intervening years."

"I don't know ... that seems like I'm trying to game the system. And wasn't it you who said that I shouldn't try to plan this. That I should just let it take its course or something to that effect."

"Yes," he replies, "that's what I said. But it was bugging me so much last night. I'm trying to prove if it's real or not because now you've caused me to doubt myself. It can't be real."

"I understand what you're saying," I say calmly, "but if it is real, that isn't the way I want to deal with it."

"You should do whatever you feel is right," he concludes. "I just wanted to offer a suggestion as to how you could prove it to yourself, or not, if that's important to you."

The call ends and I become obsessed with trying to think of places one could hide something in New York City.

CHAPTER NINETEEN

Company

I had fallen asleep on my bed, which was strewn with possible artifacts for the time capsule proposition that Stuart had suggested. I had concluded that any item that I tried to plant in 1960s New York would have to be innocuous enough to remain invisible and robust enough to withstand the ravages of time. The objects were generally small and metal, including coins, souvenir keychains, and old keys. When I awoke facing Trinity Church in lower Manhattan on a spring morning, I instinctively reached into my pocket to see what object had accompanied me, if any. For a moment, I fantasize that this old church would be an ideal place to hide an item for future discovery. But none of the objects had teleported with me, ending the time capsule fantasy for now.

I meander a few blocks in search of a newsstand and come across the still incomplete World Trade Center site. It is, in fact, very far from completion with only a massive hole in the ground marking where the foundation has been excavated. There are several cranes and a lot of earth-moving equipment chugging about, and I can see the large retaining wall constructed to hold back the Hudson River just beyond. Though I realize I'm still in the late 1960s, prior to the raising of the monoliths in the early 1970s, I still need to find a *New York Times* to more specifically locate myself. Heading back toward Wall Street, I assume I'll find a vendor amidst the hustle of real and would-be financiers.

The paper dutifully orients me. It is June 4, 1968. The front page has two articles that catch my eye. One, below the fold, mentions that Andy Warhol was shot in his studio the day before by a 28-year-old actress. The doctor that is quoted puts Warhol's chance of survival at 50-50. He'll survive, but the subject of the other article I notice won't. According to *The Times*, Robert Kennedy has the edge over Eugene McCarthy in tomorrow's California Democratic Primary. He does win, but it won't matter.

I'm standing on Broad Street, just south of the New York Stock Exchange, pondering what is about to happen on the other coast when I notice the barricades just up the block. Walking toward the crowd of onlookers, I realize that a film is being shot. And from this vantage point, I spot the crew, arranging a dozen or more cast members up at the intersection of Wall and Nassau Streets. They're dressed in uniforms, band uniforms. Though I don't see Shirley MacLaine, I know that this is the day Fosse is filming the *I'm a Brass Brand* sequence. Stuart was right. I should just relax and let things unfold as they will.

Edging toward the front of the barricade, past the suited Wall Streeters who will fully report this brush with celebrity to their suburban wives, I scan the crowd looking for Gwen. Not spotting her, I catch the eye of a production assistant and start mouthing, "I'm supposed to pick up a parcel from Gwen Verdon." He approaches me and I repeat the phrase with a tone of urgency. He pulls me across the barricade and has me wait about 20 feet behind the camera set-up while he walks up toward Wall Street. I'm amazed at how easy it is to get close to a celebrity in this era. Then again, no one's heard of Manson or Mark David Chapman yet.

As the production assistant reaches the intersection where filming will occur, Fosse and Verdon make their way around the corner and into view. The PA has the briefest of conversations with Gwen, pointing in my direction. As she looks toward me, I wave and she nods her head affirmatively while gesturing for me to come closer.

She starts walking toward me and when we're about 20 feet apart she says, "What are you doing here?"

I'm a little stunned because this is the first time that she's greeted me without enthusiasm. I apologetically say, "When I realized that you were filming here, I just thought …"

She interrupts me, "Bob's got very little time to finish this. The light will be going away. I can't chat with you right now."

"Oh, I'm so sorry. I didn't realize …" I start to say before she interrupts again.

"No, it's OK. I'm glad to see you. But I can't talk. Just wait back there. We'll be finished soon."

I head back toward the barricade and, just as she said, the shooting only lasts for maybe 30 minutes before the shadows descend on the intersection and eliminate the possibility of visual continuity. The most fascinating part of this behind the scenes glimpse is watching Gwen watch Shirley lead the marching band in front of the Pantheon-like Federal Hall. Though she's standing at some distance to MacLaine, Gwen is judging every movement, every finger position, every strut at 24 frames per second. After each take, she gives an approving, if not enthusiastic, head nod. I have half a mind to go over and tell them not to bother with the last take, given that the sequence will be somewhat lackluster on screen, but the dwindling light has saved me from delivering the bad news. Shooting wraps and Gwen makes her way back toward me.

"I'm sorry I was short with you," she starts. "The shooting schedule is very tight and we had to finish this quickly."

"Please don't apologize," I respond. "I should be the one to apologize. I just show up unannounced every couple of months."

She leads me up toward the Nassau and Wall Street intersection where the filming just concluded. As I follow her, not knowing where we're heading or why, I spot something shiny on the ground and pick up what turns out to be a gold button. She turns to see me examining it.

"Oh shit. I hope that's not from her jacket," Gwen shrieks. "Wait here. I'll be right back."

I stand there, just in front of the statue of George Washington that marks the spot where our first President was inaugurated, watching as Gwen walks toward a trailer. She disappears inside. While I'm waiting for her to emerge, I glance up at the bronze statue and start to ponder. I stroke the button with my thumb as I consider where on our first President I might hide it. I know the statue will be here 30 years hence and, even with the occasional cleaning it may or may not receive, it seems like a reasonable place to hide an object for later discovery.

Washington is posed in formal Revolutionary attire consisting of a vest over a ruffled shirt, under a heavily buttoned, three-quarter length outer coat. Another duster-like topcoat is draped flamboyantly over his left shoulder, flowing behind him and waterfalling on top of a short column to Washington's right. It's an unnecessary sartorial addition and the *Diana Ross at Caesars Palace* draping of this cloak makes me laugh out loud, but only half as much as when I spot that President Washington is sporting camel toe. How is it that no one has noticed this before?

"What's so funny?" I hear Gwen say from behind me.

"Oh, I just was looking at how gay that overcoat looks on him when I spotted that unfortunate tightness in his pants," I struggle to say through continued laughing.

"Poor Martha, poor poor Martha," Gwen says as she joins my convulsion.

I compose myself and ask, "Is everything alright? Do you need the button back?"

"No," she explains. "I was just checking to make sure that that uniform button didn't come off of Shirley's jacket. If it did, Bob would spot it in the dailies and start obsessing over it. Fortunately, it didn't come off of her jacket."

"But even if it did," I start, "no one would notice that. It's tiny."

"Bob would notice," she says firmly, "and he'd start to think he needed to reshoot the entire scene."

"Well then I guess it's fortunate that it wasn't hers."

"Yes. And now you have a souvenir," she says smiling. "Maybe you should sew it there," she says pointing to an opening in the middle of my shirt where a button has popped off.

Looking down, I nod and smile at the coincidence of having a missing button on this bright red shirt. "Do you have time for a coffee or a drink?" I ask.

"Not really," she answers, "but if you want to share a cab with me uptown we can catch up during the ride."

We walk westward and then north for a few minutes and jump into a cab on Church Street. After a few blocks, after Church turns into 6th Avenue, I impulsively tell the driver to head down Christopher Street.

"Honey, I'm sorry," Gwen says, "I don't have time to stop anywhere."

"We don't have to stop," I reassure. "I just want to drive by the place I've been talking about."

As the cab passes Gay Street and then Waverly Place, I tell the driver to pull to the curb for a moment in front of the Stonewall sign.

"This is it," I announce. "This is the place that is so important to me. The place that Jimmy opens, uh, opened."

"I'm sorry but it doesn't look like much from the outside."

"It's not," I agree. "At least right now it's not. The people who run it now — the mob characters — they're just taking advantage of gay men. But that will change next year."

I tell the cab to continue the ride up to Central Park West and as we continue I feel a sense of boldness come over me.

"In a year, the gay men who are subject to so much humiliation, from the mob, from the police, they're going to fight back. And they'll be joined by lesbians and transgender ..." I start explaining.

"Trans-what?" she interrupts.

"Oh, sorry," I try to translate for the times, "all these people who are in the minority, sexually and otherwise. They take a stand. And the space will become famous for that."

"Is that what Jimmy does?" she asks confused.

"No, he takes it back later," I explain. "Actually, it's more accurate to say that he gives it back. It's so hard to explain how this all works. You just have to trust me."

"But he's dead, so how does he give it back later?" Gwen becomes more confused.

I've dug myself in a hole and don't know how to escape the timing conundrum that I've created. Instead of retreating, I double down.

"Look, forget about all that for a second," I say firmly. "I realize that I need to prove something to you. For you to understand and believe me. When I tell you that you're going to get the rights to produce *Chicago*, it's not just wishful thinking. It will happen."

"I hope that it does," Gwen replies, "but she's still adamant that we can't have it."

"OK, let me prove to you that I know what I'm talking about," I offer.

"Ok. Go ahead," she accepts.

"Someone very famous is going to be shot."

"That already happened," Gwen answers shaking her head.

"No, not Andy Warhol," I insist. "Warhol will live. But someone else. Very famous. Very important. He'll be shot and he'll die." For a second, I toy with the idea of saying that it's Bobby Kennedy. But I dismiss the idea because I know that it goes too far. If I tell her it's Kennedy, after it happens she'll wonder how I knew. And with Shirley MacLaine being such a big supporter of the campaign, I'm liable to be hauled off to FBI headquarters if I divulge that I know about the assassination of a Kennedy before it happens.

"Well who is it?"

"I don't know," I lie.

"Well then how do you know that someone will be shot?" she interrogates.

"Let's just say it's a premonition of sorts," I say with assurance. "I guarantee you it will happen."

We go back and forth about my prediction a bit more before the cab reaches her apartment. The fact that she's asking me questions as to who will be shot, who will do the shooting, why it happens, when it will happen, and whether I've had these premonitions before leads me to believe that she's skeptical but willing to entertain the possibility. The only question I answer from her barrage is as to when the shooting will occur, telling her that it's imminent. The cab pulls in front of her building, she pays the fare, and we exit. I'm hoping that she'll invite me up so that I can ask her about her time on the West Coast, but she doesn't.

"Hopefully, we can get together again soon," I say, testing the ground to see if I've damaged the relationship.

"Sure, but we've got a heavy shooting schedule," she explains, "and there's hardly a day over the next few weeks when I'm not really busy."

Knowing that MacLaine will be unavailable to shoot while attending Kennedy's funeral in the coming days, I give Gwen a kiss on the cheek and say, "Well, maybe some free time will pop up and you can tell me about your stay in California."

"There's not much to tell." she answers, "I went out to work with the director. And that's what I did mostly." There's a sadness in her tone. And referring to Fosse not as Bob or her husband tells me that something has changed in their relationship.

As she walks into the building, I cross the street and head into Central Park. There was a tree that I used to enjoy sitting under during hot summer days when I lived on West 90th Street. It was a favorite spot to daydream and gaze upon the midtown skyline. I go in search of it, but find a similar enough substitute near what will become Strawberry Fields. It seems that I can't get away from assassinations today.

Sitting under the shade of an old oak, I replay today's events. I hadn't intended to take this route with Gwen, utilizing my knowledge of future events to manipulate her. Though I feel bad about the scheming, my near certainty that this episode is reality, not a dream, provides a certain moral shroud that masks any Svengali similarities. But I have no plan on how to use any influence I gain with my charade. That's what I need to focus on. Who do I save and how? It's too late to stop Kennedy's assassination, I justify to myself. Besides, he's only one person, not thousands. I doze off for just a bit and when I awaken I head back to Central Park West to catch a cab downtown to Stonewall, thinking that the answer lies there.

"You're wearing the same clothes," I hear from a familiar voice behind me.

I look down and see the same jeans and red shirt, sans one button, that I've had on all day as I turn around to see Gwen's face. She's extremely animated.

"Did you know it was Bobby Kennedy?" she pleads.

Now I'm the one that's confused and she spots my disorientation. "I ... ah ... no ... I didn't ... it's happened?" I stumble incoherently.

"Are you OK?" Gwen asks in a calming voice. "I couldn't believe it. I just wanted to call you to talk. But I don't have your number. And now you're here and wearing the same shirt from the other day."

"I'm fine, really," I say without conviction. "What day is it? I fell asleep in the park and now I'm a little confused."

"Come upstairs," she says grabbing me by the hand and leading me the half block to the entrance of her building. "It's Thursday."

She puts me in a comfortable chair in the living room and goes to retrieve something in the kitchen. A few minutes later, she brings a cup of tea and sets it down in front of me.

"Did you know it was going to be Bobby Kennedy?" she repeats.

"No," I say emphatically. "I just knew something very bad was going to happen to someone important. That there'd be a shooting. And that the victim would die." I'm unhappy that I have to improvise my answers, wanting to have had more time to better plan this conversation.

"Why are you still wearing that shirt from the other day?" she asks. "Haven't you been home since then?"

"No, I haven't been home," I answer truthfully. "I don't know what happened to me. I just lost track of time." I wonder whether this unexpected double episode is in response to my entertaining the time capsule test.

"Were you hit on the head or something?" she asks, almost motherly. "How could you not know that Bobby Kennedy is dead? It's all over the news."

"I don't think I hit my head," I reply, ignoring the other question. "I'll be fine. Really. I have been home. I'm just a little groggy. I fell asleep in the park. I guess I was still dreaming about the other day when you saw me downstairs. There's nothing to worry about." I decide that I need to end the concern that I've been wandering the streets of New York for two days in order to re-focus the conversation to her.

"I think the world is coming to an end," she reveals. "How else could it be possible that people keep getting killed like this?"

"It's so sad. I know," I try to pivot. "The world is so violent. But it's always been that way, I guess. We just get to see it play out on TV now."

"But he was such a good man," Gwen says near tears. "He was trying to help so many people."

I get out of the chair and sidle up to her, putting my arm around her to comfort her.

"How do these things come to you?" she asks.

"They're just impressions," I concoct. "I get an overwhelming sense of something that is about to happen. Sometimes it comes in the form of a dream. I think lots of people have the ability, they just don't recognize it. It's a gut feeling but stronger. Have you ever had a sense of something that's about to happen?"

"Not like you," she says deadpan.

"Maybe to a lesser extent?" I try again to push the conversation back to her. "Did you have any impressions of what your time in California was going to be like before you left?"

"I was just apprehensive, that's all," Gwen starts to open up. "Bob had gone out earlier. It started getting harder to talk to him. He was always busy meeting with people, putting the picture together. I didn't know what to expect once I got there."

"I don't know how I'd deal with all those wanna-be starlets clamoring for my husband's attention," I inject, trying to dig for some insecurities.

"Oh, that happens in New York too," she says matter-of-factly. "It's not something that I dwell on. It's part of the business. Bob is who he is. And we are who we are, I guess."

"It always made me crazy. When Jimmy opened the bar, all sorts of guys would throw themselves at him. And he'd be getting high all the time, so I worried that he'd just succumb to their influences."

"Did he cheat on you?" she asks with intention.

"No, I don't think so," I say. "His appetites were insatiable in so many ways, but that wasn't one that I had to contend with."

"Men with big appetites." she shrugs. "They're so attractive, aren't they?"

"Yes, they are," I say, acknowledging the unsaid.

"This gift you have," she starts, "it must be such a burden. When you say that I'll get *Chicago*, how did that come to you?"

"I've just seen that Watkins will die next year and I've seen you dressed as Roxie," I say feeding her interest. "And in terms of it being a burden ... I guess that it is. But what I'm struggling with is how to do something good with it. To help people."

"How?"

Recognizing that this is the moment, I make my move. "I think I've met you because you're a part of what I'm supposed to do. I sense that I'm supposed to enlist your help in preventing people from dying. Lots of people."

"I don't understand," she murmurs.

"I'm not sure I understand either," I admit. "I don't know if we can change something that is supposed to happen."

"Like what?" she responds.

"If you knew that someone was going to die," I try to explain, "could you warn them and prevent it? If, let's say, I knew that it was going to be Kennedy and I had told you. Even if *you* believed me and got word to him or his people. I'm not sure that anyone would believe it and that it would have changed anything."

"I think I understand," Gwen nods. "But don't we have to try?"

"I suppose we do," I say, full of hope that she's agreed to be my accomplice.

"Have you seen anything else about me?" she reverts. "Anything about me and Bob?"

"You will always be the most important part of his life," I reassure her. "Even if you're not the same couple as when you married, but then again, what couple is? You'll be his partner in the truest sense of the word. Until he dies."

"You've seen him die?" she asks, choking up.

"It's not for a long time," I reassure again.

"Do you know how he dies, where and when?" she pushes.

"No," I lie, knowing full well that she'll be at his side on a September evening in 1987 on a Washington, D.C., street. On the opening night of a *Sweet Charity* revival.

"I'm so bad," she stands flustered. "I need to get you something to eat. I'm such a bad hostess."

"Except in dance halls," I smile.

She excuses herself to the kitchen to make me something to eat. I use the time to figure out how much further I should go with my plan during this encounter. I decide that I can push a little further but, as I still don't know what the plan is myself, that I need to keep my options open.

Returning with a fresh spring salad and some more tea, she sits across from me again.

"Does that bar have something to do with all this?" she probes. "You said in the cab that the people there fight back. Is that how people are going to die? In some sort of riot or something?"

I silently applaud her sleuthing, "What happens next year ... nobody dies in that event. It happens later."

As I munch on the organic greens, we sit in the midst of an awkward silence until the phone rings. She takes the call in the other room, returning 10 minutes later.

"Thank you for the salad and the tea," I stand, taking the empty plate and cup and saucer toward the kitchen.

"Here let me," she says taking them from me. "You should rest a bit. I'm worried about you. Why don't you lay down in the spare bedroom while I go out? I'll only be gone an hour or so."

"I'm fine, really," I protest, but not too much. "I can't believe you're so nice to me. I don't mean that you're not nice generally. You're maybe the kindest person I know. Just that I'd never imagined getting to know you in this way."

"Don't give it another thought," she smiles. "You gave me that baseball cap. You've given me something to look forward to."

"Listen, I may or may not be here when you get back," I say to pre-empt another rude-ish disappearance should this episode end as suddenly as they often do.

With a sad look wiping down her face she says, "OK. But I thought we could talk more. I thought you wanted my help."

"I do," I reply. "I just don't know how yet."

She heads back toward her bedroom and I follow, but just a far as the elevator door in the rotunda. When she emerges, she's carrying a black purse and the *Chicago* cap. Tucking her famously fiery tresses under the black and red cap, she looks like she's channeling Lola.

"Make yourself at home," she says planting an affectionate kiss on my cheek.

"Next time, let's do something fun," I smile. "Maybe we can go see a show."

"But I'm not in anything right now," she laughs as the elevator door closes.

I can't believe my good fortune, standing alone in this iconic apartment. Though I'm free to explore it all, with no one ever being the wiser, I won't do that to my friend. I shuffle back to the living room and lay down on the couch, knowing I'll be gone before she returns.

CHAPTER TWENTY

The Ladies Who Lunch

Since I hadn't gone out the night before, I wake up very early on Sunday with the short-listed objects for the time capsule all around me on the bed. While the coffee brews, I decide that I must enlist the help of others to figure out how to execute the plan, a plan that has no name and some vague but noble goal of stopping AIDS. I call Stuart first, given that he's the only friend who won't crucify me for calling at 9 a.m. on a Sunday.

"This is rather early for you," Stuart ribs before saying hello.

"You just love caller-ID, don't you? Dorothy Parker would be proud."

"I've always been known for my acerbic wit," he corrects. "Caller-ID just makes it a bit more personalized."

"I've had another," I start but struggle with how now to characterize these events before settling on "episode."

"And you're calling me at 9 a.m. to tell me this why?"

"I can give you the details later, but suffice it to say that Gwen has agreed to help me."

"Help you do what?"

"That's what I'm not sure of," I hesitate. "That's why I want to convene a summit."

"A what?"

"I want to get together a group of people," I explain. "A group that I trust, that knows Stonewall and me and Jimmy and all that. I'm going to pose the question to the group as to what I should do now that I have the ability to warn people about AIDS."

"Oh, Tom, I don't know what you're thinking anymore."

"I'm thinking that I need to get other people's ideas and opinions," I say with equal seriousness.

"When is this meeting of the minds taking place?"

"Today. At a brunch," I insist.

"You're going to call all your Stonewall friends early on a Sunday morning to get together for brunch today to figure out how to stop people from getting AIDS? Have I got that right?" he replies with more sarcasm than necessary.

"Look," I pounce, "I've just had the most remarkable visit. Gwen trusts me because I've started telling her about the future. She's open to helping me. I told her I want to stop people from dying. I want to act on this right now. I don't know when I'll see her again, but I want to be prepared. I can't go back again and be all wishy-washy about what I want her to do."

"Tom, you're my friend and I'll do whatever you ask," Stuart assures. "You're just lucky I don't already have plans for today. Just tell me where and when."

"Come to my apartment at noon," I direct. "I'll fill you in on all that happened before we all get together for brunch. You're the only person who knows everything, and I don't want to tell everyone else what you know. It would just complicate the process of getting an answer."

After the call ends, I pull together a mental roundtable of the others who I want to participate.

I call Buddy around 9:45 a.m., a time I deem too early, but not too, too early, to extend an invitation to a 1 o'clock brunch. Jimmy's best friend Bobby is my next call. Though I hadn't socialized with him a lot after my time at Stonewall ended, we remained close. He agreed to come to brunch but seemed a bit surprised at the suddenness and urgency of the last-minute invitation. I find Ben's phone number, to my surprise, and to my greater surprise, he picks up the phone, clear-minded, at 10:20 a.m. and agrees to come. I don't have a phone number for Adam and debate the merits of trying to find him at the fleabag I banished him to weeks earlier. At last sighting, he had his hooks into the Jerry Seinfeld printer and, if he's still as good as he used to be, could have taken up residence with the mark by now. Weighing the probabilities, I mentally disinvite Adam.

Six seems to be a good number of people for brunch and for getting a diversity of ideas. I need one more participant, but can't think of who to call until it occurs to me that I don't have anyone from present-day Stonewall on the panel. Mentally scanning through the current staff provides no obvious choice. It's then I realize that I need to invite Dominick, the original builder of Jimmy's Stonewall and the man I left its fate to upon my departure. He's the only other person who had skin in the game, who made the effort to keep it alive when others walked away, including myself. I hadn't seen him much in the past five years, but I felt confident that if I called, he'd come. It took a half hour to find his number, but when I called he acted as though no time had passed and agreed to join my impromptu get-together. I told him who was coming and that he'd be the only straight guy at the table. True to form, he couldn't have cared less. He was just happy to be included. To give him time to come in from Staten Island, I pushed back brunch to 2 p.m.

I had told everyone but Stuart about the delayed brunch, asking them to meet me at Knickerbocker. There were other more brunchy places I could have chosen, but Knickerbocker would be a little quieter and less eager to turn the table given our patronage. At 11:55 a.m., the doorman announces Stuart and I greet him with, "This is rather early for you." But it comes off flat and, kindly, Stuart doesn't remind me who's the Parker of the group.

"So, who's coming to your little Manhattan Project?" he asks.

"Buddy, Bobby, Ben and," I say with a pause, "Dominick."

"Dominick? What do you expect him to contribute to this? He builds houses," Stuart asks, not surprisingly. Dominick could come off as rough and coarse some of the time, and his heavy Staten Island Italian accent only reinforced any similarities he bore with Paul Sorvino. But much like Jimmy, he fancied himself an impresario, and however unlikely the route that brought him there, he was the champion of Stonewall in the latter half of the 1990s.

"He knows how to get hard shit done," I justify. "He's kept that place open since I left. Added the upstairs. Pushed for a cabaret license to allow dancing."

"Yes, I know," Stuart interrupts. "But you're looking for a way to stop people from getting AIDS."

"True," I concur, "but nobody else at the table is exactly Jonas Salk either."

"Touché," he replies before switching subjects. "How are you planning to get them to talk about this? Are you going to tell them about your dreams, uh excuse me, *episodes*?"

"Buddy and Ben know pieces, but only in the gay man's theatre fantasy realm," I establish. "Bobby and Dominick don't know anything. I think I'll focus the conversation on the pictures that I want to donate and the idea of bringing Jimmy's role as the man who revived Stonewall to the public's attention."

"Be careful," Stuart advises, "some of them might think that you're ignoring their role in the revival of Stonewall. Bobby was a partner of Jimmy's. He invested money and worked there. Buddy was a good customer and informal promoter of the place. I'm sure in his mind, he should be carved into the Stonewall Mt. Rushmore too."

"Yes, and holding Frank Sinatra's martini shaker."

"Seriously," Stuart continues, "Dominick has kept the place running longer than Jimmy and you combined. He built the interior, didn't he? From a media perspective, he's a better story than Jimmy is. He's running the place. He's straight. He can be quite charming. He's got that macho brutishness that can be very attractive …"

"And he's not dead," I continue the string. "Which is both good and bad, from a media perspective. Good because you can actually speak to him about Stonewall. But, it's not as sympathetic as reporting about the gay guy who died miserably from AIDS who opened Stonewall again and never saw it become successful. But I get your point about people feeling slighted."

"Just trying to help."

"I think I'll focus on the pictures first," I propose. "They're all in those pictures, so that should mitigate any small jealousies. Then, I'll find a way to transition to the question."

"And the question is?" he volleys as good as any Park Avenue therapist.

"If you could go back to the beginning, before AIDS took off, how would you warn people or stop it or make it less lethal," I say without full confidence that I've identified the right opening to the discussion.

"Shouldn't we be leaving soon?"

"I pushed the reservation to two o'clock to allow Dominick time to drive in."

"Well, you don't expect me to wait until then to get a Bloody Maria, do you?" he says with raised eyebrow.

"No, of course not. We can go over now and sit at the bar until everyone shows up."

It was helpful, and not, to arrive so early for our reservation. Stuart and I put away two Bloody Marys and two Bloody Marias, and we're just starting a third round when Buddy and Bobby arrive. I had outlined, with Stuart's help, how to get into the discussion and asked him to play my doubles partner if things started to go off course. Dominick was the next to arrive, just after two. We decided to sit at our table, rather than wait for Ben. He shows up twenty minutes later with that I've-been-fucking-all-night chipper look that one gets despite the lack of sleep.

When I had called for the reservation, I had asked for one of the round tables toward the back of the room. I thought it would facilitate conversation in a Charlie Rose sort of way. Everyone seemed genuinely happy to break bread together, with Dominick dubbing the gathering The Stonewall Reunion.

"I was so surprised when you called this morning," Bobby says. "I'm glad that you did, but it was so sudden. I was worried that you were going to tell us bad news."

"No, no bad news," I smile. "I just had this urge to get together."

"Easy for you, honey," Buddy jumps in, "you weren't at Stonewall 'til all hours. A girl needs her beauty sleep."

"And how many hours is that?" Ben drops the first bitchy remark of the afternoon.

"Never you mind, Miss Thing," Buddy fires back. "I didn't follow some greasy biker around the bar all night trying to get him to come home with me." Apparently, Buddy was witness to Ben's mating ritual from the night before.

"The only thing greasy was my dick when he spun around on it," Ben responds, dragging the conversation to something decidedly not like a Charlie Rose sit down.

"I hope you wore a condom," Buddy chides.

"You gay guys," Dominick laughs, "is that all you talk about? Sex. And who's suckin' your dicks." The remark brings a cease-fire to the Buddy-Ben escalation.

"So, who *is* sucking your dick, Dominick?" Stuart drolly lobs.

The table erupts into laughter as the waitress approaches to take our orders. Fortunately, her arrival suspends further talk of male anatomy. I use the pause to switch back to Bobby.

"I wanted to get together because I've been looking at all these old photos I have. From when Stonewall re-opened," I say to him and to Dominick. "I've shown some of the collection to Buddy and Ben and Stuart. I think something should be done with them. For posterity."

"We could put them up in the bar," Dominick offers.

"Yes, that would be a nice idea," I say, "but I also thought that something bigger and more permanent should be done with them. After all, they tell an important story."

"You mean like making a book of them?" Dominick asks.

"No, he means that he wants to donate them to The Center over on 13th Street," Buddy jumps in, trying to help but also trying to show that he's in-the-know.

"Actually, I've given up on that idea," I cut him off. "I went to see their archive and, well, it's just not … it's not what I had in mind," I say trying to not shut Buddy down entirely. Instinctively, I start treating the conversation like I'm one of the many focus group moderators I've observed at my job. Lead the conversation, don't let any single respondent take over the conversation, and dismiss unwanted ideas without being dismissive.

"It would be nice to see those pictures again," Bobby reflects. "It's been a long time. I may even have a few that you don't have … to add to the collection."

"That would be great," I say and looking around the table add, "If any of you have anything that you think would tell the story. About Jimmy and the very beginning. I'm sure I don't have every photo, every memory captured."

"Maybe you should put a bio together about Jimmy to include with the pictures," Stuart offers up. "He's not around tell the story of how he came to find the space and re-open it as a bar."

"That's a great idea," Buddy chimes in. "Maybe we could all write something about the beginning of the new Stonewall. Lord knows I was there from day one."

Buddy's ego is starting to inflate. I hesitate, thinking of how to shut down this idea, when Ben comes to the rescue. "He's dead. He can't speak for himself anymore. It should be about him. It's not about us."

"Speak for yourself," Buddy gets agitated. "I've been the unofficial ambassador for that place since it opened. I've probably spent more money there than anyone."

"Perhaps," Stuart interjects helpfully, "you could help with some of the captions. For the photos that you're in. Explaining what they are, who's in the picture, what's the significance."

"That's a great idea," I jump in. "I hadn't thought about the need to write descriptions. Probably because I know what's going on in most of them. But for someone looking at the collection — who wasn't there — there needs to be explanation and context. All of you could help with that."

Food and drink orders start to arrive and everyone digs in. Some catching-up conversation ensues between Bobby and Dominick. Bobby seems to be probing on how Dominick is able to keep the place open, what agreements he'd made with the Duell family, the owner and landlord for the property, and whether the place will ever be profitable. Dominick shrewdly side-steps the financial questions, knowing that Bobby still feels cheated by never having received anything from his investment in Jimmy's bar, by emphasizing all the investments he'd made to convert the upstairs apartment into a secondary bar and to secure a cabaret license.

Stuart keeps Buddy occupied with talk of theatre and celebrities, allowing Buddy's penchant for self-aggrandizement to be focused in another direction. Ben mostly stays silent, chowing down his steak and eggs to replenish the energy he expended the night before. As I sense the meal coming to an end, I suggest another round of drinks and propose we play a game.

"What kind of game?" Bobby asks.

"Truth or dare?" Buddy suggests.

"Who would you rather?" Stuart says, adding to the mix his latest favorite party game where players go 'round having to pick someone to have sex with from among two horrid choices given to them. It's a game he always wins because he's amassed an arsenal of no-win choices like Nancy Reagan, Mother Teresa, and Janet Reno.

"No," I reply. "It's not an official game. It's kinda based on a dream I had." I explain the episode where I meet Dick in Stonewall and warn him about AIDS. "It got me thinking, if you knew what you know now and could go back to, say, the late 1970s, what would you do to ... what *could* you do to prevent the AIDS epidemic?"

"That's a buzz kill," Ben grunts.

"It's an interesting premise," Stuart adds, trying to stir the crowd. "Maybe I'd go to a famous doctor, someone with credibility, and get him to investigate the first cases."

"Or maybe you could go to a newspaper and get them to report on it," Bobby joins in. "If it becomes known faster ..."

"What about that first guy," Dominick struggles to recall.

"Patient Zero?" I ask.

"Yeah, the first guy. Wasn't he a flight attendant? If you stopped the first guy ..." Dominick starts to hypothesize.

"His name was Gaetan Dugas," Stuart explains. "Randy Shilts wrote about him in *And the Band Played On*. I'm not sure I believe it was him, that one person was responsible for all of it, but even if that's true, how would you stop him from spreading the virus?"

"First, you'd talk to him and explain that he's got an incurable disease and that he'll be responsible for millions of deaths if he has unprotected sex," Dominick summarizes succinctly.

"And if he doesn't listen to you?" Bobby asks.

"Then I'd kill him," Dominick states point blank.

Everyone falls silent. Dominick has never dissuaded people from thinking he was a tough guy, that he knew people. After many years of going back and forth, I concluded that it was all part of the show. If people wanted to assume things about him, he wouldn't endorse it or deny it because it only served to create an air of invincibility. And if he was going to make a go of Stonewall, he needed to be invincible. But hearing the words come out of his mouth, in a delivery that would make Joe Pesci proud, has brought things to a standstill.

"But you'd probably get caught and go to jail," Bobby breaks the silence. It's remarkable how quickly they're treating this game as real life.

"I wouldn't care," Dominick replies defiantly. "It would save Jimmy from dying." Pause. "It would save Kevin from dying. And Tony, he's infected now, he wouldn't die. Even that crazy drag queen, what was his name, yeah Vee Martense, that fucking loon, I wouldn't even want him or her to die." Dominick begins to create his *Schindler's List* of people, who worked at Stonewall or were friends of the bar, to save from certain death.

"That's so brave of you," Buddy says, as if speaking for the group.

"Yeah, brave," Ben says, without conviction. "But I don't think it was him. Dugas. I think that's bullshit. I still think the government was testing some sort of chemical weapon. That it's all a big cover-up."

"Most people have dismissed that conspiracy theory," Stuart states. "But even if it were true, what difference does that make to the thing we're discussing?"

"None," Ben says flatly.

Trying to be helpful to Ben, whose demeanor has turned defensive and testy, Bobby offers, "Well if it were true, maybe you could get close to someone in the government or at the CDC. Seduce them into giving you the evidence. Or steal it from them and bring it to *The Times*."

"I know what I would do," Buddy pipes up with a broad smile suggesting he has the perfect solution.

"And what would that be?" I take the bait.

"I'd get everyone to wear condoms," Buddy begins. "I'd contact some celebrities ..."

"Here we go," Ben says sarcastically.

"Shut up and let him finish," I say, growing tired of Ben's lack of engagement.

"Thanks, honey," Buddy says while giving a death stare to Ben. "Elizabeth Taylor, I would call her. Everyone knows she basically started amfAR so she's sympathetic to doing something."

"You know Elizabeth Taylor?" Dominick asks, while the rest of us silently groan that he's opened the floodgates.

"I know how to get in contact with her," Buddy says cagily, knowing that if he says something too over-the-top that he'll get called on it, given the seriousness of the discussion. It's one thing to insist that, as a child, you were in the midst of all kinds of Rat Pack and other celebrities when it's just harmless bar talk. It's entirely another thing to treat the subject of AIDS and death as a platform for your never-to-be-written celebrity tell-all.

"Go back to your original remark," I say, adopting the moderator tone. "The bit about getting everyone to wear condoms."

"Well," Buddy continues, "if you could get everyone to wear condoms, you wouldn't have to worry about Patient Zero or a government conspiracy or anything like that. The disease wouldn't get transmitted."

"So, you're plopped back in 1978, '79," I redirect Buddy. "What do you specifically do to get gay men to wear condoms when they have sex?"

"Considering, at the time, you're in the height of the sexual revolution," Stuart adds with historical authority. "There's Studio 54. Drugs. Cruising the piers. Backrooms. Trucks parked by the West Side Highway. It was hedonistic."

"I'd make it fashionable," Buddy declares, not backing down from his premise. "I'd go to Halston. He was *the* designer at the time. And Calvin. I'd get them to make designer condoms."

"What happened to Liz?" Ben continues his snarkiness.

"Let it go," I demand.

Ignoring the bait from Ben, Buddy continues, "They'd design these amazing condoms. Colored. Ribbed. With the rainbow flag. And they'd advertise them to make it instantly fashionable."

Even Dominick is tiring of Buddy's celebrity-obsessed solution. "You could get Brooke Shields to say that nothing comes between her and her Calvins except this rubber," Dominick says, mockingly holding up the white linen napkin from his lap in the shape of a tube.

Cutting through the laughter that follows, I redirect, "It is a different take on the challenge. Instead of trying to stop the disease or trying to build awareness about it much faster than happened, you accept the fact that you can't stop the disease and accelerate prevention of transmission."

"I don't know," Bobby adds. "I'm skeptical that people would wear them. Even with the designer versions and the advertising. How would you even convince Halston and Calvin Klein to do it?"

"I'd convince them that I was psychic," Buddy bounces back. I glance inconspicuously at Stuart and I see that he too is startled at how my admission to him about predicting Bobby Kennedy's assassination to Gwen is finding its way into this conversation.

"By telling them about something that you know is about to happen?" Stuart dangles.

"Like what?" Bobby plays along unwittingly.

"I'd tell them about John Lennon getting shot," Buddy fires back after just a moment of mentally scanning the big events of that time.

"So, instead of preventing John Lennon from dying," Dominick enters the exchange, adding the former Beatle to his expanding list, "you'd use that to make them think you're psychic?"

Everyone starts to talk at once. Principally, they've gotten into the dilemma of discussing how much you could potentially alter the future to prevent a tragedy. Some are weighing the value of a life, in this case Lennon's, versus the lives of known and unknown others. In the quietness of the 4 p.m. after-brunch lull at Knickerbocker, the commotion coming from the Charlie Rose table at the back of the room starts catching the attention of the bar patrons at the front of the house. I've lost control of the group and, looking at Stuart, see that even he has abandoned his previously agreed upon role and joined the philosophical fray.

"You idiots," Ben screams, slicing through the cross conversation. "What makes you think you could stop it back *then* if we can't stop it *today. Everybody* knows about how it's transmitted now. Known for years. Sooo fucking what. Hasn't stopped the 50,000 people this year that were infected with HIV from getting it."

"Fifty thousand and one?" Buddy plunges a dagger in retribution for the mockery he's endured.

"Fuck you, you psychotic faggot," Ben fires, standing from his chair.

Dominick stands to prevent Ben from leaping across the table. Bobby soon joins him to get Ben to retake his seat. The bartender starts to make his way back toward the anticipated brawl, but my vigorous head shaking and Ben's retreat to his seat causes the bartender to stop, mid-way to the table, and just observe.

Uncharacteristically, Buddy says, "I'm sorry. I shouldn't have said that." The words are left to linger in the air in total silence.

I motion to the bartender to bring the check and he walks back to bar.

"What about the people who didn't know that what they were doing was going to kill them?" I say very quietly to no one in particular.

"Do we owe them some special obligation?" Stuart asks, returning to his role.

"What do you mean?" Bobby asks.

"Does it make a difference that people who were infected in the 1970s and '80s didn't know that what they were doing would cause them to die?" I say in a barely audible whisper. "Are all deaths created equal? Or is a naïve death somehow more sympathetic?"

"So says the smoker," Ben responds quietly, indicating that he's contained his outrage for the moment.

"It's different," I correct. "You knew what you were doing. Even if you were high or drunk at the time. Jimmy didn't. Sex is a basic human function. You can choose not to smoke or not to drink but …"

"Is that what it says in the Philip Morris handbook?" Ben responds.

"You're clearly hurt," I terminate the exchange, "and I don't want to hurt you any further."

The waiter brings the check and, without looking at the total, I toss him my credit card so that we can all move on.

"I don't know why I get to keep on going," Bobby confesses, "when other people like Jimmy got infected and went so quickly."

"You've got survivor's guilt," Stuart diagnoses.

"Whatever you want to call it," Bobby accepts. "Why this person versus that person? What did I do or not do?"

The credit card has been run through, and I sign the statement. Rising from the table, I look at everyone and say, "Thanks for coming. I thought it would be nice to get together again. Outside that bar. We have this unique shared experience. I'm sorry if the game distracted from what was supposed to be a nice reunion."

"If you guys had only let me kill that flight attendant in the beginning," Dominick mutters.

A few chuckles result and a collective exhale, as we hug and kiss goodbye. Filing out of Knickerbocker onto 9th Street, the ensemble starts to dissipate. Dominick and I are the last to depart.

"You know I really meant it," he starts, "when I said I'd like to see those pictures and get them hung in the bar."

"I know you meant it," I smile. "You always did the right thing. Even when I thought you were doing the wrong thing. You kept it open. Past the point of no return. It's forever Stonewall now. I can't thank you enough for that. But, to be clear, I think that Jimmy's never gotten his due, and I'm going to rectify that."

CHAPTER TWENTY-ONE

Every Day a Little Death

I awaken seated on the same couch in Penthouse B at 91 Central Park West and, if not for the dark suit I'm wearing, might be misled to believe that this episode is a continuation of the last. From the table in front of me I pick up a newspaper clipping. It's dated Saturday, January 18, 1969 and the obituary for Lawrence Carr, producer of many Broadway shows including *Sweet Charity*, is directly below the date. *The Times* states that he died yesterday from a cerebral hemorrhage at just 51 years of age. The black and white photo that accompanies shows a stunningly handsome man. I gather, from my attire, that we're going to the funeral. Gwen enters the living room, dressed in black.

"Well, you said you wanted to see a show with me."

"Well, yes, but ..." I try to be non-committal given that I don't understand the circumstances I'm in with her.

"So, you've never seen *Mame*?" she asks.

"No, I haven't," I admit. "But it was definitely on my list."

"Too bad you didn't see Lansbury, but Morgan does a good job."

"Morgan?"

"Jane Morgan's doing it now. Where have you been?" she looks at me quizzically.

"Great. I finally get to see Fashion Ball no-show Jane Morgan," I say sarcastically.

"Let's go. We need to leave now so I can go over my part at the memorial with Jerry," she tells me, as though it was a reminder of something previously said.

In the elevator ride down, I ask enough open-ended questions to understand, without looking foolish, that we're headed to a memorial service for Lawrence Carr at the Winter Garden Theatre that will take place just before today's matinee performance of *Mame*. It's actually Wednesday, January 22nd, contrary to what I had assumed from the clipping. Jerry Herman will be an emcee of sorts at a predominantly theatre community tribute to one of their own. Gwen is supposed to deliver some remarks about Carr, but it doesn't seem like she's got her script finalized yet.

In the cab I ask her, "So what was he like? The picture in the paper ... well, he was handsome for sure."

"He was a kind soul, especially for this business," she elaborates. "He was certainly handsome enough to be a leading man, but his acting work didn't amount to much. That's when he became a producer. But he always missed performing I think. To know what it's like to hear that applause night after night."

"*The Times* said he was a bachelor," I say, looking at her with raised eyebrow.

"That's what they say when you're 51, work in the theatre, and have never been married," she responds in kind. "He was the picture of health. That's what makes it all the more shocking. To be cut down in your prime."

"And if you could have done something to prevent it?" I inquire.

"What's that supposed to mean? Did you see that he was going to die?" she asks for clarity.

"No, I really knew nothing of him. It's just that when you see someone cut down so suddenly, it gives you pause."

"Is this part of the 'lots of gay men dying' thing that you told me about?" she asks.

"No, I don't think that happens for a while yet," I respond, not wanting to sound so definitive about the future to ruin the appearance of it being a premonition. "Any idea of what he'd want you to say about him?"

"No, who talks about those things when you're alive and healthy?"

"What does your gut tell you?"

"He did ask me once," she struggles to remember, "something about what it was like to get a standing ovation. Even though he was a successful producer, I guess all he really wanted to be was a performer. Someone who got the standing ovation."

"Then why don't you give it to him."

"What do you mean?" she asks but is clearly tracking with the idea. "I should ask everyone to get up and give him a standing ovation?"

"Exactly," I nod. "Give him the recognition he didn't get in life."

She smiles broadly as the cab pulls up to the Winter Garden. Dorothy Loudon is heading toward the stage door and pauses when she sees Gwen exit the cab first. I follow just behind, hoping to be introduced before heading inside with them. But it isn't until we've gone inside the theatre and out on the stage of the Winter Garden, where Jerry Herman is sitting at a piano, that Gwen introduces me around before asking me to have a seat in the audience.

I park myself in Row E, on the aisle, to be able to see what's happening on stage. Herman, in addition to Sondheim, is one of my favorites and I'm delighted to see him now, as a young man at the very top of his game. Two years earlier, in present time, in 1998, I went to see *An Evening With Jerry Herman on Broadway* at the Booth Theatre. It was more of a revue than a full-scale show, just an evening of Jerry sitting at the piano playing his numerous hits, with veterans Lee Roy Reams and Florence Lacey providing the vocal accompaniment. It was one of those sorry-grateful moments in the theatre.

On the night I attended, the house was far from full which I considered a serious affront to the raging talents of this man. And while the show was a bit hokey, like sitting in someone's living room listening to show tunes, I relished the enthusiasm that poured from Herman. It was as though he was every one of those upbeat songs that he'd written. The applause from those there was heartfelt, but the empty sounds from the empty seats cast a shadow. Watching the show, I thought of how Jerry, upon winning the Tony for *La Cage Aux Folles* in 1984, accepted his award and boasted about how his kind of music was still alive and well and living on Broadway at the Palace. That moment was his retribution for all the Sondheim and Webber adulation that marked the previous 15 or so years.

But in 1998, even the ever-ebullient Herman couldn't make anyone believe that. When the show had ended, I walked a few feet down Shubert Alley and into the unmanned stage door of the Booth. There was no one around to ask if Mr. Herman would be coming out to sign the *Mame* souvenir that I had brought with me. Backstage felt lonely and abandoned. I started searching for Jerry Herman's dressing room door. It was half ajar and I could see a handful of old queens, probably longtime friends or associates, chatting with him. He looked up, eyes beaming, and called me to him. I asked if he'd autograph the CD jacket that I'd brought and it was though I had brought him Christmas. He asked my name, signed it with a flourish, and handed it back with an enormous smile. It was sadly beautiful.

Now in January of 1969, he's rehearsing an accompaniment to Loudon's "I'll Buy You a Star," one of the songs that will be played at this tribute. Verdon chats with him afterward, but I can't make out what they're saying. They leave the stage as the house doors open and a crowd makes its way down the aisles of the orchestra. The entire tribute lasts just over a half hour and Herman plays what he says are three of Carr's favorite songs, "Where Am I Going?" from *Sweet Charity*, "Merely Marvelous" from *Redhead,* and "If He Walked Into My Life" from *Mame*. Loudon does her segment and Gwen wraps up her tribute by asking the audience to give Carr a standing ovation because "he always wanted to know what it felt like to get one." I can't believe my good luck at hearing Herman's playing to thunderous applause and watching Gwen asking for and getting the audience to give a standing ovation for a dead man.

The crowd doesn't dissipate, as would be normal at the end of a show, because they all seem to know each other from working in the theatre, though I don't recognize many of the faces. Gwen makes a gesture at me, moving her hand in a circular motion to indicate that I should go around outside to the stage door. I'm not certain whether she meant for me to wait for her outside or not, so I take the initiative and head inside to find her backstage. She's talking to Loudon and some others when Jerry Herman walks up to her. Loudon and the others move away, and it's just the three of us standing in a circle.

"Great job, Jerry," Gwen kisses him.

"You were the star of the show," he defers. "That standing ovation was a brilliant idea."

"It was a lovely tribute," I say extending my hand, "and it was such a pleasure to see you play."

"Have we met before?" Herman asks.

"Well, yes, we've met," I start, deleting the *before* from my reply, "but it was very brief and you couldn't possibly remember me from that."

"Do you ever go out to Fire Island?" he asks.

Gwen interrupts with, "I don't recall getting an invitation to your place," and they both laugh.

"That's because you're a Hamptons girl, you're always out there," he replies.

"I have," I respond to the unexpected flirtation, "sometimes in The Pines, sometimes in The Grove."

"He throws the best parties," she teases, "or so I hear."

"Well, let me then officially invite you both out to my place in The Pines. June or July is good. I'm going to have a guest staying with me in August."

"That's very generous," I acknowledge. "I'd love to, if it works out. And, by the way, she won't be coming to stay with you."

Herman looks at me with a puzzled expression.

"I'm not trying to snag an invitation for August," I explain. "It's just that your guest ... she won't be there. I have a sixth sense about these things."

"He does," Gwen concurs.

There's a bit of shop talk between them about *Dear World*, Jerry's next show opening the following month. Herman ends the encounter pleasantly enough, but I sense that my remark changed the dynamics and that no invite to Fire Island would be forthcoming.

As Gwen and I leave, I ask, "Did I go too far telling him ..."

"What was *that* about?" she asks as we exit the stage door.

"He thinks that Judy Garland will spend part of the summer with him," I explain. "But she won't. She'll be dead by then."

"How?" Gwen looks horrified.

"A drug overdose," I reply. "They say it will be accidental, but you know ..."

"Then we have to stop it from happening," she starts. "She's too young and she's got children to take care of."

"I don't think we could stop it," I say coldly, "and the fact is that it happens at the same time as that uprising I told you about at Stonewall. I wouldn't do anything that could potentially interfere with that."

She hails a cab and, without saying anything, we both get into it for the drive back up to her apartment. "So, this uprising is because she dies?"

"I don't know," I admit. "Some will say that they're related. I'm not sure I believe it. It sounds too much like a PR story written with the benefit of hindsight. But, I won't take the chance."

I sense that I'm not going to see her for a while and it makes me want to tell her far more than I'd originally intended. "Your friend Jerry Herman," I explain, "he'll become infected with a disease that will kill millions of people. But he'll get treated and that will keep him alive. There will be millions of other people though that will die very quickly. Even with treatment. It will start with gay men, but it will cross into the general population. No one will be safe. You'll be going to more funerals and tributes than you ever imagined."

There's silence in the cab as she processes the information overload. I have no idea what she's thinking, when she finally says, "You've been holding back. You know much more than you're telling me. About everything."

"I have," I admit. "I wasn't sure how much I could say without jeopardizing ..."

"You knew it was Kennedy," she starts to speak frantically. "You know how Bob is going to die, you know about Judy, about Watkins ... are you going to start telling me the truth or is this some sort of game?"

"It's not a game," I insist. "If we could go upstairs for a little while, I'll explain everything as best I can. I'm just trying to get you to do me a favor," I plead as the cab pulls in front of her building.

"A favor?" she repeats. "What could any of this have to do with asking me a favor?"

She invites me upstairs, brings us both something to drink, situates herself opposite me in the living room, and looks directly into my eyes. "OK. Go ahead and explain all this and the favor."

"When I first met you," I begin, "it was like a dream. I'd wanted to see you perform and then there I was watching you create Charity at the Palace. And then I started seeing you more and you've been so nice to me, someone you didn't know from a hole in the wall, inviting me into your home and all. At first, I thought it was just going to be something fun. Something to enjoy. Palling around with Gwen Verdon. And then it started to occur to me that maybe meeting you ... that there was something else to this. That I was supposed to enlist you to help me stop this bad thing from happening. I know it sounds crazy. That's why I've been telling you things in bits and pieces. The disease I talked about, it's true. It's coming. I started thinking that with your help, your influence, that maybe I could stop it or make it less bad. That's the favor. I was going to ask you to help me. But I didn't know what to ask you to do."

"Did Jimmy die from this disease?" she asks and, at first, I'm uncertain how to answer.

"He *will* die from this disease," I elect to speak the truth. "He dies in 1994, we'll have been together for a little over four years."

"I'm sorry," she starts, and I think that she's offering sympathy, "but I don't know what to say. This is all a little much. You're a very nice person ... and I've enjoyed spending a little time with you. But this isn't something I can continue."

I'm not sure if it's the conversation that she doesn't want to continue or our unlikely relationship. "I don't understand," I start, "you asked me to tell you everything ..."

"I just can't continue this," she trembles as though she's going to cry. "I don't know. I don't want to know."

I've shaken her and that has shaken me. I've pushed something beyond the point of reasonableness. I get up from the couch. Her head hangs forward, with her face almost in her lap.

"I'll just leave then," I announce as I walk to the elevator. She doesn't stop me or say anything, and the last glimpse I catch is of her in that almost prone position. I feel like I've wounded her and I'm sick to my stomach.

CHAPTER TWENTY-TWO

On the Steps of the Palace

I've been up since 4 a.m., sitting in front of the computer that's stationed on a small glass table in my bedroom. Yesterday's brunch with the guys is a foggy memory. Far more vivid is my last encounter with Gwen. In a few hours, I'll have to face the workweek, but for now all I want to do is repair the damage I did in 1969. Instead of sleeping until seven, I go in search of proof and reconciliation. Proof that what I had told her was true and reconciliation via *Chicago*.

I had no luck finding an obituary for Maurine Dallas Watkins using Yahoo or Ask Jeeves. Yes, there were references to her death, but nothing official looking that would stand up to scrutiny. Everything I had printed from my searches looked no more authentic than something I could have typed up myself. I had convinced myself that if I could show Gwen an obituary for Watkins, something that might make her think I'd helped her gain another coveted Broadway role, that we could go back to the way things were when I first met her at the Palace. After all, it was that cap with the *Chicago* logo that had intrigued her initially.

By 8 a.m., I had become incredibly frustrated. Frustrated that I'd be late to work again, as in the days of stewarding Stonewall, and frustrated in finding no leads. I decided to head to the main branch of the New York Public Library, just two blocks from the office, during lunch, not that someone arriving after ten deserved a lunch hour. Patience and Fortitude, the lions anchoring the entrance on 5th Avenue, greet me. My computer searches earlier that morning were focused on Watkins and the period surrounding her death. Here, at this decidedly brick and mortar web, I elected to change tactics, researching the 1975 production in hopes of finding a mention of how the rights to *Chicago* were eventually secured. It took most of my lunch hour to find the microfilm reel for *The Times'* original review of the show. With all of the film readers occupied by other researchers, I had no choice but to pocket the bulky film reel and return later.

Shortly before five, I excused myself from work, unrepentant for leaving so early on a day I arrived so late. Back at the library, I secure a microfilm reader and the wheels start spinning. Clive Barnes' June 4th review of the show mentions Watkins, but nothing more than that she was the author. For an instant, I consider printing out the review as my evidence. But Barnes' review is critical of the show, and I see no reason to create further angst with someone I'm trying to court.

An earlier *Times* article from late 1972 mentions that Verdon will star in the musicalized version of the show, slated to go into rehearsal the following fall. It does mention that Watkins had died in 1969 and that the rights were obtained through her estate. A print-out of this from the microfilm reader would be sufficient evidence. But I know I can't try to show her this article, assuming that I'll be permitted to carry a present-day artifact into the past which for some unknown reason I've taken for granted, because the show will be delayed to 1975 due to Fosse's heart attack in 1974. I don't want to have to explain the delay. To regain her trust, and possible help with my cause, will take finesse. There will be no more blurting out stories of people sick or dying.

My vision is blurry from the endless pages of *The Times* that have carouseled past my eyes. I'm almost ready to call it quits when I find the most comprehensive description of the rights transfer buried in another theatre article. In a January 28, 1973 piece, I pore over what is called the "Chicago Saga." The story is itself worth of musical adaptation. Watkins had purportedly given an option to the producing team of Robert Fryer and Lawrence Carr, whose tribute I'd just attended, back in 1956. Another *Times* article, from February 3, 1956, confirmed this and indicated that it was Gwen's interest in it at the end of her *Damn Yankees* run that had pushed them to secure the rights to turn Watkins' play into a musical for Verdon. At some point, that option must have lapsed.

The 1973 article went on to describe how Watkins' religious conversion and, later, fascination with astrology influenced her to withhold the rights to *Chicago* despite repeated interest in the property in the 1960s. In an almost *Grey Gardens* tone, the story describes how Watkins had become a recluse in Jacksonville and went out of her way to hide herself from the world, communicating with her agent only through a post office box address. A former FBI private detective is hired to track her down. The detective discovers where she lives and had even learned that Watkins and her mother had been writing greeting cards for Hallmark for income, as if the story wasn't bizarre enough already.

Upon determining her whereabouts, numerous attempts were made to secure the rights again, but all efforts, even one from Verdon herself, failed. Upon Watkins' death, the rights to *Chicago* remained in her estate, controlled by her mother. And when I read the next line of the article, my heart falls. Apparently, Watkins' mother also refused to sell the rights to her daughter's play. It's not until sometime after the mother's death that the bank administering the estate allows the property to be made into Gwen Verdon's last Broadway musical.

I've screwed up royally. I've told Gwen that she'll be able to get *Chicago* after Watkins dies in 1969, but I've now learned that that isn't true. It will take more time. Much more time. To tell her that now, assuming she'd even see me, would only further erode whatever little trust I might have had. Defeated and exhausted, I return the microfilm reels and leave.

A half hour later, I'm nursing a gin and tonic at Stonewall, not wanting to go home to see all the wasted print-outs and notes I'd littered across the apartment. Charlie, the bartender, tries to engage me, but I'm just a void.

"Let me know when you want your second drink."

"Huh?" I look up from staring at the ice cubes in my tall glass.

"It's Happy Hour. Two-for-one. But, if you won't smile, I can't give you your free drink," he tries to raise my spirits.

"I'll do my best," I say, forcing the worst fake smile.

"What's bothering you?"

"I thought I had a solution to a problem," I recount, "but I've realized that it won't work."

"Is it your job or a guy?"

"Neither."

"Well, what's the problem?"

"I told someone some things that they didn't want to hear," I try to vaguely explain. Charlie is a kind-hearted soul and perhaps the most level-headed person working at Stonewall, but I don't want to get into my problems with him. "She didn't want to believe what I was telling her."

"A picture's worth a thousand words," he says instinctively.

"What?"

"Can you show her, with a picture?" he continues. "Sometimes people don't believe things until they see them with their own eyes. Can you show her what you're talking about with a picture?"

"I wasn't thinking along those lines," I reply.

As he makes further efforts to talk me into a better mood, I start concocting a plan to get a picture of Watkins' grave. Surely there'd be a headstone. All I needed to do was find out where she's buried and offer to pay someone at the cemetery to snap a picture. It would show the day of her death and I wouldn't have to grapple with all the unpleasant truths that the *New York Times* would reveal to her. The fact that Watkins' mother would continue to withhold the rights was something I'd have to deal with later I told myself.

"Thanks for trying to cheer me up and giving me some ideas," I call out to Charlie as I leave the bar. Stepping into that mid-October chill, I have a renewed sense of hope.

Tuesday after work was likewise spent with Patience and Fortitude. For someone who had written a play that became a red-hot revival in 1996, there was surprisingly little detail about Watkins to be found. Ultimately, I did come to learn that Maurine Dallas Watkins was buried in a small cemetery in Missouri, where her father and mother were also interred.

On Wednesday, I got to work extra early so that I could place some calls to Oak Lawn Cemetery. While sipping coffee, I jotted down some talking points for the phone call, to make my unusual request seem slightly less peculiar. The first person who answered didn't seem put off by my request for a photo of Watkins' grave marker. Perhaps I wasn't the first person to ask, I thought. But he declined to provide a definitive answer, relaying that I'd have to call back later to speak with someone in management. In between ad agency meetings, I'd hunker down in my office, trying to decide how much later "later" was.

I had gotten into an odd habit of subsisting on two dirty water dogs and a Diet Coke for lunch, to the point where everyone in the office made fun of my addiction. It had been going on for years. That day I went downstairs a bit later than usual, around 2:30, to get my usual from the ever-present vendor at 41st and Park. Without having to speak a word to each other, he starts to prepare my fix as I walk across the street to his cart. It was while he was lathering them in mustard that I heard it come over the old radio that he had hanging from his Sabrett umbrella. The 1010 news reporter was saying that Broadway legend Gwen Verdon had died at 75.

The next day, *The Times* would run a glowing tribute on page C21. It included two pictures, one from *Can Can* and another from *Damn Yankees*. The obituary, titled "Gwen Verdon, Redhead Who High-Kicked Her Way to Stardom, Dies At 75," covered a good 60% of the page. I deemed it of sufficient scale, but insufficient placement, for a woman of her achievements. The *Post* ran better pictures, including a pose from *Sweet Charity*, but the placement on page 45 and the text, by Clive Barnes, was not sufficiently reverential, I thought.

I never called Oak Lawn Cemetery back on the day she died, or ever. After I left work, I went home and changed into casual clothing. I picked up one of my most prized theatre possessions, a black handbag autographed by each of the five women who performed as Charity during the 1998 benefit concert at Lincoln Center. It was a one-of-a-kind treasure, auctioned at the end of the performance. Even more than the Merman *Gypsy* script, the handbag was precious because I had actually seen that one-night-only performance and had met all of them, except for Debbie Allen, at various times over the years. Verdon, in the past, and Rivera, McKechnie and Neuwirth during the 1980s and '90s.

I grabbed a cab uptown, to the most fitting place I could go. At 8 p.m. on October 18, 2000, I stood under the marquee of the Palace when the lights were dimmed, as they were at all the Broadway houses. The late arrivals for that night's performance of *AIDA* were trickling by me, but I mentally erased their presence as I clutched the bag. In the dark and in silence, I said goodbye to the friend I had never really met.

CHAPTER TWENTY-THREE

Before the Parade Passes By

I fully expected that, on the night of her death, I'd return to the past. After the lights came back on above my head, I had left the Palace and returned to 12th Street and fell asleep after scouring the web for all the coverage that I could find.

I awoke sitting at the edge of the Revlon fountain at Lincoln Center, clutching not a handbag but a copy of the *New York Times*. It was thick, so I knew it was a Sunday even before looking below the masthead. June 29, 1969. Arts & Leisure sat on top of the numerous sections, with a Vincent Canby piece titled "Judy Garland: Loneliness and Loss" catching my eye first. It was a fairly sober assessment, only questioning how it was possible that she lived as long as she did.

Gravitational forces pull from two directions. The primordial one from downtown. Another, in retrograde, from 69th Street. As I'd never been gifted with a newspaper before, I decide not to decide and start leafing through *The Times*. On page 33, I find what I'm supposed to find. "Four Policemen Hurt in 'Village' Raid," it says. The first coverage in the paper of record. It says nothing that I don't already know. Considering that the reporting claims that almost 400 young men were involved in the rampage, their word not mine, you'd think that it would be more newsworthy. But it's not.

I must have spent an hour ravaging the paper, determined not to miss any other article or ad that the theatre gods might have wanted me to discover in their gift. The only item of interest, an ad for *The Boys in the Band*, momentarily had me consider taking in the

3 p.m. matinee. My front pockets are devoid of cash and, checking the back pockets of my trousers, I discover not cash but some artifacts. It apparently was possible to bring something back from the future.

Instead of a print-out from my home computer or the library's microfilm reader, the kind of items I had envisioned bringing here, I find two photos. One is an external view of the bar in 1990 with the balloons that enabled me to date the photo. And in my other back pocket is a picture of Jimmy, inside the bar, proudly holding a sign celebrating gay pride at the place "where it all began." Contrary to my instincts, the evidence I was seeking was there all along. Charlie was right about a picture's worth.

I dump most of the paper in a trash can save for the front section with the Stonewall article and the Arts & Leisure section. Despite the drive to run downtown to see the continued protesting in Sheridan Square, I make my way toward Central Park West. Still unsure as to what I will say or do once I get to 69th Street, I pray an idea will come.

One of the doormen who I've conversed with previously is on duty. I walk up to him with a smile of recognition.

"Hi," I begin, "How have you been?"

"Fine, sir," he responds, a touch too formally. "Miss Verdon is not here."

I wonder whether I've been banished and if this response is something he's been instructed to deliver no matter how many times I might come looking for her. "I have some things to show her."

"I'm sorry," he says, resuming the more casual tone I had had previously with him. "She's been spending time out on the east end. Not sure when she'll return."

"Oh, that's OK," I nod. "Do you happen to have a large envelope? I'd like to leave this for her to see when she returns."

He starts looking for one as I ponder what I've just said. Leaving the press clipping of the first reporting of the Stonewall riots from

The New York Times is a certainty. But I am unsure about leaving the photos because they're a key part of the collection that I plan to donate to some unknown institution. After a few moments, he faces me with a large manila envelope and the moment of truth has arrived.

I tear the page 33 article from the front section, including the masthead and date. It forms an L-shaped scrap that I place in the envelope. It looks so tiny and insignificant inside. I realize that I must also include the photos, the evidence, to complete the package — to connect the present and the future. I want to ask for a pen to write something on the outside of the envelope. I even wonder whether I should circle Jimmy's face in the photo of three people holding the banner. In short order, I conclude that I have no suitable message to write and that it should be obvious who Jimmy is in the photo. I hand it back to the doorman, thank him, and trust that she'll put the pieces together when she returns from Long Island. Before departing, I sheepishly ask if I can borrow subway fare and he hands me a quarter.

I decide to get off at 14th Street, rather than taking the train directly to Christopher. Walking the remaining blocks will help clear my head and allow me to absorb what's going on in the Village beyond Sheridan Square on this warm and sunny Sunday afternoon. From 14th Street to 12th, hardly anything looks out of the ordinary. People are walking about casually. As I move beyond St. Vincent's Hospital, I feel something stirring in the distance, a sense of a large crowd. Near the corner of Christopher and 7th Avenue, outside the *Village Voice* office, I see a contingent of police offers. Sidestepping them, I cross Christopher and plant myself at the edge of the park, where Christopher and West 4th meet.

The police contingent is stonewalling, but not barring, passage. A gathering of people outside of the bar doesn't look like the mob I expect. Congregating seems to be a better description of their presence. I'm expecting a protest, like the ones I'd seen ACT UP perform regularly during the late '80s and '90s, and I feel let down.

There is no show, no mob, no chanting, and fewer barricades than I'd see during six Gay Pride marches from 1990-1995. I want to approach ground zero, but not directly, so I walk around the Grove Street side of the park. While there are some shards and other remnants of the rampage on the ground, there will be far more from the broken Budweiser bottles and confetti that mark future celebrations.

Rounding the park, back onto Christopher heading west, I come upon a thirty-ish man who is likewise surveying the scene. If I didn't know it was 1969, I could easily mistake him for a denizen of my time. Stopping beside him, I give a nod and pause. We're both staring at the front of Stonewall, across the street, from about thirty yards away.

"What's going on?" I ask.

"I'm watching to see if anything happens," he responds.

"What do you expect to happen?"

"I don't know," he replies, "something, anything."

"Were you here the other night, during the riot?"

"Riot?" he says turning to look at me. "I wouldn't exactly call it a riot. More like fighting back."

"It looks like the bar is open," I say, incredulous.

"Why wouldn't it be?" he responds. "They came in yesterday and cleaned it up, well hardly cleaned it, and wrote 'Open' on the boarded-up window."

"So, it's business as usual?"

"That's what I came to see," he explains. "This has to stop. The raids. The fear. I thought that the fighting back might amount to something. I don't think it will."

"It's not over yet," I try to reassure, without providing evidence.

"I'm Jason," he extends his hand.

"I'm Tom."

"So, you think this will amount to something?" Jason asks, reporter-like.

"In fits and starts," I opine. "The Civil Rights Act hasn't exactly put an end to discrimination now, has it?" I reference, trying to find parallels.

"They're waiting for Godot," he observes, looking at the crowd gathered outside Stonewall.

"In fifty years or so, it's gonna change ya know," I volley, though admittedly less highbrow than my companion.

"In fifty years or so, we'll all be dead ya know," he plays back to me.

"It's inevitable," I smile. "This will end. But with equality and acceptance, we'll lose something too.

"What's there to lose, aside from discrimination and beatings?" Jason says sarcastically. "Or are you one of those self-loathing *Boys in the Band* faggots?"

"I don't know," I admit. "There was a time when I was afraid for people to know who I was. I don't know if that's self-loathing or just fear."

"And now you're not fearful of people knowing you're gay?" he asks.

"When I saw my partner die, things changed. Death is the great leveler," I tell him. "How can someone make you afraid of anything after you've see the moment that everything ends?"

We walk a bit closer toward Stonewall, still comfortably along the fence of Christopher Street Park, maintaining an observer's distance to the milling police and congregators.

"Do you wanna go inside?" Jason asks.

"Maybe, in a minute. I'm just trying to soak in this moment. It's not what I was expecting."

"What were *you* expecting?" he probes.

"Something more significant," I try to explain.

"Exactly!" he punctuates. "They've just gone back inside, too meek to demand something more than the filthy cage they've been put in."

"Perhaps," I say putting my hand on Jason's shoulder to comfort him. "But I'm not looking forward to the day when we're just like everyone else."

"How can you say that when we are so *not* like everyone else?" Jason erupts, drawing the glance of a policeman across the street.

"Exactly," I whisper, trying to lower the volume so that we remain near-invisible. "In time, we'll be different, but not special. When gay is passé."

"You like talking in rhymes," Jason chuckles.

"No, really," I say. "Every group faces it. When the Italians and the Irish first came over to this country, they kept their culture. Yes, it was in the ghettos and they were treated like shit. But their specialness was authentic and valued within their community. Today, being Italian means eating pizza and veal parm. And being Irish means vomiting on the Long Island Railroad going home from the St. Patrick's Day Parade. It all gets reduced to cliché and hollow symbols."

"And they don't live in ghettos and they don't get beaten for being who they are," Jason reminds me.

"Yeah, something's lost but something's gained," I agree. "I get it. I'm not saying that I don't want it. Just that there's a price for everything."

My eye wanders above the boarded window to the second floor of Stonewall. The windows to the apartment that will become part of the second-floor expansion are partially obscured by grime, but I see a figure looking down through the sooty glass. It's Jimmy. At least, I'd swear it's Jimmy from this distance.

"Let's go inside," Jason says, stepping away. When I don't answer or follow, he turns to see me staring up to the second floor. "What are you looking at?"

Still silent as I shake my head back and forth in disbelief, I raise my hand to wave at the figure looking down on the crowd. It's a younger version of Jimmy, someone in his twenties rather than the man I knew in his late thirties.

"Do you see him?" I ask Jason.

"See who?" he asks turning around and trying to find the subject of my gaze.

"Jimmy," I start and then correct myself, "that guy staring out the window upstairs."

"I don't see anyone."

"On the left. He's looking down through that filthy window on the left," I direct Jason. I start to wave frantically, trying to catch the attention of the man looking down on the crowd below.

"Someone's just looking out at the crowd," Jason replies, looking up toward the second-floor windows. "Do you know him?"

"Yes, I think so. But I can't believe it. Can you see him?"

"Yes," he says, annoyed. "What's the matter? Why are you so fixated on him? Who is Jimmy?"

"Do you think he sees me?" I ask, continuing to wave frantically in hopes of getting some recognition from the second floor.

"I don't know. If you know him, why don't you just go upstairs?"

"I will. I will," I insist. "But I want him to acknowledge me first. Why won't he wave back? He's looking in this direction. Why doesn't he see me?"

"I don't know what the fuck you're talking about," Jason says, even more annoyed. "Either go upstairs or come into the bar with me. This is getting ridiculous."

"I gave away his picture today," I say, moving into the street to try to catch Jimmy's attention. "I shouldn't have given it away. It was the best evidence of what he did for this place."

"Look, man," Jason writes me off, "I don't know what your problem is. We were having a great conversation. Get out of the fucking street. You'll get yourself arrested."

"I didn't think I'd see him again," I explain, trying to use words that don't make me sound totally insane. "I thought he was gone and there he is. But he's not looking at me."

"Tom," Jason raises his voice, "I'm going inside." With that, Jason crosses into the doorway and disappears from view.

I look up again to the second floor and I see no one at the window anymore. I dart across the street to the archway at the leftmost side of 53 Christopher where I know a set of stairs leads to the apartment. The door has been severely damaged, probably from the crowd that raged against the police huddled inside Stonewall early Saturday morning, but it's firmly locked now. I shake and pound on the old wood until a police officer pulls me away.

"What do you think you're doing?" he demands.

"I need to get inside," I plead.

"The door is over there," he says, pointing to the entrance to the bar.

"I know that," I shout, "I used to run this place. I'm trying to go upstairs." Some of the congregators start to taunt the policeman and the crowd starts circling in on us.

"I'm going to take you in," he threatens as three more policemen move toward us to back him up.

I push my way past him and the gaggle of chanters and dart back across the street. I look up to the windows above the bar, hoping to get another glimpse of Jimmy. I don't see him, but I do see the policemen stepping off the curb to cross the street toward me. I run toward 6th Avenue, looking to escape the commotion and hide. With only a nickel left from my borrowed subway ride, I head to the only safe place I know, 59 West 12th Street.

The doorman asks who I'm here to see and I pause far too long, trying to think of who of my future neighbors has lived in the building the longest, though I'm not sure I know anyone who'd lived here since the 1960s.

"Who are you looking for?" the doorman asks a second time.

Without thought, I blurt out, "I'm here to see Jimi Hendrix." In a building that will be the future home of Isaac Mizrahi, John Waters, and many other notables, he is the first celebrity resident.

The doorman stares at me in disbelief, no doubt from my panicked demeanor, and tells me, "He's not here."

I'm relieved that Hendrix is not home because I need a place to sit for a few minutes and had he been home my charade would have ended all too quickly.

"He told me to wait for him. I can just sit there until he comes," I say pointing to a chair in the lobby opposite the elevators.

"I don't think he's in town," the doorman explains.

"He told me to wait for him at his apartment," I say calmly. "If he's not here in an hour, I'll leave. But if I leave now and he comes through that door looking for me, you'll have to explain why you sent me away."

The bluff has worked, and I sink into an uncomfortable chair next to the fireplace, grateful for a familiar place to quietly gather my thoughts. The doorman goes back to his post. I try to make sense of the last hour. Why was I seeing Jimmy above Stonewall? Why wouldn't he look or wave back at me? How could people still be going back into that bar after the drama of the previous nights? Emotionally and physically exhausted, I close my eyes and drift back to the apartment directly above.

CHAPTER TWENTY-FOUR

With So Little to Be Sure Of

The lights, the TV, and the computer were all still on from the night before when I awoke, still clothed, in my bed. Seeing that it was after eight, I reach for the phone to call in sick. I sound like the dead, so perhaps this time they'll believe that I'm really not well. The morning news programs have moved on and there are no further mentions of Gwen before the programming shifts to game shows, talk shows, and soap operas.

I'm still feeling devastated from seeing Jimmy above Stonewall. The gift of having arrived on the weekend of the famed riots, whether or not they were living up to the hype, has been eclipsed by a near psychotic obsession to understand what I'm meant to do. Pulling out all the old Stonewall photos from the closet, I expect to find two missing, joining the hat and the watch from before. Yet there they sit under the protective plastic of the album, negating everything I've come to believe. My dreams had become a reality that now returned to reverie.

Still wearing yesterday's clothes, I head out to pick up the trinity of papers that will carry the obituary. The news shop between 12th and 13th Streets doesn't tolerate reading in the small store, either before or after purchase. So, I toss *The Times*, the *Post* and the *Daily News* under my arm after paying and step back onto 6th Avenue. Not wanting to go home, I walk back to the corner for something to eat and a place to read through rote tributes. Their structure is always the same, leading with the deceased's most famous attribute, followed by paragraphs about childhood and the road to stardom, counterpunched with whatever failure, divorce, sickness, downfall or other proof point that demonstrates that life isn't just a bowl of cherries, and, thankfully, finally closed with a lesser known anecdote that sounds like it's meant to validate the deceased's legacy but is, in actuality, a way for the author to demonstrate their authority of the subject matter. Such is the state of the fourth estate. At the counter in Joe Jr.'s, I separate the wheat from the chaff over a feta omelet. I take the three pages that I will save and leave the rest for the next diner.

Without a reason why, I walk to Stonewall. At this hour, the bar is closed but I'll be able to look up to the second story windows from the same vantage point that I shared with Jason. Past and present are mixing into disorientation. Though it's not even noon, I see that the padlocks that usually secure the premises are gone and the lights inside are blaring through the shutters that are always pulled across the front window when the bar is closed. After looking up to the still empty window, I venture inside to see what's going on.

Immediately I recognize that a GI is taking place, a top to bottom cleaning of the premises by the entire staff. In the early days, Jimmy was diligent about scheduling them regularly. Over time, as he became more disengaged, they became far less frequent and the staff far less interested in spending six hours or more of their free time scrubbing everything in sight. I spot Charlie behind the bar, sanitizing the sinks and speed racks. Everyone else seems to ignore my presence, but he looks up and greets me with a broad, affectionate smile.

"What are you doing here? Come to help out?" he asks laughing.

"No. I've been paroled from Stonewall. I did my time," I joke back. "I was just walking by and saw all the lights on."

"No work today?"

"I didn't feel like going in," I say, holding up one of the papers for him to see what I had collected for posterity.

"What's that?" he asks, still scrubbing away as he talks.

"It's Gwen Verdon's obituary in *The Times*."

"Who was that?" he asks.

I look at him in disbelief. If it were someone else, I might have started telling him what an asshole he was for not knowing or ranting about how gay men have totally lost touch with their gayness. But I like Charlie because he's an innocent, someone wholly devoid of ill will or malice.

"She was one of the most remarkable performers that ever lived," I explain, electing to turn this into a teaching moment. "She came to fame on Broadway as a dancer. She was the original Roxie in *Chicago*," I offer, hoping that a more modern reference will connect. "She was married to Bob Fosse and was his muse, his partner, and the person that has helped secure his legacy."

"Wow. Did you know her?" he asks, as if on cue.

"No," I say, convinced that everything, including the sight of Jimmy in the window, has been an elaborate hallucination. "But people don't devote themselves to things today like that. To their craft or profession. To their relationships with other people. To preserving and teaching. There was a selflessness about her that I find, found, so remarkable." I begin to sound like I'm delivering a eulogy.

"Can I see?" he asks, drying off his hands and reaching out for the paper. I hand *The Times* tribute to him and take one of the bar stools that has been placed upside-down on the bar for floor cleaning purposes and place it gently on the still wet floor. As he starts to read the lengthy piece, I sit down and lean in to guide the lesson.

"She was pretty incredible," he acknowledges after I elaborate on what *The Times* did and did not say. The dirty looks from the other staff members who have been dutifully mopping and polishing during our exchange have gotten the better of him and Charlie resumes his cleaning behind the bar.

"Have you given any more thought to what I said the other day?" he asks.

"To what?"

"To using a picture to prove something. For your friend who didn't believe you," he reminds me.

"Oh, yeah. I think I would feel very bad parting with them. They're the only record that exists of what Jimmy did re-opening this place. I'm afraid to lose them."

"You can make a copy of them, can't you?" he answers sensibly.

"Well, yes, but even then I'd have to give them to somebody to make the copies," I vacillate. "I just am too scared to part with them. I was planning on donating them to some archive at some point, but I'm not even sure about that anymore. What if they don't take care of them or tell the story properly."

"If you want people to see them and to tell the story," he begins *my* lesson of the day, "why don't you buy a scanner and set up your own website?" I pause to consider his simple solution.

"I guess I could do that," I half-heartedly admit, "but I always imagined something more prestigious. If they were part of some institution's collection of gay history, that would make them more important, more legitimate than if I put them on some personal website."

"Sounds like you have to figure out what's most important to you," he explains. "If you want the whole world to know about Jimmy re-opening this place and what he went through to keep it open, then let the world have access. If you want them to be stored in some prestigious museum or library or whatever, then that's a different thing. Why is that important to you?"

"I don't know. I guess maybe because I've seen his memory wiped away from this place."

"We both know what he did," Charlie concludes. "Why do you need other people to validate that?"

"I guess I shouldn't."

One of the managers has come over to the end of the bar, near the sound system, and raised the volume of the music that had been playing to a level that prohibits further conversation in a not so subtle effort to get Charlie back to work without distraction. I return the bar stool to the top of the bar and head out.

I cab to the B&H photography store uptown and purchase a high-quality scanner to hook up to my computer at home. Within an hour, I'm back at 12th Street ready to share my collection, my evidence, with the world.

On Yahoo, I find a way to create a simple website with templates that allow photo-sharing with some text. It's not a perfect solution, but I accept its imperfections hoping that I will be able to improve the presentation over time. Several decisions have to be made to create this live archive, the first of which being what to call the name of the website. From my run-in with the Stonewall 25 Committee that threatened to sue me over selling t-shirts in the bar, I'm leery about using the Stonewall name. Surely, by 2000, any number of commercial interests, gay-related and not, have swooped in to monetize a name that has recognition. Initially, I start the process by using my own name as the domain of this archive, but as I start the painfully long process of scanning all of the images to my computer, I become emboldened to call this archive what it is. It's about the Stonewall Revival, and that's what it will be called. Fortunately, no one has bought up that name in anticipation of making a few bucks on the backs of others.

As I scan each memory into bytes, I vacillate over whether I need to identify people in the pictures, at least those associated with the bar, and whether I could be disturbing the privacy of people that might prefer not to be identified with that place at that time. My compromise is that, as these pictures were all taken in a public place, sharing them on the internet is fine, but that I will not name anyone in the pictures unless they give me their specific permission to do so. Jimmy's name will be the only one to appear on the site initially. Over time, others can decide whether they want to take credit for being at the revival. From day one, I'll have one more name identifying my pictures than Fred McDarrah had when he published his photos of the Stonewall Riots over that weekend in 1969.

As the hours unfold, I order a burger from the usual suspect to provide sustenance for the long night ahead. It takes me a good 15 minutes to select, capture, and organize each image that I'm digitizing. Without peeing, smoking, or otherwise jerking off, I can process four memories per hour. Some of the images have the scars of less than perfect handling over the years. I struggle with whether I should have them repaired, eliminating the scratch, stain, or dogear that makes them less than archival. I know that Ben-Ness Photo over on University Place could probably make the repairs, but I'm not ready to stop the assembly line of scanning and uploading to introduce another step in this process. I've already decided that I will call in sick again tomorrow, a Friday, to enable me to forge on with my duty.

I had fallen asleep sometime in the middle of the night and awoke mid-morning to the phone ringing. Stuart was checking in on me.

"I called the office and they said you were sick yesterday and that they hadn't heard from you this morning. Everything OK?"

"Yeah, I'm OK," I assure. "I was up late doing some stuff and forgot to set the alarm."

"I haven't called because I didn't know what to say to you," Stuart consoles.

"Yeah, I don't know exactly how I feel either. But there's so much stuff to tell you about, the dreams ..."

"I thought you'd decided that they were real," he interrupts. "You were calling them episodes. Now they're dreams?"

"A lot has gone on," I say wearily.

"Are we still on for tonight?" he asks, confirming our usual Friday arrangement.

"Yes, but" I hesitate, "I've got so much work to do. I've been scanning all the photos to put on the internet and I haven't really made a dent in it yet."

"You sure you're alright?" he asks again.

"Yes, I think so," I say, coming out of the fog of sleep. "Look, come over tonight. I'll show you what I'm doing. Maybe we'll go to the dump as usual. Maybe we'll order in."

After coffee, I plow back into work, and it's not until 5 p.m. that I realize that I haven't eaten or showered yet. I allow myself a 30-minute respite to make myself look human again, but by the time I've dressed the buzzer rings from downstairs. Stuart, knowing that I wasn't at work today, has come early. Opening the door, I see he has a large folder.

"I'm sure you have them, but I brought the clippings from yesterday's papers," he says, handing it to me. "So now you'll have two copies. I thought *The Times* piece was very good."

"Thanks," I say, taking the set and putting them under the lid of the piano bench. "It was fine, but I would have started it on the front page and then continued it inside. There wasn't anything all that earth shattering on the front page yesterday that she didn't deserve better placement."

"I guess there aren't any theatre queens among all the editors at *The Times*," he says drolly.

"Just old gray ladies, I guess," falling into repartee. "No fabulous invalids."

By half past seven, I have recounted the highlights of my week, both in 2000 and in 1969. For the most part, Stuart hasn't questioned or challenged anything. He's just let me talk. There are print-outs about photo scanning and website creation and photos from my Stonewall collection all over. As I conclude with my discussion with Charlie and the aftermath of that, clearly visible on every flat surface in the apartment, he starts to engage.

"I'm relieved that you're thinking more rationally about this. You almost had me convinced that you were really there, all those times. It was so vivid."

"I convinced myself ... because I *wanted* to believe it and because I couldn't find a few items that I thought I'd given away back then. It took giving away the photos and finding them still here to make me realize that it wasn't truly real."

"That bit about seeing Jimmy in the window," he adds, "I think that also shook you back to reality. Seeing him. Not being seen by him. That just threw it *way* over the edge."

"I still don't understand that part. Having him show up to look down over the original riots, like an apparition. It sounds like bad sci-fi."

"It does," Stuart laughs. "Or a Lifetime movie with Joan Van Ark or Sharon Lawrence."

"It does. I thought my imagination was a little more HBO than that."

"Do you think you can tear yourself away for dinner? You don't have to finish all of this in the next three days."

"You're right," I say, relieved. "I've gotten it off to a good start. I can resume tomorrow or Sunday. StonewallRevival.com will still be there, awaiting more pictures."

"I think it's a great idea to put them on the internet," Stuart commends. "It's very egalitarian, sharing it freely with the world. Very Jimmy. He wasn't into pomp and formality. I still don't know why you laid him out in that tuxedo."

"I was 32. I hadn't planned a wake before," I shake my head. "I wasn't going to put him in a t-shirt and jeans. He never wore suits. And the very first wake I ever saw, for a great uncle … he was laid out in a tuxedo. I must have been eight or nine-years-old. It made an impression, I guess."

"I guess it did," Stuart nods.

"I do wish though that, in the dream, he would have looked at me," I say quietly as we leave. "That he would have seen me."

"I'm sure he sees you," Stuart assures.

"Yeah," I say in the same muted voice, still unconvinced.

CHAPTER TWENTY-FIVE

The Apple Doesn't Fall (Very Far from the Tree)

Dinner at La Dolce Vita was a little more liquor infused than usual. Two martinis, followed by a bottle of wine, followed by two after-dinner drinks ensured that I'd be asleep on the couch before Chris Meloni had time to strip down to a guinea tee on the season two opener. As before, Stuart will let himself out silently, not that a *Noises Off* door slam would have woken me.

My eyes open, and I'm back where I started. In the same spot in Times Square where this mini-series began. It's warm, about 80 degrees, and while the surroundings look different, they are not unfamiliar. The Castro Convertibles sign still sits below Coca-Cola, though this square neony version, with the dynamic ribbon symbol below the logo, is decidedly more modern than its disc predecessor. I don't bother to utilize the titles of the movies and shows that I see advertised to locate myself. I walk to the newsstand.

It's August 8, 1975. *The Times* has some above-the-fold article about Gerald Ford's first year in office and there's reference in other headlines to inflation, budget cuts, and hostages. I mentally riff, "in the recession was I repressed, nowhere near." Reaching into my pocket to find what my financier has bestowed, a ticket or cash or hocked jewelry to be re-hocked, I feel the cardboard. It's a new decade, so maybe this is the season opener for another theatre slash Stonewall — though it doesn't exist in this decade or the next — adventure.

Oddly enough, there are two pieces of cardboard. Each ducat for center orchestra seating is priced at $16, a significant increase in just a few years. It doesn't surprise me in the least that the show I'm going to see is *Chicago*. Instead of a new plotline, it seems we're going to play this one out. As luck would have it, in this scripted saga, there's also enough cash for a bite to eat and a couple of cab rides.

"And where should I go?" I say out loud to no one in particular, amusing myself. It's much more relaxing to enjoy this as a dream.

A ride downtown. St. Vincent's on the left. Village Cigars on the right. Exit.

Per the director's staging, I find my mark just outside the former birthplace of the gay rights movement. Though it's still technically the site of that, the space has transitioned. Manny Duell is renting the space to non-bar tenants, as will happen over and over. The space is now split for two historically irrelevant squatters. At 53 Christopher sits Bowl and Board, a '70s post-hippie, pre-Pottery Barn shop with hand-carved, wooden kitchen utensils. Hooray for gay rights.

To the right, at 51 Christopher, is where I'll grab a bite before showtime. It is now the site of one of numerous bagel eateries that will pop up all over Manhattan during the '70s. This one, too cleverly called Bagel And, will provide some confusion to some less diligent historians who will mistakenly refer to it as Bageland in their superficial recounting of the squatter history. It's an understandable and largely irrelevant mistake owing to the renovation of the Stonewall Inn sign, which by 1975 had become fatally deteriorated. When the bagel squatter took residence, the famous sign was resurfaced with BAGELAND written vertically, as the word Stonewall had been. The vertical orientation of the text provoked the misunderstanding of the name of the overly mirrored and wood-paneled noshateria. Thanks to Mimi Sheraton's review of the bagel eatery phenomenon of the mid-1970s, including a picture of a horizontal logo above the 51 Christopher window showing the proper name of the restaurant, I'm probably the only person who knows or cares about this.

I enter, take a seat, and peruse the menu. It's more or less standard deli fare. The shtick, it seems, is that everything can be served on a bagel. I disagree with the premise and order my bagel with just lox and cream cheese, the way God intended. While the schmearing and slicing go on beyond my line of sight, I amuse myself by imagining that I will go over to the other diners, enjoying their pastrami or egg salad or whatever, and tell them about what unsanitary, if not immoral, act took place in the very spot that they're eating. Maybe on the same table for all I know.

The food arrives and I dig in, continuing the sacrilege of the icon. I wish Manny would have rented this shrine to the Mafia instead of proper tenants. At least the Mafia afforded my ancestors the right to dance in a bar of their own. And while they also overcharged for watered down drinks, they've got a thing to learn from the two that run this joint. According to Mimi, they're charging 30% more for the same thing you can get elsewhere. "Who's the real criminal?" I ask you.

As I chow down on the last bite, I give a thought to the unexpected second ticket. This is a plot twist that can take a number of turns. Will I meet some ticketless, not-yet-famous-but-going-to-be-very-big-someday person outside the theatre and have a special guest seatmate to share the performance and, perhaps, more with later? Am I supposed to sell the seat for cash that I will need after the show? I'm oddly indifferent and uncaring about the path to come, a recent gift from knowing that none of this really matters. Dream your dream. Baby, dream your dream.

I kill a little more time wandering the Village until seven and then head uptown. The 46th Street Theatre holds lots of meaning to me. As a child, I saw my very first show, *1776*, there. It was a second home during *Nine*. Now, I get to see Gwen fulfilling the prophecy — and Chita and Jerry to boot. The crowd outside the theatre is enormous, considering that the curtain won't rise for another 50 minutes or so. Coming from 8th Avenue, I make my way past the back end of the Imperial Theatre, where *Pippin* is still running, past the stage door of the 46th, and below the marquee for my show. It is then that I understand the crowd size and plot twist, having nothing to do with the second ticket.

For the second time today, I get to see a sign that I'd only read about in books and newspapers. Earlier, it was the Bagel And sign. Now, it is a small placard. It's way too small given the size of the news, but more impactful, more show-bizzy, in the diminutive. There are nine lines of text. It reads:

> At this performance
> of
> CHICAGO
> the role of
> ROXIE HART
> usually played by
> GWEN VERDON
> will be played by
> LIZA MINNELLI

The front doors are open and the longest chorus line of ticket purchasers I've ever seen spill out onto the street and up the block. They're all here to beg, borrow, steal, or purchase, if they have to, one of the 52,760 seats available for this five week run. Cleverly, this has been billed as Liza stepping into the role rather than as a "replacement." As a favor to friends. Fosse, the master choreographer, finessed the stars' orbits with the same attention to detail as a finger snap. With the understated announcement a week earlier in *The Times* that Liza would have just one week of rehearsal, all tickets to this run vanished. Today's line of buyers will see Gwen when she returns, recuperated from throat surgery.

I step out of the throng and cross the street to assess the situation, standing in the same small parking lot that I'll park my car in during the untold number of times that I will see *Nine*. To see the opening night of this brief theatre engagement is a gift for sure, but the lack of seeing Gwen in the role bothers me. It would have been far more entertaining to complete this arc seeing her perform the role, as a bookend to seeing *Charity*, even if the dream no longer provided a personal conversation with her to wrap things up. I'll simply have to register my dissatisfaction with the author in my subsequent review.

I look at the line of Liza fans to see if there's anyone who should join me for tonight's performance. Crossing back to the south side of the street, I walk up the line to assess the cattle call. There are more than a couple of cute guys who would make for a fine date or dinner companion, but I refuse to ruin this evening by miscasting the role with a chatty queen who has no real appreciation for the theatre or this moment. A few of them, those with a sixth sense I gather, unabashedly flirt and ask me if I have an extra ticket. One, summoning a dance hall hostess appeal, promises fun, laughs, and a good time. It's worthy of a call back, but he doesn't snag the role.

With the lobby doors open, the assemblage under the marquee flows inside and I follow the current. I find the pair of seats in the still relatively empty row down front. People who occupy this territory, I understand, don't claim their seats until much closer to curtain time. Looking around for the famous or future famous, I recognize no one until they enter. I see Fred Ebb first as he stops at the row in which I'm seated. John Kander is right behind. Remarkably, they possess the pair of seats next to mine, though the absence of a person in my second seat causes some initial confusion.

"Is someone sitting there?" Ebb asks, pointing to the empty seat to my left.

"Not really," I respond, "but that's my seat too. Yours must be the next one." Ebb sits and Kander takes the next seat to his left.

I'd never met either of them before, except for seeing them enter this very same theatre 20 years hence for the opening night of *Steel Pier*. It would be the only opening night I'd ever been to and a major letdown because the title song's lyrics, "Life is a party. Why don't you come to the Steel Pier?" will sound so much like *Cabaret*, but not in the good, riffing-off-a-classic way.

"So, that seat's not going to be used?" Ebb asks, looking dashing.

Fearful that he might be eyeing this as an opportunity to move some friend seated further back into the space between us, I explain, "I didn't know this would be Liza's first night when I got the tickets. I tried to find someone worthy of a moment like this but, in the end, I decided that it was too important to risk someone distracting me from what's going on on-stage."

He purses his lips. I don't know if he's impressed with my respect of the moment or whether he thinks I'm crazy. "She's going to be dynamite," he says, providing no clue.

"I can't imagine having the parents that she's had, that DNA," I offer. "When I saw her mother open the Felt Forum on Christmas, it was remarkable, even though Judy wasn't in full form."

"The Carnegie Hall run, or even The Palace," he boasts, "those were the shows to see. I think Liza has the potential to be even greater than Judy."

"What's it like, being able to guide someone with that much raw talent?" I ask, knowing that he will be her most significant mentor.

"It's remarkable. Like harnessing an explosion," he beams. "I changed the end of the first act back to the way it was supposed to be originally. Wait 'til you see it. She kills it."

I'm not sure what he's referring to, as there are few detailed accounts of Liza's stint save for a *Times* re-review of the show that had a decidedly more positive spin than the original assessment of the production. *A Chorus Line* was the darling of this season and all of the razzle dazzle that the *Chicago* team could bring to bear wouldn't change that.

"I can't wait. I'm also dying to see Chita and her together," I say, though I've had the privilege. Back in 1984, I took my cousin, Diane, to see *The Rink*. For two theatre fans, the idea of seeing Chita and Liza in a new Kander and Ebb musical was a necessity, regardless of the bad reviews and gossip about Liza's drug and alcohol problems. That night, we saw what we came to see, a big fat Broadway show with two legends.

It wasn't until after I drove Diane home to East Meadow and was making my way back to my parents' home in New Jersey that I saw the dark side. Driving through the Midtown Tunnel on my way to the Lincoln, I decided to take 45th Street to traverse the island. It's nearing 1 a.m. as I cross 8th Avenue, spotting a black limousine parked outside the stage door of the Martin Beck Theatre. Instinctively, I pull up behind it and park, engine idling, instead of continuing my trek home. Within a minute, the stage door opens and two beefy guys emerge, followed by Liza hobbling out on crutches. I grab the Playbill from the passenger seat, jump out of the car and run over to Liza, who is still only halfway to her awaiting limo. At this hour, there is no one else around.

Holding the Playbill toward her, I tell her that my cousin and I loved her performance. She smiles and slurs a "Thank you." Realizing that I haven't provided a pen to sign the Playbill and that neither she nor the beefy guys would be providing one, I say, "Just a minute, I'll get a pen from the car." Miraculously, they all stand there in the middle of the sidewalk waiting for me to bring a pen back from my car. When I return, moments later, I hand it to her and ask if she would "Make it out to Anthony, my friend and college roommate." Anthony and I had shared much of the *Nine* experience together and I wanted to give him this theatre souvenir as a thank you for allowing me to keep the 6-foot-tall *Nine* poster that we had stolen from the subway and had autographed by the cast.

Liza was unfortunately unable to understand what I was saying. She autographs the Playbill and says, "Thank you, Anthony." I try to correct her, tell her my name, and explain again that the autograph is for my friend. But she's in a complete daze. It's another sorry-grateful moment.

"They're my two best friends," Ebb smiles. "It doesn't get any better than this."

"It certainly doesn't," I smile back.

The house lights dim and Chita delivers "All That Jazz" like nothing I'd ever seen. Bebe's version will be more precise, more perfect. Chita's is more fluid and more gritty. It's at the end of the first act that I see what Fred Ebb was talking about, giving him the briefest of nods as it begins. Liza delivers the "I Am My Own Best Friend" duet as a solo. It's an interesting twist on the song, becoming less of a parody of the "My Way" soliloquies of the day. As a solo, it's a survival song and Liza milks it for all its worth, even inserting a gasp in between the last two words a la Jennifer Holliday's Effie. It's unnecessary, but Fred apparently approves given his reaction.

The adulation at the end of the show is thunderous, almost too much so. Moments earlier, Liza's cartwheel during "Hot Honey Rag" brought frenzied cheers. I'm annoyed. In 20 years, when she's 50, she won't be able to do that. Hell, she won't be doing that at 40. Gwen's doing that and more at 50, with far less fanfare. Not fair. But that's show biz.

CHAPTER TWENTY-SIX

Open a New Window

I wake up from last night's dream and hunt for the photo. Not a Stonewall photo, but a photo I had taken of Liza in concert in 1983. It's part of my eclectic theatre collection. It captures her in one of her famous poses, framed by two adoring male dancers, at the end of a number. During the beginning of the run of *The Rink*, I had asked Chita to get Liza to autograph it, which she kindly did. The 8x10 enlargement that I had made was a bit fuzzy, stretched beyond the negative's abilities, but I wanted the finished piece to be large and frame-worthy. I still hadn't framed it or displayed it amongst the rest of my treasures. It was buried somewhere in the apartment and I had to find it.

While pulling apart the walk-in closet, I call Joe Jr.'s and, before I can open another box of memorabilia, sustenance arrives. I let the answering machine handle a ten o'clock call, and hearing Buddy's voice, I pick up.

"Why haven't you returned any of my calls?" Buddy laments. "I was worried about you."

"Sorry. I got obsessed with scanning those old Stonewall photos and loading them to a website."

"You're doing what?" Buddy panics. "I thought we were going to donate them to a gay archive." Leave it to Buddy to turn a me into a we, especially when he isn't the me.

"I had a change of heart," I explain. "I decided that I'd make the photos available on the internet to everyone. I can still donate them, but this way the story will get out."

"Oh, OK, whatever you want, hon," Buddy retreats from first-person plural. "If there's anything I can do to help ..."

"Thanks. Right now it's just a lot of time consuming work, scanning and uploading. Kind of a one-person job, but I appreciate the offer."

"What are you wearing tonight?" Buddy changes subject.

"Tonight?"

"The Halloween Party at Stonewall. Dominick mentioned it at the brunch. I've been working on my costume for days."

"I honestly forgot," I admit. "I'm not even sure that I'm going to go."

"Oh, yes you better," he insists. "Ever since our brunch, I've been trying to get in contact with as many of the old gang as possible."

"And how has that been going?"

"I'm not going to tell you," he teases. "You'll just have to see who shows up."

"And what are you wearing?" I ask, bracing myself for an answer that's sure to cause awkward laughter.

"I'm going as Peter Allen. I've got a floral shirt and tight white pants to show off the goods. It's part costume, part advertisement."

"That's actually a good costume for you," I praise. "Very 'I Go To Rio.' But don't be disappointed if those young queens don't know who Peter Allen is. I was talking to Charlie the other day and he'd never heard of Gwen."

"I know, poor thing. I felt so bad when I heard. But I don't care if nobody knows who I'm supposed to be. That's their loss, not mine."

"Well said."

"So, you're coming," he insists.

"Yes, I'll come," I give in. "But don't expect much costume-wise. There's no time to do anything creative."

"I'm sure you'll think of something. We'll have to skip Knickerbocker tonight. I wouldn't be able to eat that meal and still fit into these pants. Should I pick you up around ten?"

"No, I'll meet you there," I decide, wanting to give myself enough time to continue working on the Stonewall Revival website and coordinate a decent enough costume.

For the next twelve hours, I cycle between the website and searching through my theatre collection for an idea for tonight's costume. I'm only interrupted by Stuart's call to tell me what I missed on *SVU*. I tell him about seeing *Chicago* with Liza. He asks me about the show as though he still believes that I've actually seen it. I play along, giving him details of her performance and how I'd watched Fred Ebb from the corner of my eye silently coaching her along.

"That's it?" he says, with disappointment. "No back stage visit, no after-party?"

"That's it. I didn't expect anything more. I've seen the original *Chicago*. Told Gwen that she'd get it. She did. Not that I saw her in it. That ends the story. I didn't see her in it because it's over."

"I think there's more to come," he advises.

"Maybe so. But a different storyline for sure. By 1975 the infections are starting. I missed my window to do something."

"I don't know about that," he offers. "But I think you'll continue to have these dreams, these theatre fantasies. And, selfishly, I love hearing the stories."

"Listen, I've still got a bunch of uploading to do and I've got to figure out a costume for the Halloween Party at Stonewall."

"Ok," he signs off. "I won't call tomorrow. I'm sure you'll be banged up."

I toy with the idea of going to Abracadabra on 21st Street. They are *the* store for Halloween costumes in the city and the guy who runs the shop was a regular at Stonewall during my tenure, assuming he's still around. But I elect to forgo the chaos lurking there on the weekend before Halloween when I stumble onto a better idea hanging in my closet.

Walking into Stonewall on any other Saturday, I'd be greeted with a host of hellos from the regulars and staff. Tonight, the sea of costumes has turned the place into a masquerade party and I'm venturing into the unknown. Amidst the drag, the masks, and the props, I am decidedly under-dressed, though formally attired. In the midst of scanning, I became inspired to recreate the walk-on role that I had purchased at the Broadway Cares auction two years ago — as a member of the *Chicago* chorus. It was an easy costume owing to its simplicity, black dress pants and a tuxedo shirt opened down to there. To brace myself for the cold weather and to create an unveiling for my outfit, I donned a double-breasted, black Armani topcoat that went to the floor. And to deflect the expected criticism that I wasn't really wearing a costume, I carried the black bowler hat from the show that Bebe had autographed, the one prop that could turn the pants and shirt into wardrobe. Admittedly, when I left 59 West 12th, it looked as though I was heading to The Met rather than a gay bar.

I see Dominick, not in costume, coming from the back. He tells me that Buddy and a lot of the old Stonewall gang have assembled upstairs. After dropping the topcoat in the office, I walk back to find a dozen of them laughing and drinking along the windows overlooking Christopher Street. Everyone's there, except a man staring out the window. Amid attire running the gamut from The Village People to KISS to a New York City police officer, I spot Peter Allen.

"Don't you look sexy," Buddy flirts.

I strike a Chicago pose to show off the bowler hat and return the flirtation, "C'mon Pete, why don't we paint the town."

A good number of these guys have not worked at Stonewall in five or more years, yet they made their way back for this reunion disguised as a Halloween party. The next three or four hours fly by, finding out where everyone has landed. One has opened a bed and breakfast with his lover in New Jersey. Another started working as a dresser for Broadway shows. A former manager had become a concierge for The Four Seasons Hotel on 57th Street. None of them were bartending or otherwise working in gay bars. While age may have played a part in that, I elected to think it was because we'd all done our duty and turned this place over to another generation to tend to it.

As the group dwindles down, I huddle with Buddy and Bobby at the end of the bar nearest the windows.

"Buddy told me you've started putting the photos of Jimmy and all of us on a website," Bobby mentions.

"Yes, I hope you don't mind. I hope that nobody minds that I'm just putting them out there."

"No, I think that's a nice idea," Bobby smiles.

"I tend to overthink things. So, I'm not going to put people's names next to their pictures, except for Jimmy. Maybe later on, depending on how it's all received, I can start identifying the players."

"Why didn't you just ask people tonight if they minded?" he asks.

"I don't know," I admit. "Probably 'cause I didn't want to hear anyone shit on the idea or tell me how to do it differently or say yes when they meant no or vice versa ..."

"You're not making any sense," Bobby snipes at me. "All these people came back tonight because it meant something to them. You say you're doing this to share it, but you're still controlling it."

"Guilty," I say, raising my voice. Then, calmer, "Look, I don't know what I'm doing. Just like I didn't know what the fuck I was doing when Jimmy died. I just went on instinct. Keep the place open. That's what I'm doing now. Going on instinct. I think this is important to do, so I'm doing it. We're all here to defend our actions, he's not. This is for him, not us."

Buddy, never one to exit a dramatic scene, has uncharacteristically retreated from the escalation. I spot him making his way to the back staircase to head downstairs.

"OK, OK," Bobby reassures. "I wasn't trying to criticize you for doing it. I'm just pointing out that you have people's support. Don't assume the worst. OK?"

"OK, sorry."

"Let's do some shots," he offers, turning to get the bartender's attention.

"I don't think that's necessary," I say, but a bottle of schnapps is delivered and shot glasses are filled before I can offer a compromise.

"Cheers!" Bobby toasts. "To Stonewall. To Jimmy."

"To Stonewall and Jimmy," I echo.

Dominick, who had only intermittently joined our Stonewall reunion during the evening, acting as ringmaster to the larger assemblage of Halloween revelers downstairs, makes his way toward Bobby and myself, with arms wide open and a smile stretching nearly as far across.

"You won't believe what I've got for you," he boasts loudly.

After handing an unlabeled VHS tape to the bartender behind us, he grabs me by the shoulders to announce, "I can't believe I found it. You're gonna die when you see this."

The bartender starts to load the tape into one of those combo DVD/VCR machines located just below the TV mounted above him as Dominick instructs his manager, Tony, to cue up a quieter song on the upstairs sound system, "so we can hear him talkin'."

Standing three abreast at the bar, looking up at the monitor overhead, Bobby starts to ask Dominick what is on the tape we're about to view as the snowy static crystalizes into a picture of the bar downstairs.

"When is that from?" Bobby whispers sideways to Dominick.

"It's the beginning. From 10 years ago," Dominick swells with pride, as the three of us stare at grainy footage of the interior of New Jimmy's. I hear my voice, just barely, in the background asking where to put something, as a series of long forgotten workmen parade in and out of frame, moving furniture into place just days before the opening.

"Where did you get this?" I ask, mesmerized at these visions of the near past.

"I found it in my garage. After we had brunch. I remembered that I shot this right around the time the place was getting finished up. When I saw what was on it, I knew that I had to show it to yous guys."

"Turn it up," Dominick instructs the bartender, as the camera pans toward the man who is absent from this reunion. Jimmy, in jeans and a grey sweatshirt, is stacking boxes of glasses on top of the bar. He's calling out to someone out of view, "You don't need to do this."

I see myself, 10 years younger and wearing one of my favorite suits, carrying similar boxes of glasses and depositing them on the bar. It had been one of those lunch hours where I come down to my new boyfriend's not-yet-open bar to help out in whatever small way that I could.

"You don't have to do this," Jimmy says again, this time with both of us on screen and smiling at each other as couples do when they're newly in love. "You're gonna get messed up. You have to go back to work."

"I'm fine. I'm just trying to help a little," I see myself reply as the camera pans away to capture more of the space and the final touches being made. I've lost all awareness of my surroundings, having tunneled exclusively into the sights and sounds emanating from the monitor.

The cameraman pivots back around, shooting over my younger shoulder, directly toward Jimmy so that his face fills the screen. "I love that you want to help me," he starts as an Oleta Adams song burrows into the tunnel, "but you've done enough."

The last time I'd stared into those innocent eyes he was pleading for me to help him. In this moment, with finality in the distance, he's given me a reprieve.

I hear myself tell him, "I could stay a little longer," and he smiles.

"It's OK," he reassures me, both then and now. "It's going to be OK. You should go, if you have to."

The camera pulls away to make its way down the bar and into the newly christened kitchen. The three of us continue to stare at the images of New Jimmy's, when everything was fresh and hopeful, until another blizzard of snow returns.

Another round is placed before us. Another toast is made. After holding my breath for a decade, I finally exhale. And with a bear hug to one of them and a kiss on the cheek to the other, I allow myself, "It's time for me to go now."

CHAPTER TWENTY-SEVEN

Put on Your Sunday Best

Paparazzo. An Italian word for a buzzing mosquito. Fellini bestowed the surname to a photographer in *La Dolce Vita* and the name stuck. Now, standing in the promenade of Lincoln Center again, I fully understand the translation. I somehow had sped past the usual falling asleep at home ritual and changed, Clark Kent-style, into this black-tie costume. Unlike the Halloween party at Stonewall, everyone else here is in similar formal garb. The ticket in my pocket, priced at a whopping $250, is for a gala at The Met. It's May 9, 1976, just before 8 p.m.

The buzz of photographers is swarming so that I can't see the prey they've descended upon. I step up onto the ledge of the Revlon fountain for a better view, but the feeding frenzy is moving toward the Opera House, still obscuring the sweet nectar at its center. I make an end run around the throng and get into the lobby and up one of the dual staircases for an aerial view.

We've come almost full circle from the ballet benefit at the St. James, closing loopholes, rectifying unfinished business. Though I didn't get to see the widowed bride then, she's here now. In truth, it's not the same woman. This woman is another man's bride now and, having left the world of mere mortals, has transfigured into an object. A very rare, expensive object that must be photographed. Jacqueline Kennedy Onassis floats through the lobby, an unspeaking, ethereal idol that bears a faint Mona Lisa smile. The serenity of her presence is contradicted by the horde surrounding her. There is zero personal space between the object and its observers, yet the mass moves through the lobby as if choreographed.

We're here tonight, I come to learn, to raise money for The Performing Arts Research Center of The New York Public Library at Lincoln Center. Judging from the ticket price and capacity crowd, the goal is all but assured. My indifference to ballet notwithstanding, I actually enjoy seeing the likes of Baryshnikov, Peter Martins, Suzanne Farrell, and Natalia Makarova fly through the air. But it is the star power from the less noble arts that really excites me. Elizabeth Taylor and Nelson Rockefeller act as emcees. Paul Simon sings. Gwen and Chita perform numbers from *Chicago*. At last, I get to see the deed done, though it's a bit of a letdown. Out of the context of the show, without the proper staging, it's more like seeing a snippet of *Chicago* on Merv Griffin or Mike Douglas than it is seeing the real production.

The Star-Spangled Gala is staggeringly long. As we approach the four-hour mark, I think to myself, "I'll pay another $250 just to get it to stop," as do many other patrons apparently. The number of empty seats grows over the course of the marathon, first with extended visits to the bar and then with full retreats to Park Avenue, 5th Avenue, and the like. When it's all plié-d out, it's nearly 1 a.m.

I linger in front of the Opera House for a bit, deciding what to do next. My attire and the hour limit the options, I think, though it shouldn't matter all that much in a dream. I elect to walk over to Central Park and up to 69th Street. It's a fairly mild night, maybe 50 degrees at this hour, and the streets are expectedly quiet. I stop in front of her building, closer to the corner rather than in the line-of-sight of the doorman. After maybe 10 or 15 minutes, I assume that she's already home and that this visit will not include another chance encounter, but a car pulls up and she emerges. She notices the dapper dressed man at the corner and makes her way toward me.

"You were at the benefit tonight?" she asks.

"Yes, I finally got to see you do it. Well, do a couple of numbers at least."

"You look the same," she shakes her head. "Like you haven't aged a day."

"It's the lighting. It's all about the lighting."

"I, uh, saved the pictures," she starts. "I didn't want them, but I couldn't throw them away."

"Oh, I had no idea," I apologize. "I didn't mean to be a problem."

"I'd like to give them back to you," she says, motioning for me to follow her into the building.

As we ride up the elevator, I'm amused to have found this mistake in the dream. It's the first time. I know those pictures are safely stored in my apartment and have been launched into cyberspace. I choose to play along with this flawed storyline.

She has me sit in the living room while she fetches the photos from somewhere out of sight. Sitting in a tuxedo in this grand apartment feels swellegant. When she returns, she delicately hands me the photos, as though they were fragile.

"That's your guy, Jimmy, isn't it?"

"Yep, that was him," I nod, "in happier times. I'm surprised that you saved them. I'm even more surprised that I'm sitting here in your apartment again. After last time and after you ..."

I almost refer to her death, feeling that anything is fair game in a flawed dream, but pull back because I can't bear to be unkind to this gentle soul. I finish, "And, um, after not having seen you in so long."

"I didn't know why you left them for me. What you wanted me to do with them and that clipping. You wanted me to do you a favor. I thought the pictures were part of that."

"I left them because I wanted to show you the two beginnings. The riot in '69. And the revival in 1990."

As I'm explaining this to her, I become annoyed at being dragged back into this pointless scenario of me asking Gwen Verdon for help in preventing AIDS. The storyline had become adulterated with the apparition of Jimmy at Stonewall and the discovery of the not-lost photos in my apartment. I don't want to be mean to her, even in a dream, but I don't want to follow this script anymore.

I start to adlib, "Listen, I'm grateful that you kept these for me, but none of this is real. There is no favor to do. No point in trying to change something can't be altered. Why don't you tell me about yourself, what's been going on, how that show tonight came about. Anything else, please."

My going off-script seems to have taken her a little off-guard, but she improvises quickly. "Well, tonight was a benefit for the library. They do important work, preserving dance and theatre and music, and well, they don't have enough money. They were going to close. So, I asked James Lipton to produce a benefit ..."

"That was your idea?" I interrupt, stunned. "That whole thing was your idea?" I ask again as she nods in the affirmative.

"It needed to get done. The library needed the money. To preserve all the theatre and dance history."

"Oh my God," I say in partial disbelief. "That's amazing. I've been to a lot of benefits, but never something like that. I mean freaking Jerome Robbins created a new ballet with Baryshnikov and Makarova for *your* benefit. Dancers, singers, movie stars, politicians, and everybody else involved — it's unprecedented."

"*My* Jimmy had helped me stage a bunch of benefits for Guild Hall in East Hampton. I twisted his arm a little to do this. He really put it together. It's Lipton's work."

"Yes, I'm sure he made all of it happen," I begin. "And, by the way, you might ask him to edit it down from four and a half hours next time. Yes, he did a remarkable job. But if it wasn't for you pushing him to do this, your idea, it wouldn't have happened."

"I'm just happy to make sure this stuff is preserved. A dancer's life is short and when you can't dance anymore like you used to, you owe it to your craft to keep it alive."

"So, is this your transition? Your pivot?" I ask.

"What do you mean?" she starts to ask, then says, "Never mind, I know what you mean. *Chicago* is the end of the line for me, at least in musicals."

"I get it, you're older than you ever intended to be," I smile. "But aren't you happy about *Chicago*? Aren't you enjoying it? You waited sooo long for it."

"Well, yes. But it's different when you know it's the last time. Bittersweet. Do you want something to drink?"

"Sure, whatever you're having."

"I have some beer in the fridge or if you want a real drink …"

"Beer's fine," I reply as she disappears into the kitchen. "You don't seem angry with me anymore?"

After an awkward silence and just the sound of two beer bottles opening, she re-enters the room. "I wasn't angry with you. I just didn't want to hear the things you were telling me or were about to tell me."

"I probably shouldn't have done that," I apologize as we clink bottles.

"Why would anyone want to know about every horrible thing that was to come? Life's hard enough as it is."

"Not everything that's coming is horrible," I try to reassure. "There's lots of good things too."

"I guess I missed that part when you insisted on telling me about people dying."

"I guess I was a bit heavy handed," I apologize. "But, really, there are good things to look forward to."

"The older you get, more bad things happen than good. It's just the way it is," she explains.

"And nobody needs to be reminded of that."

"What did you mean before when you said none of this is real?" she returns to the script.

Though I'm acutely aware that I'm dreaming, the conversation feels as real as any I'd ever had.

"To me, this is all a dream. A fantasy. Somewhere is the bowels of my subconscious, I must have some survivor's guilt about being alive when people who were close to me aren't. So, I wrote a play in my head, with you in the cast, to undo all the misery. But it doesn't matter."

"I still don't understand you sometimes. There's been no plague. People aren't dying in the streets."

"I'm not going to try to convince you otherwise," I say, taking command of this misguided production. "It's too late now, anyway. Even here. Ya know, I had this dream that I saw Jimmy. *My* Jimmy, not Lipton. He was staring out of a window and as hard as I tried to wave at him, to catch his attention, he didn't see me. Do you think the dead can see us?"

She looks away, deep in thought. Then, returning to look at me, she asks, "Why do you want to know?"

At first, I'm not sure how to respond. Then, I answer, "To know if they're witnesses or judges to what we have or haven't done."

"This is going down that path again," she resists.

"Sorry," I whisper, taking the last swig from the bottle. "I guess I'm too preoccupied with knowing whether they can see the good you're trying to do for them when they're no longer here. I'm trying to do right by Jimmy. To right a wrong. It would be nice if he knew that."

"Then I'm sure he does," she answers, though I can't tell if she means it or if it's a way to end this exchange. In either case, I know this is the last time I'll be with her in this grand apartment. There will be no more Broadway shows to dream about seeing her in.

In a decade's time, when Fosse dies, she devotes herself to affirming his legacy, not because someone had erased his name from a building or from history, but simply to keep it alive.

"Listen, it's getting late and as much as I'd like to stay I probably should be going back," I begin my goodbye. I pick up the photos and hand them back to her, as though they're still the most fragile of items. "I would like you to do me a favor."

"I don't understand," she replies taking the pictures.

"I'd like you to keep these. I have another set back home."

Shaking her head, "Why?"

"It will help you remember the favor," I begin. "I want you to do something for charity."

"Is that with a big C or a small c?" she says, making light of the moment.

"Well, both, actually," I say, starting to rise from the couch and picking up the empty beer bottle to return to the kitchen. She takes it from me and motions for me to sit back down.

"What you did tonight," I smile, "that amazing freaking event. It will do so much good for so many people. At some point, you'll realize it's time to do another event. For people like Jimmy."

"You want me to do another benefit? For something that hasn't happened?" she shakes her head vigorously in disbelief.

"Yes, that's what the pictures are for," I say, putting my hand on hers, still holding the photos.

"How about another beer?" she deflects.

"Ok, sure," I say chuckling. Gwen Verdon has asked me to stay for another beer. I look around the living room, in my own disbelief as to where I am and what I've asked her to do. The clock reads quarter to three, but the song is cut short as she returns with the beers.

"What are you thinking about honey?" she asks, handing me the bottle.

"Nothing really," I say. "Just, if my friends could see me now."

CHAPTER TWENTY-EIGHT

Giants in the Sky

I had awoken far earlier on Sunday than anyone, including myself, would have guessed. Though unaware how I got home, I found myself laying crosswise across the king-size bed, on top of the comforter, still in costume. I'm not the least bit hung over, astonishingly. Panicked, I leap from the bed to find the bowler hat and, thankfully, spot it sitting propped on the dining room table. If I had lost or damaged it between the time I left Bobby and Dominick at Stonewall and left Jackie at The Met, I'd have died a thousand deaths.

I launch back into the website. Except for the occasional food delivery from my friends on the corner, I devote another 14 hours to cataloging the Bermuda Triangle in Stonewall's history. It's the final penance before I can return to the land of the living.

On Monday, I had called Buddy, Stuart, and Bobby to see if they would join me for dinner the following night. Buddy and Bobby both balked at first, given that they'd miss the Village Halloween parade. While it was a spectacle worth seeing, not unlike how tourists view the Thanksgiving Day parade or New Year's Eve in Times Square, it too had become oversized and overdone. The year I saw two dozen or so people rolling up 6th Avenue inside a full-size replica of a New York subway car, replete with interior lighting, strap handles, and seating, I knew that it was no longer our little neighborhood parade. But when I told Buddy and Bobby that I'd be taking all of us to Tavern On The Green, they acquiesced.

I had asked them to meet me at 6:15 on the corner of 69th Street and Central Park West. As the restaurant was only two blocks to the south, none of them suspected my detour. Buddy and Bobby, sharing a ride from Chelsea, were the first to arrive.

"Why did you have us meet here?" Buddy whines. Ever the embellisher, he adds, "Everyone knows Tavern is off 67th Street."

"The traffic is insane," Bobby bristles. "Why is that street closed off?" he asks pointing to 69th Street.

"Don't worry," I reassure. "Our reservation isn't until seven o'clock. All will be explained in due course."

Stuart doesn't arrive for another 10 minutes, during which we observe hundreds of costumed children accompanied by parents — more often than not likewise embellished — entering and exiting the barricaded block.

"What is this all about?" Stuart startles us from behind.

"It's the most remarkable Halloween production in New York," I announce to the threesome.

"And we're here why?" he responds.

"Before we have dinner, I wanted to show you all something," I say, motioning for them to follow me past the barricade. "It's to make a point."

Four gay men in slacks and dress shirts amidst a throng of Lilliputian revelers makes each of us an out man odd. As we head up the block toward Columbus, the questions cease as my friends take in the backlot of multi-million dollar townhouses transformed into a Halloween village. The competition amongst the homeowners to offer the creepiest, scariest, most original décor is evident, with enormous fabrications attached to the stately facades. Candy is flowing from front doors like a Willy Wonka factory. The perfection of this Halloween rendering makes its more famous downtown rival appear self-indulgent. The effect is indescribable, though Tim Burton meets Thomas Kinkade wouldn't be an unfair assessment.

"How long has this been going on?" Bobby stares in amazement.

"Since 1969, though not at this level certainly back then," I respond as docent. "It's been going on far longer than the Village parade."

In a moment of candor, Buddy offers, "I've never seen anything like this."

"It's like a movie set," Stuart adds.

"And you'll never guess how this started," I offer some bait.

"How?" Bobby nibbles.

"Well, the short answer is that Gwen Verdon wanted to provide a place for kids to go trick-or-treating that was safe and fun," I begin. "Her daughter, Nicole, was about six at the time. And the Upper West Side wasn't so gentrified. Not by a long shot."

"Gwen started this?" Stuart says with surprise.

"Yep," I affirm. "She saw something that needed to be done and she did it." Pointing to the Disneyfied display before us, I add, "This is part of her legacy. She put something in place that continues to this day. Yet no one really knows that. Can you imagine doing something like that when some of these buildings were abandoned and there were drunks and junkies around? It took a lot of courage and imagination to think you could make this block a great place for trick-or-treating back then."

"I had no idea," Buddy confesses, "but of course *you* did."

"Was that listed in her obituary?" Bobby asks, thinking he's discovered my source.

"No, not in any of the ones I read," I answer, continuing as their Munchkinland tour guide.

"How do you know all this then?" Stuart asks, expecting that it came in a dream.

"I stumbled across it when I was researching the ownership of Stonewall in 1969," I explain with a CliffNotes version of my intelligence gathering on Joel Weiser, the not so holy ghost of the trinity. "The neighborhood was in a state of transformation because of Lincoln Center. The West 69th Street Block Association was formed by residents who wanted to improve the place where they lived. In their newsletters, they credit Gwen with starting this whole thing."

As we near the end of the block, I conclude the tour and lead them to the restaurant, taking Columbus down to 67th Street. The reservation specifically requested that we be seated in the Crystal Room, and the maître d' obliges. Our waiter is actor-handsome and especially solicitous, no doubt due to his relief at serving his own tribe versus the non-natives that surround us. The martinis arrive just as we finish ordering dinner, and within minutes, the chef sends out an amuse-bouche. Fittingly, it's a shot glass of roasted red pepper soup, topped with a coiffure of flaming red shredded peppers. Very amusing.

"Why did you pick this place for dinner?" Bobby asks, taking a sip.

"The website's almost done. I'm ready to let that life die and start a new one. I've done my duty and I wanted to have a dinner here to mark the occasion," I explain. "I know this isn't a place that real New Yorkers admit going to, but it's really lovely. They had Fosse's party here after he died."

"Party?" Buddy questions. "Don't you mean memorial?"

"No, it was a party," I correct. "He left something like $25,000 to his friends, a list of specific people. Something like $300 per person to have dinner on him after he died. Gwen suggested that they all donate the money back to have a party where everyone would come together. She held it in this very room."

"That must have been quite the event," Stuart chuckles.

"That's not a bad way to go out," Buddy interjects. "Throwing one last party for all your friends. I can't imagine what it would cost me to do that or where I'd throw it."

"Let's see," Bobby starts, "eight or nine people times $10 for a burger and brew at Julius'... that's a hundred bucks."

Everyone, including Buddy, laughs at Bobby's impromptu calculations and the image of celebrating Buddy at the city's oldest gay bar, still serving great burgers off their tiny grill to, as they say, mature men and their admirers.

"Or you could have something catered at the Ninth Circle," Stuart pipes up, recalling one of the sleazier spots on the trade circuit.

"I'll have you know, I've never been there, and I don't have to pay for sex," Buddy feigns indignation.

"Oh, honey, we all pay for sex," Stuart teases. "One way or another."

While appetizers of shrimp cocktail, foie gras, escargot, and autumn salad are consumed, the conversation migrates from party planning to hustlers. Though no one admits to making a purchase, everyone offers a Zagat-style critique of the city's current and former dance halls.

Looking at Bobby, I ask, "Did Jimmy every mention Vladimir Horowitz to you?"

"That's a non-sequitur if ever I've heard one," Stuart looks up.

"No, why?" Bobby replies.

"I don't even know why I'm mentioning this, but Jimmy once told me that he'd been with Vladimir," I respond. "Literally, called him Vladimir. No last name. Like they were close."

"What do you mean 'been with'?" Buddy asks.

"That's it," I answer. "He never said anything more specific. But it seemed like a source of pride or something."

"You mean sexually?" Stuart cringes.

"He never provided any details," I explain. "But yeah, that was the gist of it. And I believed he was telling the truth. I mean why would anyone fucking make that up. I think he said he was working at a place called Cowboys."

"Well, that's true," Bobby fills in a gap. "He did work at Cowboys and Cowgirls. It was Jimmy Merry's place on the Eastside. They did get famous people there for a time."

Stuart repeats, "You think he fucked Vladimir Horowitz? Why would anyone do that? Aside from the fact that he was one of the world's greatest pianists, he had to be 80. That's disgusting. I'm losing my appetite just thinking about it."

"There was so much I didn't know about Jimmy," I confide. "He was an only child, but his mother was long dead when I met him and he never spoke about his father. He told me that he'd gotten some technical degree, in computers or something, but he wasn't what you'd call educated. I think he felt intimidated by me in that respect. I almost feel like he mentioned that he was with Horowitz as a way to demonstrate that he was sophisticated, worldly."

"Well, I knew him best and he never mentioned that to me," Bobby asserts.

"I don't even know why I brought it up," I reply. "I guess loading all those photos of him and Stonewall up on the internet has brought back a lot of memories. Snippets of things that I had forgotten."

"I took a look yesterday at your site," Buddy interrupts. "You don't have much text."

I sense that Buddy is concerned that he won't be given proper billing on the StonewallRevival.com website and I try to deflect. "It's just at the beginning. I don't know how much text I'm going to add over time. My inclination is to make it mostly pictures. I don't know that my memory is good enough to document everything. And, honestly, I've come to realize that I didn't know much about him."

"What do you mean?" Stuart frowns. "You were together for, what, four years?"

"Yeah," I nod, "but our relationship was only in the present. There was no past ... at least we never really discussed the past. I didn't even have a past. And we didn't talk about the future. It was all just that moment. I don't think I loved him."

"Of course you did," Buddy asserts.

"No, not really," I admit. "I think I was in love with the world he was in. I wanted to experience it. Taste it. But safely, from a distance. Being the boyfriend of the guy who re-opened Stonewall, that was what I was in love with."

"As I always say," Stuart reflects, "even in the most fucked up relationships, both sides are getting something out of it — even if it's not apparent to you and me."

"I know he loved you," Bobby insists. "When you guys were broken up, he was just a mess. He didn't care about the bar anymore. He didn't care about anything. It was like he thought he had screwed up the best thing that had happened to him."

"That's nice to hear," I say, "but I think it was more obsession than love. I think he loved what I represented ... someone who hadn't been tainted, someone who had gone to good schools and gotten a good job, someone who was respectable or something."

"That could all be true," Stuart assesses, "and he could have still have been legitimately in love with you."

"It's funny," I start, "but I remember the moment that he first came on to me. It was so ... transactional."

"*That's* a strange choice of words," Bobby cuts in.

"I had gone over to his apartment with the friend who had taken me to Private Eyes on New Years' Eve, where I first saw him. We're sitting around his apartment having drinks. They were doing coke. All of a sudden, he picks up these photos of a house in East Hampton that he was half-owner of with a friend. Starts showing me the interior of the place. Like a real estate broker. Starts telling me that this could be mine. That if I was with him, this was the life I could enjoy. Summers in the Hamptons."

"That was a little overt," Stuart observes. "Was this before or after the bar opened?"

"Before. And it was more than overt," I insist. "It was an exchange. A bribe. And it worked."

"What do you mean?" Bobby scowls.

"I guess he thought that there wasn't anything about him that would have been attractive to me. So, he hustled himself. I was attracted to the illicit world that he lived in and the trappings of a Hamptons life — I was hooked."

"I never saw your relationship that way," Buddy offers. "And when he died, you kept his bar open. You were working night and day. You didn't have to do that."

"That wasn't noble," I rant, "it was psychotic. It was a way to keep the party going after the host had left. The showman, the impresario, the P.T. Barnum, was gone, and I wasn't ready to return to an ordinary life or go back into the closet."

The facial expressions of my friends around the table are suddenly tinged with anger and despair. I've broken the social compact. The widower may never disparage the relationship with the canonized decedent. In speaking so freely, too objectively, I've betrayed their memories and expectations.

"I'm sorry for being so blunt," I try to recoup. "I wouldn't be trying to bring attention to what Jimmy did if none of it meant anything to me."

Bobby cuts me off, almost growling, "But you said you didn't love him."

"I know and I'm sorry about how harsh that sounds," I plead. "But I'm almost 40. I don't want to think of love the same way now. I don't want that scarring, self-destructive love again. Ten years ago, I ate it up. But it's been six years since he left the party and I was still trapped in it."

"So you did love him back then?" Bobby offers a breadcrumb.

"I don't want to answer that," I defer in a whisper. "I want to leave all of that behind me. Seeing that he gets his due is the final act. I'm hoping that it will free me to open up again."

"Regardless of your motives or whether you can say you loved him or not," Stuart interjects, coming to my rescue, "the fact of the matter is that he did something remarkable. He turned a dead icon into a living icon. And as you yourself said, it's been open now far too long for it ever to revert to something else. Even if your motives for keeping it open were selfish, it doesn't matter. It could have very easily closed again when he died. It wasn't making any money. There was a pile of debt. We could all be marching past a Starbucks every June."

Nearby tables seemed keenly interested in us, as evidenced by the sideways glances and dearth of conversation in our orbit. I assumed that it was due to our colorful dialogue, though it might just as well have been due to our receiving our entrees before other tables received their appetizers.

"If someone in the media or the gay community asks you about Jimmy, after seeing the website," Stuart begins, "are you going to be as unflattering about him and your relationship as you've been tonight?"

"I don't know," I admit. "I don't expect that to happen. I don't expect anything from this. I'm just doing something that I feel needs to be done. To write something of the pages of history that this person did something good. That's a little pompous sounding. Sorry. Think of it more like a footnote or, better yet, graffiti."

"Yes, but how truthful will you be?" Bobby asks.

"How truthful do you need to be?" Buddy chimes in.

"Since when do people who've done good things need to be saints?" I snap. "There's plenty of folks who've done remarkable things that have had sordid, imperfect lives. I don't want to paint Jimmy as some sort of hero and have any number of people point out what we all know. It shouldn't make a difference, but it will. If anyone is going to call out his flaws, I'd rather it be me."

"Still, you could polish it up a bit," Bobby suggests. "You don't need to paint him the way you have tonight."

"They say there's no such thing as bad publicity," Buddy lobs into the conversation.

"It's not about publicity or polishing," I insist. "It's about setting the record straight. There's so much misinformation about the bar's re-opening or lack of *any* information in lots of cases. The submission to nominate the site as a National Historic Landmark omits the re-opening entirely. Something else I read said that 'a bar going by the name of Stonewall opened in 1993.'"

"That's not true," Bobby becomes indignant.

"Exactly," I concur. "It's only been a few years since Jimmy re-opened it and the powers that be, these historians or whatever they are, couldn't even characterize *that* correctly. It's almost like they wanted to overlook it. That it didn't fit into whatever story they were looking to tell."

"Nobody's looking to beatify Jimmy." Stuart observes. "They were looking to make the site a landmark. I'm not surprised that they omitted the recent events. It's the riots in '69 that make the place important."

"True," I concede. "But if it was a Starbucks, I doubt that they'd have gone to the effort of trying to put it on the National Historic Register. And even on the ownership of the space — back in the '60s — I've seen things that said that Joel Weiser owned it. That's bullshit. He held the mortgage. I'm sick of all the false history and omissions."

"Fair point," Stuart tries to calm me down.

My rising agitation causes a brief lull in the conversation and a shift in focus to rack of lamb and filet of beef. Another bottle of Châteauneuf-du-Pape inevitably provides oral lubrication.

"I'm really surprised at how good everything is," Bobby notes while slicing through his beef.

"Mine is great too," Stuart adds. "I don't think I've been here since the Film Society tribute to Elizabeth Taylor. That has to be 10 years ago."

"I must have been out of town then," Buddy characteristically adds. "Otherwise I definitely would have been here for my Liz."

"Well, I just want to say thank you for taking us here," Bobby offers. "And for what you're doing to give Jimmy credit for Stonewall. I understand why you want to move on."

"You're welcome," I smile. "I was a little worried that you might be annoyed that I've focused this solely on Jimmy, given that you had given him money to start it."

"It's — what do they call it? — water under the bridge." Bobby answers. "Life isn't always fair. I'm here. He's not. I could be angry that he didn't run it well and that I lost all that money. But what's the point. He was my friend."

"Thanks," I whisper, reaching for Bobby's hand. "That's kinda how I feel. For whatever it was, or wasn't, it was a moment in my life that I wouldn't change. I couldn't change it."

"Or dream it away," Stuart inserts.

Buddy cuts in with, "You still having those dreams, about Gwen and Broadway shows?"

"Sort of," I answer. "But not like in the beginning. I think it's come to a close.

CHAPTER TWENTY-NINE

Sweet Charity

After dessert and espresso, we said our goodbyes and headed home. I took the subway, not wanting to get caught in a cab trying to navigate around the Village parade route. Before jumping into bed, I took another look around the living room at all the theatre memorabilia. I wondered where it all would go when I died. To me, it was a way of holding onto something that was inherently fleeting. Fragments of memories. In 50 years or so, would there be anyone who would want snapshots of someone else's memories?

There were no theatre dreams that night, and I awoke before the alarm summoned me. It was just after six. I amble into the kitchen to brew coffee, something usually reserved for weekend mornings, given the extra hour or so I have before the call to work. As I step out of the kitchen, I spot something on the long console table at the far end of the room. On the glass surface, I see a ticket. It's for the *Sweet Charity* Concert at Lincoln Center. At $1,000 dollars, it was the most expensive event I've ever gone to, but worth far more than they charged. Just two years ago, I had witnessed one of those most remarkable showbiz moments anyone could hope to see. I don't remember seeing it last night during the memorabilia survey.

Settling into the oversized leather chair, I flip on the TV for a few more minutes of respite. I'm still staring at the theatre prizes that cover the piano and the console across the room, for inspiration for their future fate, when I hear some mumblings about President Clinton coming from the local news talking head. I look up to the screen and see captions about impeachment and Monica. I wonder what has he done, or who, with just a week until the Bush-Gore election. It's startling to see that debacle playing out again.

As the Today Show opens, I understand the anomaly. It's not November 1, 2000. It's June of 1998, just a few days before I'll see the concert on June 15th. I've awoken in what appeared to be the present but am, in fact, in the very recent past. In the safe confines of the apartment, I couldn't see how people were dressed or what was being advertised on billboards to decipher where I was. I walk back to examine the ticket again and, looking at the buffet, don't see the prized Charity handbag. I haven't bought it yet.

I'm at a loss for what to do or where to go. Gwen is living now in Bronxville, so it would make no sense to go to 91 Central Park West. The show isn't for several days, so there's no point in going to Lincoln Center. When the alarm clock buzzes, the chatter in my head is silenced, and out of an abundance of faith, I decide to get ready for work — until the director tells me otherwise.

I'm overly confident in the office. During the morning meetings, I opine freely on brand strategy and planning for the coming year, benefitting from the knowledge that, in a few months, the Master Settlement Agreement will be signed by the tobacco companies to pay over $200 billion to the States and curtail most forms of advertising. It will be a watershed moment. While everyone else seems paralyzed by the litigation tsunami that threatens to bankrupt the industry, I sound like a genius or madman, painting a future of continuing profitability and employment.

When lunchtime rolls around, I head down for my dirty water dogs. As I skirt around the black town car illegally parked in front of his cart, I see the back window roll down and her face smiling at me.

"Get in," she calls out.

I take my cue, from her and the director, and join her in the back seat. "Where are we going?" I ask, though I actually don't care.

"I want to show you something I'm doing for charity," she responds, still in that girlish timbre though she's now in her 70's and wearing glasses.

"Would that be with a big C or a little c?"

"Both," Gwen answers with laughter. "I thought you, of all people, should see it. And how is it that you look exactly the same? Don't tell me it's the lighting."

"Good genes?" I fumble for an amusing retort. "Why ask why? Anyway, I have a ticket for Monday. I wouldn't miss it for the world."

"I'm taking you to the rehearsal," she explains. "We've had two weeks to put this together. Not a lot of time, but it's really coming together."

As the car heads to the West Side, we fall into conversation as though only 20 minutes had past, not 20 years.

"I'm sorry about Bob," I say, offering my very belated condolences.

"I am too," she says. "But that was a long time ago."

"Why now? The concert, I mean."

"Timing, I guess," she begins. "With the *Chicago* revival being such a big hit, and *Cabaret* at Studio 54, and with *Fosse* coming in January …"

"I'd love to see that. Maybe I'll go on my birthday." I interrupt.

"My birthday is the 13th. When's yours?" she asks.

"The 12th."

"That'll be easy to remember," she smiles.

"But what were you saying about the concert?" I return to the original storyline.

"Oh, just that this is the right moment. If we're really going to raise a lot of money for amfAR and Broadway Cares, now is the time."

"Tell me about it, a thousand dollars a ticket should help a lot of people," I joke.

"I never forgot what you told me," she confides.

"About people dying?" I ask to confirm.

"Yes," she replies. "How are you doing?"

"You mean, am I positive?" I try to clarify. "No, I'm not. Though not from being perfect."

"I didn't mean that. I wouldn't ask, but I'm happy for you. I meant after Jimmy died?"

"Oh, I'm about as fucked up as everyone else is standing amongst the rubble," I babble, trying to stay composed.

"I won't say that it gets better," she begins, "but it doesn't get worse, at least."

"As horrific as it was," I recount, "I still think of it as a gift. To be with someone you care about at that exact moment."

"Not in public it isn't," she says, refuting my characterization.

"Sorry, I didn't think about that," I apologize, remembering that she had cradled Fosse's head in her arms as he lay dying on a Washington street. "Mine happened in a quiet hospital room with no one else around."

"Don't be sorry," she apologizes. "It's no one's fault."

The car drops us off at the rehearsal space, and I follow her in, watching the reverence being paid to her by each passing admirer, an even grander display of affection than what I'd seen as we headed to Merman's dressing room.

There's a veritable circus of people preparing for the concert, and at the same time, a small contingent of photographers and videographers capturing it. I've never seen photos or video from the event or this rehearsal but, clearly, they exist. When I return to the present, I'll set my sights on acquiring the evidence. For now, I'll bask in the live-action.

Cy Coleman is here. Bebe Neuwirth is rehearsing in a black unitard and sporting pigtails. Debbie Allen comes in and hugs Gwen with almost motherly adoration. Allen is wearing a white blouse and black high-waisted pants. They're held up with by black spaghetti straps that emphasize her bosom. It gives the appearance that she's wearing Fosse-fashionable fisherman's waders. Her sparkly silver dance flats also draw attention. She is the most camera-ready of anyone here. In contrast, Gwen is wearing simple black pants with a near-black turtleneck top and black boots.

After some time, Gwen motions for me to come with her and Allen to a separate, quiet studio space. She tells me that Debbie will be doing "If My Friends Could See Me Now" in the concert and that she's helping her with the choreography. I sit quietly behind a camera capturing the dance lesson.

I get the sense that Allen, an accomplished choreographer in her own right, doesn't really need to be told how to do the steps. She performed the role brilliantly for about a year in the '80s. It's almost as though she's letting Gwen show her how to do it, as a tribute to a great star. It's part blessing, part investiture, and absolute generosity on both sides. At 73, Gwen is still the sole author of a character that still lives in her and will outlive us all.

Against a black backdrop, sitting together on wooden bistro chairs that act as stand-in for the bed that she'll be romping on, Allen watches as Gwen flicks the black top hat from her foot, with one perfect revolution, into her hands. In each step and gesture, I see the young Gwen Verdon emerge.

They move toward my favorite moment in the song, where Charity plants her cane on the floor directly behind her and starts stepping away from it until she's literally bent into a backwards D-shape, three feet away from the cane that she's still keeping upright with her extended left arm. When I saw it in '66, it was as though she was defying the laws of anatomy. A moment later, she'd maintain that contortion as her feet invisibly warp-drive her across the stage, defying the laws of physics.

Now, standing side by side, both facing left, Gwen plants the cane as tightly behind her as possible.

"Now, walk away from the cane," Gwen instructs, as the piano accompaniment begins. The distance is no longer three feet and the cane is no longer held completely vertical as she steps away from it. Instead of warp-drive, there's an old lady's shuffle. It's beautifully poignant, like watching the final breath. They finish the number and the handful of observers applaud wildly. It's the last time anyone will see Verdon perform the song.

We move on. There's more video to be shot, for publicity purposes I assume. Cy Coleman sits at an upright piano as the cameraman gets ready. Allen, Neuwirth, and Gwen join him. When the cameraman nods, he begins to play "If My Friends Could See Me Now," and the four of them sing their hearts out. Toward the end of the song, I get misty-eyed. This moment was another gift, the last of a string. There's nothing more beyond this. The concert will be performed one time on Monday and, after that, there is nothing more for me to see of Gwen Verdon.

When the filming finishes, she comes over to me.

"I guess I should be going," I say, wiping a tear. "Thank you for a marvelous memory."

"I loved seeing you again," she says, patting my shoulder.

"Well, break a leg," I offer as my final goodbye.

"Hey, you asked me something once," she starts. "About whether I thought that people who had gone could still see us ..."

"Yeah," I nod. "I remember you didn't want to discuss that."

"I do," she utters. "I do believe." She kisses me on the cheek, turns, and walks back to the piano.

CHAPTER THIRTY

Ever After

Once again, I awaken before the alarm. It's almost 7 a.m., and uncertain as to whether this is recent past or present, I turn on the bedroom television, still lying comfortably in bed. Katie and Matt confirm that it's November 1, 2000. When I see my mother for her birthday on Friday, she'll ask if I'd gone to church today, as though God is taking attendance. I won't. I prefer to measure in love.

The alarm buzzes and I begin the morning ritual, dismayed that I won't be quite as prescient today in the office as in yesterday's time warp. I make a mental note that I arrive early, psychologically mitigating one of the late or absent days during my 1994 Stonewall stewardship, as though Mr. Philip Morris himself was taking attendance.

There is no black town car at the hot dog stand because reality disappoints. I'm inhaling one of them at my desk, looking at Gore's hopeful smile on the cover of *The Times*, when the phone rings. It's an outside number that I don't recognize. I'd instinctively let one of the admins pick up if they weren't all away for lunch. It's Charlie from the bar.

"Hey, Charlie," I say with surprise. "What's up?"

"Sorry to call you at work," he replies. "It sure was hard tracking you down. I called an old number that they had up in the office from when you were here."

"Oh, that's been quite a while," I laugh.

"Anyway, the person who answered looked up your number in the directory or something," Charlie babbles.

"Is there something wrong?"

"No, nothing wrong," he gets back on track. "Were you expecting a package?"

"No. What do you mean? Down at Stonewall?"

"Yeah, we got a package delivered this morning," he explains. "A box. It's addressed to Tom at Stonewall, 53 Christopher Street. No last name. Nobody here can figure out who it's for."

"Doesn't it say who it's from?" I ask. "A return address or something?"

"Nope," Charlie responds. "You're the only person I thought of. You're the only Tom that's been here."

"That's weird," I'm intrigued, but fearful. "It's a box, not a letter, right?"

"Yes, a box," he confirms. "About one foot by one foot by one foot."

"As long as it isn't something from a bill collector," I joke. "I'm still paranoid that one of the people that Jimmy stiffed will come after me."

"No, it's nothing official looking," he describes. "The name and address are handwritten, like it's something personal."

"Oh, that is really strange," I hesitate, not knowing what to do.

"Do you want me to put it aside? For the next time you come in?"

"Sure. That would be great. I doubt it's for me. But who knows?"

"Sure thing," he says, and the exchange ends.

I spend the remainder of my day wracking my brain as to what the mysterious package could contain, assuming it is actually for me. Though I had had no plans to stop in at Stonewall that evening, my curiosity gets the better of me. Shortly after six, I head downtown for a cocktail and a look-see.

Charlie greets me with the same beaming smile that I've enjoyed for almost a decade. After he pours a gin and tonic, he dashes upstairs to the office. The box he places before me on the bar is exactly as described. Brown cardboard. Handwritten.

It's not taped all that securely, and I'm able to open it without scissors or a knife. Charlie stares at me from behind the bar as I pull out some crumpled newspaper that was inserted to protect the contents. He watches as I unfold a note attached to a framed picture.

"It *is* for you!" he says, congratulating himself.

I don't answer, but nod my head in the affirmative, as I gaze over the four lines and twenty-two words. There is no signature on the note, but it doesn't need one.

> *I meant to give this to you last year*
> *but I didn't see you then*
> *I misplaced it*
> *Better late than never*

Still holding the note, I look up and say, "I love you Charlie."

Confused, he replies with the requisite, "I love you too."

"For me," I try to explain. "It's for me."

"What's in the box?" he asks, trying to peer over the bar.

"It's from some friends," I answer, putting the note back inside the box and folding the flaps closed. I step up from the bar stool and pull out my wallet to pay for the drink.

"You don't need to do that," Charlie insists. "It's on me."

"Thanks, Charlie," I wave goodbye.

Back at the apartment, I place the box on the glass dining table. I take the framed picture and position it on top of the piano, alongside the other theatre treasures.

There's only one more decision to make. Reaching into the box, I remove the worn *Chicago* cap. Walking back into the bedroom and into the walk-in closet, I place the hat back on the shelf from which it came — because they'd never believe me.

Notes

AMUSE ROUGE
This alternate naming of the prologue, and its play on words to the culinary teaser, is my tribute to Gwen Verdon. Though I never had the pleasure of knowing or meeting her, I've long admired her devotion to her craft and how she helped reaffirm her husband's legacy. Without mentioning her name, this page is intended to provide some examples as to how she was uncredited or under-credited for a number of accomplishments. It is meant to lay a foundation for presenting why Jimmy Pisano deserves at least some recognition for re-opening Stonewall and keeping the bar open long enough to ensure that it would never revert to being something other than the place where gay liberation began.

91 Central Park West is a storied building. An article by columnist Earl Wilson in August of 1959 describes the penthouse apartment that Gwen Verdon has just moved into, including the reference to Hearst. There are also many articles and real estate listings on the internet that refer to Hearst's ownership of the penthouse and Marion Davies' having lived there. Sometime subsequent to that, the penthouse was divided into two units. In 2017, the Corcoran real estate website showed a non-active listing of Verdon's former apartment, Penthouse B, including the floorplan. This provided a basis for describing the apartment. In March of 2015, *The Observer* ran an article about Penthouse A, the other half of the original Davies' residence, which had been put up for sale by the family that had resided there for decades. In that article, reference is made to Hearst having owned the entire building and that the monthly rental income had been Davies' allowance.

A Rex Reed article in the *New York Times* (Feb 6, 1966) is the source for Verdon's achievements that are largely unknown. In addition, there are *Life* and other magazine photographs showing Verdon coaching Marilyn Monroe to substantiate Reed's text. I found the remarkable coincidence of Verdon having danced for Davies at three-years-old at an MGM Christmas party too good to not include.

1. BABY, DREAM YOUR DREAM
There are numerous photographs on the internet showing Times Square in late 1965, early 1966. These formed the basis of my description.

I'd like pay homage, in addition to my subscription fee, to the *New York Times Archive*. Remarkably, one can read any day's *New York Times*, through 1980, as a TimesMachine digital replica. Though *Times* articles from 1981 onward are captured as well, only in text format, the ability to virtually page through the actual newspaper from the 1960s and 1970s helped me construct certain aspects of this novel.

The long road to acquiring the rights to *Chicago* from its author, Maurine Dallas Watkins, is best explained by a *Times* piece from Jan 28, 1973. "Chicago Saga" appears within an article titled "Remarque's Play Comes 'Full Circle.'"

2. WHERE THE UNDERWORLD CAN MEET THE ELITE

Among others sources, Getty Images has pictures of the intersection of Christopher Street and 7th Avenue during the 1960s. Some are credited to Fred McDarrah, the prime photographic chronicler of the Stonewall Riots. This provided background for describing the intersection. In addition to all the black and white photos of the Stonewall Inn sign in 1969 on the internet, there is a very brief sequence in the film *The Best of Everything* that shows the sign illuminated and in color.

Martin Duberman's 1993 book *Stonewall* was the first detailed accounting of the riots that I ever read. Duberman's extensive interviews of six people provide a background of the events that led to the riots and what followed. He indicated that "Fat Tony" Lauria was a pseudonym for one of the Mafia figures in his description of the underworld characters associated with the bar. David Carter's *Stonewall*, in 2010, continues the story of the Mafia connection.

Within this chapter, I've been able to add information about the ownership of the property on Christopher Street, where Stonewall stands, to that which has been reported elsewhere. The basis of this research comes from a website called ACRIS (Automated City Register Information System). ACRIS is essentially a search engine for real estate transactions in the City of New York. Using a variety of parameters including names, addresses, and parcel numbers, one can find far more information about who owns or owned what pieces of property than some people may find comfortable. Using this search engine enabled me to find out about Handelsman, Duell, Sandler, and Weiser. Cross checking their names with *The Times* provided further background on the transactions and also led me to Harper. To my knowledge, this has not been reported before in any accounting of the history of the bar, though all this information is publicly available.

Special thanks to Michael Worden at Alfred Music for this chapter title.

To the Agreement dated October 24, 2017 between ALFRED PUBLISHING LLC and Thomas Garguilo:
FORTY-SECOND STREET
Words by AL DUBIN
Music by HARRY WARREN
Copyright © 1932 (Renewed) WB MUSIC CORP.
All Rights Reserved
Used By Permission of ALFRED MUSIC

3. WELCOME TO THE THEATRE

Though I've yet to discover film footage of the original production, there are a number of bootleg copies of subsequent productions of *Sweet Charity* that can be found on the internet. I specifically looked at those revivals when Verdon was still alive, given that she is reported to have coached her successors on the choreography. There was remarkable consistency in the show's opening sequence as performed by Debbie Allen, Ann Reinking, and Donna McKechnie to give me the confidence to describe Verdon's performance of "Charity's Theme."

In March of 1967, Gwen performed "If My Friends Could See Me Now" on the *Ed Sullivan Show*. Unlike the song snippets that one can find on popular talk shows of the day, the Broadway performances on Sullivan's show tended to be more elaborate and, I believe, more faithful to the actual productions.

Descriptions of the Palace Theatre's renovation come from a *New York Times* article (Jan 30, 1966) by Vincent Canby.

4. HEY BIG SPENDER

I moved into a one-bedroom apartment at 59 West 12th Street in 1998. I had no idea when I bought the apartment that so many notable people were living in the building. Over time, an even greater number of celebrities became residents. All of this information has been reported extensively elsewhere.

The reference to the short-lived Stonewall bar that resurrected for a brief time at 51 Christopher Street in the late 1980s is from the Landmarks Preservation Commission. Regrettably, I could find no other information about that brief attempt to revive the bar. I was uncertain as to whether to include its brief existence as a proof point as to why Jimmy Pisano's efforts to keep his bar open, in spite of insufficient business, is something that should be publicly recognized in the history of Stonewall because other elements in the LPC report are not entirely accurate. They state that Jimmy's bar opened "by 1993" and, in the '60s, that the building was sold to "real estate investor Joel Weiser." Neither of these statements is entirely correct. The bar was opened in 1990 as New Jimmy's and converted back to the Stonewall name about a year later. Weiser, according to the records on ACRIS, was the mortgage-holder on the Christopher Street properties. Despite these inconsistencies, I assumed that their reference to the existence of this "nanosecond" Stonewall is true.

The original *Gypsy* script was purchased during a 1998 tribute to Ethel Merman. Numerous stars appeared at this one-night-only benefit performance to raise money for Gay Men's Health Crisis. During the evening, a few Merman artifacts were auctioned. Arthur Laurents, who wrote the book for *Gypsy* and was a supporter of GMHC, signed the script.

5. I HOPE I GET IT

The description of the apartment and some furnishings comes from photographs and from some references to the apartment in several Fosse biographies and articles.

6. I AM WHAT I AM

Joe Jr.'s was a wonderful diner/luncheonette/greasy spoon that lived on the corner of 12th Street and 6th Avenue for 35 years. Sadly, it closed in 2009.

The Beach was a day spa at 112 Christopher Street during the 1990s.

Electra, also known to me as Electra St. Jill, was still performing in South Florida as of 2017.

7. There's No Business Like Show Business
A September 7, 1970 article in the *New York Times* chronicles the growing interest in organic foods, citing Gwen Verdon as one of its early fans. Photos accompanying the article show Verdon's organic roof garden atop 91 Central Park West.

8. Doin' What Comes Natur'lly
A lot has been written about Rao's over the years. A *New York Post* article from November 2015 is one of my favorites to describe just how unique it was. I was very grateful to have been invited by one of the regulars, who held a standing weekly table, to experience it on several occasions, including the night with Mottola and Carcy.

9. Beautiful Girls
After reading about "A Fashion Show in Dance" in *The New York Times*, I was lucky enough to find a copy of the program from a vintage bookseller. While *The Times* did carry some details about the event, it was the program insert that really provided the background for this passage. A torn ticket stub was also buried in the program for seat B114 in the second balcony. It seemed only fitting to use that as an element of the story.

10. Sunday
The reference to Jane Morgan's non-appearance at the benefit comes from a *Times* review.

Giorgio Armani does indeed own Verdon's former Penthouse B apartment at 91 Central Park West. An April 2002 layout in *Architectural Digest* shows how Armani renovated and designed the space. Penthouse A recently came on the market after having been the residence of one family for decades. Thanks to the longevity of their ownership and preservation of many of the original Hearst touches, one can see many elements of the original space that Hearst built for Marion Davies on the various real estate websites that still show the property listing.

11. Love Changes Everything
The description of Gwen Verdon's dressing room and the backstage areas of the Palace come from the Rex Reed article in *The Times* and various *Life* photographs. One of the photos, from March 25, 1966, shows a portion of the dressing room from the beginning of the run. An especially vivid shot from 1967 captures Verdon just after a performance, standing before her dressing room mirror. The items on her dressing table are clearly visible, including the pack of Marlboro cigarettes, and much of the rest of the room can be seen in the mirror's reflection.

12. Not A Day Goes By
Stuart is a dear friend who graciously allowed me to borrow stories from his life, all of them true, for this novel.

13. Diamonds Are A Girl's Best Friend
The conversation that Dick relates about being teased by the bartender for having small hands comes from a conversation I had recently with a man who went to Stonewall sometime in 1967 or 1968. He described his experience so vividly and in such detail that I absolutely believe that his exchange with the bartender took place. I had to memorialize it in this book.

Ed Murphy has been written about extensively in other books and articles about Stonewall.

14. Pretty Little Picture
To keep the price of this book affordable, the photographs in this chapter and throughout the novel are printed in black and white. The original full-color photos are available for viewing at StonewallRevival.com.

15. What I Did For Love
Though Marsha P. Johnson and Sylvia Rivera have been written about in various articles and books about the riots, I don't believe that they have yet fully received the recognition they are due. Both lived long enough to see Stonewall reopen, but not long enough to see it receive national recognition. I wanted to honor them by including their doppelgangers in this chapter.

16. Be On Your Own
When I first started going through all the photos of New Jimmy's / Stonewall, I had some difficulty identifying some of the events that had been captured more than 20 years ago. The scene in this chapter where certain photos are identified as a result of looking at the tiny print on some pink balloons mirrors my own experience in recalling details from so long ago.

17. We Need A Little Christmas
I was fortunate to find articles and photos in the *New York Times* describing what Christmas at Rockefeller Center and Lord & Taylor looked like in 1967.

The *New York Times* review of the Garland performance, Stuart's recollections and photos from the night, and a bootleg recording of the concert formed the basis for my description.

18. Everything's Coming Up Roses
The idea of hiding an object in New York City for retrieval years or decades later is intriguing to me. It's become an informal party game among my New York friends.

19. COMPANY

A number of sources cite that the on-location filming of *Sweet Charity* at various sites around New York occurred in the spring of 1968. I was unable to find a shooting schedule to determine the exact date(s) that the "I'm A Brass Band" number was filmed. I resorted to finding publicity photos taken during the filming of that sequence, from Getty and Alamy, to select a day on which to craft this chapter. Unfortunately, Getty and Alamy listed multiple dates, including May 5, 19, 23, and June 4, as the dates when the sequence was purportedly shot. While I wouldn't have been surprised to find multiple dates for shooting that scene, the fact that they weren't contiguous or consistent caused me some discomfort because I wanted the date I chose for this scene in the book to be accurate. Ultimately, I elected to use June 4, 1968 as the date for this chapter because the front page of the *New York Times* that day provided some interesting fodder for the story.

And, yes, if you look at the statue of George Washington that stands before Federal Hall, you do in fact see that our first President is sporting camel toe.

20. THE LADIES WHO LUNCH

I wanted to include Knickerbocker Bar & Grill, located at 33 University Place, in this novel because it's been a favorite place of mine for many years. Whenever I go back to New York, I always make sure to pay a visit.

21. EVERY DAY A LITTLE DEATH

In addition to the Jan 18, 1969 *Times* announcement of Carr's death, a follow-up article on Jan 23, 1969 provides details of the tribute held at the Winter Garden. The details surrounding the tribute, including Verdon's request of the audience to give Carr a posthumous standing ovation, formed the background for this chapter.

In a June 10, 2002 interview in the *Chicago Tribune* and elsewhere, Jerry Herman spoke about his HIV diagnosis in 1984 and subsequent treatment. He is quoted as saying, "I really don't mind talking about it, because I want other people in my situation to realize it's possible to live a normal life with this disease. I know that everybody has different genetics and different strains of the HIV, but in my case I'm healthier now than I was when I was diagnosed. It's all because of the new drugs and my initial willingness to be a guinea pig."

In Scott Schechter's *Judy Garland: The Day-by-day Chronicle of a Legend*, the author notes that Garland was planning on flying back from London in August to spend the remainder of the summer at Jerry Herman's Fire Island home.

22. ON THE STEPS OF THE PALACE

The Find A Grave website shows Maurine Dallas Watkins as having been buried at Oak Lawn Cemetery, Buffalo, Dallas County, Missouri. The grave marker shows her date of death as August 10, 1969.

The January 28, 1973 *Times* information about the "Chicago Saga" is buried in an article titled "Remarque's Play Comes 'Full Circle.'" It appears on page five of the

Arts and Leisure section. This article refers to the optioning of *Chicago* for Gwen Verdon in 1956. The Feb 3, 1956 *Times* reported on a "long-range project," buried in an article titled "New Role Slated For Kim Stanley," stating that the option for *Chicago* had been obtained from Maurine Dallas Watkins by Fryer and Carr specifically for Gwen Verdon. Though other sources refute that an option existed for a musical version of *Chicago* that early, I chose to take inspiration from *The New York Times*.

The autographed *Sweet Charity* 1998 benefit concert handbag was acquired immediately after the performance as part of the fundraising efforts of the evening.

23. BEFORE THE PARADE PASSES BY

There are a number of accounts of what happened at the Stonewall Riots. Though the first night's rebellion is the one that typically gets cited, the rebellion actually lasted for several nights over the course of almost one week. This sequence is based on one particular account where I read that the bar was re-opened on Sunday, only serving soft drinks, and that the police had actually been encouraging people to go back into the bar. Though some have written that there were substantial crowds protesting outside the bar over that weekend and during the following week, I chose not to dramatize that perspective. I found the fact that part of the community would go back inside a bar that had been the scene of a rebellion some 36 hours before, a bar that had been wrecked in the process, despite the crowds protesting outside, to be a more interesting contradiction to focus upon.

Several sources, including *The Observer*, state the Hendrix retreated to his 59 West 12th Street apartment after his appearance at Woodstock in August of 1969. The Jimi Hendrix website states that he moved in on November 1st. I elected to assume that Hendrix did live in the building on June 29th, the date of this chapter, despite the discrepancies.

24. WITH SO LITTLE TO BE SURE OF

I purchased the domain StonewallRevival.com as a place to post the pictures that document Jimmy Pisano's re-opening of Stonewall. It is my hope that readers will be curious enough after reading this chapter to explore the site and enjoy the abundance of pictures that I have been storing for more than 20 years. The website is meant to be an online archive of this period of Stonewall's history, not a selling tool for this book. In many ways, the launch of this archive resulted from my personal journey to try to find an appropriate repository for the material. Like the character in the book, I didn't find any one particular institution that felt just right.

While keeping StonewallRevival.com free of advertising, I have elected to use Facebook and other social media platforms to promote the novel.

25. THE APPLE DOESN'T FALL (VERY FAR FROM THE TREE)

An August 31, 1976 review by Mimi Sheraton in *The Times* provided the background to the description of Bagel And.

A Clive Barnes article in *The Times* about Minnelli's stepping into *Chicago* from August 15, 1975 set the tone for the passage describing the outside of the 46th Street Theatre. A photo of the brilliantly understated announcement outside the theatre was especially evocative.

The exchange with Fred Ebb is based partially on his own words, principally from the book *Colored Lights*.

Liza's appearance on Sammy Davis Jr.'s *Sammy and Company* in 1975 featured a performance of "My Own Best Friend." Having seen Liza perform many times over the years, I was confident that the delivery of the song on that TV show was consistent with how she performed it on stage.

26. OPEN A NEW WINDOW
Sadly, there is no video tape that I know of showing the early days of New Jimmy's. For now, it's existence remains solely in the memories of those who were there and in a handful of photos.

27. PUT ON YOUR SUNDAY BEST
Getty Images has several Ron Galella photographs of Jackie Onassis attending *The Star-Spangled Gala*.

The New York Times covered *The Star-Spangled Gala* in at least three articles: a review by Clive Barnes on May 11, 1976, a description under "Briefs on the Arts" on April 7, 1976, and a C. Gerald Fraser lengthier description on March 29, 1976.

In James Lipton's *Inside Inside*, he gives credit to Verdon for the event.

28. GIANTS IN THE SKY
Gwen Verdon's role in the establishment of the West 69th Street Block Association is documented in several of their newsletters from 2002-2008. She is credited with starting the Halloween event by another early participant, Bob Anderson. These newsletters are archived on their website w69st.com.

29. SWEET CHARITY
A video of the 1998 *Sweet Charity* benefit concert is for sale from reeltimevideoproduction.com. The evening is beautifully captured, including a wonderful segment showing the rehearsals.

30. EVER AFTER
The photo at the end of the book is real. It was given to me in 1999 by my friend Stuart.

Made in the USA
Middletown, DE
24 July 2018